Before I tell You

A LOVE STORY BY

ASHLEY ELIZABETH

To anyone living with a mental illness, thinking they are unworthy of love, I promise that there is someone out there who will fight for you and with you on your stormiest days.
They will never let you drown.

Author's note

Thank you for giving my debut novel a chance.
For the past few years, I put my heart into this book.
I let anxiety keep me from pursuing my dreams for far too long.
But not anymore.

I present to you Natalie and Nathan's love story.

xoxo Ashley Elizabeth

This book contains references to abuse, gun violence, sexual assault, sexually explicit scenes, suicide, and topics that may be sensitive to some readers.

Reading is an escape for many of us, so if you feel that the mention of any of the above will upset you, please put this book down.

NATALIE

I ran like a girl whose life depended on it.

And mine did.

I ran down the giant spiral staircase, I ran over passed-out bodies on the floor, I ran through the ornate French doors, and I ran for another five blocks until I found it physically impossible to breathe anymore.

After making sure the danger hasn't followed me, I force myself to stop next to a giant oak tree to catch my breath, feeling the coldness on my skin as tiny snowflakes fall slowly around me from the dark, ominous sky. A dusting of snow covers the streets. It's a little early for this time of year, but that's what happens when you live in New England.

My body begins to shake from the cold but even more so from the adrenaline and shock spreading throughout it like an unrelenting wildfire. I'm holding my head in my shaking hands as I try to wrap my mind around what has just happened.

It feels like I'm *drowning*, gasping for air, as every labored breath I exhale is seen in the frigid night engulfing me. I reach for the tree next to me for support and notice my trembling hand feels slightly wet and sticky. When I turn it over, all color drains from my face.

There's blood smeared on my palm, and the sight of it causes my knees to buckle and shake. A wave of nausea washes over me as I start to lose consciousness, and I lean my body against the tree so as not to collapse on the hard ground. Slowly, I slide down it, resting my head against the cold, rough bark, and gradually close my eyes.

The oversized, flimsy football jersey fails to protect my body from the unkind elements, as seen in my fingers, which, when I open my eyes, notice that they are beginning to turn a light shade of blue. My bare feet are surrounded by snow, making my teeth chatter uncontrollably.

A cool, tiny trickle of blood slides down my left cheek and drips onto the pure white snow beside me. An unrelenting sob grips my throat and gradually escapes from my lips.

I turn my head to the side when I faintly hear a voice yelling in the distance. It sounds like they are saying my name, but I can't be sure because a high-pitched ringing begins to resonate in my ears.

My attention then immediately turns to the flashing red and blue lights moving down the street at an alarming rate, which is the last thing I remember.

One

NATALIE

TEN MONTHS LATER

Boston is always a good idea.

Or wait, is it Paris? Either way, Boston is my new home.

"Mom, I don't need anything else. This place is amazing," I say for what feels like the hundredth time today. Looking around my new apartment, I realize how amazing it actually is with its exposed brick walls and massive windows overlooking the Charles River.

It's perfect.

"Natalie, I'm your mother and just want to ensure you have everything you need before we leave you here all alone. We are not just down the street, you know." My mom says this as she throws her well-manicured hands up in the air to be dramatic.

"I know, mom." I give her a slight smile and see that her eyes are beginning to brim with tears, so I look away before I start to cry too.

It's move-in week for students at Linrey University, which is why my family helped me pack a U-Haul and transport my things almost three hours away from my hometown of Greenwich, CT, to live here in Boston, MA.

When I made the decision to attend LU, my mom felt the

distance would be too much for me to handle. She had pleaded with me to apply to every school in Connecticut so that I would never leave home. She even tried to bribe me with a beautiful new car that now resides in the garage of my parents' house.

But staying close to home wasn't what I wanted or needed for the next stage of my life. I needed to be someplace where I could have a fresh start. A place where I wouldn't know anyone and no one would know me. And finally, after much convincing on my part, my parents accepted that this was where I wanted to be for the next four years.

However, if I was going to be living three hours from home, my parents insisted on renting an apartment for me so that I wouldn't have to live in a dorm room on campus. I protested, telling them I wanted the whole college experience, but at the same time, I was somewhat relieved at the thought of having a space all to myself and not adjusting to a roommate, which is why I gave in fairly quickly.

And now, as I take in my new home, I'm so glad I gave in.

My dad spent the afternoon connecting all the appliances and ensuring they worked properly. Jason, my not-so-little brother, was in charge of all the heavy lifting of furniture while my mother and I pointed to where it should be placed. And eventually, after a few hours of bringing in and setting up everything, we were finished.

It's not until I sit down on the sofa, feeling exhausted, and look around the space, that the realization hits.

I'm going to be living on my own.

Alone.

I'm not too thrilled about this notion, but I know that this is something I need to do for myself.

"I am going to miss you so much, Natalie," my mom says through a layer of tissues she holds in front of her face.

"Mom, I am always just a phone call away, and I'll be home to visit as much as possible," I say, knowing it is a lie. I have no intention of going home anytime soon, though I realize I will have to make the trip eventually.

Standing up from the sofa, I embrace my mom in a hug, setting the waterworks in full motion for the both of us.

She starts to part from me, and although the tears are still running down her flawless cheeks, she smiles. "You're going to be just fine. I know you will be."

"Thanks, mom. I love you," I manage to say through a quiet sob.

God, this is going to be harder than I thought.

"I love you too, sweetie." She wipes away all the tears from my face before pulling out the compact mirror from her purse to examine her reflection.

I hear my dad clear his throat, bringing my attention to him. "Well, Natalie, make sure you never leave the oven on when you aren't home and always keep your door locked at night. I watch the news, and I know what … well, what I mean is, I love you, kid, and I hope you have a great time."

He kisses my forehead and wraps his arms tightly around me before looking over at my mom. "Well, come on, Nancy. We're going to hit traffic if we don't start heading home soon."

"I love you too, Dad," I respond. I can't be sure, but I think I see him wipe a tear from his cheek as he feigns a cough. My parents both leave with their sunglasses on, even though the sky is blanketed with massive grey clouds.

"My turn," I hear Jason say from behind me. I turn to see him casually standing against the kitchen island with his burly arms crossed in front of his chest.

I have almost a year on him, but he towers over me by nearly a foot. And although his blonde hair and ocean-grey eyes mirror mine, those are the only physical similarities we share. His lanky frame filled out a few years ago after he joined the football team at our high school, which made me seem even smaller when I stood next to him. His height and stature are why I have difficulty looking at him like he's my *little* brother.

Instead, I tend to see him as my *big* brother, my protector.

"Don't you get sappy on me too," I tease and pull him in for a hug. "You know you are always more than welcome to come over whenever you want, right?"

"I know," he says as I feel his hug get tighter. "You'll call me if you need anything?"

"Yes, of course. Can't … breathe," I joke, trying to diminish the sadness in the air.

"It's not going to be the same at home without you, Nat." His grip around me loosens, and as he pulls away, I notice his eyes are glazed with tears. "What perfume do you have on? It's driving my nose crazy." He grabs a tissue and heads toward the door.

"I'm going to miss you too, Jason." The truth is, he really has no idea how much I will miss having him around, especially after how much I have relied on him recently.

He smiles and puts his hand on the doorknob but then releases the handle and takes a detour to the kitchen. He opens the door to the fridge and sticks his arm inside, pulling out a silver can of beer. "For later," he says as he shoves the can into his coat pocket and exits my apartment.

I laugh as I lock the door behind Jason and go into the living room because I know my mother will kill him if she catches him drinking. I wasn't much of a drinker these days, but my mom insisted I have a stocked fridge of different beverage options in case I ever have company over. She also left me a frozen pizza for later so I wouldn't spend my first night alone, starving.

Digging into one of the boxes left by my desk, I find a framed picture of my family from a few years ago at a theme park in Florida. The four of us are on a water ride, zooming down a mountain in a faux log, and getting soaked. We all have huge smiles on our faces as we laugh uncontrollably from the thrill of free-falling down the waterslide.

The photo had recently become one of my favorites and instantly lifted my mood whenever I saw it. It wasn't some stuffy family portrait; it was a genuine, happy memory framed for us to remember that wonderful day for years to come. I'm assuming my mom snuck it into the box for me, so I put the picture on the end table by the sofa where it looks perfect.

But almost instantly, homesickness washes over me, and my eyes fill involuntarily with tears.

Get a hold of yourself, Natalie. It has only been five minutes since they left.

Taking a tissue from the box on the coffee table, I blot away at the additional tears trying to escape before they have a chance.

I pull my phone out of my back pocket to distract myself and see it's only 7 p.m., but exhaustion takes over when I sit on the sofa and lie back.

Tomorrow I will have time to get all my textbooks and school supplies from the campus bookstore and then make a trip to the local grocery store to get some real food to eat. But for now, I make the conscious decision to stay in for the night instead of venturing into the neighborhood.

Making my way into the bathroom, I stare into the mirror after washing my face and throwing my hair in a messy bun on the very top of my head. The tiny scar above my left eye is more prominent without any makeup covering it, making me feel vulnerable. Without thinking, I run my fingers over the tiny indent in my skin. It's small enough that most people wouldn't notice it, especially not from afar, but I always know it's there, reminding me every day.

Every. Single. Damn. Day.

Feeling ashamed, I quickly look away from the mirror, shut the light off, and close the door behind me.

I venture into my new room and rummage through the dresser until I find my favorite old, tattered oversized T-shirt and throw it on. It's a concert tee that belonged to my dad back in his rock and roll days while growing up in California. Whenever I had sleepovers as a kid, I used to bring this T-shirt with me so that I wouldn't feel homesick, and it usually worked. So, I'm hopeful that it will help me get through my first night on my own.

A loud, growling noise vibrates throughout my stomach, telling me I need to eat before I go to bed. After putting on my fuzzy bathrobe, I go into the kitchen to preheat the oven and take a pizza out of the freezer. I see the wine sitting on the counter that my mom left but decide against it and pour myself a glass of water instead. I plop myself on the sofa, which used to reside in my parents' basement, and start flicking away with the remote to see if there is anything worth watching on TV.

After about thirty minutes of scrolling through movie options aimlessly and wolfing down half of the pizza, I close my eyes while pulling the folded blanket on the sofa over my legs. But suddenly, my eyes open in a panic when I hear yelling outside the apartment building.

I get up to peer out the wall-sized window in my living room, down the five stories, and realize it's a bunch of college students who look to be having fun. They're coming from the direction of the baseball stadium nearby, and from the loud cheers and screams, I am assuming they are celebrating a win.

A tiny part of me thinks I should be down there having fun and making friends. And the fact that this thought even crosses my mind surprises me. I keep staring out the window until I see a group of guys with beer cans in their hands being rowdy. They're climbing up light poles and smashing bottles, which causes an anxious feeling to build inside me.

Everything is fine. I close my eyes and take a deep breath. *You're safe.*

But then my dad's stern voice echoes through my head, saying, *always keep your door locked at night,* and that's all I can think about.

A heavy sigh escapes me as I make my way over to the big metal door with my blanket still wrapped around me. I recheck the bolt I had locked after Jason left and then attach the chain lock to the top. As I start to walk back to the sofa, I get the idea that pushing the bookcase in front of the door might be a good fail-safe if the locks aren't enough to keep someone out.

Just in case.

After struggling for a while to move the massive bookcase, I finally get it directly in front of the door. Probably not to fire code standards, but it seems like the best option at the moment.

I then go into the kitchen and make sure the oven is turned off, shut off all the lights, and finally head to my bedroom.

The enormous white cloud in the center of the room calls out to me. Taking a few quick steps, I jump into my new bed, which is layered with an oversized white comforter and several grey throws that I picked out just days ago. My head fits comfortably on one of the many pillows as I turn onto my side and stare out the window, which presents an incredible view of the Charles River sparkling from the reflections of the city lights.

I know how lucky I am that my parents can afford a place like this and feel extremely fortunate, but as I look at the view, I'm somehow reminded of this past year, and it makes me feel a little sad.

Or I guess the truth would be that thinking about this past year makes me feel … lonely.

My lifelong friendship with my best friend, Vanessa, had ended. I was forced to resign from the tennis team after missing too many matches. And after getting asked to prom by three different guys, I chose to spend my prom night safely in my room with a box of pizza and my Netflix account.

The sad truth is these things are all my doing. There is no one for me to blame — no one to point my finger at. And if I ever decide to point my finger at anyone, I better look in a mirror.

I spent the past ten months isolating myself, preferring the comforts of home and a good book over any high school social gathering. The only positive came from my rising grades since I spent most of my time studying at the local library. It became a place of comfort for me.

A place where no one could find me.

Most parents would probably interrogate their child over this kind of behavior with assumptions of drugs and alcohol to blame. But my parents knew that wasn't me. They reminded me that they were always available to talk and knew I would eventually work through whatever I was going through. I just needed time.

Not to say they weren't concerned. They both constantly tried to get me to join them on their weekend outings and made sure the four of us ate dinner together every night.

However, one morning after my mom slipped printouts of a few local therapists under my door, I knew I had to make more of an effort. So, I began joining my parents on occasional outings and consciously smiling whenever I was around them. Eventually, I became quite good at pretending everything was ok.

I knew that time would help me. With every passing day, I was feeling more and more like my old self. And in this new city, I was determined to — eventually — really feel ok again and no longer pretend like I was.

But tonight, I just need to get through being alone for the first time, especially since there will be many lonely nights to come. So, I close my heavy eyes and pull the covers up around me, hoping to sleep through the night as I let exhaustion win.

* * *

A few hours later, I bolt upright in terror.

Sweat is dripping down my forehead, and my heart feels like it's ready to pop out of my chest as I throw off my covers to escape the engulfing heat. I put my hand to my forehead, trying to catch my breath, and begin practicing some breathing exercises I've had to do so many times before. It feels too hot in here, so I get up and walk across the room to open the window.

The cool air that whips into my room brings me back to reality, to the present moment, where I am safe from the horrible night trapped inside my memory.

I stare outside, realizing how silly it is of me to think that my nightmares wouldn't follow me here to Boston. But, of course, they did. I've had nightmares continuously for the past ten months, and no matter how many at-home remedies or tricks I try before bed, I can't get them to stop. They are always about the same thing, bringing the past back to haunt me, no matter how hard I try to forget.

When I had these nightmares at home, I had the reassurance

of knowing that my brother's room was right across the hall. Sometimes they would make me scream so loud that I would wake up Jason, who would then run into my room to wake me, saving me from the monster in my dreams.

He would stay with me, sitting on the edge of my bed, and help calm me down. Then, after waiting for me to fall back to sleep, he would go back to his room, always leaving my door open a couple of inches in case it happened again.

Hence one of my many reasons for seeing him as my *big* brother. My whole life, he has always been looking out for me.

Now, standing alone in my room, I realize it is just me and that it will always be this way from now on. There would be no one to wake me up from these horrifying nightmares anymore.

As I continue looking out at the river, a single tear escapes from my eye, and I let it make its way steadily down my cheek. With one last deep breath, I head back to my bed, leaving the window open. I lie down and pull the blankets around my body.

Turning my head to the side, I see the clock on my nightstand showing it is 3 a.m., but I know I won't be able to fall back to sleep anytime soon. So, I pull the covers off, walk over to my desk, and retrieve my current read. Bringing it over to my bed, I take out the bookmark, flipping the pages to my last spot, when I hear my phone buzz on my nightstand.

I pick it up and see Jason's name on the screen.

Jason: Can't sleep. Assuming you're up too?

NATHAN

Is this what death feels like?

I wake up with what can only be described as the worst hangover I've ever had. There's a dull throbbing in my head. My stomach is ready to hurl whatever is inside of me, and my throat feels as dry as the fucking Sahara Desert. Not to mention the excruciating aches running up and down my entire body.

Slowly, I open my eyes, avoiding any direct light, look around, and realize I passed out on someone's couch. Someone's very small and uncomfortable couch, explaining the aches in my now incredibly stiff back.

But whose couch?

As I sit up, the events from the night before slowly start to return.

I remember moving into my dorm room yesterday evening. Then my roommate, Steven, convinced me to go out with him and his friend Kevin to a frat party near campus. I figured a few drinks would help me release some tension I had been holding in, so I joined them. That part is all clear to me.

However, what happened the rest of the night is pretty blurry, and my pounding headache isn't helping the situation.

Scanning the room, I find my blue pullover next to a few people who decided to make the floor their bed. I pick it up and quickly throw it on before any of these people I don't know wake up, then pull my phone out of my pocket to see it is a few minutes after 1 p.m.

"Shit," I say quietly. I was supposed to be at the administration building an hour ago to finish picking my classes for the semester.

Hopefully, a pleading email will take care of this.

I walk out the front door and let it thud behind me as I head to my car in the driveway. Getting in the driver's seat, I glance at my face in the rear view mirror and notice how disheveled I look.

Not my proudest moment. I throw my sunglasses on, turn the keys in the ignition, and get the hell out of here.

* * *

It's a beautiful, crisp fall day in Boston as I drive back to my dorm room with the car windows rolled all the way down. The cool fresh air feels good on my skin, helping me feel more alive with each passing minute.

I pass by a big vibrant sign for the campus coffee shop, which catches my eye, and decide to make a quick stop. I do a U-turn and park my car next to the little shop.

The line of customers ends at the store's front door, but I'm in desperate need of some caffeine, so I wait. Finally, after fifteen minutes in line, the overzealous little barista behind the register takes my order and hands me a large black iced coffee.

"Have a great day!" she shouts at me as I turn to leave.

Walking toward the exit, something bright shines directly into my eyes, so I quickly block the glare with my hand. I look around for the light source but realize it's just a reflection of the sun bouncing off a phone screen sitting on a little table in front of a window. My eyes move up to the person who owns the phone, and that's when I see her.

"Natalie Spencer," I say so quietly that only I can hear her name spoken from my lips.

It's *her.*

She's sitting right in front of me in this very coffee shop. My mouth hangs open in surprise as I stare at her. She's sitting all by herself in the corner, and she's just as beautiful as I remember, if not more so.

But what is she doing in Boston?

I've known Natalie for years through my best friend, Brian Gordon. His little sister, Vanessa, was best friends with Natalie. The two were inseparable; finding one without the other was impossible.

As Natalie grew older, I saw how guys constantly gawked at her. And I mean constantly. In fact, once or twice a few guys found my fist in their faces after I heard some vulgar comments they made about her in the locker room.

And because of that, I always felt like I needed to protect her from all the creeps in the world. There was even a time last October when I had to basically rip some unwanted asshole off her.

But that day would live in my head as the best day of my life because that was the day Natalie and I kissed.

It wasn't some peck or quick kiss either. It was a *kiss*. A real kiss that I find myself thinking about quite frequently. Maybe more times than I care to admit.

But I never saw her again after that night.

Well, come to think of it, that's not true. Because I saw her at the Halloween party Brian threw at his house for my birthday about *ten months ago*. But that was also the night that … I shake my head to rid myself of that awful memory.

This past summer, I noticed Natalie wasn't hanging out with Vanessa anymore. So, one night when I was over at the Gordons' home, I asked Vanessa where her sidekick had been. She told me she hadn't talked to her in months, which surprised me. But it wasn't my business, so I didn't bring it up again.

People change. Sometimes they just outgrow different relationships and places. They move on with their lives, looking for a fresh start. I mean, that's what I'm trying to do, anyways.

What the hell, I think as I take a deep breath and walk over to the little table in the corner of the coffee shop.

She's fully engaged in a book she holds in one hand; a coffee is in her other one. Her legs are crossed in a tight pair of jeans that show off her curvy figure, and she has on a thin white sweater that hugs the silhouette of her chest. She has minimal makeup on, and her long blonde hair is pushed back behind her ears.

Goddamn. Even just sitting there reading a book she looks gorgeous.

"Hey, Natalie," I say, giving her my best smile while also trying to sound casual.

She looks up at me, and her face immediately pales as if she has just seen a ghost.

Maybe this wasn't a good idea.

But within an instant, she puts on a smile and tucks her long shiny blonde hair further behind her ear.

"Nathan? What are you doing here?" she asks. "I thought you went to school in New Hampshire?"

"I did, but I, umm, actually transferred kind of last minute to Linrey University. I wasn't feeling the whole wilderness thing, you know?" I joke with her, trying to ease the tension that I am starting to feel between us. I decide she doesn't need to know the real reason why I had to transfer to this school.

She begins to laugh a little, and I can feel the pressure lift.

"Do you mind if I sit here?" I ask, pointing to the seat directly across from her.

"Of course," she responds, gesturing toward the chair.

I take a seat and put my coffee down. My thumb traces the logo of the cup. I don't know what to say, so I start simple. "So, how have you been?"

She begins twirling a piece of her hair around her finger and takes a breath. "I've been good," she says. I can tell she is thinking over her words. "I am also attending Linrey University, and I just moved into my apartment last night right next to the river down the street. I just came here to get a head start with the reading for my English class." She slightly lifts the book in her hands to show the title *Persuasion* displayed on the cover.

As she's talking, I can't help but stare. She is perfect. From her beautiful smile to her adorable laugh.

God, why didn't I ever ask her out? I'm a moron. That's for sure. She easily could be the most beautiful woman I've ever seen.

Suddenly, I have a flashback to a time when Natalie was sunning herself with Vanessa by the Gordons' pool a few years ago. She was wearing nothing but a tiny pink bikini that barely contained all of her. I had walked outside to a group of people having fun in the pool, and when I looked over at her lying on one of the lawn chairs, I almost tripped over the sprinkler like an idiot. I will never be able to get that image of her out of my mind, and I was thankful for that.

She notices me staring, so I quickly speak. "Oh, did you get one of those new units that they just finished building? I hear the view is amazing." I know Natalie's family has money, and lots of it, so it doesn't surprise me to hear she's living there. Rumor has it that there is a ten-year wait list for one of those units.

"Yeah." Her facial expression turns into one of embarrassment as she looks down at her coffee. "I got a chance last night to see the view, and it's pretty incredible. I … umm, I'm looking forward to being on my own," she says. But, for whatever reason, I don't feel like she's telling the truth.

Maybe it's the small bags I notice under her eyes that catch my attention, but the thought occurs to me that this must be Natalie's first time living alone.

"So, do you have a roommate?" I ask to keep the conversation going.

"Actually, no." She shakes her head and reveals a smile. "I'm not really a roommate type of person."

"Yeah, believe me, I wish I could live alone. Unfortunately, I'm staying in the dorms over on the south side of campus and have to do the whole roommate thing. But, so far, the guy seems ok," I say with a laugh as an image of my roommate doing an awkward-looking keg stand at the party last night flashes back to me.

"NATE!" I hear a thunderous voice yell across the coffee shop.

Oh great.

Turning my head, I see both Steven and Kevin coming toward me. They both look like hell, and they both look like they spend way too much time in the gym.

"Dude, where were you? You were supposed to be my ride home today," Steven announces.

"Sorry, I had some things I had to take care of," I reply.

Steven's attention immediately turns to Natalie. I swear drool is running down his chin.

"Well, well, well. Who do we have here? I've never seen you around campus." The way he looks at her has me rolling my eyes. I notice her cheeks flush with embarrassment.

"Dude, take it down a notch and wipe the drool from your chin. This is Natalie. Natalie, this is Steven, my roommate I was just telling you about. And the guy next to him is Kevin," I say, leaving out the part about Kevin being Steven's inseparable shadow.

"It's nice to meet you both," she says politely.

Kevin quickly jumps in. "So are you coming to the party tonight at the Theta Phi house?" He looks like a pathetic little puppy waiting for her to answer.

"Yeah, what about it? I could be your escort for the evening?" Steven winks, puckering his lips like a duck while standing in a Superman pose.

"No, I'm sorry. I have to get some reading done tonight. Maybe another time," Natalie replies, clearly trying to stifle a laugh.

"That's too bad," Steven says, frowning. "Well, we'll see you later, Nate. And, Natalie, hope to see you soon." Steven gives another wink, then he and Kevin turn to the coffee line and sulk up to the counter.

"You really should come to the party tonight," I say. "I've never seen a guy look so heartbroken."

She looks at her hands, which are now intertwined on the table in front of her. "Oh, I'm not really a party type of person." Then, looking up at me, she gives just a tiny smile. "Besides," she places her hands on her book, "I really need to get some reading done tonight, or I'll never finish in time."

I can't help but glance at her lips as she speaks. Those same perfect lips I had kissed less than a year ago.

"Well, that really is too bad." I shake my head, disappointed. But then a small smile forms as a memory from a couple of years ago comes back to me. "Hey, remember that summer a few years ago at the Gordons' house when you and Vanessa made all those water balloons and then—"

She cuts me off. "I'm sorry, I just realized the time and need to get going. It was nice seeing you, though, Nathan." She smiles and picks up her things, then walks out the door so fast that she doesn't even give me a chance to stop her.

What the hell just happened?

Grabbing the napkin and pen in front of me, I scribble on it quickly and run after her.

"Natalie!" I yell.

She stops abruptly and turns to face me but misses the sidewalk's edge and falls toward me. I take a giant step and catch her in my arms, holding her tightly against my chest. I hear her breath falter as I look down into her intoxicating grey eyes.

And for a moment, as our eyes meet, it feels like we are the only two people on this busy sidewalk.

There's an unusual energy increasing between us that's filled with a sensual desire unlike anything I've ever felt before. I feel my heartbeat accelerate, and I realize she must too since her hands reside on my chest.

Quickly, I try to regain my composure and release her from my arms while taking a step back. I run my hand through my hair, and with my other, I hold out the folded napkin for her.

"Take this," I say, "in case you change your mind."

Without a word, she takes the napkin from my hand, then I turn and walk to my car.

When I reach it, I look back to watch her. She's still standing on the sidewalk, staring down at the napkin in confusion, until she finally unfolds it and sees my number scribbled inside.

NATALIE

Did Nathan Thomas just give me his number?

I stare at the writing on the folded napkin and feel my cheeks flush, though I'm trying to get my heartbeat back to a normal pace. I look up to see Nathan slide into his car and then drive away, heading toward campus.

When I was sitting in the coffee shop reading *Persuasion*, my mind was miles away — overseas in the early 1800s — engulfed in a romance. That was until my thoughts were interrupted by that familiar masculine voice saying my name. The same voice that used to turn my stomach into an oasis of butterflies.

But as I looked up from my book, I instantly felt my stomach drop. No, not drop. More like plummet.

Why did it have to be him? I think, letting out a rather considerable sigh.

In middle school, I spent many hours doodling his name throughout my journals. It started with just his name, Nathan Thomas. Then it became both our names. Nathan and Natalie. And eventually, it became a combined name. Natalie Thomas.

Natalie Thomas.

I was pretty certain Natalie Thomas had a nice ring to it.

His friends always called him Nate, but I referred to him by his full name, Nathan. I don't know why, but it made me feel closer to him. Like we shared some kind of private secret.

And in high school, I spent my summers by Vanessa's pool wearing the most revealing bikinis to catch his attention. But no matter what I did, he never seemed to notice me as more than probably just Vanessa's annoying friend.

When he went off to college, I figured he forgot about me and moved on with his life outside of Greenwich, so that's what I planned on doing too. I forgot about him. Or at least I tried to.

I hadn't even seen him since his—

But I cut off my train of thought with a shake of my head. I can't think about *that* night right now. Not when I am in public surrounded by strangers. Not now. And not here.

My eyes are beginning to brim with tears, and my throat tightens and burns as I try to hold in every emotion as hard as I possibly can. I start feeling lightheaded, which is making me panic. I notice an empty bench a few feet away and immediately walk over to it.

Thankfully, the instant I sit down, the dizzy feeling subsides. *Breathe, Natalie.*

I take some deep inhales and exhales and appreciate the gentle wind that is now pushing my hair behind my shoulders. But as I close my eyes, all I can see is Nathan's face.

Just ten minutes ago, he was standing right in front of me with his gorgeous smile. The one that makes my heart instantly flutter.

And then, only two minutes ago, he rescued me from the complete humiliation of falling face-first in front of him. He moved quicker than I had ever seen anyone move, just so he could catch me.

Catch me and hold me in his arms.

His strong arms.

His arms that held me tight against his chest, making sure I was safe.

There might have been cars driving by and people talking loudly on their phones and whatever else around us, but the only thing I heard at that moment was both of our heartbeats pounding faster and faster. Matching each other's rhythm.

And when he looked down at me with his incredibly dark eyes, I swear I could feel something building between us.

Something I had never felt before.

Nathan had changed over the past year, as evident from his athletic figure. The blue pullover hugged the contours of his toned body without being too tight, and his jeans hung on him just right.

Not that Nathan wasn't in shape in high school, because he certainly was. He was probably the most attractive guy in school, if not the whole town for that matter. But I had never seen him look this fit, this muscular.

And not the kind of muscular body you obtain from spending too much time in the gym. No. This kind of muscular body was created by the gods. Well, that and probably hard work.

I knew he was involved with almost every sports team back in his high school days, including baseball. He was especially good at baseball. Probably even the best on the team, which is how he earned himself a full scholarship to the school he had been attending in New Hampshire.

So why did he leave? I wonder.

Yet, even with the noticeable physical changes, Nathan still looked like the same guy I had always known.

His dark brown hair was pushed back, a little longer than I'd seen before, but I'm not complaining. I wasn't used to the stubble on his face, but it only enhances his chiseled jawline, so again, I'm not complaining. And his deep brown eyes still held the same trance over me as they always had.

But it was his smile I remember most. His smile could make your worst day seem like a distant memory. When he smiled, you couldn't help but smile too.

Damn Nathan Thomas.

I bury my face in my hands, feeling so confused.

The whole point of me going to school in Boston was to have

less chance of seeing someone I know. Especially someone like Nathan.

I put the napkin I realize I am still clutching in the very bottom of my bag, planning to forget about it, and start walking to the campus bookstore just down the road.

* * *

The bookstore is filled with young, ambitious students trying to purchase all of their textbooks before classes begin in just a couple of days. I walk around, familiarizing myself with what the whole store has to offer. There's a smoothie shop in the back, a lounge area to the left, and hundreds of books stacked neatly on shelves.

The irresistible smell of new books fills the air, which has always been one of my favorite scents, instantly bringing a sort of calmness to my mind.

After only a few minutes, I find all the textbooks I need and head to the counter to pay for my items.

A young couple in front of me in line shows no embarrassment about the amount of PDA they are putting on display for everyone. The girl has her hands wrapped around the guy's neck, and he's bent down, kissing her over and over again.

And once again, Nathan pops into my head.

Why, of all the billions of people in this whole gigantic damn world, did it have to be Nathan Thomas who would find me? The world must have a cruel sense of humor.

A daydream starts playing in my head in which Nathan and I are the couple in front of me. As I run my fingers through his dark thick hair, Nathan wraps his arms firmly around me. His head tilts down, bringing his soft lips closer to mine, and then …

The loud ding from the nearby cash register brings me back to reality. I realize I have been staring at the couple and turn crimson red when the guy notices and smiles. I turn my head, pretending I wasn't looking their way, and reach in my bag to find that damn napkin with Nathan's phone number so that I can toss it in the closest trash can.

But just as I begin to dig around, I feel the whole bag vibrate and realize it's my phone. I pull it out and see my mom's name displayed on the screen.

"Hey, mom."

"Hi, honey! How is your first day on your own going?" she asks.

"It's fine. I was just having a coffee down at the local coffee shop and getting ahead on some reading." She does not need to know who else was there. "And I'm actually at the bookstore now getting everything for my classes."

"Well, that's nice. Did you go out last night and meet anyone?" she asks. There's a hint of desperation in her voice.

"No, I was pretty tired after you guys left, so I stayed in for the night. I'm sure I will meet some people when classes start on Monday." I wasn't too confident about this, and I'm sure my mom wasn't either. We both know I'm not the best at making friends since I always come off as being pretty shy.

"You're right, sweetie. Sorry. You know I just miss you. The house felt so empty last night without you. The boys wouldn't watch any of my shows with me."

"I miss you too, mom." I feel my chest tighten a little from this realization.

"Sweetie, I was also wondering … how did you sleep last night?"

I knew this was the real reason why she had called. I had to lie. I couldn't tell her the truth and make her worry about me while I'm away from home. She saw firsthand what the nightmares would do to me.

What *anxiety* has done to me.

When it got bad, it felt like I was *drowning*. That's the only word I can think of to explain it. Gasping for air but unable to find the surface.

Before this past year, it was manageable. Undetectable even. *That* night only heightened my anxiety and made it obvious to most of those around me. Those closest to me.

But because of *that* night, I could no longer hide it from others, forcing me to crave solitude over company.

"I slept great! No issues, I promise." I tried to sound as convincing as I possibly could.

"Oh, that's great news! Maybe going to school in Boston will be good after all." I imagine her smiling at home with the phone pressed against her cheek as she says this.

My eyes begin to water, and my throat tightens for the second time today. I don't want to start crying while I stand in line surrounded by people I don't know, so I decide to end the call. "Mom, I'm about to be next in line. I'll call you later, ok?"

"Ok, Natalie. I love you. Have a great day!"

"Love you too, mom." I throw my phone back in my bag and walk up to the available cashier who is now waving me over.

* * *

I carry all of the textbooks back to my apartment, and by the time I reach the elevator doors, my arms feel like jelly. The concierge had asked if I needed any help, but I assured him I could manage, and boy was I wrong.

The elevator seems to be taking its time getting to the fifth floor. And when the doors finally open, I take one step into the hallway, not seeing the slight gap, and lose my balance, which then causes my textbooks to slide out of my hands straight down to the ground.

Great. I groan, placing my hands on my hips in frustration. I bend down to pick up my books and hear footsteps coming toward me.

"Oh hey, let me help you with those."

I look up and see a girl about my age with wavy black hair and wearing a pair of extremely skinny jeans with a plain white tee. She helps me gather my things and introduces herself.

"I'm Sarah. I'm *your* neighbor right across the hall." She points to the door opposite mine. "I meant to come by yesterday and introduce myself, but, you know … one thing led to another, and before I knew it, the day escaped me." She laughs a little. "I noticed your lights were off when I was leaving for the night, so I figured you were out at a party too." Her arms, covered in delicate floral-looking tattoos, are hugging a few of my textbooks tightly to her chest.

"Oh, no, I was just so tired from moving in yesterday. I passed out pretty early." I must sound like a complete loser. "I'm Natalie," I say as I extend my hand.

"It's nice to meet you, Natalie," she says and shakes my hand with her free one.

After our hands separate, Sarah follows me to my apartment with the other half of my textbooks. I somehow manage to get the key out of my pocket and push the door open with my hip. I place the books on the kitchen island, and she does the same.

"Wow, that is one beautiful view," I hear her say. She's standing in the open living room staring out the massive wall-sized window.

She looks at me and says, "So who'd you have to sleep with to get it?"

For a split second, I think she's serious, but then she starts laughing. I'm relieved and laugh with her. "I assure you, I didn't have to go to any extremes." I can feel my cheeks flush a little. "My parents are actually the ones who picked this place out. I think they know the architect of the building or something," I say a little uncomfortably.

"That's pretty sweet," she replies. "Well, on my side, I have a not-so-lovely view of an abandoned building that's in the process of being demolished. So, hopefully when it is, I'll have a view like this."

I walk over to the window and admire the view of the river beside her. "Yeah, this is pretty amazing." We both stand there in silence, neither of us feeling uncomfortable as we enjoy the sight.

"So, what brought you here?" Sarah asks, breaking the silence in the room.

"Well, I'm attending Linrey University this semester. I

thought I would be doing the whole dorm thing, but then this sort of happened," I say, gesturing with my hands at my new apartment.

"Hey, I go to LU too!" She has an ecstatic look on her face.

"Really?"

"Yeah! I'm a sophomore. I lived on campus last year, and believe me, one year was enough." She rolls her eyes at that thought. "What are you majoring in?"

"English literature," I respond. "What about you?"

"I'm in finance. And I know what you're thinking. I don't really look the accounting type, but I've somehow always been good with numbers, so I thought I would give it a try. Who knows?" Sarah shrugs. "I also have a backup plan. If the whole college thing doesn't work out for me, I'll just marry a rich guy. So, fingers crossed," she jokes.

We both laugh, and then she turns away from the window and makes her way toward the door.

"Well, it's Saturday, so I'm sure you have plans. But anytime you need anything or just want to grab a drink, just come right over," she says with a friendly smile.

Little does she know, my Saturday night plans involve me reading some more of my book and then soaking in a warm bubble bath. "I will. Thanks again for helping me bring my books inside," I say as I open the door for her.

"Oh, forget about it. What are neighbors for?" She gives a small wave and then leaves, closing the door behind her.

I walk over to the kitchen island where my textbooks are and take them to my desk. Making a stack, I drop each one with a loud thud on top of the others. The last book slides from the top and manages to knock my bag off the desk, causing its entire contents to spill onto the floor.

Damn.

I'm gathering everything up to put back into my bag when I see the crumpled white napkin. It looks like it's starting to tear, so I gently pick it up.

Why is this bothering me so much?

I open the napkin and read the number one more time.

But you do know why pops into my head.

I slam the napkin down on my desk and walk away, feeling mad at myself for even letting this get to me.

But I know why I'm bothered. For years I crushed hard on this man. For years I would have done anything for him to notice me. To ask me out on a date. To ask for my number. Anything!

And now it's too late.

It's too late because everything changed after that night.

Ugh. No. I can't think about that right now.

Deep breaths. You're safe.

My stomach starts grumbling, distracting me from my thoughts, and I realize I haven't eaten much today. So, I grab my wallet and head down to the lobby. There is a sandwich shop by the main entrance I want to try, and after grabbing a pesto grilled cheese sandwich, I sit on a bench by the window and again admire the view as I had done the night before. My frustration dwindles as my hunger subsides, so I go back up to my place.

My place.

I take my phone out of my pocket and see it's only 8 p.m. Most people my age are probably starting to get ready to go out, especially since it's the weekend before the fall semester begins.

But not me.

After shutting myself into my apartment, I go straight to the bathtub, turn on the faucet, and wait for the hot water to fill the tub. Steam permeates the room, and I pour some lavender-scented bath salts into the water. I slip out of my clothes and slide into the inviting tub, resting my head against the back of it while closing my eyes. Taking some deep breaths, I try to clear my mind as subtle scents of lavender take over the bathroom, but images of memories with Nathan won't stop appearing.

Except for this time, I let them.

Like the day many years ago when my parents and the Gordons' parents had taken all of us kids out for ice cream. Nathan had tagged along with Brian, which had made me secretly happy.

He was standing by the car eating his ice cream, and Brian threw a football right at him. Nathan didn't notice, so the football crashed right into his ice cream cone. He stood still as his whole ice cream dripped from his shirt to his pants. I laughed so hard I had actual tears coming out of my eyes. Nathan saw this and came over to hug me just to get the ice cream smeared all over my pink sundress. I pretended to try as hard as I could to get out of his grasp, but the truth was, I wasn't really trying.

Or there was the time Vanessa, Nathan, Brian, and I went to our town's annual summer carnival. Brian convinced Vanessa and me that we would be fine on the fastest ride and told us we were babies if we didn't go on, which, of course, motivated us to get in line. However, at the end of the ride, I had tears running down my cheeks and nausea invading me. I felt like I was going to vomit any minute. Nathan felt so bad he took me home right away, leaving Vanessa and Brian at the carnival. I kept my eyes closed the whole car ride out of sheer embarrassment as he kept asking me every five minutes if I was ok.

But the memory making my pulse speed up at this very moment was from the previous October. A week before Halloween, to be precise.

Vanessa and I had spent the weekend at her family's second home in Cape Cod. We had every intention of it being a strict girls-only weekend that included painting our nails and watching sappy rom-coms, that is until Brian and Nathan showed up. So, instead, we spent our girls-only weekend with the boys, playing drinking games on the beach and sitting around a small bonfire.

Vanessa eventually started complaining about how hungry she was, so she and Brian went to the store to get some burgers. Which just left Nathan and me sitting by the fire.

Alone.

The only sound came from the ocean as we both sat there in silence. I tried to find the courage to say something, but after a few minutes, a group of guys we didn't know came over and decided to join us. They were pretty obnoxious and drunk. One of them even sat right next to me and put his arm over my shoulder.

I had told the guy to leave and tried nudging his arm off me, but he didn't budge. That's when Nathan stood up and warned him that it would be best for him to go. But, of course, the guy didn't move. So, without any problem, Nathan picked him up by his sweatshirt and tossed him to the side as if he weighed nothing. The guy quickly scrambled to his feet and stumbled off with his other insufferable friends.

After that, Nathan took a seat right next to me on the sand, leaving no space between us. There was a strong tension growing, and I could feel the heat from his body as our legs faintly touched.

I remember staring at the sand, feeling his gaze down on me, but I was too nervous to look up at him. That's when his hand came up softly, cupping my chin to turn my face so that my eyes locked with his. My chest had tightened and my pulse had quickened when I realized he was going to kiss me.

Nathan Thomas was *finally* going to kiss me.

It's not that I had never kissed guys before, because I had. But something with Nathan felt different from the others.

His face started moving closer to mine, but then he stopped and asked, "Are you ok? You're shaking."

I lied to him and said, "I'm just a little chilly."

He took his jacket off and put it over my shoulders. I was disappointed, thinking the magical movie moment between us was over. But he slowly zipped the jacket up on me, and when he reached the top, I looked up, locking eyes with him again just as his lips came down on mine.

He was so gentle and soft. I remember he tasted of mint, which I liked very much. His hand stayed on my cheek caressingly as we slowly started to part, and his forehead pressed against mine as I caught my breath.

"You have no idea how long I've been wanting to do that," Nathan had said in only a whisper.

The truth was, he had no idea how long I had been waiting for him to do that.

But the sound of Vanessa and Brian's voices made us immediately separate. Thankfully, they hadn't witnessed anything, and the two of us never spoke of that moment again.

Did he ever think about our kiss?

But it wasn't the last time I saw him.

No. The last time I saw him, he never even noticed me. He was busy being the birthday boy and … But I make this thought immediately disappear, open my eyes, and hold my head in both hands.

"See! This is exactly why I can't call him. Because every time I think of him, I think of *that* night," I ramble to myself.

I bolt out of the tub, wrap a towel around my body, and walk to my desk. Without a second thought, I grab the crumpled white napkin that has been sitting there taunting me, and push it deep down into the bottom of the trash barrel.

Problem solved.

NATHAN

"Nate, you're not playing very fair," Natasha says with a pout, her hands on her narrow hips. She introduced herself to me as soon as I walked into the frat house about an hour ago, and I was already annoyed with her.

"Then go bother someone else," I say as my ping pong ball flies in the air and lands perfectly inside the last standing red solo cup. I just won again.

She walks away sulking, which makes me feel relieved.

"Nate, man, long time no see!" I hear from behind me.

I turn to see a familiar face. "Hey, Tim," I say as he grabs my shoulder. "You go to school here?" Tim and I were on the same baseball team in high school, and we always had a good time, so it's pretty cool running into him here.

"Yeah, actually, I live here," he says, gesturing at the house. "It's not much, but it's home."

"That's pretty sweet." Admittedly, it wasn't my ideal living situation, but to each their own, I guess.

"It has its perks." His eyes dart over to a group of scantily clad girls who just entered the room. "But what are you doing here? I thought you were up at school with Brian?" Tim asks before guzzling down his beer.

"I was, but I guess I somehow ended up here," I say with a shrug, hoping he'll drop the subject.

"Well, that's cool, man. Glad to see a hometown face. Maybe we can hit up the batting cages soon." He picks up two red solo cups on the table beside him. "Come have a drink with us." He nods in the direction of a group of guys sitting on the couches in the other room.

I chug the beer I already have in my hand and toss the can to the side. Tim hands me one of the cups, and I gladly accept without asking what it contains.

I head to the living room area and recognize a few people who were here last night, including the tan brunette in the hot pink strapless dress.

Shit.

A memory comes back to me within an instant, and I definitely recognize her now. She is hot. That's obvious. But the girl blew up my phone as soon as I left the house this afternoon, so I finally had to shut it off to get some peace and quiet.

"Fuck," I say out loud, making a few heads turn in my direction.

I had given Natalie my number this afternoon to call me in case she wanted to come out tonight, and like a dumbass, I had shut my phone off. Quickly, I pull it out of my pocket before taking a seat on the small, familiar couch (aka the couch I used as my bed last night) and turn it back on. But I have no missed calls or texts from her.

I instantly feel, well, I'm not exactly sure. I've never checked my phone hoping to see a message from a particular girl before. So, I think this feeling is called … disappointment?

"What's with the face?" Steven asks as he takes the little available space next to me on the couch. He smells like weed, and looking into his glossy red eyes lets me know he's as high as a kite.

"Nothing. I just realized I never signed up for my classes today." I put my phone back in my pocket and take a chug from the drink in my hand.

"Screw classes!" Steven yells, clearly already trashed.

"Yeah, everyone knows it's about the PARTIES!" His sidekick, Kevin, who is now sitting on the other side of Steven, forcefully yells so that everyone can hear him. He gets cheers from a lot of wasted people standing nearby as he chugs the rest of his drink and then proceeds to smash the can on top of his head.

"Real nice," I say. These two make *Dumb and Dumber* look smart.

"What's your problem?" Kevin asks.

"Nothing, I'm going to go get another drink." I make my way to the kitchen and fill my cup up with the dark liquid concoction in the punch bowl. I'm about to leave the room when I hear a familiar voice.

"Well, there you are."

Fuck. Fuck. Fuck.

"Veronica, hi," I say, keeping my voice even as I turn around to face her.

"It's Victoria," she says with a sour look. She crosses her tan arms across her chest, pushing everything up and distracting me for a moment.

"That's, umm, what I meant," I lie.

"Well, Nate, you never returned any of my texts. What's up with that?" She starts getting closer to me and uncrosses her arms so that she can put her hand on my bicep.

Ok, time to nip this in the ass.

"So, Victoria, last night was great. Really, it was. But I'm not looking for anything serious right now, and I'm sorry if I gave you the wrong impression." I run my hand through my hair, watching her reaction. "I hope that's ok?" I can instantly tell that it is, in fact, not ok from how wide her eyes have suddenly become.

The chilling look on her face tells me precisely what is about to happen. She slaps me hard across the cheek, and I let her because I deserve it. I mean, we didn't sleep together, just fooled around, but I still feel bad.

She storms off in a fit of anger as I take a swig from my drink. I'm used to girls always throwing themselves at me. I mean, I'm not blind. I know I'm a good-looking guy, but what I'm not used to is rejection.

And rejected is exactly how Natalie is making me feel.

God, she practically bolted out of that coffee shop this afternoon, and I don't know why. Shaking my head, I try to get her image out of my mind but fail.

Why can't I stop thinking about her?

I look down at my phone and notice it's getting late, so I walk back to the room where the couches are to find a place to sit. Unfortunately, when I get there, all the seats are full. As I look around, I see the place getting packed with bodies of young, drunk, and horny people, so I go to the backyard to get some air.

I spot a stone wall on the far end of the yard and head over to it. I zip my pullover up as a slight gust of cold air whips around me, making me wish I had worn an actual coat tonight. Sitting on the stone wall, I bring my drink up to my lips and turn my eyes up toward the clear night sky.

This is my favorite time of year in New England.

For a brief moment, as I stare at the stars, I wonder what Natalie is doing at this very moment. Does she have a boyfriend? A girl like that couldn't possibly be spending her nights alone.

I finish my drink, lie back on the stone wall, using my hands under my head as a pillow, and close my eyes.

Does she ever think about that kiss?

I had wanted to kiss Natalie for so long, but we were always with groups of people. Not until that night on the beach, that is.

Something took over me that night when I got lost looking down into her perfect grey eyes. At that moment, I realized how much I needed her. Maybe it was the fact that the two of us were finally alone with each other for the first time, but I did it.

And I would be able to die happy just knowing I had kissed her sweet lips, even just that one time.

We didn't see each other again until my birthday a week later. Well, actually, I saw her that night. She never saw me.

But that was something I had been trying to get out of my head.

The image of Natalie from that night had haunted me for months afterward. So I was relieved to see her today, just as beautiful as ever.

A loud sigh escapes me as I struggle to get the thought of her out of my head. I wish she had come tonight.

I feel my phone vibrate in my pocket, so I instantly look at it, hoping it might be her. But instead, it's my younger brother, Nick.

Nick: He's out.

* * *

Twelve hours later, I'm parking my car at the Boston Yacht Club that's just twenty minutes away from school. I get out and head toward the entrance, noticing how pristine and regal everything looks. As I get closer, I see a man standing by the docks holding paperwork in his hands. He seems to be evaluating all the employees busy cleaning and inspecting the massive boats and yachts docked.

My instincts tell me this is the guy I'm supposed to be introducing myself to. As I approach him from behind, he turns around and displays an ultra-white smile.

"So, you must be the new guy," he says as he holds out his hand to me. He's tall, slender, and wearing a khaki pair of pants with a navy polo shirt and a new-looking pair of Sperry boat shoes. His hair is combed back with a little too much gel, so no one strand is out of place, and his wire-rimmed glasses make him appear older than I believe he actually is.

"Hi. Yes, I'm Nathan. But most people call me Nate," I respond as I shake his hand.

"Nice to meet you, Nate. I'm Tom Anderson, the general manager around here." He turns his head and looks around at everything before bringing his attention back to me. "Mark had a lot of nice things to say about you. He tells me you're one of the hardest working employees he has ever had. Never missed a shift."

"Well, to be honest, Mark has been more of a mentor to me than a boss over the years." I run my hand through my hair and look off in the distance before saying, "He's a really great guy."

Mark is the manager at the Greenwich Yacht Club where I have spent the past five summers working. But more importantly, he has been the only real father figure in my life.

At sixteen years old, I decided to get a job to help my mom out. And on the way home from school one day, I spotted a big "Help Wanted" sign on a light pole for the local yacht club not far from my house. The rest is history.

Mark and I always got along well, and he must have seen something in me — maybe the son he never had — because he took me under his wing and taught me everything he knew about boats. I picked up the skills fast and found working with boats to be physically demanding, proving useful when I needed to let off a little steam.

A few months ago, Mark had called Tom (without me knowing) to help me find a job close to school. He knew that me going to college this year would depend on whether I could find work, so he did everything he could to make this happen for me. No words could describe how appreciative I felt when he told me what he had done.

Tom smiles. "He said I'd be horribly mistaken if I didn't give you a job here, so no pressure, but don't screw up." He chuckles to himself. "He and I were childhood friends, so I'm only happy to help when he asks a favor of me."

"I won't let you down, sir. I promise," I respond.

"Just call me Tom, ok? Sir makes me feel so old," he says as he watches a beautiful yacht pull up next to the dock behind me. He continues to look off at the boat when he says, "Well, you'll pretty much have the same responsibilities that you had in Greenwich, so I expect you'll know your way around everything."

"Yes, sir. I mean, Tom. I know my way around boats pretty well."

"Great, I have some things I need to take care of in the office, but Greg," he points to a skinny guy cleaning a boat nearby, "can show you where everything is."

Tom looks down at his glistening Rolex. "So make yourself at home, and oh yeah, we're pretty flexible about the schedule here, especially while you're in school. If you put the work in, there won't be any issues with things. So, just let Greg know your availability, and he should be able to find shifts for you to fill. Any issues with anything, just let me know." He smiles, and I nod back in understanding, then he leaves for the main building.

The place is pretty impressive, and it isn't hard to see why people pay big money to become members here.

There is a high-top bar overlooking the water, an upscale restaurant to the side where a live jazz band performs, sailboats lined up on another side, and multimillion-dollar yachts awaiting their daily inspections and cleanings. This place is at least three times the size of the yacht club back in Greenwich, but I'm confident I will have no problem keeping up with the workload.

After taking everything in, I set out in Greg's direction to introduce myself.

"Hey, Greg. I'm Nate Thomas, the new guy," I say, reaching out my hand.

Greg has a surprisingly firm grip. "Well, we are sure glad you're here. We've recently been a little short-staffed, so it's nice to have someone on board who knows what they're doing."

"Yeah, I've spent quite a bit of my time working with boats." I turn my attention to the vessel Greg is in the middle of cleaning. "I can't say any of them have ever been this big, though."

"Oh yeah, this one is a beauty," Greg says, "Just showed up a few hours ago." He puts the rag in his hand over his shoulder and looks at me. "I could use a break with this. Let's head over to the main building so I can show you around, and then we can get your schedule taken care of."

"That would be great." As I follow Greg, I peer over my shoulder for one last look at the massive ships lined up against the docks.

It isn't Mark's place. That's for sure. But for some reason, I'm starting to feel like maybe Boston is exactly where I'm supposed to be.

NATALIE

I t's finally Monday, the first day of classes.

I feel like a little kid getting ready for my first day of school as I pick out my outfit and make sure I have all the correct textbooks in my bag. And after deciding on a dark pair of jeans, a long beige sweater with a white camisole, and a dark brown pair of ankle boots, I feel ready to start my freshman year.

Closing my apartment door behind me, I walk to the elevator and hit the button for the doors to open. While I wait, I feel my phone vibrate in the back pocket of my jeans. I take it out and see Jason's name on the screen.

Jason: Don't flunk out.
Me: I'll try not to!

"Natalie, are you on your way to campus too?"

I look up from my phone and see Sarah coming toward me with textbooks in her hands.

"Yeah, I'm on my way to my creative writing class, which is over on the far side of campus," I say.

"Awesome! I'm heading that way too. What time is your last class today?"

The elevator doors open, and we both step inside. Sarah hits the button for the lobby, then the elevator slowly descends.

"Umm, it's at two and ends at four." I respond. The doors open again, so we exit the elevator and enter the lobby.

"Oh, good! That's when my class ends too. Let's meet at the campus coffee shop so we can walk back together."

"That would be great!" I answer.

It takes about fifteen minutes to get to the main campus. We exchange numbers before parting, and then Sarah waves goodbye as she heads to her class.

"Good luck!" She yells over her shoulder.

"You too!" I yell back before going the opposite direction.

I walk briskly toward the building where my first class will be and admire the fall foliage beginning to appear. The leaves are just starting to transform into beautiful red hues, and there's a familiar New England chill in the air.

The campus is bustling with anxious students trying to find their classes. I'm the first person to arrive for my creative writing course, so I grab a chair near the middle section and wait for everyone else to file into the room.

The professor makes a mundane entrance and begins his lecture immediately with no formal introduction. I pull my pen and notebook out of my bag and start copying down every word he says. After nearly two hours of frantically writing in my notebook, the class is dismissed, and every student bolts out of their seat and rushes to their next class.

The rest of the day goes by in a blur. Some professors make us play the embarrassing ice breaker games to get to know one another, and other professors act like they don't care that we are even there. A few people in my classes introduce themselves to me, and I start to think I might enjoy this whole college thing.

After my statistics class, I grab a sandwich at the cafeteria then head to my last class of the day, History of Films. I have actually been looking forward to this one.

I walk into the room and see a few students have already taken their seats, so I find an empty chair near the back and take out the textbook from my bag, placing it on the top of the desk directly in front of me.

Flipping slowly through its pages, I am captivated by images of films, new and old.

That is until I hear *his* voice.

"Is this seat taken?" Nathan asks as he makes himself comfortable in the chair beside me. Or at least as comfortable as a person who is well over six feet tall with broad shoulders and a very muscular body can be in these tiny seats.

I swear my heart just skipped a beat. Either that or it stopped working altogether as I feel butterflies forming colonies in my stomach.

Stay calm, Natalie.

But the second I look up, I see that beautiful smile and melt faster than butter on a hot summer's day in Georgia.

"Looks like it is now," I respond with a smile.

"How are your classes going?" he asks.

"They're actually going pretty well. This is my last class for the day. How about you?" I ask. He runs his hand through his hair, and I find myself wishing it was my hand.

Get a hold of yourself, Natalie!

"They're ok. Can't complain. I signed up pretty late for classes, so I got stuck with whatever was left." He shrugs. "Kind of been looking forward to this class, though. I've always loved getting lost in movies."

"I've been looking forward to this class too," I reply.

He smiles at me, and I immediately feel my insides going crazy. What is he doing to me? I quickly bring my attention back down to my textbook, continuing to flip through the pages, pretending to read.

"By the way," he says, "I must have missed your call the other night."

"Oh, I umm …" I can't think of what to say, and I can feel my cheeks begin to flush.

"I'm just teasing," he remarks with a playful wink.

I'm relieved and show a slight smile back at him. Then the teacher walks into the classroom and addresses the class.

"Good afternoon. My name is Professor Clark." He picks up a marker and writes his name on the board behind him. "The seat you are in today will be your seat for the rest of the semester, every Monday and Friday afternoon, and I expect to see every one of your smiling faces present in class." He walks over to his desk and starts fiddling with his computer.

Staring at the screen, he says, "Now, the general objective of this class is to bring classic films to life before your very eyes, to evaluate the use of technology present at that current time, and to discover what made it so successful even decades later. We will watch some current films that have had a successful impact on the film industry as well, but overall, the films we will be watching are from many years prior. This class is not meant to be difficult, and as long as you put in the time and have an appreciation for film, I believe you may enjoy your time in this class." He clicks down hard on his mouse before turning his attention back to the classroom full of students.

"Today, we will watch *Casablanca*, which just happens to be one of my favorite films. We won't have time to watch the whole movie today, but I expect a three-page paper on your observations turned in at the start of our next class. Who stood out to you the most? What is happening in the world at the time? Are there any current films that show a similar theme? How does Rick represent the United States in 1941? These are just some questions I would like for you to consider. And with that, I present to you *Casablanca*." Professor Clark shuts the lights off as the movie projects onto the giant white screen at the front of the class.

Casablanca is one of my favorite films too, so I can already tell I am going to like this class. I close my textbook and put it in my bag, which is sitting next to my feet, when I feel someone's breath close to my neck. Instantly, I know it's Nathan.

"It would have been nice to see you, though," he says in just a whisper, only inches from my ear, so only I can hear him.

I turn my head to look up at him, and his piercing eyes stare right back at me, not looking away. It's intimidating. But also … a complete turn-on. There's a feeling in the pit of my stomach that I can't describe. My whole body seems to be going numb, and I can't find the words to say anything because my mouth has gone completely dry.

A beeping sound from the phone of the girl in front of me brings me back to reality. I quickly compose myself, sitting straight in my seat like nothing has just fazed me. I know or used to know Nathan better than most people, which means I know his level of experience with girls, and I wasn't about to let him turn me into a big puddle of mush with a dumb line like that.

Tossing my hair over my shoulder, I say pretty sarcastically, "Oh, I'm sure there were plenty of girls there to keep you entertained." I turn back around and pretend to watch the film. I'm not sure, but I think I saw a look of disappointment pass across his face. I imagine he is not used to girls giving him the cold shoulder, but he will have to start getting used to it with me.

The rest of the class goes by in silence as everyone focuses on the film.

Finally, with five minutes left of class, the professor turns off the movie and turns on the light.

"Now don't forget about the three-page paper I expect at the start of your next class. We will finish *Casablanca* on Friday." And with that, he picks up his briefcase and walks out the classroom door.

I'm picking up my bag from the floor when I hear Nathan clear his throat. Looking up at him, he runs his hand through his dark hair and looks down at the ground before bringing his gaze up to me.

"I wasn't trying to give you some kind of line, Natalie. I really meant what I said." His eyes are begging me to believe him.

I look away from him but can feel his gaze still on me, so I look back and instantly regret it. He has no idea what those dark eyes do to me, and after only an instant, I'm lost inside them. Those eyes that, for years, I've dreamed about.

If only you knew why nothing could ever happen between us.

He looks like he is about to say something, so I hastily cut him off before he has a chance.

"Well, I better be going." I move my eyes back down to the floor. "I'm supposed to meet a friend for coffee. I guess I'll see you in class." I get up from my chair and leave as quickly as possible, not giving him a chance to say anything else. As soon as I exit the room, a weight lifts off my chest, and I feel like I can breathe again.

I snag a seat on a bench outside the library entrance and take a deep breath, waiting for my heartbeat to slow down. I grip the edges of the bench and let my head rest against the brick wall behind me until my breathing returns to normal.

How am I going to make it through a whole semester with Nathan only sitting inches away from me?

I let out one final big breath, tuck the loose strands of hair behind my ears and then make my way to the campus coffee shop.

Entering it, I see Sarah sitting at a table with a coffee in her hand and wave to her as I go up to the counter to order an iced caramel latte, one of my favorite treats. After the barista hands me my drink, Sarah and I walk back to our apartment building.

"So, how was your first day? I remember mine. I didn't want to be late, so I started running when I heard the bell go off from the clock tower in the center of campus and ended up tripping into my first class, falling face first in front of everyone already in their seats. I was so horrified that I skipped the rest of my classes that day," she says, laughing.

"Well, it's safe to say mine wasn't nearly as traumatic. Overall, I'd say it wasn't so bad. It was actually kind of … enjoyable." That is until I found out I would be spending the rest of the semester sitting by Nathan several days a week. The one man I had always wanted and now couldn't have.

Torture. That's what this semester is going to be. Absolute torture.

"That's great! Sarah says enthusiastically. "Tomorrow, I start my internship at a big fancy bank, so unfortunately, I won't be on campus, but if you want to grab drinks or anything tomorrow night, just let me know."

"Wow, that's so exciting. Is it far?" I ask as we enter the main lobby of our apartment building. The concierge gives us both friendly smiles as we wave to him on our way to the elevator.

"No, it's just a few blocks away. Plus, my boss is a real babe, so at least I'll have some eye candy to keep me occupied." We both laugh at this.

I'm happy for Sarah, but now that means I have no one to walk with me to and from campus tomorrow.

We say our goodbyes after we get to our floor, and I step inside my apartment, pleased to be home. I drop my bag on the kitchen island and lie down on my sofa, pulling a blanket up around me as tiredness washes over me. I'm relieved that the first day of classes went pretty smoothly.

Well, except for the Nathan part.

Why did he have to be in my class?

When I was younger, I always daydreamed about being one of the girls Nathan took out on a date. Sometimes I would hear him talk about those nights with his friends. They would try so hard to get him to spill details about any intimate moments, but he never did. They couldn't get a word out of him.

It made me like him even more.

But I knew I would never be one of those lucky girls. Nathan would never see me as more than his best friend's sister's friend.

"It would have been nice to see you, though."

That line keeps playing in my head until I convince myself he didn't mean anything by it and that I'm *overthinking* everything like I usually do.

And even if he did mean it, there is no way Nathan and I could be friends or even more, for that matter. Not after *that* night when … But I sit up in a panic and try to think of anything else but *that* night. A night that Nathan and everyone else I know could *never* find out about.

I pick up my copy of *Persuasion*, which is lying on the coffee table in front of me, and spend fifteen minutes reading, but I'm finding it hard to focus on the words. They all start blurring together, so I put the book down, curl up on the sofa, and close my eyes, dreaming of a handsome Humphrey Bogart.

Only what should be Humphrey's face is instead Nathan's. He's wearing a trench coat as the rain comes down hard around us. His arms are wrapped around me so tight, and his dark eyes look deep into mine as he says, "We will always have Paris."

NATHAN

y phone on the small wooden nightstand beside my bed wakes me up at noon to let me know it's finally Friday. *Thank God,* I think as I roll over and shut off the loud, obnoxious alarm.

The week went by in a blur with every new class I sat in and every new face I met. My courses seem like they will be ok, and my roommate, Steven, was never actually around, so I usually had the place to myself, which was great. I had a couple of shifts at the yacht club that were easy overall, and my coworker, Greg, actually seems like a cool guy.

There was just one thing I couldn't get out of my head.

Natalie.

Why did it feel like she was purposely avoiding me? Even last Monday at the end of class, she practically bulldozed people out of her way to get away from me. Or at least that's what it felt like she was trying to get away from. I also wasn't sure why I cared so much.

But you do know why.

The truth is, I used to have a massive crush on Natalie when we were in high school. A crush that I'm starting to realize I never really got over. And a crush that was honestly more than just a crush.

She was a sophomore when I was a senior, and even though she was younger than me, it didn't change the fact that she was way out of my league, simply because she was Natalie Spencer. The girl was admired by all at our high school, whether she wanted to be or not. I knew she never liked the attention and pretty much always kept to herself. Still, her family's money and her desirable looks made her noticeable to everyone, especially horny high school boys.

Once or twice, I saw her getting rides home from the captain of the football team or the captain of the basketball team. I know she never asked the baseball captain for a ride home, though, since that was me. Maybe she just never liked me that way, but I had always wondered what it would be like to give Natalie Spencer a ride home.

I lie in bed and stare at the ceiling for a few minutes wondering why Natalie would be avoiding me. Was it the night we kissed? Did I say something to make her uncomfortable?

Then it occurs to me; does she remember seeing me *that* night? The night I try so hard not to think of. Is that why she has been avoiding me? But, no, there was no possible way she remembers seeing me. She could barely keep her eyes open when they put her in the back of the …

No!

I shake my head, making the image of Natalie from *that* night disappear completely. My hands instinctively go up to my face as frustration takes over.

I start replaying our conversations at the coffee shop and in our film class and nothing comes to mind that I think would have made her upset with me.

Shit.

This girl seems to want nothing to do with me, which is probably why I can't get her out of my head.

"This is not going to be easy," I stress as I jump off the tiny twin mattress to get ready for class.

After taking a hot shower, I throw on a new grey pullover and a pair of jeans, then spray the slightest bit of my cologne in the air around me. I push my hair back, pick up my backpack, plug in my headphones, and yes, I'm one of the few people left in the world who still uses headphones, and leave my dorm room.

On the walk to class, I decide to make a last-minute trip to the campus coffee shop.

That should do the trick. Five minutes later, I walk out with not one but two coffees in my hands.

I'm a few minutes early to class, which is not like me at all, but I go in and take my assigned seat. I place both coffees on my desk, and my leg starts bouncing up and down in anticipation.

As students start filing in, I look around but don't see Natalie among the sea of faces. Maybe she's not coming to class today. Did she drop this course after finding out I was in it?

Would she really go to this extreme to avoid me?

But just as the professor walks into the room, Natalie quietly takes the seat beside me.

"Hey," I whisper just loud enough for her to hear. Her long blonde hair is pulled back, but a loose strand dangles by the side of her left eye, giving me the urge to gently push it behind her ear. I don't, of course, and instead, resist while I wait in anguish for her to say something.

"Hi," she politely responds, but she looks down at her bag and pulls out her assignment.

"You like caramel, right?" I ask. I can tell I've caught her off guard, and she looks at me in confusion. "I stopped by the coffee shop on my way to class, so I grabbed you an iced caramel latte. I'm pretty sure that's what you used to drink." I hand it to her, and she cautiously takes it.

"Wow," she says. "You … you remembered that?" Her eyes are glued to the drink in her hand, but her mind looks like it's elsewhere. She finally blinks and turns her attention back to me.

"Yeah, of course," I respond with a smile, and thankfully, she smiles back.

"Thank you," she says quietly. The tension between us instantly lifts.

Professor Clark walks to the front of the class. "Please pass your papers to the front so I can collect them."

I take my paper out of my bag and pass it to the person in front of me.

"Also, if anyone is interested in earning some extra credit, tonight at the Boston Common, there will be a showing of a film you may all be familiar with: *The Dark Knight*. If you attend and then present to me on Monday with your ticket as evidence along with a one-page detailed paper on why you either like or dislike the film, I will give you twenty points to use on any future assignment or test."

While much of the class cheers at this bit of news, a lightbulb goes off for me.

An evening at the Boston Common while lying under the stars next to a beautiful girl might not be such a bad way to spend my Friday night, especially if that girl is Natalie.

"Ok, ok, settle down. Now we will be finishing the classic film, *Casablanca*." He stands in front of his computer until the film starts projecting on the white screen and then walks over to the door to shut the lights off. I'm starting to think this might be the best class I have ever had.

The silence between Natalie and me during the film feels deafening. I want to say something but know not to, so I spend the next hour looking straight ahead at the movie.

A soft rhythmic noise comes from her direction, making me turn my head. I notice her fingers drumming gently against her desk, and when I look up at her face, she seems lost in thought, staring out the window beside her. And just as I turn back to the screen, Humphrey Bogart is watching a vintage plane fly away, and suddenly the lights in the classroom turn on.

"There is no assignment for tonight, so have a good weekend. I will see you all on Monday," Professor Clark says before being the first one to exit the classroom.

I throw my book into my bag and get out of my seat, noticing Natalie packing her things too. But it doesn't seem like she is rushing to leave this time. Turning to make my way out the door, I stop when I hear her soft voice behind me.

"Thanks again for the coffee," she says. "I didn't realize how much I needed one." She gives a little lighthearted laugh, automatically making me smile.

I turn back around. "Yeah, it's really no big deal." I adjust the strap of my bag over my shoulder, but she makes no motion to leave. "Is this your last class today?" I ask.

"Yes, I was just going to head back to my apartment," she says, now gazing down at the floor, avoiding eye contact. She looks like she is trying to think of something to say as she twirls a piece of blonde hair between her fingers.

She also bites down tenderly on her bottom lip, which drives me crazy.

What I would give to taste those lips again.

"Would you want me to … walk you back to your apartment?" I ask. I hope I didn't just make things weird. But relief washes over me as a small smile appears on her face.

"I'd like that," she answers.

We leave the classroom side by side. The walk goes by quickly as we make small talk about our courses and teachers. But when we near her building, I hear someone yell my name. I look around and see Tim leaning against a wire fence that surrounds a basketball court. There's a pickup game going on behind him that he must be playing in.

"Dude, will I see you at Danny's house party tonight?" He screams across the way, loud enough so I and everyone else nearby can hear him.

"No, man, I don't think so," I yell back. I have other intentions in mind for tonight.

"Come on, man! It's going to be a full-out rave!" He pleads with me. "You can bring that fine-looking thing next to you! Wait a second … is that Natalie Spencer?"

I look over at Natalie, who I can tell is completely mortified. "No, sorry, another time," I say and continue with Natalie to her apartment. We walk through the entrance, and I notice the building even has a concierge service.

Of course, it does.

"Sorry about him. He's not a bad guy. He just doesn't know when to shut his mouth," I say with a slight shrug.

She keeps her gaze straight ahead and says, "I'd be lying if I said I wasn't used to it." Then she glances up at me. "Was that Tim Horgan from high school?"

"Yeah, it was. I ran into him last weekend. He lives at one of the frat houses nearby." I'm relieved she isn't upset by his stupid comment, and I decide this is the moment to ask her about tonight. "You know, I was thinking ..." My heart feels like it is beating faster than it should be. "Would you maybe be interested in going to the Boston Common tonight? You know, for the extra credit." I look around, too nervous to make eye contact with her, and when I finally do, I can tell the wheels in her head are spinning. "I'm not exactly sure how busy it will be, but it could be fun, and who knows what—"

But she quickly cuts me off and says, "Yes. I'd love to." The genuine smile on her face tells me she means it.

"Great!" I exclaim, maybe a little too excitedly. "I mean, yeah, that's great. I'll come back here around seven to pick you up."

"Ok, I'll see you then," she says and, in a nervous gesture, tucks a small strand of hair behind her ear. Then she turns and heads to the elevator.

I leave Natalie's building and start walking in the direction of my dorm room. I'm looking forward to tonight, but I'm also feeling ... what is this feeling?

Nervous? Am I feeling nervous?

I can't remember ever feeling this way about a girl before. But I could live with it, especially if it meant I would be spending my Friday night with Natalie.

Seven

NATALIE

At 7 p.m. on the dot, the concierge calls to let me know a gentleman is waiting downstairs for me. I tell him I'll be right down then grab my bag and stop in front of the full-length mirror in my bedroom. I take one last look at myself, which causes my stomach to twist into a thousand anxious little knots.

When Nathan asked to see me tonight, I immediately thought *no*. I had spent all week trying to bury my feelings for him way down. I mean, like *way* down. Further than I knew possible. The thing was, the harder I tried to stop thinking about him, the more he made his way back into my head. Back into my heart.

But about thirty seconds after Nathan asked me to go to the Boston Common with him, and about thirty seconds after I had immediately thought it was a bad idea, I heard a small voice in my head say, *yes*.

So that's exactly what I said.

Though, after I made it inside my apartment, I realized I only had a few hours to pick out an outfit, shower, and do my hair and makeup before he picked me up. So, I took a quick, hot shower, and when I got out, I found myself standing in front of my closet for twenty minutes without any clue as to what I should wear. But then it occurred to me that I have a very stylish neighbor who could help with my dilemma.

I marched over to Sarah's apartment in my bathrobe and knocked a few times on her door, hoping she would be home. When she, thankfully, opened her door, I explained my predicament while slightly begging for her assistance. Her face lit up with excitement at my request, and she returned with me to my closet.

Sarah and I ended up choosing a dark pair of high-rise jeans, a white blouse I could tuck in, and a black pair of ballet flats. The shirt was just the slightest bit see-through, but we thought it still looked classy with a white lace bra underneath. After putting everything on and looking in the mirror, I found that my nerves were starting to evaporate.

Sarah looked me up and down, proud of her work, and said, "I expect a full report when you get back." She left after wishing me good luck, and that's when the nerves returned.

After one final look in the mirror, I take a deep breath and begin my trip down to the lobby.

When I step out of the elevator, I see Nathan standing against the wall, and my breath catches. He's wearing a black pullover with a dark pair of jeans, looking like he just left a Calvin Klein photo shoot. He notices me walking over to him, and an adorable smile appears on his face.

Goddamn.

"You look … well, you look great, Natalie," Nathan says, and his cheeks redden.

"Thanks." I lightly pull on my shirt sleeve and look anywhere but at him.

Nathan leads the way to the lobby door and holds it open for me. "After you."

We step outside, and I see his car parked in front of the building. He opens the passenger door for me and waits for me to get in before shutting it. After he jumps in the driver's side, he starts the car, and we are on our way.

There is a silence between us that I don't like, so I say the first thing that comes to mind. "I'm still kind of surprised that you wanted to go out with me tonight." I turn my attention to the passenger window, instantly regretting my choice of words.

"You're surprised?" he asks.

"Well, to be honest, yes, I am." I shrug. "I mean, I haven't seen you since … well, in a long time." I can feel my cheeks burn at the mere thought of that moment on the beach.

"Well, if we're being honest with each other, I'm surprised you agreed to come. Don't get me wrong, I'm glad you're here right now, but I'm still surprised." He pauses. "Why did you agree to come with me tonight?" He looks over at me quickly but then puts his eyes back on the road.

"I umm … I don't know." I stare out the window, unable to come up with a reason as to why I was here. Or a reason I could admit out loud in front of him without completely embarrassing myself. I couldn't admit that, for the past week, it had been virtually impossible for me to even get the thought of him out of my head.

"You think about that night too, don't you?" He doesn't look at me, but I notice his grip on the steering wheel tightens.

I know right away what night he's referring to. The night I wish I could relive over and over again, also known as the night we shared our first kiss. I look first at him and then down to my lap as I slowly shake my head up and down. "Yes," comes out of my mouth in only a whisper, but I know he heard me.

"I thought you … never mind."

"You thought what?" I ask, bringing my eyes up to him.

He hesitates before answering. "Did I do something wrong that night?"

"Wrong?" I ask in surprise. There was absolutely nothing wrong about that kiss.

His eyes make their way over to my face as we stop at a red light. "It's just, I never heard from you after that night. I thought maybe I did something wrong. I mean, when I saw you at the coffee shop last week, you seemed like you couldn't get away from me fast enough, and then again at our film class. I don't know. I just thought—"

I cut him off before he can finish. "Nathan, I'm so sorry." I look away from him, embarrassed. After all this time, he thought I had stopped talking to him because of that kiss. My heart starts to ache. If only he knew the real reason why I had distanced myself from him and everyone else this past year. "That night on the beach with you was honestly one of the best nights of my life. I didn't think it meant anything to you, though, like it did to me. So I tried to forget about it, which kind of proved impossible for me to do."

His hand gently cups my chin and lifts my face, so my eyes connect with his. "You're wrong. That kiss did mean something to me. It meant everything to me."

We sit in silence, staring into each other's eyes. Nathan's palm rests against my cheek as his thumb brushes away a piece of hair hanging in front of my face. I start feeling self-conscious, so I bite my bottom lip out of habit, which he notices immediately because his gaze moves down to my lips. His hand moves softly against my skin until his thumb reaches my bottom lip, tracing it back and forth. My breath hitches and my pulse quickens in anticipation as he moves closer to me. But just as I close my eyes, the car behind us honks, letting Nathan know the light has turned green.

"Damn," escapes quietly from Nathan's lips. He shakes his head in frustration and turns back to the road.

I lean my head on the window beside me, hoping the glass's coolness will help slow down my heartbeat for the remainder of the ride.

I replay the conversation in my head and can't help but feel excited that he had been thinking about that kiss this whole time too. It also bothers me that he thought I stopped showing my face this past year because of that night on the beach when it was actually because … But then a large sign for the Boston Common catches my attention.

Nathan parks his car as close as possible to the Common, but we still have a short distance to walk. I open my door and step out into the chilly night air, quickly realizing I left my jacket back at my apartment. A tiny frown emerges as I wrap my arms around myself, and Nathan sees.

"Don't worry," I hear him say. "I always keep extra sweatshirts in my car." He reaches in his trunk and then turns back around, standing only inches in front of me as he hands me his oversized sweatshirt.

"Th-thank you," I reply, looking up at him. I'm worried that things are now awkward again between us after what just happened in his car, but his smile tells me not to be.

"No problem."

He then pulls out a big thick plaid blanket and a rather large cooler. I give him a confused look, and he responds, "I brought some food and drinks for us to have during the movie." This show of effort causes my tummy to do a few happy summersaults.

As we make the walk over to the ticket booth, I see lots of people sprawled out on blankets nearby, getting ready for the movie to begin. We find an open space near the back of the park, and Nathan spreads the blanket on the grass. I start feeling a little anxious when I realize what the seating arrangements may entail.

Looking around, I notice couples all over the place who show no concern that they are in a public place as they wrap their bodies around each other, using this event as their personal make-out session.

Nathan sits down and then lightly pats the spot next to him, while I awkwardly stand to the side.

"I don't bite, Natalie."

I laugh nervously at his comment and sit cross-legged beside him on the blanket. The chill in the air makes my body start to shiver, so I put on the sweatshirt Nathan had given me to wear. It is about three sizes too big for me but very soft and comfortable.

A familiar smell emits from the sweatshirt, and immediately, I recognize it as the same light-scented cologne he even wore when we were younger.

I remember a few years ago when I was at Vanessa's for a sleepover. Nathan was outside playing basketball with Brian, so I took his bottle of cologne out of his gym bag before he noticed and sprayed it on my pillow. Thinking about it now, I can't decide if it was romantic or creepy, making me laugh a little aloud.

"What's so funny?" he asks casually, opening the cooler in front of him.

"Oh, nothing." I look down at the blanket and pick up a small leaf that has made its way next to me. "I don't know. I just never would have guessed this is where I would be spending my Friday night. Here. With *you.*" I bite my lip and then look over at him.

"Yeah, I guess you're right." He laughs a little but then looks down at the ground before asking, "Is it weird? You and me?" He plucks a piece of grass and tosses it to the side.

You and me.

"No." I shake my head. "It doesn't feel weird to me."

"Ok good because it doesn't feel weird to me either. It actually feels … the opposite of weird." His smile kindles a warmth through me like I've never felt before.

I turn my face down, hoping he won't see the blush spreading over my cheeks.

We sit silently for a few seconds before Nathan gets up and opens the cooler. "So, what would you like to drink? I brought beer, wine, water …" He digs his hand through the cooler looking for something.

"I'll take a water, please."

"Are you sure you wouldn't rather I pop this wine bottle open for you? The guy at the liquor store said it was pretty good." His hand comes out of the cooler holding a corkscrew.

"How did you buy alcohol when you're not twenty-one yet?" I ask teasingly.

"Oh, I already know what places to go to around here," he says with a smirk. "Besides, next month, I won't have to worry about that."

"That's right. Your birthday is on Halloween."

"Yeah." He looks out over the park like he is trying to think of something. "And yours is only a few days after mine on …

November 5, right?" he asks, turning back to me.

"Very good," I say, impressed by his memory.

"So, how about it?" He's holding the bottle of wine in his hands while displaying a playful grin.

"Maybe just a little bit." I haven't had a drink in a while, but being around Nathan like this … I don't know how to explain it. There's just something about him that has always made me feel comfortable whenever I'm with him. I don't have to keep my guard up, and it's a really nice feeling.

I grab the bottle of wine and the corkscrew out of his hands. Then, after struggling with the corkscrew, I pour a decent amount into one of the red solo cups he hands me and take a long sip. The sweet, refreshing taste slides smoothly down my throat, and I savor every drop.

"I guess one drink won't hurt," I say, making him chuckle.

"So, I wasn't sure what you were in the mood for, but I brought us some food too." He starts pulling out everything he packed in the cooler and tells me my options. "There is cheese and crackers, grapes, a vegetable platter, and of course, some popcorn and candy because how can you watch a movie without popcorn and candy?"

"Oh no, Nathan, I didn't even think to bring anything," I respond, embarrassed.

"Don't worry. I wanted to do this." He places everything neatly in front of us and then looks at me. "Besides, what kind of date would this be if we didn't have food?"

So this is a date.

"A date, huh? I thought you said this was just for the extra credit?" A little giggle escapes me as I reach for the grapes.

"I might have only said that so you would say yes to going out with me. Looks like it worked, right?" He winks at me.

"Oh, you think you're so smooth, don't you?" I throw a grape at him, which he catches with his hand and then pops into his mouth.

And then we both laugh. The genuine, not-holding-anything-back kind of laughter. Laughter that shows how comfortable you are with someone.

"So, I was thinking this might be a good chance for us to get to know each other," Nathan says before putting another grape in his mouth.

"How so?" The sound of a giggle catches my attention, causing me to turn my head and get a visual of our neighbors rolling around on their blanket. I wonder if this is what Nathan has in mind for us tonight.

"Don't worry, Natalie." A smile flickers across his face when he notices me staring at the couple. I turn away instantly, embarrassed that he caught me. "I mean, get to know each other by asking some questions."

I'm relieved when I hear this. "What do you want to know?"

"Well, I feel like we spent a lot of time around each other over the years, but, to be honest, I want to know more about what hides underneath that beautiful surface." His dark, consuming eyes are fixated right on me. "I mean, I know you like ice caramel lattes, don't do well on roller coasters, and could kick anyone's ass in tennis, but I'd like to know more."

"S-so, ask away." I hope he doesn't know what his eyes are doing to the speed of my heartbeat.

"Ok, hmm." He brings his hand to his chiseled chin like he is thinking hard about something. "What do you want to do after college?"

"Umm, well … I would really like to write professionally." I tuck my hair behind my ear. "I've always loved reading. I use books as an escape, and I would love to be able to provide that same experience for people." I don't mention that reading provides me with a much-needed calmness I can't find anywhere else. It silences all worries in my head when I'm too overwhelmed to think straight.

"That's pretty awesome. Have you written anything?"

"I thought it was my turn?" I tease.

"Yes, yes, sorry, your turn," he says, laughing as he puts his hands in the air in defense.

"Ok, let's see." I look around and spot a group of guys playing basketball in the distance when it hits me. "I know. Who do you want to be like when you grow up?"

He takes a second to think about this one. "That would be my mom." He takes a can of beer out of the cooler and takes a sip before continuing. "She's one of the strongest and bravest women I know. I wouldn't be here today without her. I would do anything for her."

I was expecting to hear an athlete's name, but instead, I'm caught off guard by his answer. "Wow, she sounds pretty lucky to have you as a son."

He drinks another mouthful before saying, "Alright, my turn." He stares into the distance, thinking about what to ask. "Where is the one place in the world you would like to go?"

"That's easy. Paris," I say immediately. "I've always wanted to go there, ever since I was a little girl. But I guess I've never made time in my life, or maybe I just never had someone to go with, I don't know." I look up to the sky. "To stay in a room that overlooks the Eiffel Tower so that I can see it twinkle at night, eat a crepe from every outdoor food stand, spend a whole day exploring the Louvre, and dress up for dinner and a show at the Moulin rouge … I'm babbling, aren't I?" I shift uncomfortably on the blanket, feeling like I've said too much.

"Not at all. I enjoy watching you talk about something you're so passionate about," he responds with a look that tells me he is processing every word I just said.

I notice that we somehow seem to be sitting closer to each other on the blanket. Did he move closer, or did I?

"Ok, my turn," I say, starting to enjoy this game. "Hmm, let me think." I take the final sip of my drink and then place the empty cup on the ground beside me. "Alright. I have one. Where is your happy place?"

"My happy place?" His expression is one of confusion.

"You know, like the one place in the world that makes you the happiest no matter what might be going on in life."

He starts thinking, but for whatever reason, I feel like he is fighting with himself to answer my question. Sitting in silence, not knowing what to say, I'm relieved when *The Dark Knight* begins projecting on the giant screen.

Nathan positions himself lying down on his back with his hands under his head for support. His pullover comes up just a bit, revealing rock-hard abs that make my insides tingle. I turn away from him and continue sitting cross-legged with my chin in my hands.

"That doesn't look too comfortable," Nathan says. "Here, use this as a pillow." He tosses me the jacket he had brought for himself.

I look around at everyone else, who are also lying down to watch the movie. Then, placing the folded jacket on the edge of the blanket, I lie down slowly until it supports my head.

"Better?" he asks with a knowing smile.

"Much better." We both turn toward the screen, our bodies only a couple of inches apart.

* * *

The movie is about halfway through when I start wishing that time would slow down, if only for tonight.

Nathan keeps making little comments. It usually annoys me when people talk during movies, but for some reason, when he does it, I enjoy it.

Probably because every time he says something to me, he moves his mouth close to my ear and whispers tenderly against my skin. And every time his voice resonates there, it sends shivers down my whole body. So yeah, that's probably why.

I end up having a second glass of wine, which makes me feel even more relaxed, and I boldly inch closer to Nathan, feeling the warmth from his body.

In response, Nathan moves closer to me, eliminating the space between us.

He turns to me and begins to whisper in my ear when something wet drops on my face. *Rain.* And I don't mean like a drizzle but a sudden torrential downpour.

"Shit," I hear Nathan say as he jumps up and begins to throw everything in the cooler.

I pull the sweatshirt off me and hold it over my head to protect myself from the rain and try to help pick up our things.

"Forget it. Let's go!" Nathan shouts over the thunder that is now booming in the background.

He grabs my hand, and we bolt in the opposite direction of his car.

There's an abandoned-looking brick building covered by vines with a small roof sticking out between the alleyway that Nathan notices and takes us to. No one else at the Common seems to see this spot as they all dash for their cars on the other side of the park, leaving only us two standing here. Good thing, too, because the roof barely covers the both of us.

I drop what items I had managed to save, along with the sweatshirt that was still in my hands, then look up at Nathan. His eyes are wide and staring right at me, and his mouth is slightly parted. *Oh no.* I look down and see that the white blouse I had chosen to wear was no longer slightly see-through but now completely see-through, revealing everything, including my white lace bra.

Nathan shakes his head, looks away, and takes his pullover off. The black T-shirt he has on underneath is damp and sticking to every contour of his chest. His arms appear solid, like he could pick me up without any problem, and for a split second, I want to know what that would feel like.

My thought is interrupted when he hands me his pullover to put on. I take it from him, eager to cover myself, but then, without thought, I drop it to the ground.

Nathan narrows his eyes in question until I take one daring step closer to him, filling in the small space between us. My head is level with his chest, and I can see my breath in the frigid air coming out quickly as my pulse races.

We remain frozen in place until his hand slowly rises and begins to graze my skin at the opening of my blouse, where the top button has come undone, sending shivers down my spine. I feel my breath catch as his hand slides, ever so slowly, up my neck and to my chin, which he then tilts upward, making me meet his dark eyes. And every second spent staring into them causes my heart to pound louder, comparable to the thunder in the distance.

Slowly, I place my shaking hands on his chest and feel his heartbeat matching my own.

And that's when his lips finally crash down on mine.

Nathans lips move soft and slow as he tastes me, but then quickly turn hard and hungry. His hands travel down my body to my thighs where he grips me and picks me up into his arms. My back is pressed against the brick wall, and my legs wrap tightly around his solid torso as we mold together perfectly. He pulls his mouth away from mine, allowing me a moment to breathe, and he continues his assault of kisses from my jawline all the way down to my collar bone.

"Nathan," escapes from my lips in a trembling breath. He responds by grinding his hips roughly against my own, allowing me to feel his hard length trapped inside his jeans. Letting me know how badly he wants me, which ignites a desire between my legs, accompanied by a dampness that was not created by the rain.

I move my hands over every part of his defined arms before sliding them under his shirt, feeling every inch of his ripped chest. His powerful body is holding me up with no issue, and without a doubt in my mind, I know this is where I am meant to be.

In his arms.

I somehow manage to pull his shirt off and run my hands up and down his toned back. His hand fiercely pushes aside my bra, and his lips journey down my chest. My fingers rake through his hair as his tongue glides over my skin, over my stiff nipples, and I can't take it anymore.

"Kiss me," I gasp.

And that's all it takes for his lips to rush back to mine with an urgency I have never experienced before.

As I am about to pull him harder against me, an alarm sound

from a car on the other side of the building brings us back to reality. Nathan removes his lips from mine and sets me down, leaving me breathing hard and craving more. My eyes open to find him looking cautiously down at me.

He rests his forehead against mine and whispers softly, "I never thought I'd have a second chance with you."

NATHAN

When Natalie and I get back into my car, both of us are soaked to the bone. I notice she is shivering and immediately reach into the back of my car to find another sweatshirt hiding under the seat.

"Here. Wear this." I hold it out for her.

"No, I'm fine. You should wear it," she says as her teeth begin to chatter uncontrollably.

"Natalie, besides the fact that your whole body is shaking, if I have to drive with you sitting next to me in that extremely see-through shirt, I am going to get very distracted, which would not be good for either of us." A playful smile comes to my lips, and she takes the sweatshirt without hesitation.

Her cheeks turn a light shade of pink as she quietly looks over at me.

"What's wrong?" I ask.

"Can you … can you close your eyes, please?"

"May I ask why?"

"Well … I want to take my shirt off and put this dry sweatshirt on," she responds, looking down at her hands self-consciously.

"Oh. Yeah, no problem." I close my eyes and face away from

her. Of course, every part of me wishes I could keep my eyes open for this, but the most significant part of me, the gentleman part, forces me to keep them closed.

"Ok, you can open your eyes," Natalie's sweet voice says a few seconds later.

I open them. She looks so good in my sweatshirt with her wet hair trailing over her shoulders. I reach over and lightly push her hair back behind her ear.

"This sweatshirt definitely looks better on you than it does on me," I tell her.

She smiles shyly then faces the window, probably trying to hide the deep flush on her cheeks.

I turn the car on and adjust the heat to as high as it will go, holding my hands in front of the vents for a moment to make them stop shaking.

"Here, let me help," Natalie offers as she takes my hands in hers and rubs them between her own. Her hands are like satin, rubbing back and forth against my rough skin. And whatever she is doing, it's sending even more shivers down my body.

"How about you drive with one hand?" She playfully sticks one of my hands in the front pocket of my sweatshirt she is wearing.

"W-works for me," I say, trying not to get too excited about where she just placed my hand. Her hands slide into the front pocket too and one of them holds mine tightly. Our fingers interlock, but I use my thumb to rub little circles on her soft skin.

The rain starts to lessen as I pull out of the parking spot and head in the direction of Natalie's apartment. I don't want this night to end, so I drive slowly, taking a longer route back to her place, when an idea comes to mind.

"Any plans this weekend?" I ask.

"No. I'll probably just be at the library reading and writing some papers. What about you?"

"Well, tomorrow morning, I'm driving back home. There are some things I have to take care of, so if you want a ride home for the weekend, you're more than welcome to join me. I'll be coming back on Sunday night, and I'm not going to lie, it would be nice to have some company on the ride." I look over and see her smile.

She thinks things through before she responds, though. "Ok. I'm in."

"Great," I say as we pull up outside her apartment building. "I'll come by in the morning around 9 a.m. Does that work?"

"Yeah, that works for me." Natalie makes no move to leave my car. She stares at the front pocket where her hands are still holding onto mine while biting down on her bottom lip.

Damn those perfect lips.

I move my free hand to her chin and gently lift her face so our eyes meet. "Goodnight, Natalie," I say and bring my lips to hers one more time. She takes her hands out of the pocket and wraps them around my neck, pulling me closer. After a few seconds, I slowly part my lips from hers before things intensify.

She pushes her hair out of her face before saying, "Goodnight, Nathan." She puts one hand on the door handle but then turns back to face me. "Oh, your sweatshirt. I almost forgot." She looks like she is about to take it off, forgetting that she no longer has a shirt on under it, so I place my hand on hers to stop her.

"Keep it."

"Ok," she says without hesitation. She opens the door and sprints under the light rain to the lobby door. Within seconds, I can no longer see her.

With some soft music playing in the background, I drive back to my dorm room and pull into the parking lot. As I walk into my room, exhaustion hits me, and I jump into my bed, relieved that once again, I seem to have the place to myself for the night.

A soft buzzing comes from my pocket, and I pull out my phone to see who's texting me.

Unknown Number: Thanks for tonight. I had a really nice time.

I quickly add Natalie into my contacts.

Me: I had a really great time too. Thanks again for helping me earn some extra credit.

Natalie: Haha I thought you said this was a date?

Me: Oh this was definitely a date. In fact, it was the best date I've ever had.

Natalie: Goodnight Nathan.

Me: Goodnight Natalie. See you tomorrow.

I shut my phone off and toss it on the nightstand next to my bed. My eyes feel heavy and close slowly as my mind begins to wander into a dream.

The scene appears in black and white. I'm wearing a trench coat and holding Natalie tightly while rain pours down, and our lips lock with an intensity unknown to most.

* * *

At 9 a.m. on the dot, I pull my car up to Natalie's apartment building, and she comes running out with her bag in hand.

"I'm glad you asked me to come. I know it's only been a week, but I can't wait to see my family." She tosses her bag in the back and then gets settled in the passenger seat.

"Yeah, no problem. I'm glad you're here," I say as I start the car and head toward Connecticut. I've always envied how close Natalie and her family are.

After not even an hour on the road, Natalie falls asleep with her head tilted against the headrest. She looks so peaceful, but the slight bags under her eyes make me think she didn't sleep well last night. When I stop at the next red light, I unzip my jacket and place it over her body.

A few hours later, I pull into the driveway of Natalie's family home. The house resembles more of a mansion than a typical home.

"We're here, Natalie," I say softly as I rub her cheek with the back of my hand.

Her eyes open cautiously, but after she looks around, she realizes where she is. "Oh my God. Did I sleep the whole way here?"

"Pretty much," I say, giving a small smile.

"Oh, Nathan, I'm so sorry. I guess I didn't really sleep well last night." Her hands fly up to her face in embarrassment.

"Hey," I gently wrap my fingers around her wrists and move her hands away from her face, "it's no big deal."

"Ok," she says. "I've never fallen asleep in front of someone before, but I guess I just feel …"

"Feel what?"

She hesitates before saying, "I feel *safe* with you."

I gaze into her eyes, wishing I could read her thoughts because her word choice emits concern. Yes, she should always feel safe with me, but what would have incited her to use that word? Why not the word *comfortable*? Or any other word in the English dictionary, for that matter.

What or who would make her not feel safe?

I want to ask, but I notice her shift nervously in her seat, realizing her mistake, so I decide not to.

"Well, whenever you need to take a nap, you just let me know. That's what I'm here for." I wink, which makes her smile, and I observe the bags under her eyes have started to fade. "So, after I get some stuff done at home, I was planning on going to the Lonely Tavern tonight. If you want to come," I run my hand through my hair, feeling nervous, "just call me later, but if not, it's no big deal."

"Can I think about it?" she asks. "Not that I wouldn't love to spend tonight with you, it's just this is the longest I have gone without seeing my family, and I just want to …"

"Natalie, don't worry. I promise it's not a big deal." I hope she doesn't hear the disappointment in my voice, so I lean in close to kiss her soft lips.

I had every intention of it just being a simple kiss before she left my car, but the second our lips touch, I need more. We begin to move in unison, both of us ravenous for the other person. Natalie grabs my shirt and pulls me into her. I feel every part of me beginning to throb for her, so I quickly pull away before anything more can happen.

I watch as Natalie opens her eyes and rests her head on my chest. "Wow, I don't think I will ever get tired of that." I can't see her face, but I know a beautiful smile is on it.

"Me neither." I hold her against me, wishing she wasn't about to leave.

But after only a few seconds, she slowly lifts her head and smooths out her shirt. "Well, thanks again for the ride and for the best nap I've ever had," she teases, making me grin. She hops out of the car, grabs her bag, and walks to her house. Already, I miss her presence.

I back my car out of Natalie's driveway and start toward my house, which is only a few blocks away. I know this will not be a pleasant visit, and I can feel my stomach turn when I arrive.

"Hello?" I ask after unlocking the door and walking in.

"In here," I hear my brother, Nick, respond.

Nick is my newly seventeen-year-old brother who has just started his junior year of high school as a straight-A student and a very talented basketball player. He has the same dark hair, brown eyes, and angular jaw that I have, but he stands a couple of inches shorter than me and is only just beginning to bulk up. He comes off as shy and guarded to most, probably due to our unfortunate upbringing, but with me, he has always been the complete opposite.

He is, without question, the best brother I could have ever asked for.

I enter the kitchen and see Nick making a sandwich. "What's up, dude?" he asks before he stuffs a big bite into his mouth.

"Nothing much. Just thought I'd stop by to take care of some things." I look around the house to see if anyone else is home.

Nick nods his head in understanding. He knows the real reason why I came home.

"Where's mom?" I ask.

"She's out running some errands," he responds. "She probably won't be home for a few hours."

I nod my head. "Let me see the note."

Nick retrieves a small envelope out of his pocket, which he

hands to me. Opening the envelope, I see the familiar handwriting, and that's all it takes to make my insides boil with rage. Every muscle in my body tightens furiously from the small words I'm staring at. I hit the counter hard with my fist, doing more damage to myself than the solid surface.

"Dude, you know I'm going with you," Nick says.

I stare down at the piece of paper in my hand. "I think you're going to have to so I don't kill him."

NATALIE

I stand awkwardly in front of the door, not knowing if I should knock or just walk in. But impulsively, my finger gently pushes on the doorbell, and I wait anxiously for the door to open.

I hadn't seen my family in a whole week, which was starting to feel like an eternity, being that it was the longest time I had spent away from them. I laugh, remembering how I told myself I wouldn't be going home anytime soon, and now I find myself standing on the front porch, only one week later.

My mom opens the door like she is expecting to see a door salesman, but when she realizes it's me, her face lights up like it's Christmas morning.

"Hi, mom!"

"Natalie! Oh, my goodness." She wraps me up in her arms. "Why didn't you tell me you were coming home?"

"I wanted to surprise you."

"Well, this is certainly a happy surprise!" She lets go of me and looks me up and down. "Come in. You must be hungry. Let me make you some lunch."

"That would be great." A familiar, comfortable feeling washes over me as I enter the house. My family's home is massive, there is no denying that, but it always feels welcoming to me. Of course, this probably has more to do with the people living in it.

I follow my mom through the entryway, past the living room and dining room, and into the kitchen where she pulls out a counter stool at the island for me to sit on.

"How about I make you your favorite: grilled cheese and tomato soup?" she asks, despite her already pulling out the frying pan from the bottom drawer.

"Yes, please." I hear footsteps coming down the stairs, and I look over to see my dad enter the kitchen.

"Guess who decided to make a surprise visit, Robert?" My mom announces as she reaches for a can of tomato soup in the cabinets.

"Well, from the look of it, I would guess it's my favorite daughter." He plants a quick kiss on my forehead. "How are you doing, kid?"

"I'm really good," I respond. "My classes are going well, and I made friends with my neighbor, Sarah." I leave the part out about making out last night with Nathan, which would be the real reason why I was *really* good. I don't think they would want to hear about that.

He takes a seat beside me, and my mom hands him the morning newspaper along with a mug full of hot coffee.

"We are so glad to hear that," my mom adds. She walks back to the stove and flips the grilled cheese on the frying pan. I can hear the recognizable sound of the butter sizzling, which causes my stomach to rumble in excitement.

"Glad everything is working out well," my dad states.

When I look at him, I'm suddenly aware that my dad is still in his plaid pajama bottoms and bathrobe, which is very unlike him for this time of day. He's usually the first one in the family out of bed in the morning.

"Umm, dad, did you just wake up?" I ask.

"Oh, ah, yes, I did." He looks down at his pajama bottoms and bathrobe. "What gave it away?" he chuckles before adding, "I was out late last night with Peter Gordon working on his boat. He was having some engine troubles, so I stayed to help him until we had it up and running again. Took some energy out of me, I guess."

"Oh," is all I can manage to say. Just hearing the Gordon name makes me queasy.

"Hey, do you think I could get one of those?" Jason asks as he walks into the kitchen.

"Jason!" I jump off the stool and run over to him, wrap my arms tightly around him, and squeeze him as tight as I possibly can. I didn't realize how much I've missed him until now.

"It's only been one week," he says through gasps. I smile and loosen my grip before sitting back at the counter. He pulls out an empty stool next to me and sits. "But I've missed you too, Nat."

I see my parents both give each other fond looks.

"Jason, did you tell your sister about the incredible game you had last night?" my mom asks.

"Wait, was it the first game of the season? How did it go?"

On cue, my dad slides a section of the newspaper in front of me where I see the headline, *THREE CHEERS; WE MEAN TOUCHDOWNS FOR JASON SPENCER!* A large black and white photo of Jason in his uniform is displayed underneath.

"Oh my God, Jason! This is so exciting!" I beam with pride for my brother.

"It was nothing," Jason says casually. "The other team was playing horrible defense, so it really wasn't difficult to do."

He's always so modest about his achievements.

"Well, I think it's amazing. In fact, I'm taking this section of the paper and framing it." I rip the section out and hand the rest of the newspaper back to my dad. "Maybe later we can look at your schedule to see what games I can make this season."

Jason smiles. "Sounds good to me."

My mom hands me a plate with a grilled cheese sandwich and then a bowl of tomato soup. The smell alone makes my mouth water. "Thanks, mom." I dip my sandwich into the soup and take a bite. The gooey melted cheese combined with the rich and creamy tomato mixture tastes like heaven.

"Of course," my mom says with an affectionate smile. She starts preparing Jason's grilled cheese next. "So, how did you get home today, Natalie? I hope you didn't take the bus the whole way here. They always have such mechanical issues with those old things. They're so dangerous and unreliable."

Shoot. I didn't think about them asking this question.

"Oh, a friend from school lives in this area, and they were coming home for the weekend, so they offered to give me a ride home too." I take another bite of my sandwich, secretly praying they drop the subject.

"Oh, I see." My mom looks to my dad, who is now hiding his face behind the paper in his hands. Most likely trying to avoid where this conversation is going.

"Do we know this friend?" my mom asks, careful not to push the subject too far.

"Umm," I say, pretending to be thinking hard about this. "No, I don't think so."

It was a lie, of course. They know Nathan from constantly being at the Gordons' home, but for whatever reason, I don't want them to know it was him who drove me. Maybe because I don't even know what it is that Nathan and I are doing. Last night was the first time the two of us actually started getting to know each other.

And it was nice.

No, it was better than nice.

It was perfect.

Jason's voice interjects to rescue me. "So, any plans for today?"

"No, I hadn't really thought about it. I was just looking forward to seeing you guys," I respond with a small shrug.

"Oh, good!" my mom exclaims. "Would you want to go on some errands with me? Then maybe we could get our nails done later?"

"I would love that," I say before putting the last mouthwatering bite of my grilled cheese sandwich in my mouth.

"And then maybe the four of us can go to dinner?" she asks.

"Actually," I look over at Jason, "I was thinking Jason and I could have dinner at the Lonely Tavern tonight for some brother and sister time."

Jason looks at me, confused, so I kick him lightly on the shin. "Oh yeah, sounds good to me." He shakes his head and rubs his shin before turning his attention to the grilled cheese sandwich my mom just placed in front of him.

"That sounds lovely! Maybe your father and I will go out to dinner too. It's been ages since we have been out, just the two of us." My mom looks over at my dad with pleading eyes.

My dad lowers the newspapers in his hands and says, "Whatever you want, dear."

* * *

A few hours later, after accompanying my mom on some errands and getting our nails done, I'm back home.

"I'm going to see if I can find Jason," I tell my mom as I walk up the stairs.

I knock on the door to Jason's room but hear no answer. My hand turns the doorknob, and I open the door a few inches, disappointed to find that he is not inside. I sulk over to my room across the hall, and when I walk in, I'm startled.

"Jason, you scared me," I say, bringing my hand to my chest.

"I didn't even do anything. I'm just sitting here." He's lounging on the extra-long bench attached to the big bay window in my room, which overlooks the backyard. I've spent so much time reading in that same spot.

"What are you doing?" I ask, taking a seat on the other side of the bench. The bench is long enough for both of us to have our legs stretched out fully without touching.

"I could ask you the same thing," he says, with a slight smirk. "Want to explain to me why we are going to the Lonely Tavern tonight for dinner?"

"Well ..." I look out the window and try to decide how I should explain this.

"Let me guess. It has to do with the guy who drove you home today?" Jason asks.

"How'd you know?"

"Call it a brotherly intuition."

"Ok. Maybe, it has to do with that," I say as my cheeks flush.

"Well, are you going to let me know who he is? I am your *big* brother, after all." He crosses his burly arms over his chest.

"Ok fine, but please don't say anything to mom and dad," I plead.

"Oh, so they do know who he is. Well, this is getting interesting." He scratches his chin like he's deep in thought.

"Yes, and actually …" I pause and take a deep breath, worried what he is going to think. "You know him too."

"Go on," he says hesitantly.

"Wait, you have to promise me you won't say anything," I insist before continuing.

"Nat, you know I won't say anything. I promise." He looks reassuringly at me.

"Ok. You're right. I know you won't." I take another deep breath, trying to find the courage to say his name out loud. "It's Nathan. Nathan Thomas. You might know him as Nate." I look at Jason, who shows no emotion and sits in silence for what feels like an eternity. "Well, are you going to say something?"

He bursts out laughing. "Sorry, I couldn't help it. I wanted to see you sweat it out." I roll my eyes before crossing my arms over my chest in annoyance. "I like the guy. He seems pretty cool." He shrugs his shoulders. "I mean, I don't personally know him, but I remember him being pretty damn good at baseball, and sometimes I would see him working at the yacht club when I went there with Dad. I've seen him around town a few times with friends." He looks out the window and then back at me. "And oh yeah, his brother, Nick, is in the grade below me. We've played some pickup basketball games at school every now and then."

I nod my head in acknowledgment. "Alright, well, now that we've gotten that out of the way, I feel better." In fact, I'm relieved.

"You know your opinion means more to me than anyone else's would."

"Well, someone's got to look out for you and your horrible taste in men," he teases.

"Hey, not true," I say as I inch my foot closer to him to kick his, but I can barely reach, so it's more of just a light tap.

"My foot!" He rolls off the bench and onto the floor with a loud thud and holds his foot in the air. "How will I ever play football again?"

"If that hurt, then what do you do when a three-hundred-pound guy charges at you on the field?"

"Run for dear life and never look back," he responds, making us both laugh.

Jason gets up from the ground, pretends to limp, and then sits back on the bench. "So, what's the game plan for tonight?"

"Well, I was hoping you might be able to drive me to the Lonely Tavern? And possibly back home too? Nathan is planning on being there tonight, and I didn't give him a definite answer on whether I could go or not, but I would like to see him."

"Alright, I guess I could get a few of my friends to meet me there." He pulls out his phone and starts swiping his finger over the screen.

"Thanks, Jason." He gives me a knowing smile.

"If he hurts you, though, I will have to kill him. You know that right?" he asks, his tone serious.

"I know. That's what *big* brothers are for."

ten

NATHAN

I check my phone for what feels like the thousandth time and see that there is still no text from Natalie.

This girl is becoming my weakness.

My attention turns to the old rusted brown grandfather clock that resides in the corner of the living room. Its loud, obnoxious chimes are letting me know it is now 8 o'clock. *Time to go*, it says to me over and over again. As I get up from the couch, a loud and disappointed sigh escapes me, causing Nick to glance over for a split second before returning his attention to the TV.

"What?" he asks. His eyes remain glued to the screen as he molds even further into the couch.

"Nothing." I grab my jacket hanging over the back of the recliner and put it on. "Ready to go?"

He jumps up from the couch with ease and picks up his coat from the floor. "Want me to drive?" he asks as the two of us walk outside to my car.

"Not a chance in hell." He only got his license a week ago, but the disappointment on his face causes me to cave. "How about you be the designated driver home tonight?"

His face lights up. "Works for me!"

When we get to the Lonely Tavern, I can tell the place is

already packed since there are barely any parking spots left.

We walk in and both recognize plenty of familiar faces from around town. I take a seat on a stool at the bar, and Nick does the same next to me. He orders a sprite, and I order a beer, which the bartender brings over quickly.

No bartender in this whole town has ever asked to see my ID.

"Hope you enjoy it," she says with a flirty smile as she leans on the counter in front of me, clearly trying to display her cleavage in the extremely low-cut top she is wearing.

"Thanks." I take the beer and bring it up to my mouth. The cold liquid slides down my throat, helping erase the long and very draining day from my mind.

Nick finds the booth in the corner of the tavern where a group of his friends from school are sitting. "I'll be over there." He is about to get out of his seat when I stop him.

"Wait," I say, "take this." I hand him the key to my car. "Don't forget you're driving us home tonight."

"Thanks, man." He jumps off the barstool and heads over to his friends.

I keep my phone on the counter in front of me, hoping Natalie might text, but with every passing minute, it seems more likely that she will not be joining me tonight.

The baseball team on the TV screen above me scores another homerun, and cheers can be heard throughout the bar. I cheer along and bring my now second beer to my lips when I hear a soft voice behind me.

"Hi, Nathan." I turn to find Natalie standing behind me. She's wearing a low-cut black top tucked into a dark pair of skin-tight jeans. It takes all my self-control to remind myself that we are in a public place.

"Natalie, you made it." My smile is probably too big, but I can't hide how happy I am that she's here.

"Well, I had nothing better to do," she teases. "Is it ok that I'm here?" Her beautiful grey eyes look into mine for confirmation.

"Yeah, it's more than ok that you're here," I respond. She

blushes. "Would you like a drink?" I ask. "I can order you whatever you'd like."

"Hmm." She looks around to see what everyone else is drinking when she spots a girl in the corner with a pink frozen drink. "I'll have that!"

"You got it." I catch the bartender's attention and then point to the pink beverage in the girl's hand for reference. The bartender acknowledges this and then walks away to make the drink.

Natalie continues to stand next to me, and I realize there isn't anywhere for her to sit. I also notice all the men in here are eyeing her up and down. So I jump up and offer her my seat, which she takes, and stand over her, blocking the views of everyone in the bar. But the guy sitting next to her is blatantly gawking, so I give him a death stare as a warning, and he immediately gazes down at his drink in front of him.

The bartender hands Natalie the pink fruity-looking beverage, and Natalie takes a sip. "Wow, that has quite the kick to it." Her eyes go wide as she swallows.

I laugh at her expression. "If you don't like it, I can get you something else."

"No, this is perfect! Especially with the mini pink umbrella," she says before bringing the drink back up to her lips. I watch her take a sip and realize this girl has no idea how sexy she is. The bar lights are dim, but it feels like every spotlight is on her in this moment.

She gives me a questioning look. "What?"

"Nothing." I run my hand through my hair and feel my cheeks begin to flush. I can't even begin to tell her the thoughts that were just running through my mind. "So, how did you get here anyway? I would have picked you up."

"I had my brother, Jason, bring me." She points to the far side of the bar where he sits with some friends. I recognize him from school sports and his occasional appearance at the yacht club with his dad. "He likes this place, so it was really no problem for him to take me."

"I really am glad you came." I look down, and the second my

eyes lock with hers, I can feel my heart trip over itself.

"I'm glad I came too."

* * *

After a few drinks for each of us and a lot of laughs, Natalie tells me she needs to run to the restroom. She starts to jump off the stool, but I can tell what is about to happen. I grab her by the waist as she loses her balance and miscalculates how far down the step is. I bring her down slowly, facing me, and I can hear her breath falter. When her feet reach the ground, I push her hair out of her face so I can look into her eyes.

"Come here," is all I need to say before her mouth is on mine. Her lips move fiercely, just the way I like, but I bring her speed down, knowing what a kiss like that can lead to. We pull away slowly, and she smiles.

"I'll be right back."

A smile forms on my face without realizing it as I watch her walk away.

Goddamn.

Who would have guessed it would be Natalie Spencer I would be spending two nights in a row with? That it would be thoughts of Natalie keeping me up at night. And boy, were they good thoughts …

"Hey, Nate!" I hear a familiar girl's voice over my shoulder and turn around to see Vanessa Gordon.

"Vanessa! How are you?" She jumps up to hug me.

"I'm good! I'm just here with my family." She points to a big group that's taking up a whole section of the tavern in the back. "We came home for the weekend for a family birthday party."

"We? Does that mean Brian is here too?" I ask, looking around the bar excitedly. I hadn't seen him in a few weeks, and it was weird to go that long since we had spent a lot of time together at school in New Hampshire for the past two years.

"Yeah, he should be here any minute!" she responds. "But, hey, can I ask you something?" She waits for me to nod my head. "Did

I just see you here with Natalie a few minutes ago?"

"Actually, yeah," I say. "We kind of ran into each other on campus. I had no idea she was also attending LU, and well …" I shrug my shoulders and laugh a little at the situation's awkwardness. "Is it weird?"

"No, I think it's great! I always knew Natalie had a crush on you, so I was glad to see you two together. I was just surprised," she says with a genuine smile.

"She used to have a crush on me?" I ask, unaware of this news.

"Oh jeez, don't play stupid with me." She rolls her eyes. "You must be dumber than I thought if you didn't know that." She punches my arm playfully as I feign injury. "I miss her a lot, actually, so I'm glad to know she's doing well." Vanessa looks down at the drink in her hand.

"If you don't mind me asking, why aren't you and Natalie friends anymore? I mean, you guys used to do everything together. Did something happen?"

"That's the thing, Nate. Nothing happened. Nothing I can even think of. The last night I saw her, she was over at my house for a party, and then, that was it. I never heard from her or saw her again." She shrugs her shoulders, and a defeated look passes over her face.

"Do you happen to know which party this was?" I ask, already feeling like I know the answer.

"Umm, I think it was the Halloween party last year." She thinks for a bit longer. "Yeah, that's exactly when it was because it was for your birthday."

"I see." I start to flash back to that night, which makes my stomach drop.

So, something did happen that night.

"I used to try calling her, but she never answered or called me back. I left her voicemails and texts, but I never got any response. So, I don't know." Her eyes begin to water. "If something had happened, if there was something I did to upset her, I would maybe understand, but I just don't have any idea what happened."

I put my hand lightly on her shoulder. "Hey, I'm sorry. I didn't mean to upset you. I was honestly just curious."

"Oh, stop. You know you're like a brother to me," she says with a smile as she wipes one tear from her cheek, acting like it was never there. "I better get back to my family, but let me know the next time you stop by so we can catch up." She hugs me again and walks to the other side of the tavern.

A few minutes later, Natalie appears by my side.

"Sorry, there was a huge line," she says and takes a seat on the stool I saved for her.

"Don't worry. I survived." I stand over her and place both my hands on her thighs as I lean down to kiss her slowly.

"Oh, really?" she teases as our lips part. I notice her cheeks look a little flushed. Probably from the alcohol running through her body.

"Yeah. Umm, actually, Vanessa Gordon came over. I guess she is here for a birthday or something." I watch Natalie's face for a reaction.

"Oh …" She turns her attention to the drink in her hands.

"Yeah, she umm … she said she misses you."

"She did?" Her eyes light up with surprise and eagerness, but then she quickly regains her composure.

"Yeah, she said she tried to call you a few times." I leave off the fact that she also has no idea why they stopped being friends in the first place.

"I must have missed the calls," she says with a bit of annoyance.

I raise my hands in the air in defense. "Woah, don't shoot the messenger." This makes her laugh, which relieves me.

"So, how can a girl get another drink around here?" she asks, raising her empty glass in my face.

"Ok … ok, but this is the last one. I would hate to have to carry you out of here." I chuckle and order her another pink drink from the bartender.

"You wouldn't want to carry me out of here?" She pouts her luscious lips and looks up at me with those damn bedroom eyes.

Her arms wrap around my neck, pulling my face toward her. Within a second, her mouth is next to my ear, and she whispers, "I think that would be kind of hot. Don't you?"

I stand there with my mouth open, turned on as fuck. "You're drunk, aren't you?"

"No, not me, Nate." She giggles as the bartender slides another drink in her direction. She takes a sip of the beverage, which makes her face light up.

"Ok, now I know you're drunk. You called me Nate, and you never call me Nate."

"I meant Nathan." She puts her hand on my chest and looks up at me. "Nathan, you want me, don't you?" Her hand slowly travels down my chest, but I stop her before she gets too far down.

"Natalie." I take her hand off my body and hold it in mine. Then, putting my mouth right up against her ear, I speak only loud enough for her to hear. "If you weren't drunk, I would take you right fucking here and now on top of this bar. Filling your tight little pussy with my cock, making you come over and over again. I wouldn't stop until I knew with certainty that you were fully satisfied. So, yes, I want you."

There's plenty more I want to add, but I decide to practice restraint and save it for another time.

Natalie's mouth opens in shock. She looks up at me with an expression I am unable to read. "I wish you would," escapes from her mouth in only a whisper.

I cup her face gently in my hands and look longingly into her eyes. "Someday, beautiful." I move my thumb deliberately side to side across her bottom lip, feeling her pulse speed up in the palm of my hand. "But not tonight. Not when you're drunk. Because believe me when I say you'll want to remember every second of it." Then, I brush my mouth against hers, back and forth, before I press down gently, tasting the fruity flavor on her lips.

"You taste so sweet," I say as I pull back. "I like it."

She laughs, but suddenly, her face turns ghostly white and her body freezes.

"What's wrong?" I ask. But we're interrupted by someone screaming my name from across the bar. I turn around and immediately get excited to see a familiar face approaching me. *Brian.* His enormous stature makes him impossible to miss in any size crowd.

"NATE!" Brian yells for a second time. He tries to pick me up in a bear hug but only manages to lift me a couple of inches from the floor. He would have succeeded too, if not for me being taller than him. What Brian lacks in height, he makes up for in brute strength.

"Brian! It's been too long, my man," I say as he puts me firmly back on the ground. I turn to include Natalie in the conversation, but when I look at where she was sitting just five seconds ago, she's gone.

Eleven

NATALIE

I left the tavern before Nathan even had a chance to notice that I was missing.

Now, my body is shaking uncontrollably in the passenger seat of Jason's car. I look in the back seat and find Jason's football jacket, which I wrap around my body like a blanket while I wait.

"How could I be so stupid?" I say out loud in anger.

When Brian walked into the tavern, I thought I was seeing things. There was no way he was here. Not right now. And not in the very same place as me.

I closed my eyes to make the image of him disappear, but when I opened them, Brian was still there. Haunting me. I don't think he saw me sitting behind Nathan, but I knew I had to get out of there when he started walking over. So, the second Nathan turned away from me, I ducked and slipped off the barstool, sneaking out the back entrance without being noticed.

I stumbled a few times in the parking lot while looking for Jason's car, but I located it on the far side of the lot after only a few minutes. Thankfully, he never locks his doors, so I was instantly relieved when I was able to open the door and hop in.

The letters on my phone all looked blurry, but somehow, I managed to text Jason.

Me: Can we please leave?
Jason: Everything ok?
Me: Yes. But I want to go home.
Jason: Where are you?
Me: In your car.
Jason: Ok. Be right there.

And now I wait, I think, wrapping the jacket tighter around me.

I lean back in the leather seat and position my head against the headrest, but suddenly, the car begins to spin. Not sure if it's the extreme nerves pulsating in my body or the amount of alcohol I drank that's making me feel this way, but I whip the jacket off and open the door, moving cautiously to the side to get some air. My feet land firmly on the ground as I try to make the dizziness stop. I close my eyes and put my head between my knees, taking deep breaths.

"Natalie, are you ok?" Nathan asks with concern in his voice. I open my eyes and see his feet in front of me. "You were sitting right next to me, and then suddenly you were gone." He sounds out of breath like he might have just been running around looking for me.

"Yeah, I'm fine," is all I manage to say. My eyes instantly close again, and I keep my head locked between my knees, hoping he will leave before I heave all over his feet.

"You look it." He lifts my body out of the seat, gently pulling me up to stand beside him. Then his body slides down onto the seat he just pulled me from.

I'm not going to be able to stand up for much longer, so I ask, "What are you doing?"

He reclines the seat all the way back and then carefully pulls me down to sit on his lap. The door is left open so my legs can stick out of the car, allowing me to still feel the cool breeze. He lets the right side of my head rest against his chest while he rubs my back in a slow circular motion. His other arm is positioned across my lap, holding me against him like a seat belt.

"I am so embarrassed," I say as I nuzzle my head into his chest.

"Don't be. It's my fault. Just close your eyes."

"Why are you being so nice to me? You never even noticed me until recently."

I feel his chest rise as he takes a deep breath before speaking. "I like you, Natalie … a lot," he adds with certainty.

I definitely drank too much because I know I heard him wrong.

"You like me?"

"Yes. I know I shouldn't, but I do." His hands have stopped forming circles on my back and are now moving tenderly up and down.

"Why shouldn't you like me?" I ask, placing my hand on his solid arm that's wrapped around me, feeling the heat radiating off of him.

"Well, you know …" He lets out a sigh. "You've always been Natalie Spencer. The girl that everyone either wanted to be or be with. You were … how do I say this without sounding like a total asshole? You were, well, I mean, you are perfect. I don't deserve to be with someone like you. You … you deserve better than me."

Me, perfect? If only he knew.

"You must be drunker than me," I say as I process what he just said.

The spinning is beginning to fade the more I focus on how nice his hand feels on my back. The motion sends tiny shivers down my spine.

"No, it's true." He goes silent for a moment like he is thinking about something. "All those years, I watched guys drool over you, and I always felt this insane need to protect you from assholes like that, and I never understood why. But now I do. Having you in my arms now … I've never felt like this with anyone."

I am having a really hard time understanding what he is saying with the ringing echoing in my ears, so I don't say anything.

"Natalie, can I ask you a question?" His hand slowly moves higher up my back.

"Mhmm …" is the only noise I manage to make.

He pauses his movement. "Why did you and Vanessa stop being friends?"

"Because of him … and that night. The snow was so cold," I mumble into his chest as I burrow into him closer.

"Because of who?" he asks.

I can feel the muscles in his arms tense, but I have nothing left in me. Exhaustion wins.

The last thing I feel are his lips kissing my forehead before he whispers, "Goodnight, beautiful."

* * *

My head is throbbing. No, more like pounding. No, it's throbbing *and* pounding. It's like someone took a jackhammer to my skull and forgot to shut it off.

Ugh.

I slowly pull my comforter off while keeping one hand in the air to block any and all sunlight from hitting my eyes as I shuffle to the bathroom. When I squint in the mirror, I see that my makeup is still on from the night before. It's smudged around my eyes, making me look like a zombie raccoon. I'm wearing the same outfit I had on last night too, plus an oversized grey sweatshirt that smells of Nathan. I inhale his scent and instantly start to relax.

I take everything off and jump into a scalding hot shower. The smell of apples and peaches fills the air as I lather body wash on my loofa and begin wiping last night's humiliation off my skin. After filling the bathroom with steam, I turn off the water and step out of the shower feeling the tiniest bit refreshed. I put on my big white bathrobe and matching slippers before going down the main staircase, following the heavenly coffee aroma to the kitchen.

"Hey," I say when I see Jason sitting at the kitchen island with a mug of coffee in his hand. His hair is ruffled, and he is wearing a pair of plaid pajama bottoms with a white T-shirt, looking like he just rolled out of bed.

"Hey, Natalie," he says, hiding a smile behind his coffee.

"Don't start with me." I grab a mug from inside the cabinet and fill it with coffee. Then after fiddling in the medicine cabinet, I find something to help with my headache. "How are you even up right now, and where are mom and dad?"

"Well, first, I didn't drink last night," he says with an annoying grin. "And mom and dad left a few hours ago. They didn't want to wake you, but they had plans to spend the day with Mr. and Mrs. Gordon on their boat." Jason finishes his coffee and walks over to the sink to clean out the mug. "Oh yeah, mom left you some money in an envelope over there if you need it."

My stomach drops at the mention of the Gordons, but I act like it doesn't faze me. I pick up the envelope with my name on it and then place it back on the counter without giving it a second thought. A sigh escapes me before I ask the question that's really on my mind. "So, how did I get home last night?"

"You really don't remember, do you?" Jason crosses his arms in front of his chest.

"The last thing I remember is finding your car in the parking lot, and then it's kind of fuzzy after that." Of course, I don't mention that I vaguely remember the conversation Nathan and I had inside Jason's car or the fact that I basically admitted to Nathan in the bar that I wanted to have sex with him. I hold my head in embarrassment when I remember that last part.

"So …" Jason scratches his head and takes a seat at the counter before continuing. "I walked out to my car a few minutes after you had texted me and saw Nate sitting in the passenger seat with you on his lap, passed out. I didn't know what was going on, so I was pretty pissed and started yelling at him. But then Nate explained that you might have had a few too many drinks, so I drove you both back home after he laid you down in the backseat. When we got home, he carried you up to your room. I told him to just crash here for the night since he looked pretty exhausted." He finishes with a casual shrug.

"Wait," I look around wide-eyed before I whisper, "he's here?"

"Yeah, up in the guestroom. His brother just dropped off his car." Jason gets up and puts a piece of bread in the toaster before turning around to face me. "What's going on with the two of you anyway?"

"Nothing." I jump off my seat and rush out of the kitchen, feeling annoyed about the situation but more with myself.

How could I have let myself drink so much after what happened last year?

I walk quietly up the stairs. The guest room door is open just a little bit, so I peek inside. I don't see him, so I open the door further to get a better look but realize that Nathan isn't here.

The edge of the bed creaks as I sit down and lie back, feeling frustrated that I was hoping he would still be here. I stretch my arms out above my head and let out a deep breath, becoming mesmerized by the ceiling fan above me, lost in thought.

What happened last night can't happen again. It was too close to the truth being revealed, and it was my own fault. The two of them are best friends. Brian and Nathan. Two peas in a pod. They have always been best friends and will always be best friends. I was stupid for thinking that this wouldn't be a problem.

Just then, a tiny voice whispers in my head, *tell him.*

But I can't.

Because even if I tell Nathan the truth, he might not believe me. Or worse, he might hate me because of it.

So there is only one thing I can do, and it makes my stomach turn just thinking about it. I need to end whatever is happening between us before it goes too far. I need to end this before Nathan finds out about *that* night. I try to convince myself it's for the best, but the tear that rolls down my cheek and hits the pillow tells me otherwise.

Suddenly, I hear the door shut, and I jump up to see Nathan standing in front of me with nothing but a white towel wrapped around his waist. My mouth drops open, and I don't have a chance to compose myself before he sees my expression. He has the body of an Olympic god, and I know he can tell exactly what I am thinking from the way I can't take my eyes off him.

"N-Nathan," I begin to say before words tumble out of my mouth faster than I anticipate. "I'm so sorry. I had no idea you were still here. Jason told me you stayed in the guest room last night, and I was just checking to see if you were still here, and I'm so sorry about last night. I shouldn't have—"

"Natalie, it's ok," he says calmly, stopping me in the middle of my apology. He looks down at his body and then back at me before a huge grin spreads across his face. "Want to take a picture before I have to put clothes on?"

"Why, you little …" I reach for one of the pillows next to me and toss it hard across the room at him.

He takes a single step to the side, avoiding the pillow altogether. "Are you trying to make my towel fall off, Miss Spencer?" he asks with an annoyingly cute smirk.

I can feel my cheeks turn crimson. "Of course not! I was just checking to see if you were still here, and clearly, you are, so I'll go now." I stand up in embarrassment, ready to walk out the door, but the knot that's holding my bathrobe in place loosens, and I can feel the robe falling from my skin before I can think about stopping it.

In just a single second, Nathan takes one huge stride toward me and holds together the fabric of my bathrobe before it reveals all of me. I quickly re-tie the knot around my waist, and Nathan takes a step back. Looking from my bathrobe to Nathan, I notice he's staring at the ceiling.

"Nathan?"

"Yes," he answers.

"What are you doing?"

"Oh, I just wanted to make sure you were umm … covered first." He looks back down at me, and I notice his cheeks turning a soft shade of pink. We both share a small, nervous laugh.

I look down at the belt around my robe and find myself playing with it, unable to find the courage to make eye contact with him. We stand there, unsure what to say, as a certain sexual tension builds in the air around us. Nathan runs one hand through his hair and takes a deep breath before taking a single step closer to me, closing the space between us. He places one hand gently on my cheek, then he lifts my chin, so I'm now looking up at him, and that's when he comes down fast on my lips.

I wrap my hands around his neck and pull him in harder as his lips explore mine. But only seconds later, he is already pulling away from me, leaving me wanting more.

His forehead rests against mine as he breathlessly says, "You have no idea what you are doing to me."

twelve

NATHAN

Natalie leaves the room and shuts the door quietly behind her before I let the towel around my waist fall to the ground.

After sliding my jeans on, I sit on the edge of the bed with my head in my hands, feeling like I need to process everything that has happened these past few days.

And damn, it was a lot to process.

On Friday night, lying side by side with Natalie under the picturesque starry night sky, it felt like what I had always imagined a night with Natalie would feel like.

Perfect.

Why did it take me so long to finally ask her out?

All these years, we had known each other without actually knowing each other. I could kick myself for letting so much time go by.

But I guess luck was on my side when the skies opened up that night. As I held her firmly in my arms against that brick wall, her delicious lips on mine, everything felt dreamlike. Like we were the main characters of our own movie, finally having our big scene together.

I didn't want that moment between us to end, but like all great films, it had to. Only, when I let her out of my grasp, I had a strange feeling it wouldn't be the last time she was in my arms, and I was right.

I woke up yesterday morning feeling like I was on cloud nine for the first time in my life. But after dropping Natalie off at her house, my mood severely shifted after spending all afternoon with Nick looking for *him* …

The man who was the reason why I needed to come home this weekend.

The man who has continuously ruined my life.

The man who has always brought out the worst in me.

I can feel my body tense just thinking about this fact and immediately begin to take some deep breaths. Slowly in and out. My hand, which now has a fistful of the pillow beside me, gradually opens, but I can still feel my pulse intensifying with each passing second.

I hate how much control this man has over me.

Don't let him win. Think of Natalie.

And that's all it takes for me to clear my head and gradually calm down.

Last night at the tavern, I had never seen Natalie radiate so much confidence. She laughed, smiled, and flirted with me like no one else was in the bar but us. Of course, I saw every look she was getting from the random creeps who were probably at least twice her age, and yes, I wanted to punch each and every one of them on the spot for even daring to look at Natalie, but the only guy she was looking at, the whole night, was me.

And everything had been going really well. That is until she disappeared.

A small part of me knew it wasn't the alcohol that made her leave so quickly. Instead, someone or something in that bar was why she ran out of there. I was sure of it, but I just couldn't figure out what or who it was.

I had told Brian I would be right back before searching for her throughout the entire bar, and after a few minutes with no luck, I went outside to the parking lot. It only took a minute before I heard someone quietly making sounds of distress.

And after moving in that direction, I found her, halfway outside of her brother's car. The poor thing had her head between her legs, and I could see her body trembling as I approached.

She was so light when I picked her up and put her on my lap that I had to remind myself to be extra gentle. I rubbed her back in circular motions, the way my mom used to rub mine when I wasn't feeling well. Her body continued to shiver under my touch until she finally fell asleep.

Did she remember what I had said to her?

Probably not.

I wouldn't remember anything with that amount of alcohol in my system either.

I had never just straight up told someone I liked them before, but the words practically jumped from my lips before I could stop them. A part of me also knew she might not remember anything, which made it less daunting to say the words out loud. She didn't say anything back to me, but that was no surprise as she could barely utter two syllables at that point.

Realizing she probably wouldn't remember our conversation, I took the opportunity to see if I could find out why she and Vanessa were no longer friends. For some reason, it was really bothering me. Those two used to be inseparable, and something serious had to have happened to cause such a rift between them.

But her response to my question took me by surprise.

"Because of him ... and that night. The snow was so cold."

My stomach clenches because her words had confirmed that something did happen *that* night.

Something bad.

Her words replay in my head, bringing an unpleasant and unwelcomed memory to my mind. A memory I had tried so hard to forget.

That night.

An image of Natalie leaning lifeless against a solid tree invades my mind. I grasp my head hard, trying to make it stop, but it's no use.

It was the night of the Halloween party last year at the Gordons' house. Or, more accurately, my birthday night, which, for many years now, Brian had used as an excuse to hold an all-out Halloween rager.

I feel like I am about to heave as the memory unfolds.

Natalie was running so fast.

I chased after her, knowing something wasn't right. But the frost had made the roads slick, and I came close to having a complete wipeout a couple of times, so I stopped.

Breathing hard, bent over with my hands on my knees, and trying to catch my breath, I barely noticed the falling snow as my body temperature radiated heat and welcomed the cold's touch. I tried calling Natalie's name over and over again and looked in every direction she could possibly have run, but she was gone.

I yelled her name one last time with an urgency I'd never felt before, and that's when I heard her. My head moved in the direction of the small cry. A cry that I was thankfully able to hear.

In the distance, I first saw only her legs next to a tree, and I swear my heart stopped beating. And then I ran like I was fucking Usain Bolt.

She was lying motionless against the tree with her eyes closed and her arms wrapped around herself when I arrived. Blood had trickled down the left side of her face and dripped onto the snow beside her. Her legs were left bare to the elements since she was only wearing what looked like an old football jersey, which might have been a part of her Halloween costume, and her shoeless feet were in the beginning stages of turning blue.

I dropped to my knees and reached for her with shaking hands, instantly relieved when I could feel a pulse. I was so scared as I said Natalie's name repeatedly and tried to wake her up, that I never even heard the sirens getting closer until the ambulance pulled up beside us.

Fuck!

I run my hand through my hair and stand up suddenly to open the window for some fresh air. A slight breeze makes its way into the room, allowing me to escape that horrible vision.

Did she know it was me who found her?

That it was me who wrapped her in my jacket before I picked her up and placed her in the ambulance? That it was me who tried to visit her in the hospital, only to be told by staff members that just immediate family could see her? Or that it was me who left a bouquet of pink roses on her porch, too much of a coward to knock on the front door and hand them to her?

No. She wouldn't know any of this.

She has never mentioned that day to me, so I've been assuming she has no idea it was me who found her. And I would never bring it up to her. I mean, how do you casually bring up something like this? Especially since I never saw her after that night. Not until just recently, that is.

But now, the thought of what might have happened to her that night was eating away at me.

Natalie had told the paramedics that she slipped on some ice as she fell in and out of consciousness, but I knew she was lying. My gut was telling me something wasn't right, but I chose to believe her words so that I could selfishly try to get that image of her lying helplessly against the tree out of my head.

If something *had* happened to her that night, I would never be able to forgive myself, especially knowing we had been in the same house.

But that's the thing. I was pretty sure I knew everyone at that party, and there wasn't anyone there who would have hurt her.

Or was there?

I shake my head, trying to make this thought disappear because it makes my heart pound and my insides boil with unyielding rage.

Think of Natalie.

The image of Natalie lying on the bed in this room earlier appears and makes my wrath subside. I lean against the window frame and appreciate the coolness from the glass on my skin.

When I opened the bathroom door and saw her lying on the bed in nothing but her figure-hugging bathrobe, I nearly lost my towel on purpose. Her robe left little to the imagination, showing off her long legs and hourglass figure. And the never-ending slit in the center of her robe was only an inch away from ultimately revealing her.

The things I wanted to do to her would surely have made her blush if I had said them out loud.

I don't know anything about Natalie's sexual history and honestly don't want to because thinking about Natalie with another guy makes my jaw reluctantly clench in pain. Still, I couldn't deny I was curious.

Had she ever …?

I knew that all the guys back in high school would have done anything to be with her. There were even a few I had to put in their place when I had heard them talk about their intentions with Natalie in the locker room.

But that's how I had always been with her. I always felt like I needed to protect her since she was part of our little group with the Gordons. At the time, I was young and stupid and didn't understand why, but now, I was beginning to. I had feelings for her, feelings I didn't know were actually possible to have for someone else.

An involuntary sigh escapes me as I look to my left and see the clock on the nightstand showing 11 a.m. My pullover is in the corner of the room on the floor, so I throw it on before making my way downstairs. But as I walk through the hallway, I see Natalie's bedroom door open and glance inside.

Last night, after Jason pulled into the driveway, I wrapped Natalie in my sweatshirt before picking her up and carrying her through the front door. I was sure to follow Jason's directions to her room and not wake her parents up.

That was the last thing I needed.

After approaching the end of the hall, I opened the third door on the left, revealing a glimpse into Natalie's life.

A massive white bed was pushed against one of the walls and covered with decorative pillows and blankets. A rather large bay window with a long bench overlooking the expansive backyard was on the opposite wall from her bed, and bookcases filled with every book imaginable stood on both sides of the room.

I placed her gently in the center of her bed and wrapped the blankets over her body, careful not to wake her.

But as I turned around to leave, I heard her whisper, "Nathan." I looked back as her eyes began to flutter open. "Will you stay with me?" she asked, sounding so weak.

I didn't say anything. I knew I should turn around and walk straight to the guest room, especially with her parents' room just down the hall, but then she whispered, "Please?"

I lifted the blankets and slid my body beside her, molding into her incredible curves. She moved closer to me and rested her head on my chest as I wrapped my arms around her protectively. As soon as she fell asleep, I told myself that I would leave and sleep in the guest room, but my eyes were heavy, and the calming feeling of having Natalie beside me put me right to sleep.

I didn't wake up until dawn when the sun was already shining brightly through the bay window. Natalie was sleeping so peacefully on my chest. Her long silky hair was smoothed out against my arm, and her hand was tightly clutching my sweatshirt. I bent my head toward her, placing a kiss on her forehead, and then slowly sneaked out from under her grip. I then went to the guest room where I tossed and turned in bed without Natalie's presence.

That all seemed like such a long time ago.

Now, going down the enormous staircase, I hear laughter and follow the sound. I poke my head into the living room and find Jason watching something on the massive TV.

"Hey, is your sister around?" I ask.

He looks over at me and answers before spooning cereal into his mouth. "Yeah, she's in the kitchen." He points behind me.

"Great. Thanks." I turn around to leave but hear Jason say something.

"Thanks for taking care of my sister last night." He puts his bowl of cereal on the table beside him. "She had a tough year last year, and it's nice to see her finally happy again."

"Yeah, of course," I respond.

What does he mean by a tough year?

As I head to the kitchen, I put that comment on the back burner for another time.

When I walk in, Natalie is sitting on a counter stool at the island, immersed in the book in her hands. She's changed out of her bathrobe and into a thin blue sweater and jeans. Even dressed casually, she looks beautiful.

"Reading anything good?" I ask.

She looks up, a little surprised. "Oh, hi." She smiles. "Here's your sweatshirt from last night." She puts down her book and hands me the folded sweatshirt, which now smells pleasantly like her.

I pull up a counter stool beside her, and she starts pouring a cup of coffee for me. "Thanks," I say, taking the warm mug in my hands.

She begins tracing a circle on the counter with her finger, probably trying to think of something to say.

"So, I was thinking about taking a ride along the coast today." I sip some coffee while observing Natalie.

"That sounds nice," she responds, still looking at her hand.

"Yeah, I just want to clear my head a bit, but I think you should come with me. There is something I'd like to show you."

"Really?" she asks. There's excitement in her eyes as they meet mine.

I pull her counter stool closer to me, causing her breath to weaken. My lips are just inches from hers, but I let the seconds toll and anticipation build. My hands grip her thighs, rubbing them up and down. Then, just as she thinks I'm about to go in for a kiss, I move my lips to her ear and whisper, "Yes, really," before jumping up from my seat and making my way to the front door.

I don't grasp how fast she is, though, because just as I'm about to pull the handle on the door, she turns my body and pushes me against the wall in a single motion. I can easily get out of her hold if I really want to, but I don't want to.

She presses her hands against my chest, looks up at me, and says with a playful tone, "You think you're so smooth, don't you?"

A sly smile makes its way to my lips as I bring my hand up to her jawline and slowly trace it back and forth with my finger. Instead of responding, I bring my lips as close as possible to hers without letting them touch. Our eyes are in a deadlock as I let the anticipation build for a second time.

Both of us are waiting to see who gives in first.

My lips move slowly to her jawline, where I now start placing a line of small kisses, taking my time with each one. Eventually, I lead the trail of kisses further down her neck. I can feel her pulse quicken with each kiss, but she is standing perfectly still, pretending this isn't affecting her in the slightest. She's trying to win this little war we've started of who can hold out the longest.

And she probably would have won, too, if my mouth hadn't made its way down to her delicate skin that was previously hidden under her blue sweater and black lace bra. And maybe if my tongue hadn't licked her just one time across her very stiff nipple.

Yeah, that's when she lost the war.

Because that's when she breathlessly begs, "Please, Nathan."

And that's all it takes.

My lips are on hers within a second.

Her soft lips taste so damn delectable, and her body pressed right up against mine feels so damn good. She has her hands in my hair as my hands hold tightly onto her hips, pulling her harder into me. She slides just one finger down my neck, past my chest, and further down my abdomen, sending blood pulsing to the southern region of my body.

I can feel all of *me* throbbing for her.

Wanting her.

Needing her.

Goddamn.

Her finger slides back and forth on my skin just above the

button of my jeans, causing my pants to become almost painfully tight, but just as my hands slide over her waist and down her back, she pulls away from me, out of my grasp, and opens the front door.

Smoothing out her hair, she turns around with a devilish smile before saying, "You're going to have to do better than that."

I'm left standing stunned and harder than I have ever been in my entire life as she saunters mercilessly over to my car.

Holy fuck.

thirteen

I roll the window down and feel the warm breeze move through Nathan's car as we drive along the coast. It's a little warm for it being almost October, but I'm not one to complain. My cheek rests freely against the door as I close my eyes, welcoming the sun's warmth on my skin while breathing in the familiar and comforting smell of the ocean.

For the first time in a while, I feel … happy.

In the driver's seat, Nathan looks handsome and relaxed, with the breeze pushing his hair back and the sun casting him in a perfect early afternoon glow. There's soft jazz music on the radio, which Nathan hums along to as he takes us along back roads I've never noticed before. He places his hand on the middle console with his palm facing up, and I immediately place mine on top of his. This makes him look over at me with a pleased smile before wrapping my hand inside his.

"What are you thinking about?" he asks.

"Oh, nothing," I respond with a soft smile. He lightly squeezes my hand, sending goosebumps up my arm.

There is something about how he makes me feel whenever I'm with him. It's like I'm the only one in the whole world he's thinking about. The only one he wants to be with. And I was more than ok with it.

But it will never work between us.

My subconscious is trying to ruin this moment, but I let the worry dissipate as soon as Nathan brings my hand up to his lips and places a gentle kiss on the back of it.

I just want to be here with Nathan, without worrying about what could possibly go wrong. I could freak out about all of that another time. But not now. Not today.

Nathan takes a turn down what appears to be a deserted trail in the middle of the woods, barely big enough for his car to fit through.

"Where are we going?"

"You'll see," he says.

After five more minutes of driving down the dirt path, he suddenly stops and tells me we have to walk the rest of the way. After I get out of the car, he takes my hand and leads me further down the trail.

"It feels like we're in the middle of a horror movie," I tell him after almost tripping over a tree root.

"What do you mean?" he asks.

"Oh, you know, the naïve girl follows the hot guy into the woods only to go missing, and she's never seen again."

Nathan stops walking abruptly. I look up at him to find he's smiling with a gleam in his eye. "So, you think I'm hot?"

My cheeks instantly flush. "That's not what I was … just keep walking," I tell him. And he does, while keeping the same irresistible smile plastered on his face.

We eventually come upon a thick mess of vines and branches, which Nathan pushes aside to reveal why he brought me here.

I gasp. "Where are we?"

"Remember when you asked me where my favorite place to go is? Or, actually, I think you called it my *happy place*, right?" He lets out a small laugh.

I nod my head, mesmerized by the sight.

"Well, this is it."

"This place is so beautiful," I say while I look around, taking everything in.

There's a small area of white sand that looks like it has never been stepped on. The space is surrounded by boulders of different sizes, which has turned the beach into a private cove, hiding it from the outside world. The ocean water is crystal clear, and there isn't anyone or anything in sight. And the only sound I hear is the soft rumble of each ocean wave coming to shore.

"I thought you might like it," he says with certainty. "This place has been my little hideout whenever I needed an escape. No one has ever bothered me here." He pushes his hair back and looks off like he's deep in thought. "I came across it as a kid when my family first moved here. Actually, I ran away from home and found it by accident. At the time, I thought I would stay here forever, but eventually, I got hungry. And after realizing I wasn't going to be able to catch any fish with my hands, I went back home." He laughs at the memory.

"What would you need to escape from?" I ask. From what I know of Nathan, he has a nice family, did well in school, and excelled in sports. So I find it odd he would need a place to hide.

Nathan looks away from me. "We all have secrets, Natalie." For some reason, I feel like he is referring to my secret, but surely not. "Come to think of it, I've never brought anyone here before."

"You-you never took anyone here?" I'm surprised by this information.

"No, not until today." He turns to look at me with a shy smile.

Then he takes my hand and leads us to the sand where we sit. The sun is hiding behind some clouds, which makes it a little chilly, so Nathan automatically unzips his jacket and wraps it around my shoulders. I lean my head against him, and we both sit silently for some time, listening to the small waves crash against the rocks.

"I think this is now my new favorite spot," I reveal.

A small gust of wind presses my hair in front of my face, so Nathan gently pushes it back. "I'm so glad to hear that. Any time you want to come here, just let me know."

"Oh, good, because I will never remember how we got here." This causes us both to laugh, and wow, do I love hearing Nathan's laugh.

"Well, should we get going?" he asks.

"No," I whine, then begrudgingly say, "alright, if we have to."

Nathan stands up, brushing the sand from his pants. He offers me a hand, which I take, and he pulls me up with ease.

"Thank you for coming here with me." He wraps his strong arms around my waist as he looks at me with warmth in his eyes.

"Thank you for bringing me here," I say.

His hands cup my face as he places a tender kiss on my lips. Our mouths mold together perfectly. And then, instead of our usual hot and heavy action, we begin to move slowly and more intimately with each other. And I'm thoroughly enjoying it.

Eventually, his lips part ever so gradually from mine, and he says, "Let's go, beautiful."

Nathan leads us back to his car, hand in hand, and we continue our drive. He takes a few back roads, bringing us more inland where we're no longer able to see the ocean. I am about to close my eyes when I see a giant sign for fresh cider donuts and apple picking down the road.

My eyes open wide, and I look over at Nathan. "Can we?" I ask with a little more enthusiasm than I intend. "Please?"

Nathan smiles and turns the car into the farm entrance, making my tummy and heart very happy.

"Wow, I guess this is a popular place to be," he says as he looks for a parking spot in the overcrowded lot.

He finds one near an old red barn in the back, and we both jump out and head over to the little store where we see people coming out with donuts in hand. My mouth starts watering when I see someone bite into the decadent sugar-covered donut, revealing a soft, cakey inside.

When we get to the counter, Nathan asks for a bag of cider donuts. Not one. Not two. But a whole bag of donuts.

I knew I liked this guy.

The older woman behind the counter tells us that a fresh batch of donuts will be out shortly and hands us each a cup of cider to drink while we wait. I see a picnic table outside, so I grab Nathan's hand and lead him over to it where we sit across from each other, relishing our cider.

"I've really enjoyed myself this weekend," I say. What I don't tell him is that it's also the most alive I've felt this past year.

"Me too," he responds. "I don't know how to explain it, Natalie, but just being with you, I feel …"

"I know," I say. "I feel the same way."

Nathan puts his cider down and reaches for my hand across the table. "I'm so glad I ran into you in that little coffee shop." He traces the inside of my palm, and I feel my heart flutter.

"Nathan," I say, feeling my cheeks heat up because of what I am about to say. I don't know why I am about to say what I am going to say, but it has been on my mind, and after what happened before leaving the house … I shiver, remembering the pleasurable feeling of his tongue on me. I feel like it is now or never. "I don't remember everything from last night, but I do remember one part I'd like to … discuss a little further."

"And what part is that?"

"Well," my cheeks are definitely fully crimson now, "the part about you taking me right there and now on top of the bar and then mentioning 'someday.' Well, I guess what I'm trying to ask is … did you mean it?" I feel the heat radiate from my cheeks down my chest as I anxiously await his response. "I mean, not like the part about actually doing it on top of the bar, but I guess more about the part of *someday*."

He laughs a little, making me feel embarrassed that I even brought it up. "Never mind, that was stupid of me." I start to pull my hand away from his.

"No," he says and holds onto my hand firmly. His smile fades completely. "I'm sorry. I didn't mean to laugh. It's just, well," he starts looking around, "you want to talk about that here with everyone around us?"

"Oh, I didn't even realize …" I look around and, for the first time, notice we aren't the only ones sitting in this area.

Nathan brings his voice down to a little more than a whisper. "Natalie, you have no idea how badly I want to be with you. I haven't been able to get you off my mind, and to be honest, I don't want to." His eyes drop to our intertwining hands, and his thumb starts tracing little circles in my palm, sending a shiver up my spine. "I'd like to sound like a gentleman and say we should try not to rush *things,* but I don't even know if that's possible with us." The corners of his lips turn up in a mischievous smile, which causes the insides of my thighs to start pulsing. "Every time I'm near you, I just … want you. So fucking much. And it scares me a little because I've never felt this way about anyone before." His eyes meet mine with identical hunger.

I want to tell him how much I want him. How I've thought of him and *only* him before going to bed. How badly I want to feel his hands sliding over every curve of my body while his mouth devours me in places I've never been touched.

And let's be honest, if this were anyone else but Nathan, I would say even thinking about this would be moving too fast. But it's *Nathan.*

The same guy I've had a crush on for years. I've known him for half of my life. If there was ever going to be a guy I wanted to have sex with, it would be him.

But there is one problem.

I've never had sex.

And Nathan has. Probably more times than I ever want to know about.

That said, there are bigger concerns than Nathan's level of experience. Like what if I don't know what to do? What if it makes things awkward between us? Or what if I'm the worst sex Nathan has ever had?

Ugh.

I realize he is watching me cautiously, which makes me wonder if he can hear my heart beating as fast as my overanxious mind is working.

"Nathan, everything you're feeling, I'm feeling too. I have never felt more myself than when I'm with you." Relief washes over him, and he relaxes his shoulders.

"But there is something I should tell you, and I'm sure I'm probably making it feel like a bigger deal than it is, but you definitely should know." My eyes look away from him as nerves invade every part of me.

"Hey, beautiful, you can tell me anything." His hand is on my chin, gently bringing my face up to meet his gaze while his other hand squeezes my hand in encouragement.

Just tell him.

"Ok. S-so you see … well, the thing is, I've never—" But I'm cut off by a voice that we both hear approaching.

"Well, well, well … what do we have here?" I know this voice so well that I don't even need to look to know who it is. All the color drains from my face, and my whole body instinctively freezes.

"Hey, man. Two days in a row," Nathan says as he takes his hand away from mine to shake Brian's. His beefy physique only makes him appear more intimidating standing right next to the table, towering over me.

"Hey, Natalie," Brian says, staring right at me with his beady green eyes. "I haven't seen you in quite some time. You're looking really good." He eyes me up and down, making me glad that I am still wearing Nathan's jacket.

"H-hi," is all I can say before looking away, keeping my eyes glued to the table.

Don't panic. Don't panic. Don't panic.

"So, what happened to you last night?" Brian asks, looking back at Nathan.

"Oh, yeah, sorry about that. Wasn't feeling so great. I guess I had one too many." He gives a lighthearted smile, but when he looks over at me, his smile recedes, and a worried frown takes its place.

"Hey, man, I've been there. I get it." Brian puts his hand on Nathan's shoulder. "I remember this one time …"

As Brian starts rambling off, I can feel my chest tightening, and my heart begins beating erratically. I roll up the sleeves of Nathan's jacket as extreme heat spreads throughout my body. Am I about to have a panic attack in the middle of an apple orchard?

Stay calm.

Nathan's hand falls on top of mine, causing me to look up at him. He mouths the words, "Are you ok?"

I somehow manage a small smile and nod my head reassuringly, but he doesn't look convinced.

Don't let him see the truth.

After Brian finishes telling his story, I hear Nathan ask, "So, what are you doing here, anyway?"

"Oh, I got dragged here with my family before I head back to school. They're out somewhere in the orchards. But," he looks down at me and then back at Nathan, "what are you two doing here … together?"

Nathan runs one hand through his hair before he answers. "Oh, we umm ran into each other at school and …"

"Your donuts are ready, dear!" I hear the woman from the store shout through the open window to get my attention.

My *savior.*

I mechanically jump up and head over to the pickup window in a hurry. The woman hands me the donuts, and I turn around to walk back to the picnic table then stop. Where do I go? Brian and Nathan are still engaged in conversation. I can't go over there. But I also can't leave since Nathan was the one who drove us here.

You're such an idiot, Natalie. Two times in two days! You knew something like this would happen. How could it not? They're best friends.

I move in the opposite direction, looking for an escape, when I see a sign that reads "Corn Maze Fun," and a hasty plan comes to mind. I'll just kill a few minutes in there until Brian goes back to his family, and everything will be fine.

I walk through the entrance of the corn maze, and after only taking a few turns, I realize I may not have thought this plan all the way through. I have never actually been through a corn maze before and assumed it would be easy for me to find the exit. But after walking past the same purple flag for the third time, I know I'm lost.

I pull my phone out of my pocket and find that twenty minutes have passed.

Fuck.

I also have two missed calls from Nathan.

Fuck. Fuck.

I sit on the ground, drop the bag of cider donuts beside me, and run my hands anxiously through my hair. It has now been twenty-five minutes, and the panic attack is in full swing. My body is trembling, beads of sweat trickle down the back of my neck, and my airway feels one second away from closing.

I'm on the verge of passing out in a fucking corn maze.

Deep breaths, Natalie. Inhale. Exhale.

I can't!

"Natalie!" I hear Nathan's voice and realize he must be looking for me in the maze. Only his voice doesn't create the same comfort it usually gives me. Instead, he sounds worried and … angry.

"Nathan!"

"Stay where you are! I'm coming!" he yells.

In less than two minutes, he runs around one of the corners, out of breath, and spots me. He scoops me into his arms, holding me securely against his chest. "Natalie, what happened?" he demands. "Are you ok?" There's worry in his eyes as he looks me over, so I timidly nod my head up and down. "I tried calling your phone, and you didn't answer. So, I went into the store, and the woman told me she saw you head in this direction. Why?"

I can't find the courage inside of me to say anything.

"Natalie?"

"I g-got lost. I'm sorry. Can you …" My voice is so soft that I can barely hear it myself. It doesn't help that I'm also staring at his chest, too afraid to look up into his eyes.

"Can I what, Natalie?" He is mad and frustrated — that is obvious — but at least his voice has returned to its normal comforting tone.

"Can you please take me home?"

He hesitates before saying, "Why won't you tell me?"

"Tell you what?"

I look up and find him shaking his head in frustration. "Nothing, forget it." He releases me from his arms, and once my feet land firmly on the ground, he kisses my forehead and gently grabs my hand. "Let's go."

The car ride back to my house is completely silent.

Painfully silent.

I know what I need to do, but just thinking about it makes me anxious. There is no way I can be a part of Nathan's life while Brian is a part of his. I look out the window, trying to muster up any courage I have left inside me because I'm going to need it in order to say goodbye.

Nathan's car pulls into my driveway, and he is the first one to break the prolonged silence between us.

"So, I can come back here around seven tonight to pick you up and head back to school," he says, making no direct eye contact with me. Instead, he continues looking straight ahead over the steering wheel.

"Nathan, th-this isn't going to work." I place my hands in my lap, trying to keep my composure.

"I can get you at eight then, if that's better?"

"No, I mean this." I point at the two of us. "You and me. It can't happen."

"What? I don't understand." He turns toward me, and I can tell he is thinking over what he is about to say as he takes a deep breath. "I know something is going on, Natalie, and instead of talking to me, you … you keep trying to push me away," he says dejectedly.

"Wh-what do you mean?" I try to keep myself calm, but I can hear my voice shaking, and I know Nathan can too.

"I'm not dumb, Natalie. I'm just having a hard time piecing everything together." He grips his fingers tightly around the faded leather steering wheel. He's focused, like he is trying to piece everything together precisely at this very moment. "You may have succeeded in pushing everyone else away, including Vanessa, but you sure as hell will not succeed in pushing me away."

His words have just cracked open the flood gates.

I feel one tear slide down my cheek and onto my chest before I have a moment to stop it. "Nathan, I …" I look down at my lap in a panic. As much as I want to tell him everything, I can't. Everyone close to me will be affected by this, and I don't want that. Not when this is my burden and my burden to bear alone.

"Talk to me, Natalie, please."

"I can't," I whisper. A second tear slides down my other cheek, but just as I reach up to wipe it away, Nathan's thumb slides softly across my cheek. He frames my head in his hands, but I keep my eyes firmly closed because I can't find the strength to look at him.

"Please look at me, baby," he says softly.

I do as he says, and the second our eyes meet, my heart crumbles into tiny pieces.

He stares at me intently as if he is trying to read my mind, and boy, how I wish he could.

And then he asks me something. Something I have been hoping would never come up between us.

"Did something happen between you and Brian?"

"What?" My heart is pounding like a drum.

"Brian. Brian Gordon. Did something *happen* between the two of you?" he asks, emphasizing the word *happen* like he already knows. But that's impossible. He doesn't know. And he can't know, which is why a lie leaves my lips faster than I mean it to.

"No." I shake my head adamantly.

"It just seems like you get a little … *anxious* when he's around, and if something did happen, you just need to tell me—"

"No, nothing happened. I don't know why you would think that. So please stop. You don't understand." I can feel the tears begging to escape, so I look away, doing everything in my power to hold them in as my throat burns.

"But that's just it, Natalie. You won't let me understand." And that's when I make the horrible decision to look up into his eyes. They are pleading with me to tell him what happened, which reluctantly destroys me. "Please tell me, Natalie. I want to help you, but I can't if you don't tell me what's going on. I know something happened last year. It was me *that* night who—"

But I cut him off before he can finish because I am getting too close to breaking, divulging everything to him. "It's like you said last night. You don't deserve to be with someone like me. I deserve better than you. It's that simple."

The pain flashing across his face is an immediate stab to my already aching heart.

I open the passenger door and jump out of his car, reaching the front door of my house within seconds, slamming the door behind me, and leaning back against it for full support. Tears are streaming down my cheeks and onto Nathan's jacket that I am still wearing.

What did I just do?

The hurt in his eyes, now embedded in my mind, makes my chest throb, and the tears only intensify. I run up the stairs and into my room where I sob uncontrollably into my pillow for the next few hours.

I don't know how or what he knew, but he knew something. And it's probably for the best that he never finds out the truth since it would never have worked out between us anyway.

Right?

Fourteen

NATHAN

The unsettling image of Natalie running out of my car has been stuck in my head for the past week, and there was nothing I could do to make it go away.

To make the pain stop.

Her words stung like a hard slap across the face.

You don't deserve to be with someone like me. I deserve better than you. It's that simple.

They played over and over again in my head, torturing me day and night. I tried convincing myself that she didn't mean it and had only said those words to push me away, just like she had pushed so many others away, but I was also starting to believe that maybe she did mean them.

And the worst part was, maybe … she was right.

"Why so down?" Greg asks as he takes a seat next to me on the dock at the yacht club.

I had picked up as many shifts this week as possible to try and keep my mind off Natalie, but no matter how many boats I docked or cleaned, it didn't seem to be working.

"I'm fine," I reply.

"Come on, Nate, you've been miserable all week."

"Have I been? Sorry, I didn't realize I was," I lie as I stand up and pick up the bucket beside me, looking across at the next boat to be cleaned that just docked nearby. Greg seems like a nice guy, but I don't feel like having some heart-to-heart with him at the moment. I just need to stay busy and keep my mind as far away from Natalie as I possibly can, which is turning into an impossible pursuit.

"Something is obviously on your mind. Is it a girl?" Greg asks, making me stop in place.

I shrug my shoulders. "Maybe. How'd you know?"

"Because you look exactly like I did when I thought me and my girl were over."

"What did you do to fix things?" I ask, taking a seat on the dock again.

"I apologized." He looks over at me. "I apologized over and over again and then again a little more until she finally believed I was genuinely sorry."

"What did you do, if you don't mind me asking?" Now I'm curious.

He laughs a little while he rubs his forehead. "Ah, I kind of ruined our one-year anniversary." He holds his hands up in defense. "I know. It was a big mistake on my part. She had a whole night planned out for us, but in all fairness, she didn't realize when she made the plans that our anniversary happened to fall on the same night as the World Series." He takes his glasses off to clear the lenses before putting them back on his face and continuing. "Well, let's just say I showed up to dinner a little late and a little under the weather, ruining the night. I felt like a total asshole. The next day, she packed a bag and went straight to her sister's house. It was the worst week of my life."

"Then what happened?" I ask, curiosity now getting the best of me.

"Well, that was almost three years ago. Now we're engaged with plans to be married next summer." A huge smile lights up his face. "The point is, I apologized, and she forgave me because that's what you do when you love someone. It can be that simple if you let it be."

I nod and look down at the ocean below my dangling feet, letting his words sink in.

"What happened?" Greg asks.

"Well, to be honest, I don't even know." I let out a deep sigh. "Maybe I pushed her to try and tell me something that she wasn't ready to talk about. I didn't stop to listen. I just kept pushing her like an asshole. I just … I care about her a lot actually. So much so I'd even take a bullet for her. Wouldn't even need to think about it. I've known her for almost half my life. There isn't anything I wouldn't do for her."

"Did you tell her this?" he asks.

"No, cause I'm an idiot. And I'm not sure I'll have a chance to since it kind of seems like she's avoiding me now." I run a very frustrated hand through my hair. "It feels over before it even really got started."

Greg nods in understanding before standing up. He places his hand on my shoulder and gives me an encouraging smile. "If she's the one, everything will work itself out. You'll see."

"I hope you're right," I respond.

But was he?

On Sunday, after I dropped Natalie off at her house, I drove back to school alone, which made the three-hour drive feel longer than it actually was. When I got back to my dorm room, it was empty as usual. I fought with myself for half the night to call her, but what would I even say? Eventually, I threw my phone to the other side of the room and went to bed, hoping to somehow magically wake up and find that everything was back to normal.

When my alarm went off the following day, the realization hit me that I would see Natalie in our film class that afternoon. This thought made me eager to get out of bed and start my day, which is exactly what I did. My morning classes dragged as I watched the clock tick slowly until it was finally time for History of Films.

I was one of the first people in the class and took my seat feeling pretty tense. I didn't know what I should say or do. Should I say something to her first, or should I wait for her to say something to me? I had practiced a potential conversation in my head at least a hundred times that morning, hoping to put things back to the way they were, but when the professor started the movie, I knew Natalie wouldn't be coming to class.

Was she avoiding me?

My phone sat on my desk taunting me as I argued with myself about texting her, but ultimately, I put my phone in my backpack and decided against it. If she wanted to talk, she would call or text me; I had to give her space.

Maybe space was what she needed.

The next few days had passed by in a blur. I was doing everything I could to keep my mind off Natalie, which meant hitting the batting cages with Tim and picking up more shifts at work. Both baseball and being around the ocean gave me a certain calmness I could never find in anything else.

But now, it had been almost a week since I had seen or heard from Natalie, and I could only blame myself. I knew I shouldn't have pushed her to talk to me in the car, pleading with her to tell me what was going on. I should have dropped the subject altogether. I should have waited for her to want to tell me what was bothering her and be there with open arms and a shoulder for her to cry on. Be the kind of guy she needed. But I fucked everything up.

The thing was, something inside me really needed to know what happened to her *that* night. The idea that something serious might have happened, well, it's been eating away at me every night, leaving me exhausted as I rack my brain for answers.

And I know she said it had nothing to do with Brian, but I can't help but think she was … lying.

Why?

But even if a small part of me thinks she's lying to me, I still need to believe her. I need to trust her. I need to hope that she gives me a chance to apologize, and most importantly, I need to never bring any of this up to her again. And maybe that would fix everything between us.

Although, seeing as we have class together in just a couple of hours, I guess I will find out. Of course, I don't know if she will actually be there or not, but the anticipation of it has been driving me crazy.

"Why don't you take off early?" Greg suggests, bringing me out of my daze.

"Yeah, I think I just might. Thanks." I make my way to the locker room to change out of my uniform and into my jeans and a sweatshirt before returning to campus for class.

Half of me expects her seat to be empty when I walk into the classroom, but then I see her. She's sitting in her regular seat, quietly staring out the window. My heart begins to sprint as I walk to my spot beside her.

She is dressed casually in jeans and a Linrey sweatshirt, looking as beautiful as ever. Of course, the girl could be wearing a potato sack and would still look beautiful.

I'm not sure if she'll even want me to sit next to her, but I notice that all of the other available seats are taken, so I'm left with no choice.

It's now or never.

"Hey, Natalie."

She turns to me, and that's when I take in the full sight of her.

My chest tightens. There's an unrecognizable pain right where my heart is beating.

It's her eyes.

They look lifeless and defeated. Her usual beautiful ocean-grey eyes are now faintly bloodshot, there are dark bags underneath them, and her eyelids look heavy and impossible for her to keep open like she hasn't slept at all this past week. Most people wouldn't even notice, but I do. I notice everything about her.

She looks broken.

Did I do this to her?

"Hey." She passes a little smile off and then turns her eyes to her textbook lying open in front of her.

"Ok, class. If everyone could quiet down so we can get started, that would be great," Professor Clark announces. "Today, we will be watching a film that many of you will probably be familiar with."

The professor pulls down the projection screen and then shuts the lights off as a movie I don't recognize begins to play. A person is in a boat rowing with soft music in the background as the sun rises in a marshy area and a giant white house appears overlooking the water. A man's voice begins speaking, declaring his love for another with all his heart and soul. And with that, all the girls in the room swoon.

Oh great.

Well, all the girls in the room except Natalie, who is staring unwaveringly at the screen, showing no emotion at all.

I need to talk to her. I need to fix this before it's too late.

"Natalie," I whisper.

She continues watching the film and takes no notice of me.

I try again. "Natalie?"

She turns to me, her eyes meeting mine for only a moment before she looks back at the screen and quietly says, "Please, not now." I see a single tear roll down her cheek right before she brushes it away with the sleeve of her sweatshirt.

My heart aches in seeing this, and it would remain feeling this way for the rest of the class.

After what feels like the longest class of my life, the professor shuts the movie off, turns the lights back on, and tells us to have a good weekend before he is the first to race out the door.

"Hey, it's Nate … right?" the guy next to me asks.

I look over my shoulder and recognize the guy from a pick-up basketball game I played a few weeks ago near the dorm building.

"Hey, man. Eric, right?" I ask.

"Yeah, hey, listen, there's a beer pong tournament tomorrow night at the Theta Phi house, and I'm kind of in desperate need of a new partner since mine is sick with the flu. I know it's last minute, but do you think you would be able to fill in?" he asks. "You never missed a shot at our pickup game, so I figured your beer pong skills were probably insane."

"Oh, umm, I don't know." Going to a frat party was not on

my list of priorities right now. In fact, it was the absolute last thing I wanted to be doing tomorrow night. "Maybe."

"Think about it," he says with conviction before picking up his bag and leaving the classroom.

When I lean over to pick up my own bag, I notice Natalie is still in her seat, looking directly at me. Our eyes briefly meet, but she quickly recovers and turns her head away while getting her things together. I try to think of anything to say to her, but before I can even get the words out of my mouth, her bag is packed and she is practically running out the door.

"Natalie!" I yell in desperation before the door slams behind her.

Fuck.

I'm the last one left in class, still sitting in my seat with my head in my hands, shaking in frustration. There has to be something I can do to fix everything between us.

Making no effort to get up from my seat, I pull my phone out of my bag and see that I have three missed calls, all from my brother, Nick. My stomach turns, and I know this can't be good. I call him as fast as my fingers allow, and he picks up on the first ring.

"Nate, you need to come home! He's breaking everything in the house!" Nick shouts on the other end, talking so fast I can barely understand him.

"Hold on, I'm on my way!" I throw my backpack over my shoulder and run out the classroom door.

Fifteen

NATALIE

Over the past week, I had been experiencing my own living hell. And it was my fault.

After Nathan and I had that stupid fight, I shut down. Miserably shut down. Worse than I think I ever have before.

I spent Sunday night at my family's house feigning ill when my mother asked why I wasn't going back to school. She felt so bad that she even made me her homemade vegetable soup and let me stay in my room completely undisturbed for the remainder of the night, which was truly appreciated on my part.

The next day, when Jason got home from school, I bribed him to take me back to Boston with the envelope of cash that my mom had left for me on the kitchen counter. Of course, Jason being Jason, he wouldn't take the money.

He dropped me off at my apartment in the evening, and after I finally settled into my bed, I couldn't help but feel a little guilty for missing school. It was my first time skipping classes. However, I reminded myself that it was absolutely necessary because I had no idea how I would ever be able to look Nathan in his damn gorgeous brown eyes again. Not after what I had said to him.

You don't deserve to be with someone like me. I deserve better than you. It's that simple.

I cringed remembering those horrible words I had used to end things between us. I took Nathan's own insecurity, his ridiculous belief that he didn't deserve to be with me, and I used it against him by confirming his own fear.

And I lied. I lied to the guy who was begging me to tell him the truth.

Shame doesn't even cover what I am feeling over this whole mess.

No, what I am feeling is …

Confused.

Depressed.

Frustrated.

Heartbroken.

Lonely.

Tired. Very … very tired. Emphasis on tired.

All in all, I'm a mess.

With each passing night, the nightmares only became worse. In fact, they were some of the worst ones I've had. I'm talking about waking up with my heart pounding out of my chest, sweat dripping down my neck, and tears raining from my eyes as I screamed out in fear.

I assumed the nightmares progressed because, for the first time in almost a year, I had come face to face with the man who haunted my dreams, Brian. And as true as this was, I also knew they were getting worse because I was fighting with myself to tell Nathan the truth.

But how could I?

If I told him, it would change everything.

First, it would change, or maybe even end, the relationship between my parents and Mr. and Mrs. Gordon, who have been friends for more than twenty years. Second, it would impact Vanessa, my former best friend, who I couldn't even put into words how much I have missed. I only pushed her away because I never wanted her to find out how much of a monster her brother is, and I knew seeing her face would only remind me of him. And lastly, it would affect Nathan. Nathan and Brian aren't just best friends. They're more like brothers. And if I tell Nathan, well, I'm honestly not sure who he would believe, and it terrifies me to find out.

No, telling Nathan the truth is out of the question.

Or is it?

I can't.

Yes, you can.

It will do more harm than good.

You don't know that for sure.

ENOUGH!

Anyway, to try and keep my mind off Nathan, which turned out to be impossible, I stayed busy with my studies and managed to get ahead in most of my classes. The days were passing by, and I had hoped to hear from Nathan by now, putting that whole conversation behind us, but every time I checked my phone and saw no missed texts or calls, I felt a little worse inside. Like someone was slowly twisting my heart around and around just to see how much pain I could endure before eventually breaking it.

And I honestly wasn't sure how much more pain I would be able to handle.

Besides, I highly doubted Nathan was as heartbroken as I was feeling, if he was even heartbroken at all. Because let's face it, he's a twenty-year-old, very attractive and very experienced college guy, which unfortunately means he has probably already moved on to the next best thing.

That thought brings tears to my already sobbing eyes.

Nathan and I had just started to get to know each other, and I blew it. I said such hurtful words to him, and to be honest, I couldn't blame him for not wanting to talk to me anymore. I was so mad at myself for not being honest with him, letting this secret hold me back from living my life. It was continually eating away at me, and Nathan had been right; I had been trying to push him away because of it.

Not to mention, I had a full-blown panic attack in the middle of a corn maze in front of him, so if my hurtful words didn't push him away, I'm sure the sight of me at my lowest probably did the trick.

If he ever finds out about my anxiety and how bad it can get, he'll probably realize I'm not worth it.

I can feel my chest tighten at this thought.

Deep breaths, Natalie.

But maybe I could find some way to make things right between us. I just didn't know how.

Would he ever forgive me for what I said to him?

Well, I guess I will find out eventually because it's finally Friday, which means I'll have class with Nathan in just a few hours. My stomach coils into a hundred tiny knots just thinking about this.

I grab the first sweatshirt I find in my closet to pair with some skinny jeans, throwing them on in a hurry, but even just a glimpse of myself in the mirror catches me off guard. I barely recognize the girl staring back at me. She looks exhausted. *Lifeless.* There is nothing special about this girl. Nothing that would grab Nathan's attention and make him want her.

I put concealer on to try and hide the bags under my eyes and add a sheer coat of lip gloss.

"This is as good as it is going to get," I say out loud, looking uncomfortably in the mirror.

I get to class early and am the first one there. My nerves are eating away at me as I drum my fingers on my desk and bounce my knee up and down. I look out the window next to me to try and calm down, but it's no use. Students begin entering the classroom, which only causes my heartbeat to accelerate.

I begin some deep breathing exercises I had practiced so many times recently while envisioning myself alone in the one place I have always wanted to visit, Paris. It's nighttime, and I'm standing directly in front of the Eiffel Tower. It sparkles beautifully, becoming a magnificent and overwhelming piece of artwork in the middle of the city. I take the elevator to the top and am alone when I step outside. I admire the view and run my hand over the solid metal that has been standing strong for over a century. I can feel my heartbeat beginning to slow down, and my knee stops shaking, but then I hear his voice.

"Hey, Natalie," Nathan says quietly.

I'm quickly brought back to reality, back to film class, and turn to him. *That* face. *Those* eyes. My stomach clenches.

There are a hundred things I want to say to him.

I want to beg him to forgive me for saying those horrible words I never meant. I want to cry in his arms and tell him anything and everything he wants to know. But instead, all I can manage is, "Hey."

I try to put on a smile, but I know it looks out of place on my disheveled face. I can tell from his expression that he *sees* me. And I mean really sees me. He's looking at me so attentively, like he has just noticed me for the first time. My throat tightens as I feel my eyes mist over. Immediately, I look down at my textbook, hoping he didn't see the tears ready to escape.

Thankfully, the professor starts his usual classroom announcement, and I am relieved when the lights go out and the movie begins to play. Ironically, the film choice for today is *The Notebook*.

How appropriate, I think as I roll my eyes.

I've seen this film a hundred times, but what girl in this class hasn't? Couldn't the professor have picked something more lighthearted for today or really just *anything* else?

I'm staring at the screen, pretending to watch the movie, when I think I hear my name. I continue to stare ahead, ignoring the voice by my ear. But then, I am regrettably sure I hear it again a few seconds later. My gut tells me not to look his way, but I listen to my heart and turn to face Nathan.

The moment I do, I see his dark, piercing eyes, so after quickly looking away, I quietly plead, "Please, not now." Then turn my attention back to the movie. Back to one of the greatest love stories ever told.

I wipe a single tear off my cheek before Nathan even has time to see it.

My mind is now working overtime. I thought I would be able to talk to Nathan, but clearly, I'm not ready. This whole week, I thought if I could just apologize to him, then I would feel better. But what my heart is telling me, or more accurately persuading me to do, is tell him the truth.

Tell him *everything.*

But as much as my heart is right, my gut is trying hard to convince me not to.

Because what if I tell him the truth, and it only makes things worse? It could possibly mean never seeing him again. Never feeling his strong arms wrapping me up against his chest. Never hearing that adorable, carefree laugh. Never seeing that heart-stopping smile. And of course, never tasting those soft, powerful lips on mine … ever again.

That thought scares me more than I am willing to admit.

A deep breath I didn't realize I was holding in releases as the realization of what I need to do comes to light.

I need to tell Nathan the truth.

No more putting it off, and no more excuses.

But how will I tell him?

The lights turn on, and I realize the professor has ended the film and dismissed the class. I look down at my textbook, thumbing through the pages, hoping no one has just witnessed me daydreaming.

Nathan's desk chair moves as he packs his bag. Should I ask him to talk now?

Only when I look over at him, hoping to catch his notice, a guy sitting near Nathan starts talking to him about joining a beer pong competition at one of the frat houses tomorrow night. I hear Nathan say, "Maybe," which I assume is a guy's noncommittal way of saying, "I'll be there." And a lightbulb turns on in my head.

I'll go to the party.

I could casually run into Nathan like I had no idea he would even be there, and maybe that's where we could talk. This could be my chance to tell him everything.

Without realizing that I'm still looking in Nathan's direction, he turns toward me, catching me off guard.

Damn. Here come the waterworks.

Nathan looks like he wants to say something, so I instantly throw everything in my bag before jumping out of my seat and leaving the room. I hear him call after me, but it's too late. I can't stop, and neither can the tears.

God, I am really getting tired of crying.

Students are filling up the center of campus, but I move my legs as fast as they will go, almost tripping a couple of times on the cobblestones, until I make it back to my apartment just as it starts to rain.

The concierge, per usual, welcomes me home, and I try to smile back at him as I give a slight wave. When I step onto the elevator, I can finally lean back and take a deep breath.

The doors open on the fifth floor, and when I step off, I see Sarah locking her apartment door.

"Hey, Natalie," she says.

"Hey, Sarah." Standing next to her, I realize just how frumpy I actually look. She is wearing a skin-tight black sweater with faded jeans and perfectly straight hair, looking like she just stepped out of an Instagram ad. I, on the other hand, look like I just rolled out of bed and picked the first thing I found to wear, which is exactly what I did.

I tuck a piece of hair behind my ear and hold my books in front of me to hide as much of myself as possible.

"Are you finished with classes for the day?" she asks.

"Yeah, it's been a long day. I'm ready to take a hot bubble bath and call it a night." I laugh a little at how pathetic I sound.

There's pity in her eyes as she says, "You should come out with me tonight! I'm on my way to meet some friends at a bar nearby, and you should totally come with us!"

A part of me thinks I should take her up on her offer when an idea occurs to me.

"Actually, I was going to ask you if you would want to come

with me to a party tomorrow night over at the Theta Phi house?"

Sarah looks thrilled with the idea. "Yes, of course! I haven't been to that house in a few weeks!" She looks down at the gold watch on her slender wrist. "I have to run now, but yes, definitely. I will see you tomorrow night!" The elevator doors open, and after a few people step off, she steps inside.

Just as the door closes, I say, "Can't wait!"

Operation run into Nathan at a random frat house I've never been to before is either going to be a successful mission or it is going to backfire on me completely.

"May the odds be ever in your favor" resonates in my head.

* * *

It's Saturday, the day of the party. The day I will finally tell Nathan the *truth*.

After texting Sarah about when we want to meet, I spent the whole afternoon getting ready, which I knew would take some time in my condition.

First, I soaked in a bubble bath while letting a rose face mask absorb into my skin, hoping this would take away any puffiness. Next, I applied a deep conditioning mask to my hair and took the time to shave every inch of my body. And finally, after stepping out of the bath, I painted my nails, moisturized everything, and styled my hair in loose curls. I looked in the mirror and was relieved to see I was beginning to appear like my usual self.

The next thing to do was pick out an outfit. I settled on a tight pair of dark denim jeans and a curve-hugging black off-the-shoulder V-neck top, leaving very little to the imagination. Finally, I threw on a pair of silver hoop earrings and charcoal-heeled booties and grabbed my grey velvet crossbody bag, ready to get this night, or more accurately this mission, started.

When I open the door to leave my apartment, I find Sarah sitting on a hallway bench with a drink in her hands.

"Here, this one is for you." She holds up another drink that had been sitting next to her.

"I don't know ..."

"I promise it will take the edge off. And I can tell by how ridiculously amazing you look that you're a girl on a mission tonight." She gives a playful wink.

"You're right." I take the drink from Sarah and wait for her to give the cue.

"Bottoms up," she says before we clink our cups and chug.

Thirty minutes later, we show up at the Theta Phi house along with what feels like half of the school. A group of rowdy people in the front yard are playing games, using the streetlights to see what they're doing. We walk up the cobblestone path, enter the house, and are met with music blasting from every corner and packed young bodies having a good time.

Sarah and I push through the masses of people, trying to find some space. She immediately recognizes a few faces and introduces me to everyone she knows, while I keep my eyes open for Nathan. Eventually, we walk into the kitchen, and Sarah pours us each a glass of whatever is in the punch bowl. We both yell "cheers" over the raucous music before gulping down every last drop.

"Sarah!" I hear someone shout from across the room.

She instinctively recognizes the guy calling for her. He's tall and skinny with jet black hair and tattoos all over his neck. A little too punk rock for my taste, but maybe not for Sarah's.

"Will you be ok here if I go say hi?" she asks, looking at me for confirmation.

"Yeah, of course!" I say as loud as I can. I fake a smile, but I'm a little uneasy about being left alone when I don't know anyone here. Cue social anxiety.

She lays her hand on my arm. "I'll be right back. Promise!"

But a few minutes later, I look around and realize she is nowhere in sight.

Great.

I'm also continually checking to see if Nathan is anywhere in the crowd of people, and he's not. As time goes by, I realize Sarah won't be coming back anytime soon and Nathan might not even be here. And, I'm now slightly tipsy and alone in a house full of people I don't know.

This was a horrible idea.

"Hey, gorgeous." I hear a husky and unfamiliar voice to my right.

I hesitantly look over my shoulder and see a guy who spends way too much time in the gym approaching me. As he gets closer, I realize he also likes to wear way too much cologne. A cough escapes me as I suffocate from the overwhelming putrid scent. The guy has a drink in his hand that he holds out for me to take, which I definitely do not.

"Oh, no, thank you," I say, showing him the drink I already have. The guy towers over me, and not in a sexy way but more of an intimidating way. He clearly doesn't comprehend personal space since he leaves only an inch or two between us.

"So, what is a sexy girl like you doing here all by yourself?" he asks, licking his lips.

Oh no.

"Oh, I'm not here alone. My friend should be back any minute." For the second time tonight, I fake a smile as I look around for Sarah, except this time, in a panic, but I still don't see her anywhere in the crowd.

"Well, why don't we go wait for your friend in my room?" He raises his eyebrows at me and rests his rough hand on my hip, making my insides churn.

I step away, backing myself against the wall, and say, "No, I don't think so." A few drops of my drink spill on my shirt, and when I look down at my cup, I realize my hands are trembling.

He steps toward me, now closing all space between us, and puts his mouth right up to my ear. "You look like you could use a good fucking, and I am just the guy who can help you with that."

My eyes widen, and I try to turn away from him, but I'm trapped. I drop what's left of my drink on the floor and move fast to my left, but the guy is faster and blocks me with his arm.

"Come on, stop playing games. I'm captain of the football

team for fuck's sake. Of course, you want me. So why drag out the inev-inevitable?" He slurs his words as he stares down at me. I can tell this guy has no intention of going anywhere.

There's some cheering in the other room, which must be from the beer pong tournament, and it captures the creep's attention. I use this opportunity to my advantage and push his heavy arm out of my way and begin to make a break for it, just as he forcefully grabs my arm from behind. But, as I try to pull out of his grasp with whatever strength I have, the guy is tackled to the ground, sending me back against the fridge, which I reluctantly bang the back of my head on.

Ow.

Everything happened so fast that I could barely comprehend what was going on.

"What the ..." I start to say, but then I see who tackled the creep to the floor. It's Nathan. He is standing over the asshole, who is now on the floor in the fetal position — possibly crying. No, I stand corrected. The captain of the football team is definitely crying.

"You broke my fucking nose!" the guy yells from the floor through sobs as he holds his face.

"Don't ever fucking touch her again!" Nathan shouts, which is heard over all of the beer pong cheering in the other room.

People are beginning to stare. Some of them even cheer, waiting for a fight to break out. The guy on the floor suddenly gets up, looking between Nathan and me as a trail of blood slides down his face from his nose. His fists tighten by his sides as if he is deciding how best to keep his dignity intact. But the second he realizes he has to look up at Nathan and not down or even level, he does what probably any other guy in his shoes would do.

"Fuck this. I'm out of here." He scurries off to the back of the house and disappears out of sight.

Nathan's back is to me, and he is breathing heavily. His very stiff broad shoulders are rising up and down. Gently, I place my shaking hand on Nathan's back and feel his body automatically tense under my touch, but within seconds, he starts to relax. When he turns around to face me, a gasp escapes from my mouth.

"Nathan, your eye!" He has a huge black eye. But how? The creep never had a chance to lay a hand on him, and it didn't look that fresh … so how did he get it?

Instead of answering me, he cautiously looks me up and down. Not in a sexual way, but more like he is inspecting a car for any damage after an accident.

"Are you ok, Natalie?" he asks, moving closer, intoxicating me with his presence. He pushes my hair back to look at my face for any injuries. For a second, all I feel is the warmth of his strong, reassuring hand on my cheek until I unconsciously wince a little when he brings his hand to the back of my head and touches the spot where it just banged against the fridge.

"Let me get some ice for that." He removes his hand and walks away from me then opens the freezer door and takes out a handful of ice that he wraps in a dish cloth and places tenderly against my head. Just having him in my presence for the first time in a week is already making me feel better.

"Your hair looks nice like this," he says with a little smile as he plays with one of the long curls.

"Thank you," I say, feeling a hint of warmth spread through my cheeks.

"What are you doing here anyway?" he asks, eyeing me warily but still holding the ice in place. "I thought you didn't like to go to parties?"

"Well, I was …" I cannot tell him I came here looking for him. "I was here with a friend until she ran off with some guy and …"

"Oh, ok, I just wasn't sure if it had anything to do with the conversation you might have overheard in class yesterday," he says before biting down on his lip to keep from laughing.

Busted.

Now my cheeks begin to really heat up. "Ok, I knew you were going to be here tonight, so I came here looking for you." I stare down at the ground, hoping he doesn't notice the embarrassment that is very evident on my face.

All he says is, "Let's go outside and get some air."

He waits for my approval, so I gently shake my head up and down, and he takes my hand in his, sending electric sexual shock waves throughout my body.

As we pass the makeshift bar, he grabs a bottle of water before continuing to lead us outside. His hand holds tightly onto mine as he takes me to the back of the yard where it's quiet. A stone wall encloses the property. It's pretty tall, so he picks me up to sit on the wall comfortably beside him.

We sit silently for a few minutes staring at the night sky, both of us unsure what to say or do.

That is until Nathan stretches his arms, takes a big swig from the bottle in his hand, and then tells me his secret.

Sixteen

NATHAN

What I am about to tell Natalie is either going to completely scare her away from me or — hopefully — only make us closer.

I anxiously run my hand through my hair, not knowing how to begin this difficult conversation.

But first, I need to apologize.

"Natalie, I want to start by saying I really am sorry about what happened the other day." I look at her on the stone wall beside me. She's silently swinging her legs and gazing down at the grass. "I pushed things too far. I know I did, but it's just … well, I'll just come out and say it. I feel very protective over you. And I've felt this way as long as I can remember."

A smile forms as I remember the first time we met as kids at the Gordons' home and how nervous she was to say hi to me. Even then, the color of her cheeks would give away her feelings, and it's always been one of my favorite things about her.

"When we were kids, I would spend part of the summer mowing the neighbor's lawn for cheap money to make sure I always had enough quarters on me because I knew you would want the vanilla ice cream sandwich when you heard the ice cream truck.

Seeing your smile after taking the first bite would make mowing all those lawns worth it. And when we were in high school, well, let's just say a few guys ended up with my fist to their faces for things I might have heard them … mention about you."

Her legs stop swinging, and I notice her blush then chew on her lower lip, contemplating.

"But recently, I've felt even more protective of you, if that's even possible, which is why it bothered me that something was upsetting you. Because all I wanted to do was fix things for you. Make things better. But I don't know how because I don't know what's wrong." I realize I'm rambling, so I stop to take a breath. "And I don't know why I thought it had to do with Brian. To be honest, I feel kind of bad I even brought my best friend into this, but … I don't know. You told me it had nothing to do with him, so I believe you. The thing is, how can I be mad at you for not telling me what's been upsetting you when I haven't been honest with you about what's been going on in my life."

With that, she looks up at me cautiously. God, how I've missed getting lost in those beautiful eyes. I shake my head and turn forward, so I don't get distracted from the reason why I brought her out here.

"You see, my father, or the person who I'm related to by blood, well, he's not a very nice guy." A sigh escapes me as I realize this will be the most difficult thing I have ever had to tell someone. "When I was just a kid, my father lost his job at a company he had worked for his whole life. They had a massive layoff, and I guess you could say he took it rather personally." I pause, unsure if I should continue, but the second Natalie's hand lands on top of mine, I find the courage to keep going. "He turned to alcohol, and he started drinking … a lot. The man drank like a fish. I would find empty containers outside all the time and try to get rid of them before my brother ever found them. Vodka, beer, tequila … you name it."

Images of my father drunkenly passed out around the house emerge in my head before I can make them stop.

"It affected him in ways my family and I would never have

imagined. At first, it was like he had lost all motivation to live. He would sleep all day, and when the night came, he was like some possessed zombie just aimlessly switching the channels on the TV with a beer in his hand, not acknowledging anyone around him. It really started to freak my brother and me out, but it was my mom who … who I would find crying all of the time."

I look away from Natalie, shame spreading through me.

"But then things got … worse. I would constantly hear my parents arguing while I tried to fall asleep, but I had no idea what was actually going on. There were so many signs, but I was just a kid. I didn't … I didn't know." I take my hand away from Natalie and put my head in my hands, fighting with myself to continue. "Like the sweaters my mom would wear in the summer or the dark sunglasses she would wear in the house. She was doing everything she could to make sure my brother and I didn't see the bruises. She didn't want us to know about the pain she was experiencing at his expense. And I … I never connected the dots."

Just thinking about my mom makes my eyes mist over.

"When I was about twelve, my baseball team had won a pretty big game against our rival town. So afterward, a bunch of us went to the local pizzeria to celebrate. My mom was supposed to be my ride home, but she never showed up. So, instead of waiting, I decided to walk home. I remember thinking that my mom would never normally have forgotten to pick me up. She always showed up on time or early for everything. Well, when I got to my house, I walked through the front door, and it was eerily quiet. I called out for her but heard nothing. I knew she was home, though, because her car was in the driveway. So, I walked into the kitchen, and that's where I found her."

I pause before continuing, holding in tears as tightly as possible while images from that night crash into my head.

"She was severely beaten. Could barely utter a complete sentence. I was so scared, and I remember the tears just pouring uncontrollably." A single tear manages to break out right now, and I quickly wipe it away so Natalie won't see. "As I held my mom in my arms, I heard a crash in the living room, and I knew right away that it was him. I stormed into the living room, ready to beat the living shit out of him, but I was so young and scrawny. Let's just say it didn't end well for me."

I look down at my hands, shaking as I remember every detail from that night. The physical pain that man put me through. The vile words he lashed out at me after every hit. I was so thankful Nick had been at a friend's house that night.

Natalie reaches out and tightly holds onto both of my hands, which causes the shaking to subside.

"The neighbors had heard the screaming from my mom begging him to stop, so thankfully, they called the police, who showed up and arrested my father on the spot. After that, my mom moved my brother and me to Greenwich, hoping to give us all a fresh start. She changed our last name back to her maiden name, Thomas, so no one would ever associate us with my father. And for a while, it seemed like everything was going to be ok. But recently, it's gone back to shit."

I shrug my shoulders feeling defeated.

"About a year ago, my mom's friend, who was also her lawyer during everything that went down, called to tell her that my father had completed his jail time early. She advised my mom to file a restraining order and assured her he would have no way of finding us, but I knew she was wrong."

I shake my head in anger at the court system. How could they let a man, no, a monster like this, walk away free, knowing what he did? Knowing what he was capable of doing again?

"Last spring, Brian threw a party at our off-campus house in New Hampshire. I was there and was drinking like a sailor, living off the high from a big win my baseball team had that day. But it was about midnight when my brother, Nick, called me, deflating my good mood. He told me that when he got home from school, our father was there shit-faced. He was destroying things and screaming at Nick to tell him where our mom was, who was at work, thankfully. Nick called the police, who came and took him away. I don't even know how he found us, but he did."

A wave of anger boils inside me just thinking about it.

"I was so angry that, without thinking, I jumped in my car to drive home, pushing the gas as far as it could go. However, it wasn't long before I was pulled over."

I take one of my hands out of Natalie's to rub my forehead where a slight headache has formed.

"As you probably guessed, I was slapped with a DUI. The judge let me off pretty easy, though, after hearing about the circumstances surrounding the incident, with just a community service sentence and a loss of my license for a little while."

The next part I am dreading to say out loud. I glance over at Natalie, who is looking at me encouragingly.

"The school I was attending in New Hampshire got wind of what happened. They didn't need someone like me attending their school or representing their baseball team, so I was expelled. The only people who know about me being expelled, besides my family, is Brian and, well, now you."

I'm too embarrassed to look at Natalie, so I stare at the grass.

"That's why I came here. Since I lost my athletic scholarship, I knew I would have to work if I wanted to continue attending school. Long story short, my boss in Greenwich pulled some strings and got me a job at the Yacht club here, and I knew Linrey University was close by, so it made the most sense. And after talking with the baseball coach, there's a good chance I might be able to play in the spring as long as I keep my grades up and train hard during the off-season." I wait to see if Natalie will say anything, but she lets me continue. "However," I take a deep breath, "my father was recently let out."

I hear her inhale sharply.

"Last weekend, the real reason why I went home is because he left a note on our front door that said, 'I'm back.' That's it. No signature was needed for me to know who it was from. Nick took the note down before our mom found it, and then we spent Saturday looking all over town for him, but we didn't have any luck. And then yesterday, Nick called me. He had been home alone, sleeping, when he heard loud crashes coming from downstairs. So he went into the hallway to see what the noise was, and that's when he saw him smashing framed family photos and throwing empty beer bottles at the wall. Thankfully, my mom was out of town on business, so Nick locked himself in his room and called me. He didn't call the police because he knew I wanted to deal with him myself. I wanted to do the things to him that he had done to my mother over and over again. I wanted to do to him what he had done to me so many years ago."

"When I finally got to the house, I found him passed out on the couch." Rage consumed me the minute I saw him, but I don't want Natalie to know this. "So fists were exchanged, and he managed to get a few swings in, too, as you can see from my black eye." I try to offer a little smile, but it's no use.

"Well, soon after, Nick called the police, and the instant my father heard the sirens approach our house, he bolted."

My hands cover my face as shame washes over me.

"I should have just had Nick call the police as soon as he saw him. But I was stupid and let my pride get the best of me. My mom and brother are now staying at a family member's house until the police find my dad, but it tears me apart not being home with them. Not being able to keep them safe."

A sniffle escapes before I can do anything about it, and Natalie's hand lands gently on me. She starts rubbing my back up and down, the kind of touch I've needed all week. She looks at me with pure compassion in her eyes.

"I'm so sorry, Nathan," she says. "I had no idea you were dealing with all of this. I just … I'm so sorry." Tears glide down her cheeks, shattering my heart.

"Don't cry. It's ok. Come here." I easily lift her, so she sits sideways on my lap, and her head rests comfortably against my chest while my arms wrap tightly around her body.

"Nathan, that thing I said to you the other day … I didn't mean it. Not a single word. And I don't know why I said it. Well, actually, I do know why I said it, but it was horrible of me, and I can't begin to tell you how sorry I am." The tears are now pouring down her cheeks, and her eyes are begging me to forgive her.

"Natalie, I know. It's ok." I feel her trembling in my arms, so I hold her closer to me and rub the top of her arm to keep her warm. Damn, I wish I had worn a jacket so I could wrap it around her. "When I had said, 'you deserve better than me,' I meant it because of this. This shitty situation that I can't seem to escape. I didn't want you to know any of this because I was so ashamed. Ashamed of how I've handled everything. Ashamed of who my father is. It's not something I've ever been able to tell anyone."

"So, why did you tell me?" she asks quietly.

"Because I realized if I want you to be part of my life, I have to be honest with you and let you know what's been going on so that you can make your own choice about what you want."

"You want me to be a part of your life?"

"Of course, I do, beautiful." I look down at her. "But what I really want is for you to be with someone who makes you happy. Do I … make you happy?"

Nerves fill every square inch of me as I wait for her response.

Her eyes meet mine. "Yes, you do. You have no idea how happy you make me."

I pull her tighter against my chest and find the center of her forehead with my lips.

We sit molded together, taking in everything that's been said. It's like an enormous weight has been lifted from my shoulders, and it's a surreal feeling, to say the least. This secret isn't just mine anymore. It's ours, and I know I can trust her with it.

"Thank you for telling me everything." She nuzzles up against my chest. "I know that wasn't easy to say. But Nathan, I hope you know I'm not going anywhere. You are who I want. And if we are being honest tonight, you are who I have wanted for a very long time. A very, very long time," she confesses.

"I'm sorry for making you wait." It breaks my heart knowing she has been waiting for me.

"It's ok. You were worth the wait," she says with a wink.

"Natalie?"

"Yes?"

"I like you. I *really* fucking like you." God, it felt good to tell her.

"I like you too," she says sweetly at the base of my neck. "I really fucking like you too."

That makes me laugh because I'm not sure I've ever heard this girl swear before. "You have no idea how nice that is to hear," I say as I tilt her chin up toward me. Her iridescent grey eyes stare back at me, waiting for me.

Has she missed this as much as I have?

I try to prolong the buildup, but I need her now. I need her more than I have ever needed anything in my life. And the moment our lips meet, I realize how much she needs me too.

She wraps her arms around my neck and grips my hair, tugging me closer to her. This, in turn, tightens my grip around her waist. Her luscious lips taste sweet, probably from whatever was in the punch bowl, and I'm loving it. The second our tongues meet, a fire ignites inside me, running up and down my core, craving every part of her. I loosen my hold and bring my hands to her hips, pulling her body entirely onto my lap and turning her so that she is now straddling my thighs. My hands slide lower down her back, pressing her body right up against mine. I feel the warmth between her legs as she grinds her hips deliberately onto mine, instantly making me hard.

She moans my name in a ragged breath as I move my lips to her jawline and further down her neck. Her breathing starts picking up as I find the sensitive spot below her ear, where my tongue slides across her delicate skin. I feel her hands slide down my neck and further down my chest, but I'm taken aback when she gently pushes herself away from me.

"Is everything ok?" I ask breathlessly. Maybe she changed her mind. God, I hope she didn't change her mind.

She nods but slides off my lap and stands in front of me, trying to steady her breathing. Her hands smooth out her hair and make sure her shirt is tucked back into those skin-tight jeans.

I sit back and watch her in confusion. Then she clears her throat before looking straight into my eyes.

"Nathan, there … there is something I need to tell you."

Seventeen

Standing directly in front of Nathan, who is patiently waiting for me, my stomach clenches into tiny knots. There's a good chance I could heave at any moment, and now my heart is pounding so hard that it's the only thing I can hear.

Should I start at the beginning?

Should I skip ahead to the end?

Was this a mistake?

Have I forgotten how to speak?

Breathe.

God, this is going to be so hard to say, but after everything he just confided in me, how could I not tell him?

A slight breeze pushes a loose strand of my hair in front of my face, and as I bring my hand up to move it back into place, I notice the uncontrollable trembling in my fingers. Nathan sees this as well, causing me to hastily look down at the ground.

"Natalie, you really don't have to do this if you don't want to," Nathan says with concern echoing in his voice.

"No, no. I want to," I say very matter-of-factly. But I can still feel my chest tightening, and my pulse accelerating. Last I checked, it was sixty degrees outside, so why does it feel like every pore on my body is releasing sweat like I'm the goddamn Niagara Falls over here?

I take one final deep breath and slowly exhale before I let the words find their way out of my mouth.

"Ok, so before I tell you—" I'm cut off by the sound of my phone buzzing loudly in my back pocket. I grab it with the intention of putting it on silent but freeze when I see my mom's name on the screen.

"It's after midnight. Why would she be calling me so late?" I say out loud to myself before looking up at Nathan. "I'm sorry. I think I need to take this."

"Of course," Nathan replies.

"Hi, Mom, is everything ok?" I ask, waiting to hear her familiar voice on the other end. But, instead, her usual cheerful tone is almost unrecognizable as she speaks through a stifled cry.

"Mom, I can't understand you. What's wrong?" The panic is now evident in my voice.

"It's your father," she manages to sob, and my eyes widen in horror.

* * *

A few hours later, Nathan and I are almost back in our hometown of Greenwich. It's raining wildly, ironically matching the abundance of tears cascading down my cheeks as the phone call with my mom plays on an endless loop in my mind.

I lean my head against the cool glass window, looking for comfort from anything.

After my mom was able to control her crying and take a few composing breaths, she told me that my dad had suffered a minor heart attack.

He had been cooking dinner with her at home, when he violently reached for his chest before crashing to the floor. My mom immediately called for an ambulance, and they rushed him to the emergency department where the doctors were able to stabilize him. The team on hand had insisted my mom would be fine to go home and sleep in her own bed, but she had told them the only place she would be sleeping was by my dad's side, just like she had done for the past twenty years. Once everything had settled down, she called to let me know what was happening.

I had told her I would be there as soon as possible, but the second our call ended, I realized there was no way for me to get to them. Besides the fact that I was pretty sure I had just drunk at least half of the contents of the punch bowl inside, I knew there was a bigger issue. No car.

So, amid tears, I told Nathan the whole conversation I had just had with my mom. Without even having to ask him, he grabbed my hand and led us back through the frat house, which still had an immense number of people packed inside, until we eventually squeezed our way through the front door. As soon as we were outside, he picked up the pace and took us down to the end of the road where his car was parked. Neither of us said anything as Nathan started driving in the direction of Greenwich.

He kept his right hand tightly wrapped around mine the whole drive and continuously told me that everything was going to be ok.

"I know," I said over and over again, not believing my own words. My mind kept displaying different images of my dad. Memories once forgotten were clear as day.

Why him?

My dad was the one who taught me how to ride a bike for the first time. The one who bought a record number of Girl Scout Cookies so my troop would win the grand prize trip to California. The one who never missed any of my tennis matches, even the away ones. And the one who picked me up from kindergarten early to take me to get ice cream after I was traumatized that Bobby McClain had kissed me smack on the lips, thus giving me cooties.

There was never much talk about it, but I knew he grew up not having a considerable amount of money, which is why he did everything in his power to give his children the life he never had. With nothing but hard work and determination, he started his own architecture firm, Spencer Inc., which he has overseen for thirty years. It is now the top architecture firm in New England. In my unbiased and completely impartial opinion, it's also the top architecture firm in the country. Maybe even the world. Again, just an unbiased opinion from a girl who loves her dad.

As I stare out the rain-soaked window, I realize we are pulling into the hospital parking lot. Nathan finds a spot by the front entrance and parks his car while still firmly holding onto my hand. I look at my phone to see if there are any more updates from my mom, and except for my phone alerting me that it's after three in the morning, there are no new texts.

We rush to the hospital entrance, where we both approach the front desk for assistance. An older woman with a friendly face greets us.

"Hi, I'm trying to find which room my dad is in," I say, trying to keep my voice even. I notice the badge on the woman's shirt says "Sue."

"Well, let's see here." She turns on the computer in front of her. "What's the last name, and what would he be here for, dear?"

"The last name is Spencer, and he had …" I can't say the words out loud.

Nathan jumps in for me. "He had a minor heart attack." He then squeezes my hand in encouragement.

Sue's warm smile fades when she hears this, and now sees me in a new and understanding light. "Oh honey, I'm sure everything will be just fine. Your dad is in great hands here." She types my last name into the computer and quickly locates my dad's room number. "It says he is in room 405. So, you will want to take the elevator right over there, and when you get off on the fourth floor, take a left, and your dad will be down that hallway."

"Thank you," I say as Nathan and I head to the elevator.

As I press the button for the doors to open, I hear Sue yell, "Everything will be ok!" I give her a small smile and then step into the elevator after Nathan.

I push the button for the fourth floor and lean against the wall, closing my eyes for a second as I feel my heart race with dread, not knowing what I will see behind door 405.

"Natalie?"

My eyes flutter open to find Nathan standing directly in front of me, looking down at me with sadness in his eyes.

"Come here," he says softly, holding out his arms for me to fall into, which is exactly what I do. I snuggle into his sturdy chest, inhaling his familiar scent. His arms wrap tightly around my body, and his chin rests on the top of my head.

I wish we could stay like this forever and that we were anywhere else in the world but here. Here being in a hospital on the way to see my dad who just had a heart attack.

A. Heart. Attack.

"Thank you for taking me and for coming with me." I can't stop the tears from welling up in my eyes. "I don't know what I would have done if I had to come here alone." My hands are gripping his shirt for dear life, not ready to let go as I feel the elevator rising.

"I'm here," Nathan says before leaning his head back and placing a gentle kiss on my forehead.

My stomach plummets when I hear the doors open.

But Nathan takes my hand in his and leads us off the elevator to search for room 405. We take a left and begin walking down the hallway until we both see it simultaneously and freeze. *Robert Spencer* is on the paper nameplate next to the door, triggering my breathing to waver.

It's becoming too real for me.

"I'll be right out here waiting for you," Nathan promises.

I nod and take a deep breath before pushing the door open with unsteady hands.

My heart sinks.

Sound asleep in a hospital bed, my dad is hooked up to multiple wires, which are monitoring him. The rhythmic beep of one of the scary-looking machines brings me some comfort, though, hearing his heart is now doing ok. My mom is sleeping on the chair next to him, while Jason is sprawled out on the sofa in the back of the room covered by a thin hospital blanket.

The sight of my sleeping family spreads a warmth through me that I've desperately needed since my mom's call.

I quietly close the door and walk back out into the hallway where I find Nathan sitting in a chair that is way too small for his massive body. His head is leaning back against the white wall, his legs are fully stretched out, and his eyes are closed. However, when he hears me approach, his eyes immediately open and he awkwardly jumps up from the chair.

"Everyone is asleep, including my dad," I say, feeling just the tiniest bit calmer.

"Well, that's good." He gives a reassuring smile and puts his hands in his pockets, unsure of what to say next.

"I think I should probably stay here tonight with them." I point to the room where my family is sleeping.

"Yeah, of course. I can turn this chair into my bed for the night." He glances down at the relatively small chair before looking back at me. "I want to be here for you."

My heart turns into mush.

I take a step closer to him and wrap my arms around him as far as they will reach. "I really appreciate that, but I don't want you sleeping in that tiny, uncomfortable chair in the middle of the hallway. I'd offer you the couch in the room, but it looks like Jason has staked it out as his own." I try my best to give an uplifting smile. "I'll be ok. I promise."

"Are you sure?" he asks, hoping I'll change my mind.

"I'm sure." I stand on my tiptoes to give him a light but much-needed kiss. It's like the instant our lips meet, I can feel the world aligning on its axis at a perfect 23.4 degrees. The way it's supposed to. The way it should always be.

It feels *right*.

As we slowly pull apart, I keep my eyes closed, enjoying his taste, until I hear him speak. "Well, if you're absolutely sure, then … I think I'll head back to school."

"What? Why would you do that?"

"Well, the whole situation with my dad …" He looks embarrassed about what he is going to say. "I don't think I should be staying at my house tonight … alone."

"Oh, Nathan, I didn't even think about that. How selfish of me, I can't believe—" I start to say as I bring my hands up to my face, but Nathan interjects.

"No, don't worry." He puts his large hands on my shoulders and looks directly into my eyes. "It's really not a big deal. I can come back to pick you up and bring you to school whenever you're ready."

"No, you're not driving all the way back to school at this time of night, especially in a torrential downpour." I'm trying to think of somewhere for him to go when it occurs to me that there is a place only five minutes from here where he can sleep. "I know. You'll stay at my house."

"What? No. I can't do that." He shakes his head.

"Oh, yes, you can. Trust me. My parents won't mind at all. The house key is under the blue planter on the porch, and you can sleep in the guest room or … you can sleep in my room." I leave the option open for him. "If you want to," I add.

"Your room?" He raises his eyebrows.

"Yeah, you know, so you don't feel alone." I lean against his chest and look into his dark eyes, peering down at me. "It'll be like I'm there with you."

He wraps me inside his strong arms, giving me that happily ever after feeling. You know the feeling. The one at the end of every great romance novel where, just for a moment, everything feels perfect. But the sudden swoosh of doors opening with nurses running by reminds me that we are, in fact, not experiencing our happily ever after moment … yet.

Nathan takes his time kissing my forehead before saying, "That sounds like a great idea to me."

"Ok, good." For a second, I think I hear movement from the other side of room 405's door, but it's probably just Jason snoring.

"Thank you again for bringing me and being here with me. This was, well, what I mean is …" I trail off, unsure of how to finish this sentence. How do you say thank you to someone who literally stopped everything without hesitation to drive you three hours to see your dad in the hospital — in the middle of a rainstorm, in the middle of the night? I don't have the right words for this.

"Natalie," he moves a strand of my hair behind my ear, "I would do anything for you."

I know I've turned as pink as a Starbucks passion tea.

"Is there anything I can bring you from your house?" he asks.

"No, I'll be fine. Will you text me when you get there, though, so I know you made it in one piece?"

"Of course. Try to get some sleep, ok?" His eyes glaze over my face with concern.

"I will," I reply, but if he saw the size of the couch that I am going to have to share with Jason, then he would know this is going to be a very difficult task.

His lips touch mine one last time and linger for a few seconds before he loosens his grip around my waist and leaves.

I open the door to my dad's room as quietly as possible, but when I step inside, I'm surprised to see my mom awake, standing beside my dad, observing every breath he takes.

"Hi. I hope I didn't wake you," I whisper.

"Oh, no. This chair isn't exactly the most comfortable piece of furniture to sleep on, but it's the only thing available." She gestures to my brother, who is taking up the entire length of the couch.

I look at Jason and quietly laugh at the sight of him before turning back to my mom.

"Thank you for coming so quickly, sweetie," she says. "I was so worried, and I just didn't know what to do, and then …"

"Mom, it's ok." I walk over to her, hug her slender frame, and then look down at my dad. "How is he doing?"

She lets out a big sigh. "The doctors confirmed there is partial blockage in his artery. They've put him on some medications and are fairly confident that, with some rest, he will be back up and running soon enough without needing surgery. But we will have to make some serious changes to his lifestyle when he gets home, and knowing your father, I'm sure he won't be too keen about it." She gives me a knowing look, her eyebrows raised, then puts her hand back on top of my dad's, holding it supportively "We are lucky it was only a minor heart attack compared to what it could have been." Her eyes begin to tear up. "I thought … I thought I was going to lose my best friend tonight. But this guy is not going anywhere as long as I have something to say about it." A tear slides down her cheek as she looks down at my dad with nothing but love in her eyes.

"He's going to be ok, mom," I assure her, hoping I'm right about this.

Even after all these years, their love for each other warms my heart. It's the kind of rare love most people only see in movies or read about in books. But I've been lucky enough to witness it every day of my life.

I turn around to face Jason, who is still sound asleep, and try to figure out how I can move his large body over to one side of the couch when my mom speaks up.

"So, Natalie, how long have you and Nathan Thomas been seeing each other?" she asks, still keeping her eyes on my dad.

My cheeks instantly warm up. "Oh, that well, he umm … we ran into each other, and he was with me when you called, and then I guess … he kind of drove me here."

"Oh, I see. And do you kiss every guy who gives you a ride home?" There's a hint of amusement in her voice.

"Please tell me you didn't see that?" I cover my face with my hands as redness spreads from my cheeks down to my chest like an unyielding heat wave.

"I'm just teasing, sweetie. I heard voices out in the hallway and got up to see who it was," she says with a casual tone. An almost too casual tone. "I haven't seen him around in a while. He must be a pretty nice guy, though, if he drove you here when you two were clearly at a party enjoying yourselves," she says as she surveys my outfit. "Not to mention, he's not too bad on the eyes."

I roll my eyes and laugh. "Oh, mom."

She displays a small smile. "I'll be right back. I'm just going to get some water." She looks down at my dad once more before walking out into the hallway.

I gently take off the heels I have been running around in and then push Jason over to one side of the sofa with as much strength as I can muster. The blanket is barely big enough to cover one person, but I bring half of it up over my body, leaving the other half on Jason.

"Nice of you to join us, Nat," Jason says groggily as he pulls on the blanket and shifts to his side.

"It's good to see you too, Jason." I pull hard on the blanket, fighting for my half.

"You better not snore," he says before drifting back to sleep.

"Good night, Jason."

Eighteen

"Nathan, wait!" I hear a woman's voice call just as the elevator doors are about to close. Holding them open with my arm, I step out and recognize the woman as Natalie's mom.

"Mrs. Spencer. Hi." I put my hand out awkwardly toward her for a handshake.

"Oh, come here." She pulls me in for a hug. "I haven't seen you in ages. I barely recognized you." She unwraps her slender arms from around me and takes a step back. Her eyes widen when she sees my black eye, but thankfully, she decides not to mention it. "Your mom told me you were all grown up, but she didn't tell me how tall you've become." Mrs. Spencer and my mom hit it off a few years ago at some book club in town, which resulted in frequent coffee dates between the two. "Thank you for bringing Natalie to us so quickly."

"Of course," I state. "I'm so sorry about your husband. How is he doing?" Her grey eyes, similar to Natalie's, look away pensively before she answers.

"He's going to be ok. Just needs to rest for a bit." She assures me with a slight smile, but I can't help feeling like she is really just trying to reassure herself. "I don't think he is going to be very happy with me, though, when I tell him he can't have bacon anymore," she says with amusement.

"Ah, no, taking bacon away from a man should be illegal," I joke, trying to erase any tension in the air. But I notice the slight quiver in her hand as it pushes her shoulder-length blonde hair behind her ear, which makes me ask, "And how are you doing?"

"Me? Oh, I'm … well, I've been better." She maintains her smile, but I recognize something in her eyes that I used to see all the time as a kid. Fear. Mrs. Spencer feared losing her husband, while my mom feared being abused by hers. So, it was something that, as a child, I became quite used to seeing. So much so that I became pretty good at knowing from the moment I walked through the front door of our house after school whether it was going to be a good night or a night where I would need to hide under my bed with pillows covering my ears to drown out the insistent yelling and loud bangs. Of course, at the time, I had no idea those loud bangs were my father hurting my mom.

"It was scary, that's for sure. Probably left me a little shaken up, but seeing Natalie walk through that door just now certainly helped put my mind a little more at ease," Mrs. Spencer says, releasing me from my thoughts.

"Yeah, she definitely has a way of doing that," I admit.

"Your mother mentioned you had recently transferred to a school in Boston, but I guess I didn't connect the dots. Do you attend Linrey University too?" She looks at me curiously.

"Yeah, actually, Natalie and I take a class together," I say, unsure how much more I should tell her.

"Oh, what a small world." A genuinely warm smile appears on her face but then instantly falls. She tips her head to the side, eyeing the car keys in my hand. "You're not going all the way back to campus tonight, are you?"

"Umm, actually, Natalie suggested I use the guest room at your house." I decide to leave out the part about me sleeping in her daughter's bed. "If that's ok with you, of course?"

"Of course! There's a spare house key under the blue planter, and there's plenty of food in the fridge. We probably won't be back until tomorrow afternoon. Well, I guess more like later today, and please ignore the mess in the kitchen. I'll get to that at some point." She stares into space, deep in thought. "It happened while we were making dinner …" Her voice trails off.

"Mrs. Spencer," I interject, knowing what she needs to hear, "everything is going to be ok."

She instantly puts a smile back on her face to show she's fine, but her glossy eyes convince me otherwise. "I couldn't agree with you more. And please, call me Nancy." She turns around and makes her way back through the empty hall.

I press the button for the elevator and wait for the doors to open. Once they do, I step inside and lean back against the wall, closing my eyes as exhaustion takes over from everything that's occurred these past few days.

"Nate?"

I open my eyes and see Mrs. Spencer standing in front of the elevator.

"Thank you for making my daughter happy again."

* * *

After easily locating the house key under the blue planter where Natalie and her mom had both told me to find it, I enter their home.

It doesn't matter how many times I walk through this front door, I will never get over how enormous the house is.

No, not just enormous, but insane.

There is a grand staircase that can't be missed when you walk inside, the flooring is marble, pieces of artwork, which look like they belong in a museum, line the walls, the ceilings reside high up in the heavens, and I'm pretty sure my hand is holding onto a solid gold doorknob. *Holy fuck.*

And that was all just from a first glimpse inside, never mind the rest of the house.

But even with how ornate everything seems, there is something about this house that is welcoming and warm. In fact, it doesn't just feel like a house; it feels like a home.

As I walk around, I notice that everything is spotless and seems to be in its proper place until I enter the kitchen. There's spaghetti sitting in a cold pot of water, pieces of now soggy bruschetta on a plate, a salad wilting away in a large wooden bowl, a bottle of red wine uncorked on its side on the counter with its liquid now on the floor, chopped up onions and peppers in a skillet, and what appears to be a broken plate on the floor.

This is the scene Mrs. Spencer was envisioning having to clean when she returned home.

But there is no way I would be leaving this eerie reminder for her to see after coming back from the hospital.

I start looking around until I find the pantry where the broom is hiding and get to work. The shattered pieces from the broken plate sweep effortlessly into the dustpan, and I dispose of them in the trash, along with all the soiled food sitting out. Next, I get on my hands and knees to scrub the wine off the floor before washing the dishes in the sink and wiping down the counters. At this point, I look around, pleased that the kitchen is back in its original state.

A yawn escapes from me, and I realize how drained I really am. It's been quite some time since I've stayed up this late, and I'm starting to feel the effects. So, I shut the lights off in the kitchen and begin my slow journey up Mount Kilimanjaro or, what I mean to say is, up the stairs, observing all the family pictures that line the wall until the final step.

There are a few staged family portraits that look like they've been taken over the course of several years. Everyone has perfect smiles on their faces and matching outfits like they are posing for an ad in a JC Penny catalog. But my favorite pictures are the candid ones. The ones that look like no one knew the picture was even being taken.

In particular, there is an image of Natalie that captures my attention. She is lying in a grassy field, holding a fluffy white dandelion, and laughing as if someone had just told her the funniest joke she'd ever heard. She has no makeup on and is wearing a simple white dress; her long blonde hair is splayed out around her. And she is breathtaking. Absolutely breathtaking.

Natalie's family seems very close to each other, which makes me feel a little envious. But at the same time, it comforts me to know that there really are families like this out there in the world. Normal. Happy. Loving. They aren't all messed up like mine.

Maybe Natalie and I will be lucky enough to have a family like this someday.

Wait! What? The brakes in my brain immediately slam down before I can continue this thought.

God, what happened to the guy who used to heave at the idea of being committed to one person? Who used casual hookups as a distraction from everything else going on in his life? Who didn't think he was worthy enough to be loved?

He found Natalie. And she turned his whole world upside down. That's what fucking happened.

I shake my head, laughing at myself. Then I notice a serene picture of Natalie's dad sitting in a chair at the beach. Relief fills me, knowing that he is going to be ok. It would have destroyed Natalie if anything more serious had happened to him tonight, which, in turn, would have destroyed me.

When I finally reach the top of the stairs, I go to the end of the hallway where I see Natalie's bedroom door sitting partly open. I walk in and head straight for the cloudlike bed.

I lift my shirt over my head and unzip my jeans, letting them fall to the floor. Her bed is perfectly made, so I pull back the blankets then slide under the covers, enjoying the feeling of her satin sheets against my skin. The pillows smell just like her, surrounding me with an intoxicating aroma of apples and peaches, which causes an ache in my core for Natalie.

All of my five senses are wishing she was here beside me. In fact, they are begging for her. Needing her.

Damn, I wonder what it feels like to run my hands over her soft pu—

Nope.

I am not about to jerk off in Natalie's bed.

Don't even think about it, Nate.

After running my hands over my face in frustration, I pull the covers up tightly around my turned-on body and move around until I find a comfortable position on my side. I sigh as my head molds to her thick and very supportive pillow, helping release some tension.

Today really had been quite draining.

Before I returned to campus, I spent the morning making sure my mom and brother were situated at my aunt and uncle's house, who live just a few towns over. I felt so conflicted about leaving them with my unhinged and very erratic father still out there, but my mom insisted they would be fine if I went back to school. I still couldn't help but feel guilty for not staying with them.

When I returned to my dorm, I felt pretty tired. Actually, if I'm being honest, I was completely worn out. Exhausted. Mentally and physically. My body had begged me to climb into bed, but after the week I just had, I thought going to a party would help take my mind off things. Release some of the tension that had been slowly building up.

And man, it was good I showed up at Theta Phi's house when I did. I was at the frat house for no more than ten minutes when I spotted Natalie in the kitchen.

As worn out as I am at this very moment, I still find myself getting achingly hard at the thought of her.

I remember raking my eyes over her every curve. Natalie's jeans hung on for dear life to her perfectly voluptuous hips, while her cleavage was begging to be free of the tight black top she was wearing. Her long blonde hair, usually pin straight, hung in perfect waves, framing her face. My eyes moved to her plump lips, which looked ready for a taste before my gaze moved up to her eyes.

It was her eyes that told me something was wrong.

It was fear. *Goddamn fear.*

My body began seething as I finally noticed Connor standing

uncomfortably close to her. Most people probably viewed him as the school's hero, being the captain of the football team and all, but from the moment I met the guy at a party a few weeks back, I didn't like him. Call it intuition or simply a gut feeling. Or maybe it was just from hearing the way he talked about the girls he, in his own words, *fucked senseless.* I knew something wasn't right in the head with him.

And the second this asshole put his hand on Natalie's arm, I lost it and tackled him to the ground before he even had a chance to blink. God, I really hope I did give that guy a broken nose. He deserved it.

Just thinking about that asshole gets my blood boiling all over again. Think of something else. Anything else.

Natalie.

I told Natalie something I had never told anyone before. I told her about my father. *Fuck,* I hated calling him that. That man would never be more than someone I was related to by blood. And even that was too much for me to grasp.

Did she think differently about me after I told her everything?

She only looked at me with empathy the whole time I talked, never saying a word. The tears that ran down her cheeks caused an unpleasant heaviness in my heart. I didn't want to make her cry. I just didn't want there to be any secrets between us anymore. I wanted to feel closer to her and just having her there listening to every word I spoke meant more to me than she would ever know.

I never even had the nerve to tell my best friend, Brian, about those parts of my life.

Brian. My best friend.

The thought of Brian has made me feel uneasy lately because something still feels off with that whole thing.

Even I couldn't deny that Brian had his asshole moments, and there were more than a few, but did that mean he was capable of a moment that included possibly hurting Natalie? The girl who spent the majority of her life playing one of the four pieces to our old friend group. It was too much for my head to comprehend.

And I don't think Natalie would lie to me, but maybe she would if she felt she had to. Maybe she was lying to me because something did happen between her and Brian, but it was … consensual? And now things are awkward between them? But wouldn't Brian tell me if they hooked up? I mean, unlike me, who hates talking about that stuff with other people, Brian is one of the biggest talkers I know. He would tell anyone within a mile radius about who he had just had the pleasure of hooking up with. It was like some weird high he got. Some secret pleasure. Not the actual sex part, but the part about telling people about the sex. He could never keep it to himself. In fact, one time, he was still in bed with a girl when he texted me to let me know. It was fucked up.

But Natalie and Brian?

Picturing the two of them together, on top of an abundance of questions circulating in my head, creates an instant wave of nausea.

Fuck. I really don't want to think about this right now.

I turn to my other side, hoping to stop this thought in its tracks with something more pleasant, and it works. Because now I'm facing a framed picture of Natalie on her nightstand. In the photo, she's standing with her brother who completely towers over her. I assume, from the cap and gown she is wearing, that it was the day of her high school graduation. But, besides the cap and gown, she is wearing the most heartwarming, beautiful smile.

Looking at Natalie's delicate pink lips makes me instantly think about the kiss we shared hours ago while sitting on the stone wall. And it was a good kiss. No, it was a *perfect* kiss. Exactly like every single one of our kisses has been.

At that moment, I needed her more than I had ever needed anything in my life. I needed to feel her in my hands. I needed to taste her on my lips. And above all, I needed her to need me.

Because after telling her about my father, a wave of vulnerability had swept over me. It was definitely not a pleasant feeling nor one I was entirely used to, but being consumed by Natalie with her lips, hands, and body certainly made the uneasiness wash away.

Then she pushed away from me. She stood in front of me, trying to find the courage to tell me something. Her breathing quickened and her hands began to shake. And from noticing how difficult it was for her to keep her eyes locked with mine, I had a pretty good feeling it had to do with *that* night.

Was she going to tell me what had been bothering her? Did she only want to tell me after everything I had just told her?

I hoped that wasn't why.

It was stupid of me to keep prying into something she clearly wasn't comfortable with sharing, and because of that, I have made up my mind. I'm going to drop the subject. It isn't my business, and the last thing she needs is me being an asshole and pestering her with questions. She needs someone she can trust. Someone who can take care of her and, most importantly, someone she can feel safe with. And I plan on proving to her that that guy is me.

Natalie will tell me what is bothering her when she's ready. And when she does, I will be there for her however she needs me to be.

But if she doesn't want to tell me, well, I can live with that. Right?

And if not … I'll just ask Brian.

Nineteen

NATALIE

A sound very similar to that of an angry grizzly bear wakes me up with a jolt, and I realize that the noise is, in fact, not a bear but my brother Jason who is snoring loudly beside me.

My eyes flutter open, but when I begin to remember where I am, I sit up in a panic.

The hospital.

A rush of raw emotions floods over me as I look over to where my dad was sleeping last night.

He's awake.

My dad is awake.

My eyes get misty. He's sitting upright in the bed, fixated on the TV in front of him.

"Dad!" I shove Jason's massive legs out of the way and get up from the couch. Gently, I wrap my arms around my dad, scared I might hurt him if I squeeze too tightly.

"Well, good morning, sweetheart," he responds after turning the TV off and reciprocating the hug. "I'm surprised you could even sleep through Jason's snoring." We laugh a little, but then I immediately turn the conversation back to him.

"How are you feeling? I was so worried last night when mom

called me. I got here as soon as I could." I look around at all the monitors and wires still surrounding him, beeping reliably. It's almost like they are trying to reassure me everything is ok.

"Oh, I'm fine. These things happen at my age. It's no big deal," he says calmly.

"Dad, a heart attack is a big deal. Even a minor one."

"Sweetheart, I'm not going anywhere. Not today," he says as he takes my hand in his. "But I am very glad that you're here. It means a lot to me." His eyes begin to water, which prompts my avalanche of tears. "Aww, come here, kid. You know I can't stand to see you cry." He holds out his arms wide for me.

"I can't help it," I say through a sob as I welcomingly let his arms wrap around me again. But this time, he holds on to me a little bit longer.

"You know, when you were a little girl, I could always get you to stop crying with a visit to the ice cream shop downtown. How about we make an ice cream date after I get out of here? Just the two of us. Would you like that?"

"I'd like that a lot." I wipe the tears from my eyes and allow a small smile to form.

"See, look at that. Even just the promise of ice cream makes you stop crying," he notes with a hint of laughter.

"Blame mom. She's the one I got my sweet tooth from." We both laugh in unison with equally watery eyes. "I love you, dad."

"I love you, Natalie."

The door to the room swings open, and my mom walks in humming a tune I don't recognize but stops when she sees us. She's balancing a tray of coffee cups in one hand and a glass of water in her other hand. "Oh, good morning, Natalie! Did you sleep ok?" She places the tray on the little table by the window.

I comb my hair out with my fingers and use a napkin to wipe away at the mascara stains under my eyes. "Oh, you know, as good as one can sleep on a tiny couch with their giant brother hogging the only blanket." This makes my parents chuckle, and we all glance over at Jason, who is still sleeping soundly. God, this guy can sleep through anything. Actually, no. That's not true. There is one sound that always manages to wake Jason up. Me. Or, more precisely, the screams of terror I let out in my sleep when my nightmares feel too real. It's always Jason running to my rescue on these nights. I guess I never realized that not only do these nightmares have a hold over me, but they have a hold over Jason as well, which suddenly makes me feel guilty.

My mom hands me one of the cups of coffee and my dad the glass of water. He makes a humph noise, which my mom ignores.

"Thanks," I say before taking a sip. She can probably tell how much I need some caffeine right now.

My mom looks solemnly at my dad. "So dear, the doctor says he would like to keep you here for another night or two for observation and a few more tests."

My dad rolls his eyes. "But I'm fine!"

"Robert, you may think you are, but your body is telling you otherwise." I can see her eyes glisten as she holds her tears in, trying not to show her true feelings. Trying to stay brave for all of us. "There are some changes we need to make when we return home. I have a nutritionist and personal trainer scheduled for immediate appointments this week. And I will not be hearing any complaints about it," she states with one hand on her hip while the other hand brings a cup of coffee to her lips.

My dad looks like he is going to put up a fight, but then with one look at my mom, he immediately decides against it, lets out a frustrated sigh, and drops his shoulders. "Alright. Let's talk about something else." His eyes turn to me. "So, Natalie, what time did you end up getting here last night?" He takes a big gulp of his water and then puts it beside him as he waits for my answer.

My mom looks down at her coffee, avoiding all eye contact with me.

"Umm, I don't actually remember. It was pretty late. You were sleeping when I got here." I walk back to the couch to sit down and put my shoes on. Did someone turn the heat up on the thermostat?

"Hmm …" I can tell he is finally noticing the outfit that I have on. "And may I ask how you got here last night?" He looks over at my mom who is now pretending to wipe something off her blue blouse.

"Oh, umm …" I can't lie to him after everything that just happened to him, so against my better judgment, I tell him the truth. "Nathan Thomas drove me here," I blurt out. I take longer than necessary to put my shoes on, avoiding my dad's gaze. When I finish, my fingers unconsciously reach for a piece of my hair to twirl as I nervously wait for his reaction.

"Oh …" He looks like he is mulling things over until his eyes widen like he's just comprehended the name I said. Well, I know it wasn't the name that made his eyes go wide. It's the minor detail of it being a boy's name.

He quickly composes himself, but his eyes shift between the window and me. Oh no. I recognize this look. He's weighing the pros and cons of what I just said.

Please, God, let there be more pros than cons on his list.

My mom looks nervously between us and jumps in like a lifeguard on duty for an emergency rescue. "You remember Nathan Thomas, dear? Such a polite young man. He's Linda Thomas's oldest son and friends with Peter and Joyce's son, Brian. Coincidentally, he and Natalie now go to the same school together. Isn't that great?" My mom raises her eyebrows as she nods her head at my dad, waiting for him to agree with her.

"Oh, yes, of course." He shakes his head up and down. "I've seen him a few times working at the yacht club. Seems like a hard worker. And I think I remember seeing his name in the paper a number of times when he was on the school's baseball team a couple of years ago." My dad stops talking and looks directly at me before continuing. "Well, that was … that was very nice of him to bring you here." He picks up his glass of water and holds it in his hands as a smile slowly forms on his face. He looks at my mom, who is now smiling back.

My stomach unclenches as his smile confirms there are more pros than cons on his list.

"Guys, can we please not make a big deal out of this?" I plead, leaning back into the couch in total embarrassment.

"What? I didn't say anything." My dad puts up his free hand in defense. That's when his smile stretches from ear to ear, and he begins to laugh, which is a very welcoming sight to my weary eyes.

* * *

My mom, Jason, and I leave the hospital in the afternoon to head home. Jason wants to get his things together before going to his girlfriend's house for the night. My mom wants to shower and pack an overnight bag so she can spend another night with my dad at the hospital. And I just want to collapse in my bed for the next twenty-four hours for some much-needed sleep.

As we turn down our street, I'm hoping Nathan is still at my house, but his car is nowhere in sight when we pull into the driveway. A slight ping of disappointment spreads through me as I look out the window, but my mom interrupts my thoughts.

"Everything ok?" she asks as she looks at me in the rearview mirror, seeming to read my mind.

"Yes, just a little tired." I get out of the car and make my way to the front door before she has time to say anything else.

When I walk inside, it's eerily quiet.

I know my dad will be coming home in a couple of days, but it feels weird not having him here with us right now.

My stomach rumbles, reminding me I haven't eaten anything in quite some time, so I go to the kitchen. But when I enter it, I'm surprised at the state of it. Not because it looks like a disaster, which was my mom's description of it, but because it's ... clean.

"Hey, mom, I thought you said the kitchen was a mess?" I look around, noticing how spotless everything is. It might even be cleaner than usual, if that's even possible.

"What, honey?" She walks in from around the corner. That's when her facial expression changes to one of shock. "What the ...?" Her mouth drops to the floor. "This place was in shambles when I left here." She looks around at everything in confusion. "We had been cooking dinner, and I had turned the stove off before we left, but there was a pot of spaghetti cooking and vegetables sautéing in a skillet. I was in the middle of making a salad, and I dropped a bottle of wine on the counter when your father fell, and he dropped a plate right over there, which shattered into pieces …" Her voice trails off as she points to the floor where there's not even a speck of dirt. Then, after just a moment, some sort of realization seems to have struck, which is followed by a knowing head nod.

"What is it?" I ask.

"Nathan." She looks around and connects the dots in her head. "He must have cleaned. I've never seen this place look so immaculate before," she marvels with a soft smile as her eyes water for the second time today.

"I'm sure it was no big deal," I say, suddenly no longer hungry, so I turn around and make my way for the stairs. However, the butterflies dancing in my stomach tell me it is a very big deal. I know that cleaning up that mess in the kitchen was the last thing my mom wanted to deal with when she came home. It would remind her of what had happened the night before. And how the kitchen looked just now probably made my mom feel like my dad's heart attack was just a bad dream. Like it never happened.

Almost never happened, that is.

Slowly, I head up the stairs as exhaustion overcomes me. Had there always been this many steps to get to the top?

After trudging up each one, I reach my bedroom and push open the door, looking inside, unsure of what I expect to find. But my room looks exactly the same as I left it. I walk over to my bed and sink into the extra thick mattress, drained from my lack of sleep on the unpleasant hospital couch. I turn on my side to get comfortable and notice a folded note with my name on it resting on top of my nightstand.

I pick it up and immediately know who left it for me, which causes my heart rate to increase with anticipation.

Natalie,

I hope your dad is doing well.

And you were right. Sleeping in your bed did help me feel like you were here with me last night. But I have a feeling it would have been even better if you actually were here with me, though I'm not sure how much sleep either of us would have gotten.

Looking forward to seeing you soon, beautiful.

Let me know if you need anything.

- Nathan

Every part of my body aches for Nathan. I need to feel his strong body in my hands. I need to taste his sweet lips on mine. I need to see those beautiful dark eyes staring down at me. And … I just really need Nathan. Here. Right now. With me.

I've never felt this way about anyone.

I've never needed someone the way I need Nathan.

And needing someone wasn't a feeling I had been acquainted with, especially in such a short amount of time. But then again, was it really a short amount of time? We may have just recently started to get to know each other … physically, but Nathan and I have known each other for, well, half of my life.

I want to tell Nathan how I feel, but should I? Is it too soon? Would he feel the same way about me? And how would I even tell him? But then a thought occurs to me.

Maybe I don't have to tell him how I feel. Maybe instead, I can show him how I feel. My cheeks instantly warm up from this thought.

But what if I don't know what to do? What if it's awkward? What if I'm horrible at it? What if … STOP!

But it's too late. I can feel it. The impending doom. It's happening. And I can't make it stop.

Anxiety.

Crippling, excruciating anxiety.

It begins to creep up from deep inside the abyss, making my chest tighten and my palms sweat. It's trying to take over and win like it has done so many times.

Except for this time, I fight back.

I lie back on my bed, close my eyes, and bring the weighted blanket over my waist.

This will pass.

I start to regulate my breathing with a technique I read about while doing some research a few days ago to ensure I would never embarrass myself in a corn maze again.

Inhale for four seconds.

Hold your breath for seven seconds.

Exhale for eight seconds.

I do this again and again until the pounding clatter of my heart starts to subside.

The moment I sense I can breathe again without feeling like there are five bricks stacked on top of my chest, I decide to read the note one more time, and as I do, I realize that none of those worries matter.

They're all silly intrusive thoughts just trying to scare me, but they won't work this time.

It's not possible.

Because all I know at this very moment is that I *love* Nathan Thomas.

And I always have.

twenty

NATHAN

The morning sun shines vibrantly through the big bay window this Sunday morning in Natalie's room, ending my peaceful night of sleep.

I might even note that it was one of the best nights of sleep I've had in a long time. And it didn't just have to do with how comfortable Natalie's bed was. Sleeping here, it felt like I had Natalie next to me the whole night, which is probably why I dreamed only of her.

And man, it was a *good* dream, as evident from my morning wood now rubbing up against the comforter, begging for relief, which will, unfortunately, have to wait.

I stretch my body out, feeling every muscle adjust before throwing the covers off and bringing my feet to the floor.

What should I do today?

There is one place I know I need to stop by at some point, but the thunderous rumble erupting from my stomach lets me know that my first priority needs to be food.

And fast.

I pick up my phone and call Brian, hoping he might be home from school to get some breakfast and catch up. Maybe even see if he has some insight into what might be bothering Natalie. But after the fourth ring, it goes to his voicemail, and I hang up feeling slightly disappointed.

After putting on my clothes from the night before and leaving a note for Natalie on her nightstand, I make my way out into the hallway, down the giant staircase, and out the massive front door.

I find myself driving around town until a blue neon sign for a small old diner catches my eye. I park by the front door and go inside, noticing only a handful of customers. As I take a seat at the counter, a perky young waitress comes over.

"Well, hey there, handsome. What can I get for you?" she asks while flirtatiously playing with a piece of her dark hair. Her wanting eyes travel up and down my body.

She can't be any more obvious that she wants me.

"Umm." I grab a menu and quickly scan it over. "I'll just have the Sunday special with a glass of orange juice. Thank you."

The woman continues staring at me, and when it takes longer than normal for her eyes to blink, I realize she's checked out. Unfortunately, this isn't the first time this has happened to me.

I clear my throat. "You ok?"

"Oh yes. Of course. Sure thing. Sunday Special." She shakes her head out of the fantasy she was just in, which, I would bet my life savings, was featuring me. "Is there anything else I can get for you?"

The way she looks at me tells me she isn't referring to anything offered on the menu.

"No, I think that would be it," I respond casually, trying to give her the hint that I'm not interested.

"Ok then, well, if you change your mind, just holler for me. I'm Tina." She points to her name tag, which resides right next to the cleavage spilling out of her tight shirt.

"Will do," I say and look down at my phone, hoping she will walk away. I'm relieved when she does.

Soon enough, a plate stacked high with all the breakfast essentials is brought to me. The aroma of bacon fills my nose, and

I shove my fork into the masterpiece. It isn't long before I've wolfed down the eggs, pancakes, bacon, toast, and glass of orange juice. Now I feel ready to conquer whatever the day throws at me.

Or at least ready for the next daunting task on my agenda.

As I drag my fork over the empty plate, procrastinating leaving, a young couple, probably around my age, enters the diner. They are holding hands and sit a few barstools away from me. The girl keeps her hand on the guy's thigh as they share one menu between the two of them. Every few seconds, he looks at the girl, and they both smile like they're sharing a secret.

Maybe they just fucked in the parking lot. I laugh at this thought. *If they did, good for them.*

I want Natalie in that way.

So badly I do.

The girl's body is one you only see walking down a Victoria's Secret runway. Actually, due to the fact that Natalie has meat on her bones, it's a lot better than what you would see on a runway.

A. Lot. Fucking. Better.

But besides her body, all the other things about her drive me wild. The way she laughs, the way she looks down at the ground when she's nervous with me, the adorable pink color on her cheeks that reveals her emotions, the way she feels in my arms … the list is endless.

However, as much as I want Natalie in that way, it's more important to me to take things slow with her.

I can be patient.

For her, I can wait.

But how long is the appropriate amount of time to wait?

How long would Natalie want to wait?

I know back in high school she dated a few guys, but I didn't hear about any of them being serious.

Had she ever had sex?

The question leaves me curious, and my mind begins to wander.

But then I hear the girl at the counter giggle as the guy kisses her lightly on the lips in front of everyone in the diner. I wonder if this is what will someday happen between Natalie and me. Displaying our feelings for each other in public and not caring who is around to witness.

I hope this couple is a glimpse into my future.

After getting up from my seat, I leave a twenty-dollar bill on the counter and head out to my car, no longer able to procrastinate my to-do list. I start the engine and drive in the direction of the one place in the world I wish I didn't have to go.

I park in the driveway and stare at the house where my mom, brother, and I had resided for nearly a decade. It never felt like a home to me. More like a place to hide. A place where my father could never find us. But now that he has, it feels more like a trap. A place to go only if you want to be found.

I use my key to unlock the front door and walk in, unsure about what I will face.

"Hello?" I call out, praying no one answers me. Thankfully, no one does.

As I stand alone in the middle of the kitchen, there is an unnerving silence. I survey the damage, noting the place looks exactly the way we left it just a couple of nights ago when all hell broke loose.

A kitchen chair is in pieces, and broken dishes are all over the floor. The fridge door is still open, and food is scattered about. A punctured orange juice bottle lies lifeless on the floor in a pool of its contents.

As I make my way into the living room, I notice even more damage. Sofa pillows look like scraps of cloth, and framed family photos sit broken on the floor. Window curtain rods hang detached from the walls, and there are speckles of dried blood on the carpet, probably from when I smashed my father's nose.

I sit on the chair closest to me and take everything in. My anger steadily builds. Why was this man a part of our lives? Why couldn't he leave us alone? We want nothing to do with him, yet he continues to torture us with his presence.

I hang my head in my hands, feeling frustrated with everything.

Leaving my mom and Nick while he's still out there, clearly off his rocker, makes me feel so guilty. Nick is just in high school and shouldn't have to deal with any of this. He should be out having fun with his friends and enjoying his junior year. My mom is one of the top-selling real estate agents in the state and should be able to enjoy her success instead of having to constantly check over her shoulder.

Why couldn't they catch a break?

I never understood how my mom ended up with someone like my father. And when I asked her that very question a few years ago, she told me he hadn't always been this way. He used to be sweet and gentle, but then something just snapped in him. The day he lost his job, he lost himself, only to find himself in a bottle of alcohol. And let's be honest, it wasn't something we ever talked about, but he found himself in syringes too.

I don't remember him before the rage that destroyed him. As hard as I try, I can't remember.

I never told my mom this, but a little part of me worries I will turn out to be like him. These thoughts haunt me during nights of insomnia when all I can do is stare at the ceiling and wait for the fear to pass.

However, it's the bigger part of me that convinces me otherwise. And that's only thanks to my mom. She raised Nick and me to always put others before ourselves, that kindness would get us far in life, and most importantly, to put family over everything. So, thanks to her, I know there is no chance of becoming like my father.

Standing up, I go back into the kitchen, trying to decide how to conquer this mess. The broom is standing in the same corner it always does, so I grab it and start to sweep up the broken dishes and food as a feeling of déjà vu washes over me.

I find it funny that this is how I'm spending my weekend at two different homes: sweeping up broken dishes and cleaning up other people's messes.

This thought brings me back to Natalie.

Is she home yet? Has she seen the note I left for her? Is her dad ok?

I'll call her as soon as I finish with everything here.

About an hour later, I am done with the kitchen and move on to the living room where I spend twenty minutes trying to get the dried blood out of the carpet. After no success, I move the area rug over to cover it.

No one will even know.

I reattach the curtain rods back to the wall, vacuum up the shattered glass from the broken picture frames, and toss the pillows, which are beyond repair, into the trash. Finally, the place is starting to look livable again.

I'm moving the coffee table to the side to ensure no more broken glass is hiding anywhere when my phone falls out of my pocket and lands partly under the couch. I reach down to grab it, but my hand clutches at something much bigger instead. It feels like a thick book, so I pull out the unknown object.

I recognize it immediately. It's an old photo album my mom put together when Nick and I were kids. A thick layer of dust covers the binding, clearly showing it hasn't been held by anyone in years. I wipe it off and turn to the first page where there's a picture of Nick and me from when we were toddlers.

My fingers flip the pages leisurely, and I notice an unrecognizable man in almost every photo. It takes me a second to realize who he is.

It's my father.

But the man in these pictures is not the same coward I know today.

Instead of an unkept beard, he has a clean-shaven face and a fresh haircut. Instead of wearing baggy and tattered clothes, he has on a pair of fitted pants and a polo shirt. His eyes are bright and joyful; there's no hint of the dark sunken bags he has under them now. He looks young and happy. I don't know the man in these photos, and it makes me depressed when I think about how drastically he has changed over the years.

I close the book and toss it on the couch beside me then lean back and close my eyes, waiting for the anger that is beginning to build up inside me again to subside. My mom had probably put this book together before everything changed.

Before he had changed.

A soft buzzing noise causes me to open my eyes in alarm, and I realize my phone is still under the couch. I pick it up and see I have a new text from Natalie.

Natalie: Hi.

Me: Hey, how are you? How is your dad?

Natalie: He's ok. They're keeping him for at least another night or two for observation and my mom is staying with him. Can you come over tonight around 7?

Me: Yes. Of course. Is everything ok?

Natalie: Yes. I just don't feel like being alone tonight.

Me: Ok, don't worry. I'll be there. See you beautiful.

Just hearing from Natalie makes me feel better. Something about her causes my mind to forget about everything else that's going wrong.

I run upstairs to shower and then find a fresh pair of clothes to change into before leaving. Unsure if Natalie will be hungry, I stop to pick up a pizza on the way to her house, figuring it's a safe choice.

At seven, I pull into her driveway, walk up to the door with the pizza box in my hand, and ring the doorbell. Anticipation builds in my stomach.

How is it possible that I already miss her?

I'm looking forward to a nice cuddle on the couch tonight. Holding her in my arms. Maybe even the chance to taste a little more than just her lips. Now that would be a great way to end the night.

But no sex.

Not tonight.

I can wait.

When Natalie wants to have sex, we will have sex. That's for damn sure.

But that night is not tonight.

I look at my phone and see that a couple of minutes have passed and immediately worry, so I ring the doorbell again.

Just as I'm about to call her, the door slowly opens, and Natalie pokes her head from around the side.

Damn, that gorgeous smile could make me do anything for her.

Anything.

"Hi, beautiful. I didn't know if you would be hungry or not, so I picked up a pizza for us." She holds the door open, so I walk in past her and hear her shut the door gently behind me. But when I turn around, I nearly drop the pizza box on the floor.

Natalie is leaning against the front door and wearing the sexiest fucking pink piece of lingerie I have ever seen.

"N-Nat-Natalie …" is all I can get out of my mouth before she takes the pizza box from my hands and places it on the bench beside us.

twenty-One

NATALIE

"It's show time," I say to myself, looking into the floor-length mirror in my room after hearing Nathan ring the doorbell.

The second after my mom and Jason left for the night, leaving me with the house to myself, I grabbed my phone to text Nathan, asking him to come over.

And with only a short amount of time to get ready, I somehow pulled it off.

Every inch of my body was freshly shaven, and my hair was hanging in loose curls. I had found a pink satin nightie, which I had purchased years ago with no real intention of ever wearing it, in the back of my closet with the tags still on it. It was a little tighter in the bust than I remember, causing me to spill over the edge, but it fits.

I trace my hands over the soft material, feeling confident in my skin and ready for Nathan to see me.

I turn away from the mirror and walk to the top of the stairs. It's time to let Nathan in and get this night started. But just as I take a step down, I suddenly realize I've forgotten about an essential item, which sends me into a panic.

Shit.

I forgot condoms.

I forgot the damn condoms.

Think. Think. Think.

That's it!

I rush into Jason's room, and as I open the drawer to his nightstand, I pray I don't find anything in there that will totally gross me out. Located in the very back of the drawer is an open box of condoms. So I grab a few, not knowing how many I will need, and run back to my room, pretending that I didn't just steal condoms from my brother.

If he ever finds out, I think I will be the first person in history to die of actual embarrassment.

I hear the doorbell ring again, and a complete panic sets in. My heartbeat quickly increases as I think about what I'm about to do. Then, looking in the mirror one last time, I muster my confidence and march out of my room in nothing but lingerie.

You got this.

I walk down the staircase, practicing my breathing with each step.

Inhale.

Exhale.

Inhale.

Exhale.

As I place my trembling hand on the doorknob and turn it, I take one last big breath.

Slowly I open the door while standing behind it and poke my head around so Nathan can't fully see me. I smile when I see him, and he smiles back, which instantly erases any fears I have about tonight.

God, I love his smile.

"Hi, beautiful. I didn't know if you would be hungry or not, so I picked up a pizza for us," Nathan says as he walks by me, looking straight ahead, oblivious to what I am wearing.

I shut the door and lean against it, waiting for Nathan to turn around. My eyes close for a split second, and when I open them,

Nathan is facing me with his mouth hanging open.

"N-Nat-Natalie …" Nathan utters in almost a whisper.

I take the pizza box out of his hands and place it on the bench against the wall near us.

"Do you like it?" I ask, feeling suddenly shy as I look down at myself. All of my confidence has disappeared, and I'm starting to wonder if this was a dumb idea.

I hear him clear his throat and instantly look up into his dark eyes, which are busy raking over my body. He steps toward me, closing all space between us, and then backs me firmly against the door. His breath quickens as his hand slowly reaches out to touch me.

"Do you know how to tell if a man likes what you're wearing?" he asks. He traces the thin lingerie strap with his finger, following the seam across my breasts, past my waist, and down to the laced edge at the top of my thighs, causing warmth to spread between my legs.

I timidly shake my head, shuddering beneath his touch.

"It's by how fast he takes it off you. And baby, all I want to do right now is rip this off your body," he says with no hint of humor, looking down at me with a raw intensity I've never seen before.

We aren't making eye contact because he's too busy exploring all of me, which causes my heart to race faster and faster. His finger now traces the other side of me. I hear his breath hitch as he reaches the bottom, and as if he can read my thoughts, begging him to take me, his lips come down desperately on mine.

His hands cup the sides of my face and then run all the way down my arms. Suddenly he's pulling my arms away from my sides and bringing them against the wall above my head as far as they can reach. Then, only having to use one of his hands to restrain my wrists in place, he brings his other hand back down to my waist, pulling me closer to him, allowing me to feel the hardness of his length. A small moan escapes from me as his hand finds itself between my thighs, providing a tiny amount of relief from the building pressure inside me.

And then, just like that, it stops.

Nathan pulls his mouth away, giving me a chance to catch my breath as I rest my head against the door. He looks down at me, breathless, but there's also concern etched on his face.

"Natalie, are you sure?" He removes his hand from between my legs and wraps it tightly around my waist.

I can only shake my head up and down.

His hand moves gently to my face, and his thumb begins to glide across my cheek. "You've had a lot to deal with these past few days. I just want to make sure—"

But I cut him off.

I don't want to think about anything.

I just want *him*.

I want *him* more than anything in this whole world.

I look right into his eyes. "Please. I need you."

And suddenly his lips are back on mine.

He releases my hands from the door and brings his own hands down to cup my ass as he effortlessly picks me up. I instinctively wrap my legs tightly around his torso, gripping his body to mine. With ease, he carries me up the stairs and to my room, where he delicately lays me down on the bed.

He pulls his sweatshirt and shirt off over his head, and while I wait, I run my hands over his solid body, exploring every muscle all the way down his stomach.

Oh my God. Nathan has an eight-pack.

My finger traces over every ridge of his abdomen, and I find myself wishing I was using my tongue instead.

He's watching me curiously, and I start to feel self-conscious, so I pull my hand away, but he stops me. His hand wraps around my wrist, and he places the palm of my hand back on his skin. A sly smile appears as he takes my hand and brings it further down, over his jeans, and right between his legs. "Do you feel what you do to me? You make me so fucking hard."

I bite my bottom lip and feel the warmth between my legs turn into a searing source of heat, knowing that I am the one responsible for him being so turned on.

Nathan positions himself on top of me and holds my gaze before placing delicate kisses along my jawline, making a perfect path down my neck to my collarbone. He pulls the straps down from my shoulders then brings the whole piece down to my hips, exposing my breasts. His mouth drags down my skin to attend to my breasts, sucking and licking every inch of them, making me moan uncontrollably. I pull on his hair, and he looks up at me with a little smile as he licks one of my nipples and uses the pad of his finger on the other.

As I shift against his mouth, Nathan slides the nightie down the rest of my body, tossing it on the floor. The only thing left on me is the matching pink lace thong, which Nathan looks very pleased to see.

His fingers loop through the sides of the thong, and I think he's about to pull it off until his head lowers to plant a soft kiss on top of the fabric over and over and over again.

Holy fucking hell.

After he pulls the panties off, he sits up, getting a full view of me completely naked. I have never in my life felt more vulnerable than I do at this very moment. But Nathan takes his time, gazing down at me with incredibly appreciative eyes.

He places his hands on my thighs, separating my legs more as he kneels between them, letting out a deep breath. "You have no idea how much I need you right now."

I sit up, cupping his face in my hands as I rub his stubble with my thumb and look him straight in the eyes. "Then show me."

He pushes my hair out of my face and takes a strand between his fingers. "Natalie," he looks at his hand and then back to me, "have you ever had sex?"

I'm too embarrassed to answer, so I look at his chest and shake my head slowly, indicating the answer is no.

"Hey," he tilts my chin so that I'm looking straight into his piercing eyes, "don't ever be embarrassed with me." He smiles warmly. "We'll go slow, ok?"

"Ok." Any worries I might have had immediately vanish.

He places his soft lips on mine and brings me back down so my head is comfortably against the pillow. When he knows I need a moment to breathe, he releases my lips and begins an assault of kisses down my body, making my head spin. The trail of kisses comes to an abrupt halt right before he moves between my legs. I can feel his breath on my skin, causing me to squirm in delight, but the lower his lips get, the more I panic.

I impulsively squeeze my legs shut. "You don't have to do that."

Nathan freezes, and his eyes dart up to meet mine with concern. "Do you not want me to?" he asks, his mouth hovering closely over my skin.

I didn't know it was possible, but my whole body blushes.

"Oh, no, I do. I mean, I *really* do. It's just, well, umm, no one has ever done this to me, and I know some guys don't like doing it, and, well, what I'm trying to say is you don't have to do it if you don't want to."

"Natalie?"

"Yes?"

Nathan's smirk would put the devil to shame. "I'm not some guy."

"No? I mean, no, of course not, it's just …" I feel my stomach clench as his large hands gently push my legs apart.

"And I know I don't have to." He stares between my legs, causing an instant throbbing pulse to begin. "But you see, the only thing I want to do right now is to make you come." His index finger slides slowly up and down the center of my wet folds.

Ok, that throbbing pulse between my legs has now evolved into an extreme pounding.

"And I'd really like to know how sweet your pussy tastes by warming you up with my tongue." He pierces me with lust-filled eyes. "So, that's exactly what I'm going to do."

I can't find words.

It's like the whole English language just completely erased itself from my memory. All I can do is wait for the moment his tongue touches me and …

Oh. My. God.

The pressure from his tongue sends my body into overdrive. It's the most amazing sensation I've ever felt, and I have to tightly hold onto the sheet with both hands to anchor myself down to the bed as Nathan buries his head between my thighs.

"Fuck, Natalie. You taste so damn good," he breaths against my sensitive skin.

His hands grip the top of my thighs, firmly keeping my legs parted wide for him, and his tongue strikes me repeatedly. Over and over again, causing me to lose all notion of time.

"Nathan, it feels too good," I pant, unsure how much more I can take.

He removes his lips from my skin to say, "Oh, baby, I'm not even close to being done."

My insides ignite at his words.

Every cell in my body is dizzy with pleasure.

Nathan lifts himself above me as one of his hands slides down my thigh, stopping only when it is directly between my legs. His middle finger parts my flesh, feeling how wet I am. A satisfied grin appears on his face, and he licks his bottom lip, covered in my arousal. And when our eyes connect, his large finger thrusts inside me.

"Oh God," I breathe, enjoying the feeling of his very talented hand torturing me relentlessly with a rhythm of pleasure. Then, he adds another finger inside me just as his thumb touches down on the most sensitive part of my body, causing me to whimper.

"Does that feel good, baby?" he asks, whispering in my ear, his thumb moving in tight little circles faster and faster.

"Y-yes," I say as I close my eyes and tilt my head all the way back. I can feel every muscle in my legs beginning to shake.

Euphoria. That is the only word I can use to describe this moment.

Nathan's lips devour my own as his fingers invade me again and again, and his thumb provides a much-needed vibration, creating an overwhelming buildup of pleasure.

Pure merciless pleasure.

Seconds later, it's over for me when the pressure becomes unbearable.

I lose all control, holding onto his shoulders for dear life as my legs tremble. My back arches until, all at once, I collapse back on my sheets, out of breath, reeling down from my moment of bliss.

Once the aftershocks come to an end, Nathan removes his hand from me and kisses my forehead. "I think you're all warmed up and ready for the finale. If you still want to?' he asks.

"Yes. Yes. Please, a hundred times yes." I immediately respond while eagerly shaking my head up and down. "If you need me to beg, I will," I tease.

He laughs before stepping out of bed, leaving me already missing the feeling of his body against mine. "I would never make you beg for anything, Natalie."

I bring my hands to my head, trying to catch my breath while reliving every second of that glorious orgasm.

But the instant I hear him unzip his jeans, I turn to watch him drop his pants and boxer briefs onto to the floor.

Wow. All I can think is, *wow.*

The sight of him causes that throbbing sensation between my legs to return, and I can tell from the way he is consuming my body with his eyes that he is just as turned on as I am.

During everything, he must have noticed the condoms on my nightstand because he grabs one and tears it open.

Anticipation fills me as he lowers himself on top of me. But before he does anything, he looks into my eyes, waiting for me to give the ok. Ever so slightly, I nod my head, and then he gradually enters me. A little cry escapes before I bite down on my bottom lip to hold it in.

He stops and puts one of his hands on my cheek. "Are you ok?"

"I'm ok." I take his face in my hands, bringing his lips back to mine. "Keep going," I plead. "I want to feel all of you."

Nathan starts slow, bringing a matching rhythm to both of our bodies. It hurts a little, but the more he moves, the better it begins to feel. And as my body adjusts to Nathan's rather large size, his thrusts get deeper and faster.

And for the second time tonight, I feel the same familiar pressure buildup. Except for this time, it's all-consuming.

"Nathan, I think I'm going to—"

"I know, baby. I'm right there with you."

Just as I think it can't get any better than this, Nathan takes his hand and firmly presses his thumb right on my clit.

"Oh, Nathan," I cry out as I collapse back onto the sheet, trembling beneath him. I'm completely and utterly lost in this foreign but incredible feeling.

After just a few more thrusts, I feel Nathan's body tense in my hands. A long harsh breath escapes from him, followed by a groan, then his body falls on mine and his head rests on my chest. I run my hands through his hair, not saying anything to give him a moment to wind down.

A moment he rightfully deserves.

He turns over to lie on his back and says, "Come here." His arm lifts in the air, waiting for me to snuggle beside him. With my ear pressed against his chest, I can hear the beat of his heart matching my own.

I feel a little exposed lying here with nothing on, so I start to pull the sheets back up over myself.

"Oh no, you don't," Nathan says. "Do you have any idea how long my eyes have waited to see that gorgeous body? I'm not ready for it to be over yet."

I blush and smile into his chest.

He strokes my hair with one hand while his other hand wraps tightly around my waist, and we both lie silently for a few minutes.

"Hey," he says quietly. I look up at him as he tucks a piece of hair behind my ear. "Are you ok?"

"Am I ok?" I smile. "I have never felt better."

He looks pleased. "Oh, good. I know since you had never … done this before, well, I just wanted to make it as enjoyable as possible for you."

I'm pretty sure Nathan just blushed. And it was the cutest thing I think I've ever seen.

"Was I … ok?" I ask.

He starts laughing but quickly covers his mouth to stop himself when he sees me look nervously down at his chest. "Baby, I feel like the luckiest guy on the planet right now."

I'm instantly relieved. "I like it when you call me baby."

"You do? Well, I'll be sure to do that more often then," he replies into my ear before resting his head on the pillow.

Happy butterflies fill my stomach.

"How did you know to do that thing with your … wait. I'm sorry. Don't answer that." I can't believe I just said that. Nathan shifts uncomfortably, and I know I just ruined the moment between us.

Good job, Natalie.

"Don't be sorry, Natalie." He stares at the ceiling, and the silence slowly starts to kill me. Then, finally, he lets out a sigh. "It's probably no secret that I have … experience." His hand rubs his temple before he continues. "But you should know, tonight was a first for me too. I've never had sex with someone who I truly care about. I've never felt this close to someone before. You … you mean everything to me." He lowers his brown eyes to mine. "Do you know that?"

Do I know that?

I think about his question, but it only takes a second for me to come up with my answer.

"Yes." I shift so I am lying on top of him, looking down into his dark eyes. As I bring my lips to his, a feeling of complete happiness fills me. "I really do."

His hand runs up and down my back in a smooth motion, making me feel sleepy, so I rest my head on his chest, which starts rumbling with laughter.

"What's so funny?"

"Nothing," he says, but then continues. "Well, actually, when I came here tonight, I told myself we weren't having sex. I wanted to make sure we waited until you were ready." I look up at him, knowing with every ounce of my heart that we had waited long enough. Any longer, and I probably would have exploded into a thousand very horny pieces. "Looks like I didn't have to wait too long." He chuckles.

"I'd say we waited long enough. Feels like forever if you ask me," I reply, hinting at how long I truly have been waiting for him. My hand starts tracing a small circle over his firm stomach.

"You're right. I should never have made you wait so long." He lifts his head just slightly so that his lips touch my forehead.

"So, speaking of waiting, how much longer are you going to make me wait for round two?" My finger slides down Nathan's torso, and I watch his eyes widen in surprise when I wrap my hand around the length of *him*. Hard and ready for me.

Ding! Ding! Ding!

Round two is about to begin.

NATHAN

Twelve days.

It has been twelve goddamn incredible days of nonstop sex with Natalie.

There was the before-bed sex. The morning sex. The shower sex. The between-classes sex. God, there was even that night in the car when we couldn't get to her apartment fast enough after our dinner date.

The girl could not get enough of me.

Not that I'm complaining.

And I was starting to realize that I unleashed a monster. No, I take that back. I unleashed a sex fiend, and I was enjoying every tantalizing second of it.

But unfortunately, tonight, I will be getting an unwanted break since I'm heading up to New Hampshire after class to see Brian and the old gang. It's been a while, so I'm looking forward to seeing everyone again, but I'm not happy about spending a night without Natalie in my arms. Something I had been quickly getting used to.

How pathetic do I sound?

I walk into History of Films as the clock strikes two and see Natalie in her usual seat. Just the sight of her makes my heart race.

She's wearing a short black skirt that shows off her long golden legs. The same legs that I was running my hands up and down just last night. A white button-down top tucked in and a tight black leather jacket completes her pleasing look.

She doesn't see me standing in the doorway, so I lean against the frame and pull out my phone.

Me: What are you doing to me?

I see her flip over her phone, which is lying on the desk in front of her buzzing away. She smiles slightly then looks up to find me admiring her from afar before returning to her phone. Within seconds, I feel my phone buzz.

Natalie: Just making sure you know what you'll be missing tonight.

This girl is something else.

I take my seat next to her as the professor starts discussing the next film he will be showing: *Saving Private Ryan*.

Finally, an action-packed movie. The kind of movie I like. Not that last week's sappy film didn't pull at my heartstrings, but I mean, who actually writes someone three hundred and sixty-five letters? Wouldn't that be considered harassment after the first dozen unreciprocated letters? But for some reason, every woman in this class finds it romantic.

Go figure.

"Hey," I say just loud enough so only Natalie can hear me.

"Hey," she says back.

The professor pulls down the projection screen and starts to hit some buttons on his computer until the film appears. When the lights shut off, I can feel the sexual tension between Natalie and me magnify, so I pull out my phone to keep the conversation going.

Me: I really wish there was no one in this classroom.
Natalie: Why?

Me: Cause I want you to sit on the desk in front of me so I can bury my head under that skirt.

Natalie: Oh I don't think anyone in class would mind if you did, especially me.

Me: Don't tempt me baby cause I can't even tell you how fucking hard you're making me right now.

The most beautiful blush spreads over her cheeks.

After class ends, we grab our bags and head to Natalie's apartment.

"Are you going to miss me?" I ask as we approach her building.

"Oh, I just won't know what to do with myself," she teases. "Actually, I ended up making plans with Sarah, so we're going to some bar tonight that she likes."

"That sounds like fun." I was glad she would be going out with a friend because every now and then when she gets lost in her thoughts, I can't help but feel like a piece of her is missing. That piece being Vanessa. "Can you do me a favor, though?" I ask.

"Sure."

"Can you text or call me when you get home tonight so I know you're safe?" I tilt her chin so I can look right into her stormy grey eyes.

"Of course," she says before touching her lips to mine.

God, those perfect lips.

I'm savoring every second with her, knowing I have to leave soon.

She pulls away, her eyes meeting mine. "I know you're about to leave, but do you have two minutes to run up to my apartment with me so I can give you something?"

"I always have two minutes for you."

As soon as we get off the elevator, she takes my hand in hers and pulls me inside her apartment before shutting and locking the door behind her.

"Can you sit on the sofa?" she asks.

I walk over to the sofa and take a seat, waiting for whatever it is that she wants to give me. But as soon as I sit down, Natalie takes a seat on my lap, straddling her legs over mine and wrapping her arms around my neck.

"Oh," escapes from my mouth. I now understand what she wants to give me.

"I really am going to miss you," she says in a whisper right next to my ear before she places a trail of kisses along my jawline, ending on my lips.

I pull her into me and feel her soft hair slide through my fingers like individual strands of silk. My lips part from hers and begin moving down her neck as my fingers play with the buttons on her top. One by one, I unbutton it and watch it fall off her, revealing the gorgeous curves trapped by her bra. My hands slide down to her thighs and under her skirt where I'm caught off guard.

Her breath catches, and my eyes widen in surprise.

"No underwear?" I ask, incredibly turned on. If I had known she wasn't wearing any underwear during that whole class, I probably would have buried my head under her skirt.

She shakes her head as my hand moves between her legs, discovering how wet she already is. Her eyes close, and her head rolls back as my middle finger enters her, thrusting deep inside. She bites her bottom lip, a telltale sign I've learned is her way of trying to keep herself from moaning out in pleasure. But I love her moans. In fact, it's become my favorite sound. So, I shove another finger inside her, which causes her to finally cry out. "Oh God, Nathan."

Oh God, Nathan.

Not only is her moan my new favorite sound, but hearing *Oh God, Nathan* come out of that sexy mouth has become my sole purpose for living.

She reaches down to my zipper as I continue to curve my fingers inside her, searching for her secret spot. The second I'm sprung free, she licks her lips and looks over my thick arousal with hungry eyes.

"Like what you see?" I tease. I keep one hand wrapped around her waist, holding her firmly to me while the other hand persists in its assault of pleasure.

Her hands wrap around my cock as her thumb circles the tip, creating an intense throb throughout my whole length. "I don't like it," she pants. "I love it. I really love it." She uses her delicate hands to tenderly stroke me.

God, she has no idea how *good* this feels.

I watch her enjoying every second of this like I am. I'm not just pleasuring her. And she's not just pleasuring me. We're pleasuring each other. And it's fucking amazing.

I lean my head into the side of her neck, licking a straight line up to the area right below her ear. Her pulse in this spot quickens as my fingers slide in and out of her faster and stronger, having only one objective. To make this girl come.

But the second her eyes look into mine, I see a lust that makes me harder than a slab of concrete.

She lifts herself from my fingers and slides off my lap, kneeling before me.

"Holy fuck," I groan as her beautiful mouth takes all of me.

She flattens her tongue, running it along the underside of my length before sucking on the head like a goddamn lollipop, swirling me around in her mouth. As her soft lips glide over me deeper each time and her tongue applies the perfect amount of pressure, it becomes apparent that the clock between my legs is ticking, ready to strike midnight.

"Baby, that feels so fucking good, but I'm not going to last much longer, and I really want to fuck you in that skirt."

She removes her mouth from me, displaying a mischievous grin, before bringing her hands to her bra. I think she is about to take it off, but I'm taken aback again when she pulls something out from the space between her skin and the fabric. Her smile widens as she hands me a condom.

"You had no underwear on this whole day, and you've been walking around with a condom in your bra? God, you are the sexiest woman I have ever met," I say as I quickly tear the wrapping off the condom.

An adorable blush spreads on her cheeks, and she positions herself back on my lap, sliding her skirt all the way up to her hips.

As I start to roll the condom on, Natalie's hand stops me.

"Did you want to do this part?" I ask with a grin.

"Well, I was just wondering … what are your plans for tonight in New Hampshire?"

"I don't know. Hadn't really thought about it. I'm sure it will just be a bunch of guys drinking and being stupid. Nothing too exciting," I assure her, hoping that might end the conversation since the throbbing between my legs reminds me that I desperately need to be inside her.

"It's just, speaking of being stupid—" she starts to say, but I cut her off because I know exactly where her over-anxious mind is going with this.

"If you think I would even consider being with another woman when I'm lucky enough to be with you, well, I'm going to stop you right there. You are all I want," I say right before kissing her forehead. "So please get that worry out of your head."

Natalie and I have never talked about it, but I know she has anxiety. I saw it firsthand when we were younger. There were moments when she would become eerily quiet and her eyes would look like they were on the verge of tears as she gave in to the negative voices looming in her mind. But as soon as she snapped back, she would plaster a smile on her face and pretend like nothing had just fazed her.

However, lately, it seems like her anxiety has spiraled out of her control. Like when I found her in the corn maze having a panic attack. It broke my heart to witness her huddled on the ground and shaking with tears staining her cheeks. I regret how loud my voice was when I first found her, but I was so scared. I didn't know what to do. But I promised myself I would be better prepared next time if there ever was a next time, which is why I spent a lot of time researching anxiety after that day.

Hell, it even gave me a reason to visit the campus library for the first time. I never knew how many books have been written about mental health, and thank God they exist because it helped me understand anxiety better. I compiled a list of the best therapists in the area, ordered her a monogrammed journal so she could write down everything taking up space in her head, and learned breathing exercises that can help relax her mind.

And when she's ready to talk to me about it, I'll be here for her. Because I want to be able to take care of her. No, let me rephrase that. I need to be able to take care of her. And I will.

So it pains me to think that she would worry about me being with someone else when that is never going to happen.

Never.

Her hand rolls down the rest of the condom over me. "Ok, but let's be clear on one thing. I'm the lucky one."

And with that, she slides every hard inch of me inside her.

A few moments later, the two of us are lying on the couch, catching our breath. I feel Natalie's chest rising up and down as I hold her. I lay my head back against the arm of the couch and close my eyes, exhausted from the lack of sleep I've had these past few nights.

But again … not complaining.

"Have a rough night?" she teases.

"Oh, you have no idea. Some hot blonde kept me up and had me and my dick working overtime." I laugh and hear her giggle, so I open my eyes to find her looking at me. But suddenly, her smile fades. "Hey, what are you thinking about?"

"Oh, nothing," she responds, quickly looking away and nuzzling against my chest.

"You're nervous about meeting my mom tomorrow, aren't you?" A few days ago, I let Natalie know that my mom and brother are coming to visit on Saturday, and I thought it might be a good time for them to meet. Natalie has met my mom in passing throughout the years but never officially, and never as my … well, damn, how do I introduce Natalie to my mom? I guess I haven't really thought about that part.

"Yeah, I guess I am," Natalie responds.

"Don't be. My mom is going to love you." I take her hand in mine and lightly squeeze it. "There's no way she wouldn't. It's not possible."

"I just know how important this is to you. Especially after you mentioned that you have never introduced anyone to her before."

"That's because I was never with anyone I wanted my mom to meet." I put a smile on and softly squeeze her thigh to get her to smile too, which she does.

"You kind of like me, don't you?" she playfully asks with a wink.

"Nah, I don't like you. I really fucking like you." I roll on top of Natalie and look down into her beautiful eyes before leaning down and kissing her softly on her forehead, cheeks, and finally on her perfect lips.

* * *

As the sun begins to set, I pull into the driveway of what used to be my off-campus house in New Hampshire. The place looks just the same as the day I left it. The grass is well overdue for a cut, the siding needs a fresh coat of paint, and a large crowd of people is making its way inside for the usual Friday night festivities.

It wasn't much, but it was the place I called home for the two years I went to school here.

I grab my bag out of the car and make my way up to the front door, hearing music blaring from inside the house. People are coming and going through the front door that's been left wide open. I'm immediately greeted with cheers and shouts from some familiar faces when I walk in. These are the same people I had spent many Friday and Saturday nights with over the past two years. Nostalgia overtakes me, making me feel like I never actually left this place.

"Dude, so good to see you!" My friend Paul walks up and hands me a cold beer.

"Hey, man, how have you been?" I ask, gladly taking the can.

"Oh, you know, same shit, just a different day," he says, looking around. "But what about you? How's Boston treating you?"

"Can't complain."

Paul is a pretty outgoing guy, and we always had a good time together. We spent many nights in this house getting shit-faced, trying to out-drink each other.

I always won.

"Let me take your shit, dude. I'll put it in your old room. No one lives in there yet. Brian has been very selective about who's going to be our new roommate." He grabs my bag from my hands and walks up the stairs.

"Nate. My man! You made it!" I turn around and see the only guy in this house who could ever out-drink me, Brian.

"Hey, Brian," I say as he comes in for a manly hug. "Always good to see you, man."

He turns away from me and starts making himself a drink of mostly vodka. "You ready to get shit-faced tonight?"

"That's what I came here for," I say before chugging down the rest of my drink.

Brian hands me another one and then leads us down the basement stairs where déjà vu hits me. The only light in the room comes from the stringed neon bulbs hanging from the walls. A DJ's booth is in the corner where a guy blasts shitty mixes from his outdated computer equipment. Couches are grouped in another corner, and a ping pong table resides on the other side reserved for beer pong. People are beginning to fill every square inch of the place.

I follow Brian to the couches and recognize even more faces, including Jessica.

Shit.

twenty-three

NATALIE

Sarah knocks on my door just as I finish putting on the final touches of makeup.

"Hey, Sarah," I say, inviting her in. She's exuding confidence, wearing a tight black miniskirt with an off-the-shoulder silver crop top and a pair of black stiletto heels. Her makeup is over the top but looks incredible. Her dark hair has been pulled back and draped over her slim shoulders. This is what every girl dreams of looking like.

She walks in to give me a hug and starts squealing. "Ah, I am just so excited that we are finally going out together!" She takes a step back and assesses my outfit. "Natalie, this dress looks amazing on you! I wish I had your curves," she says with an envious pout.

"Really? You don't think it's too much?" I ask, looking down at myself.

A few days ago, I was walking to the campus bookstore when a dress in the window display of a local boutique caught my eye. It was front and center, standing out among all the other dresses. The black silk stopped me in my tracks. Well, until I moved my feet into the store to try it on.

When I looked in the mirror, I saw … me.

Or, I mean, I saw the old me. The version of myself that I had been keeping hidden. The one who liked to go out and have fun, making memories with friends. Not the one who locked herself in her room, seeking refuge from her nightmares.

But wearing this dress made me feel … *confident*. A word I hadn't felt in a long time.

The hem is shorter than anything I own in my closet, but the sheer sleeves make it feel like there is more fabric to the dress than there actually is. The neckline dips scandalously low, and the cutouts in the bodice reveal more skin than I am used to showing.

I've already been trying to think of when I can wear it for Nathan.

"No way, Natalie. You look so hot!" Sarah coats her lips in a layer of vibrant red gloss and then takes a peek in her compact mirror. "Well, are we ready to get this night started?"

A big part of me wants to back out, throw on an oversized T-shirt, and curl up with a good book, but instead, I say, "Let's do this!"

* * *

Sarah and I are confined to the corner of a bar in a small, shabby pub situated close to our apartment building. This place has a reputation for not checking IDs, and it's a Friday night, so of course, it's packed with college students filling almost every seat and space available.

"Umm … what are you drinking?" Sarah asks me, looking at the wine glass in my hand as if it's a poisonous spider.

"A glass of Chardonnay. Why?" The bartender seemed surprised when I asked for a glass of wine, but I guess, looking around me, they probably don't get that request often.

"No way." She shakes her head in disapproval. "Chug that shit down. We're getting you a real drink." She calls the bartender over with a small wave and a flirtatious smile. "Hi, gorgeous, can we please each have a sex on the beach?"

I practically spit my wine out in shock. "A what?"

The bartender nods his head with a chuckle and disappears before returning with two pretty-looking beverages that he places in front of us.

I take a sip and immediately realize I have found my new favorite drink.

Sarah inches her chair closer to mine so I can hear her over the loud music playing. "So, who is the hot toddy I've seen coming and going from your apartment recently?"

"Who?" I ask, feigning confusion.

"Oh, you know, the tall guy who looks like a Calvin Klein model," she responds while pretending to fan herself.

"Oh, umm, him. Well, he and I are both from the same town, and we sort of started …" But I don't know how to finish that sentence.

What are we doing?

Are we just hooking up, or does Nathan think it's more than that? I know I do, but we haven't had *that* conversation yet. Do we need to? Or is our current relationship status just implied?

"Well, we started getting to know each other better," I finally respond and feel a slight heat on my cheeks.

"Good for you, girl! Enjoy it!" Sarah exclaims enthusiastically. "You two look perfect together."

"Thanks," I say before finishing the rest of my drink. "So, are you seeing anyone?" I ask, taking the attention off of me.

The bartender immediately brings me another drink at the sight of my empty glass.

"Oh, you know, I like to keep my options open. I've been so busy with school and work, I don't really have time for anything serious." She waves at some guy sitting across the bar. I look over and instantly recognize him from the house party a couple of weeks ago. The same guy Sarah had disappeared with. He starts walking over toward us with another guy close behind him.

"Hey, Sarah," the guy says as he approaches. He puts one of his thick tattooed arms on the back of Sarah's chair, filling all space between them. The other guy stands there awkwardly, unsure of what to do.

"Hey, John." She places her hand on his arm. "Natalie, this is my … friend, John." I can tell from the pause that they are more than just friends.

"Hi." I give a slight wave.

I look at John's friend who is still standing in the background with his hands in his pockets, looking uncomfortable. He's tall with dark, messy hair, has tattoos up and down his arms, and is wearing a pair of thick black framed glasses that hang right above his prominent cheekbones. His clothes look one size too small on his slim body, but somehow, he makes it work. He's not exactly my type, but there is no doubt about it; he is a good-looking guy. "What's your name?" I ask.

"Oh, dude, sorry," John cuts in. "This is my buddy Kyle."

"Hi, Kyle, it's nice to meet you. I'm Natalie."

"Nice to meet you, Natalie." He gives a shy smile as he steps toward the group.

"Well, don't you two look great together," John says, making things feel even more awkward.

"No way, this girl is taken," Sarah chimes in, coming to my rescue.

"Too bad," I hear Kyle say under his breath.

"You mean your boyfriend let you go out looking like that?" John asks, slowly eyeing me up and down. I cross my arms in front of my chest, feeling extremely self-conscious.

"Leave her alone, dude," Kyle says. I give him an appreciative smile.

"I didn't mean anything by it. Just a question." A tall, slender brunette walks by, distracting him until Sarah loudly clears her throat, bringing his attention back to us. "How about we join you beautiful girls and order another round of drinks?" John asks, and I notice his hand begins to slide down Sarah's back.

They both pull a chair up next to us, and John orders drinks for everyone. Twenty minutes later, I've finished my third drink and feel pretty buzzed but good. I look down at my phone, hoping to see Nathan's name on the screen, but there are no new texts or calls, which leaves me disappointed. This feeling, combined with the amount of alcohol in my system, motivates my fingers to type away on my phone and hit send before I can even think about it.

Me: I miss you.

I don't mean to sound pathetic, but I'm very tipsy in a bar with people I don't know and would much rather be with Nathan, who I'm sure is having a good time doing whatever it is he is doing.

Whatever it is he is doing … oh God.

Images of Nathan with other girls at previous parties pop into my head. Girls were always throwing themselves at him. Beautiful, skinny, flawless girls who looked like models. Girls who were confident and knew how to flirt like professionals. Girls who Nathan would have no problem flirting right back with. I watched it happen so many times before.

So why would tonight be any different? My stomach twists at this thought, giving me an overwhelming and unpleasant feeling.

"Boyfriend trouble?" I hear Kyle ask me.

I look to my right and realize Sarah and John are pretty preoccupied with each other, leaving Kyle and me to fend for ourselves.

"No, it's nothing." I smile and shrug my shoulders.

"You know, if my girlfriend looked like you, I'd never let her out of my sight," he says before taking another sip of his drink. I'm pretty positive that the beer in his hand, plus the other four beers he just drank, are giving him the courage to speak his mind now.

"Oh …" I take a sip from my fourth drink. "Do you have a girlfriend?"

"Me? No." He shakes his head adamantly, laughing at my question. "I don't do that. I'm more into … well, let's just say the opposite of relationships."

"I see." I look down at the drink in my hand, unsure what to say or do.

"So, should I be worried your boyfriend will show up here any second?"

"Oh, no." I shake my head but stop when a dizzy feeling spreads through me. "Well, to be honest, he's not my boyfriend. I actually don't know what we are."

Why did I just tell him that?

"Oh, so you're like fuck buddies or something?" he asks casually. "That's cool. We could do that too if you want." He looks me up and down like he is seeing me for the first time. "Someone like you shouldn't be tied down to just one guy, and I don't mind sharing, especially if it's you."

Ok, this just got really weird really fast. "Excuse me. I'll be right back."

I jump off my seat, feeling the effects of the alcohol the second I land on the ground. The bar is spinning more than it should be, but somehow, I make my way to the restroom located all the way in the back of the bar. I push open the door, thankful that no one is in here, and lock it behind me as I lean back and slide down the length of the door, taking deep breaths. After a few minutes of practicing my breathing until the nausea feeling subsides, I stand up and place both of my hands firmly on the edge of the sink, waiting for my equilibrium to return.

Why hasn't Nathan texted me back? I know he told me not to worry, but how can I not when I don't even know where we stand with each other?

Thoughts of another girl being with Nathan start to torture me. I pull out my phone and call him, hoping to hear his calming voice, but it goes straight to voicemail. My eyes begin to water as my stomach clenches from the thought of what he might be doing. Every breath I take is a struggle since my lungs refuse to do their job.

I'm drowning.

And suddenly, I'm flying to the toilet, gripping the seat for dear life as every drink from tonight betrays me.

This is not how I saw the evening going.

Fuck anxiety.

After nothing is left in my stomach but regret, I'm turning on the sink to splash my arms with cold water when someone begins to pound on the door.

"Natalie? It's Sarah!"

I open it to find a very concerned Sarah standing in front of me. "What did that asshole say to you?" she demands with her hands on her hips, looking like she is ready to go back and wallop him in the face on my behalf.

I knew I liked her.

"It doesn't matter. I started to get the spins, so I needed some space."

"Well, I know what will make you feel better. There's a dance club a few blocks from here. They have the best late-night snacks to soak up all the alcohol in your stomach, and they play the best music."

"I don't know …" I start to say, not really sure if I can handle much more excitement tonight.

"Please? Don't let those tools out there ruin our night. I promise we will have fun!" Her eyes are begging me to say yes, so, against my better judgment, I do.

"Ok. But I definitely need to get some food in my stomach."

"Yes!" She grabs my hand and pulls me through the crowded bar. "You won't regret this!"

Before leaving, we quickly pass by John and Kyle, still sitting in the corner but fixated on a few girls hanging on them.

Good riddance.

To my surprise, Sarah stops and yells, "Hey, boys!" And the second they look at us, she gives them the finger.

* * *

A few hours later, our Uber driver drops us off at the entrance to our building, and we both clumsily walk to our apartments in a fit of laughter, ready to end our girls night.

"I had a really fun time tonight. Let's do this again soon!" Sarah hugs me tightly.

"I had fun too," I reply as we part from each other and make our way into our own units.

And truthfully, I did. After we left the stingy pub and ventured to the nearby dance club, that is.

We spent hours dancing with each other, shoving mozzarella sticks in our faces, and taking advantage of the karaoke machine in the back of the club that no one else was using. It was truly a night to remember.

But every time Sarah and I shared a laugh, this little ping in my chest went off, a dull ache in my heart consistently reminding me of my best friend. The one I used to have this kind of fun with. The one I had dropped with no explanation, knowing the pain it would cause her. The one I hadn't seen in almost a year. And the one person I was missing more than anything or anyone at this very minute.

Vanessa.

My Vanessa.

Something damp slides down my cheeks. I bring my hand up to my face and realize I'm crying.

I guess I had worked so hard to put Vanessa in the black hole of my mind, trying to block out every happy memory with her, that it took making a new friend to realize how much I miss my old one.

This would explain why I spent so much time alone this past year, hoping I wouldn't remember what I was missing by avoiding nights like tonight. Hoping it wouldn't bring back the regret and pain of losing the person in my life who played the part of the sister I never had.

I pull out my phone, alcohol clouding my better judgment, and for a brief moment, I decide to text Vanessa. I'll tell her everything. I'll tell her how much I miss her. How sorry I am about everything. How I've spent every day for the past year wishing I could turn back time.

But as soon as I see her name on my contact list, I can't stop staring at her last name with dread.

Gordon.

And, unfortunately, realize I can't text her. And will never be able to text her.

I wipe the remaining tears from my cheeks and try to convince myself it's for the best. If I tell Vanessa what happened, it will only cause her pain, and I can't be the reason for that.

I'm about to lock my screen when a notification pops up on my phone, alerting me that I have a voicemail. I walk over to my bed and fall into it, feeling exhausted, as I press play.

"Hey, Natalie, sorry I missed your text and call. I should have called you sooner, but my phone died on my way up here, and I just finally got it charged. Anyways, I miss you too. Like really miss you. A lot. I hope that doesn't make me sound too pathetic, but it's true. I can't wait to see you tomorrow. Don't forget to text me when you get home, please. Miss you, baby."

An uncontrollable smile spreads across my face. It helps soothe that icy ache in my heart with some much-needed warmth.

My fingers type out a simple message for Nathan.

Me: I'm home. Wishing you were here.

I kick my heels off my swollen and painful feet and slide out of my dress so I can finally curl up in a ball under my blankets, ready to drift to sleep in anticipation of tomorrow.

twenty-four

NATHAN

Jessica is not someone I had planned on running into today. In fact, if I had known she would be here, I probably wouldn't have come.

"Hey, Nate," Jessica says. She's wearing the same devilish smile that used to make my dick instantly hard from knowing what that mouth can do. Doesn't have the same effect on me anymore, though.

She's sitting on the couch directly in front of me, on the lap of some poor sucker I don't recognize, tracing her dagger nails up his chest. One look at this girl should tell people she's trouble. From the skirt that barely covers her ass to the nipple piercings pressed against the thin fabric of her too-small top, she's a problem. But at least she's no longer my problem.

Not to mention, she has slept with at least half the guys in this room, me included. And normally, I wouldn't even judge someone's sleeping habits. I mean, look at me. I'm not one to talk. But this girl, well … she's sinful. And not in a good way.

"Jessica," I say, purposely not making eye contact with her.

Brian sits on the couch across from her, and I hesitantly follow his lead. Then I try to chug as much of the alcohol in my cup as possible, knowing I will need a lot more than this if I have to be anywhere near this girl tonight. From the corner of my eye, I see Paul stride across the room and look between Jessica and me, fully knowing the history between us, before he takes a seat on my other side. And as if this girl can't take a hint, she gets up from the lap she is occupying and saunters over to our couch, placing herself directly on my lap, causing me to freeze in annoyance. She puts her hands on my cheeks and moves my face so that I am looking straight into her roguish eyes.

"What are you doing?" I grumble, but she ignores my words.

"No hard feelings. Right, Nate?" She looks completely innocent with her pleading eyes and her bottom lip out.

"Oh, of course not. Why would there be any hard feelings between us?" I ask, sounding as sarcastic as possible before finishing the rest of what's in my cup.

Last year, Nick came to visit me at school for a weekend. I admit that I shouldn't have brought him to a college party. That part I will take responsibility for. The part I will not take responsibility for is what occurred at the party.

Jessica had decided to play a drinking game with Nick in the kitchen while I was in the basement. She told him that whoever took the most shots of vodka would win. To this day, I have no idea what the prize was going to be, and I don't ever want to know. Well, the conniving bitch played her game with my very underage brother, except every time she poured a shot of vodka for Nick, she poured a shot of water for herself.

Nick was over ten shots in when he collapsed to the floor.

A few people rushed to find me and tell me what had happened. I remember running up the stairs, seeing my brother lying motionless on the kitchen floor, and feeling so afraid. I tried shaking him to bring him to, but he just laid there lifeless. So, that night, instead of Nick having a good time visiting his older brother, he spent it in the emergency room getting his stomach pumped. And after I found out about their little game, I cussed Jessica out, letting her know how lucky she was that nothing more serious had happened.

I had hoped never to see her again. But here we are.

"Now, now, you two. That's all in the past," Brian says, interrupting my thoughts as he pats my back. "Nate came here to have a good time tonight, so let's show him one!"

"Cheers to that!" Paul yells before chugging the rest of his drink.

Jessica lowers her lips toward my ear, clearly trying to shove her cleavage in my face. "You know I could show you a good time … to make up for things."

"No thanks, and I think you should find somewhere else to sit." I give her a slight push off my lap, taking her by surprise.

"Well, someone's no fun." She huffs.

"I don't do that anymore." I get up from the couch to grab a bottle of beer from the fridge on the other side of the room.

"And why not?" she asks, surprised.

I notice everyone's faces have turned toward me, waiting for my response. "Well, not that it's any of your business, but I'm seeing someone." I sit back on the couch and use the bottom of my T-shirt to help remove the cap from my beer.

"You? I don't believe it." Jessica looks me dead in the eye. It's almost unnerving how long she goes without blinking.

"Do I know the lucky lady?" Brian chimes in with a smug smile on his face.

"I'll tell you later," I respond, not wanting to discuss my personal life in front of a room full of people.

"Well, who is ready for a round of ping pong?" Paul asks, clearly helping me by changing the subject.

"You're sure you want to play against me? You know I always win," I say with a proud grin.

"Eh, we will see about that, man. I've been practicing all summer. Got some new moves." He starts animatedly pretending to be swinging a paddle in his hand.

"You better watch out, Nate. He's been pretty much sleeping

with his paddle every night. Pretty sure it's the only thing he's been sleeping with all summer," Brian adds.

"Ha. Ha. Very funny. We both know that's not true since you fucking barged in on Katie and me last week, piss drunk." There's a look of annoyance on Paul's face, and I sense I'm missing something.

"Hey, not my fault you didn't lock your door. Besides, if Nate had heard those noises coming from your room, he would have done the same thing. I thought you were being attacked, for Christ's sake." Brian throws his hands up, exasperated.

Ok, clearly, there's some tension between these two.

"Whatever, man." Paul shakes his head like he's trying to forget it and looks over at me. "What about it, Nate? You ready to get your ass kicked in an epic round of ping pong?" He rolls up his sleeves, knowing I would never deny him the game we played together almost every weekend while I was here.

* * *

An hour later, after several wins in ping pong against Paul, I head upstairs with Brian to get some air. I pull my phone out of my pocket to text Natalie, but when the screen doesn't turn on, I realize it must have died on the ride up here. So I run up the stairs to what used to be my old room to charge my phone.

I look around the small space and notice that not much has changed. Actually, nothing has changed. It still has the same tiny mattress, dark bookcases, forest-green walls, and an ugly brown lamp that stands alone in the corner. This place isn't much, but it was my escape. My home.

I miss going to school here with my friends. And I miss having a place like this to myself, but considering everything that's happened this past year, I am lucky to call Boston my new home.

Besides, I would never have been given a second chance with Natalie if I still went to school here. And for that, I count my lucky stars.

I walk downstairs to see Brian standing in the kitchen talking to some girl I don't know. His hand rests on her hip as the girl whispers in his ear. I head over to them after the girl walks away.

"Who's she?" I ask.

"Just one of many," he reveals. "Let's go outside and get some air." He turns for the door at the exact moment I notice his bloodshot eyes, which lets me know that he's not just drunk but most likely high too.

I grab another can of beer before being greeted by a refreshing chill in the air as I step out through the back door. I sit on one of the old, rickety wooden chairs around the fire pit, hoping it doesn't crumble under my weight. As I sit back and take a sip of my drink, Brian gets the fire to a dull roar, so we have some heat. He sits on the chair beside mine and looks up to the night sky, bringing his drink to his mouth and then tossing it to the side when he's finished.

"So, Nate, how's everything going?"

"Well, it's certainly not what it used to be." I rest my can on the arm of the chair. "Coming here really makes me miss this place."

"Yeah, man, I know. I haven't even found anyone worthy enough to take over your room," he says with a slight laugh. "I think there's a part of me still hoping you'll somehow end up back here."

"You know that's not an option for me," I mutter, looking up toward my old bedroom window with a pang of regret.

Brian and I became instant best friends the day he hit the kid in school who made fun of me for wearing a Red Sox shirt to class. I guess I had missed the memo that everyone in my new school was a Yankees fan. But ever since that day, almost ten years ago, Brian and I had been as close as brothers. He could sometimes be a real jerk, especially to people he didn't like, but never to me. We were even lucky enough to get into the same college. But unfortunately, things changed.

I rub my forehead, trying to forget about the DUI.

"Hey, I almost forgot to mention. Unfortunately, it looks like

I won't be able to make it for your birthday this year. We have a home game that night, and coach will kill me if I miss it. But I was talking to Tim, and he wants to throw the traditional Halloween birthday rager at his place." He looks over at me before continuing. "He said his parents will be out of town that weekend, so it's perfect."

"You know how I feel about birthdays. I really don't need a party," I insist, knowing deep down Brian has always just used my birthday as an excuse to throw one. And besides, after what happened last year, having a birthday party is the last thing on my mind.

"Dude, it's your twenty-first birthday. You have to have a party. And I mean, come on, your birthday is on fucking Halloween. It's epic. Tim's already put in an order for kegs, and he's insisting on costumes for everyone."

I give him a not-so-subtle eye roll.

"I know," he chuckles. "But his house, his rules."

"I guess," I say, still not sure about this.

"Paul said he'll be there, and I'll try to make it, but the game time is going to be cutting it kind of close."

"Don't even worry about it. It's not a big deal."

His eyebrows raise in confusion at my nonchalant expression. "Come on, man. You know it will be fucking amazing like it is every year."

"Yeah, I'm sure you're right," I agree.

"I'm just jealous I won't be there. God, I was so fucked up last year, I barely remember it."

It's true. He was pretty fucked up and ended up disappearing later in the evening. I assumed he was either passed out or hooking up with a girl in his room. Never bothered to find out.

"So, I guess the real question is … are you really whipped?" Brian asks. "I never actually thought that day would come for either of us." The thought makes him chuckle.

"Yeah, about that …" I look down at my drink. Why am I nervous to tell him about Natalie?

"Well, who is she?" Brian asks. He notices the worried expression on my face. "What? Do I know her or something?"

Here goes nothing. "It's Natalie."

"Natalie who?" Brian looks like he is racking his brain for a last name, and then his eyes go wide. "Natalie Spencer?" His voice gets louder, and he sits up from his chair in shock. "Are you insane?"

"Yes, Natalie Spencer. What's the big deal?" I'm confused by his reaction.

He composes himself and leans back in his chair as his eyes stare into the fire. "Nothing, I'm just surprised in your taste. She's always been a bitch."

"When was Natalie ever a bitch?" I ask, now getting defensive.

"Oh, dude, you know how she is. Acting like the queen of everyone around her. She is as prude as they come and has always acted like she is better than everyone else." He grabs another can of beer from the cooler beside him. "Just because her daddy makes more money than everyone from that goddamn town doesn't give her the right to—" but he stops. "Whatever, man, it's your life." He begins to chug down his beer.

What the actual fuck?

This is not the reaction I was expecting from my best friend. I thought he would be happy for me. But this?

"Well, if we're being honest here, I don't remember her acting that way. *Ever.*" I finish what's left of my drink, crush the empty beer can, and toss it beside me. Natalie … a bitch? Acting like the queen of everyone around her? Nope. Never. And prude? If only Brian had any idea how very not prude Natalie is. But he will never find that part out. My lips are sealed shut with those pleasant thoughts. And Brian's in no position to be upset about how much money the Spencers have when he's living a pretty identical fiscal life to them. *What the hell?* He's never had a financial burden in his life. I have no idea where this hatred for Natalie is coming from, and then a thought immediately comes to my mind. Something I should have asked him the moment I walked through the front door. "Did something happen between you guys?"

"Who? Me and Natalie? No way," he says, shaking his head adamantly. "Not my type."

"Not your type? Ok …" Now I know something is up because Natalie has to be his type. Natalie is every guy's type. And every girl on this planet is Brian's type.

"I don't get it, man. Like, what happened? The slut got on her back for you or let me guess … her knees. Am I right? And now you've forgotten how to—"

I bolt upright in my chair, feeling the wood crack beneath me, ready to give out. "Don't ever fucking talk about Natalie like that." My fists slam down onto the arms of the chair as I practically growl at Brian. Now he's crossed the line.

"Jeez, relax, Nate." Brian laughs, which manages to piss me off more. "Didn't realize you had actual feelings for the girl. Thought you were just getting some ass."

"It's not like that with Natalie." I stare at Brian, trying to get him unsettled, but nothing about this bothers him in the slightest. "She's different."

"Ok. Right." Brian responds dryly.

I slowly lean back in my chair, willing my body to calm down. A few minutes of uncomfortable silence pass before I can't take it anymore. I reach into my pocket to pull out my phone but remember that I left it in my old room charging.

I'm out of here.

"Well, I'm going to call it a night, man. I'll find you in the morning before I leave." I stand up and make my way toward the back door, still feeling my blood boil from Brian's words.

I didn't come here tonight to fight with my best friend.

"Wait." I turn to see that Brian's caught up to me.

"Sorry, Nate, I don't know what came over me. I've probably had one too many," he rakes his hand over his buzz cut and looks from the ground back to me with eyes that remain bloodshot. "I'm happy for you. I mean it." He puts a reassuring hand on my shoulder.

"Thanks, Brian. I appreciate it." I'm sure the alcohol and

whatever else in his system made him act out the way he did. Right?

"Just be careful," he adds before turning back to his chair.

What the fuck does that mean?

But I tell myself it's not worth it. He's drunk, high, and who knows what else. Confronting him about anything right now would only end badly.

I turn toward the back door and walk into the house. Since we've been outside, even more people have arrived, making it rather difficult to get from one room to the next. I squeeze through the mass of college students and walk up the stairs to my old room, shutting the door behind me. Grabbing my phone, I turn it on and see that I have a missed text and call from Natalie.

Natalie: I miss you.

God, how is it possible that I already miss her?

I lie back on the bed and call her as I look at the clock on the nightstand and see it's almost 2 a.m. When it goes to her voicemail, I figure she's probably sleeping, so I leave her a message. After I finish, I shut my phone off and slip under the blankets. My arms crave the feeling of being wrapped around Natalie, holding her firmly to my chest, but this will sadly not be one of those nights. So, I close my eyes and hope I see her in my dreams.

And yes, I know how fucking corny that is.

twenty-five

NATALIE

I wake up with a massive headache. A headache that's so bad I know aspirin alone isn't going to fix it. I shouldn't have drunk so much last night, especially knowing I would be meeting Nathan's mom later today.

Ugh. Good job, Natalie.

At least I have plenty of time to get ready … or do I? As my stomach clenches with dread, I turn my head to look at the clock on the nightstand beside me.

It's 1:30 p.m.

Oh! My! God!

Immediately, I jump out of bed in a panic and grab my phone. Nathan texted me over an hour ago.

Nathan: Good morning beautiful. I'm on my way home and should be back to campus around 2. I'll stop by your place first. Can't wait to see you.

I look at the mirror hanging on the wall in front of me and am horrified. My hair is the actual definition of a bird's nest. My eyes are black and puffy from leaving my makeup on, and when I look down, I notice that my feet are swollen and blistered from all the dancing I did last night. There is no way I will have enough time to fix all of this before Nathan gets here.

Without thinking, I run to the bathroom, turn on the shower, and jump in under the water. Grabbing my body wash, I remove all evidence of last night and then begin to condition my hair to get all of the knots out. After a few minutes of standing under the showerhead, letting the hot water relax my body, I shut it off and towel myself dry. Just as I wrap the towel around my body, I hear a knock.

Shit.

I go to the front door, look through the tiny peephole, and see Nathan standing on the other side. Slowly, I open the door while standing behind it in case there are other people in the hallway. Nathan looks just as handsome as ever and is holding two cups of coffee in his hands.

"Please tell me one of those is for me?" I ask with desperation in my voice.

"Well don't you look nice," he says with a smile as he walks past me. "And yes. I thought you might need this." He holds out one of the coffees for me to take.

I reach for the cup with one hand while my other hand holds my towel in place, but he pulls the coffee from my reach.

"Oh, you see, it's pretty hot, so you have to use both hands to hold it." His smile has now turned into a huge grin.

"Fine, I don't want coffee anyways." I turn in the direction of my bedroom. Two can play this game.

But he comes up behind me and grabs my free hand to stop me. "I'm just kidding, beautiful." He puts the coffee in my hand at the exact moment he kisses my forehead.

"Thank you," I say before taking a sip, closing my eyes and enjoying the feeling of the hot liquid sliding down my throat. But when my eyes open, I notice Nathan staring.

"I missed you," he says then runs a hand through his hair and looks out the window. "Is that bad? I mean, it was only one night, and I fucking missed you." He brings his delicious brown eyes back to me. "I'm not used to feeling like this."

"I guess you have it pretty bad for me, huh?" I stand on my tip toes so my lips brush against his.

He smiles before pressing his lips firmly against mine, causing my heart to race as his tongue finds my own. Then, as he pulls away, he says, "I guess I do."

"Just so you know, I missed you too." I look away from his eyes before adding, "A lot."

"Well, looks like we both have it bad then, huh?" He runs his fingers through my wet hair. "You know it might be easier to make out if you take this towel off," he suggests.

"No way," I say through laughter as I take a step back, gripping my towel tighter. "I need to get ready. Go make yourself comfortable while I put some clothes on. What time will your mom and brother be here?"

"Around 3:30. I think I'll give them a tour of the campus, and then we can meet up with you before going to dinner." He's sounding very casual about the whole thing, even though I know how important this is to him.

"Sounds good to me." I smile at him and then head to my room.

"Natalie?"

I stop in my tracks and face him. "Yes?"

"What is that hanging on your doorknob?" He's looking at the dress I wore last night that, after I flung it off my body, must have somehow ended up there.

"Oh, that?" I can't pick it up and hide it because of my coffee in one hand and the towel in the other.

Nathan places his coffee on the counter beside him and reaches around me to grab the dress, letting it hang loose in the air while he examines it. "Did you … did you wear this last night?" he asks. His fingers run over the delicate fabric and even slower over each cutout.

"Y-yes. I did." Maybe wearing that dress was a bad idea. "Are you mad?"

His fingers instantly stop running over the fabric, and he looks at me with curious eyes. "Mad? No, of course I'm not mad. I just wish I had seen you in it." The cutest little smile makes its way onto his face. "Why would I be mad?"

"I don't know. We ran into one of Sarah's … friends last night, and he had said something that made me think maybe I shouldn't have worn that, and I just started thinking—"

"Natalie?"

"Yes?"

"You can wear whatever you want to wear." He steps toward me and reaches for a loose piece of damp hair before pushing it back into place. "Do I like that other guys got to see you in this? Absolutely not. Do I like that they probably had explicit fantasies about you? God, no. But guess what? At the end of the day, it's me who gets to live out every guy's dream." He lowers his head so his lips fall on the sensitive spot right below my ear where he begins to place a trail of soft kisses down my neck. "I'm the one who knows what those sweet lips taste like. I'm the one who knows what sounds come out of that sexy mouth when I make you come. And I know what to do to get your heart racing." His hands move around my waist, gripping me firmly against him. Even with the thick towel between us, I can feel how unbelievably hard he is for me. "To get you aching for me. To make you soaking wet for me. To make you feel so damn good." His tongue slides up my neck, causing my heartbeat to accelerate into hyper-speed. He brings his lips to my ear and nibbles softly before whispering, "Not them. Me. Only me."

The second I hear his possessiveness over me, the familiar throbbing starts between my legs. The throbbing that he knows is because of him and only him.

God, he's good.

"Nathan, please—"

His lips land hard on mine.

Craving me.

Needing me.

And I eagerly reciprocate.

My hands long for him, so I finally let the towel drop to the floor and place my hand on his chest, feeling his heart beating rapidly beneath my touch. Somehow, while our lips are locked, Nathan takes the coffee cup from my other hand and places it on the counter beside him before running both of his strong hands down my body, cupping my ass, and picking me up in one fluid motion. My legs tightly wrap around his torso as he pushes me up against the wall, pinning me in place with his hips.

He breaks free from our kiss, leaving both of us wanting more, and looks down at my body that he holds securely in his arms. "Fuck, Natalie. You have no idea how much I needed you last night." As one of his hands keeps a strong hold of me, his other trails leisurely over my breasts, causing that elusive throbbing between my legs to turn into a fierce pounding as his thumb rubs over one of my nipples in little circles.

He knows exactly what he is doing to me.

"Well, you can tell me, or you can show me," I somehow manage to say breathlessly, creating a playful smirk on his face. "But personally, I hope you show—"

His lips land on mine before I can finish, and he carries me swiftly to my bedroom where we spend the next hour together making up for the night we spent apart.

* * *

"Can you zip this up for me?" I ask Nathan as I look at myself in the mirror. I'm wearing a new floral dress I purchased a few days ago, hoping to make a good impression on Nathan's mom.

Nathan walks over and stands behind me, zipping the dress up slowly, probably slower than he needs to, which sends shivers down my body. "You look beautiful, Natalie," he says quietly in my ear as his chin rests on my shoulder and his arms wrap around my waist.

"Thank you." I bring my hands to his, looking at the two of us together in the mirror.

And I have to admit, we look pretty damn good together.

He spins me around so I'm now facing him and looks into my eyes. "Did you have a good time last night?"

"Actually, yes, I did. Sarah and I went to some bar down the street, which wasn't so great, but then we spent the rest of the night dancing at a small club. It was a lot of fun. I have the sore feet to prove it." I laugh, remembering how Sarah ended up losing her shoes at some point in the evening.

"I bet you looked so sexy on the dance floor." He starts tracing my jawline with his finger, making my insides go crazy.

"Did you have a good time?" I ask, trying to keep my voice steady.

"Yeah, it was … interesting. But overall, a good night. I miss going to school there." He shrugs.

Knowing the circumstances of why he doesn't go to school there anymore, my heart breaks for him.

"But I have a question for you." He runs one of his hands through his hair and scrunches his face. It looks like he is internally fighting with himself about something.

"Yes?"

"And I promise this is the last time I will ask you this, but are you sure nothing ever happened between you and Brian?" His eyes stare directly into mine, waiting for an answer. My body goes numb, and I pray to the gods that he can't hear my thoughts.

Did Brian say something to him? Does Nathan already know about that night? But if he doesn't know, I can't tell him now, not when we will be spending the night with his mom and brother.

I need to lie.

At least for right now.

I'll tell him later. I will.

"No," leaves my mouth faster than I can comprehend. Standing perfectly still, I do everything in my power to show no emotion on my face.

"Ok," he says, now looking off at something. "I believe you. It's just … I don't know. He seemed weird when I brought you up.

I thought maybe you two … well, actually, I don't know what I thought."

"You brought me up?" I ask, tilting my head in confusion.

"Oh, well," he starts to say, "ok, I'll be honest. Honesty is good." He looks down at me again, making me nervous. "So, there was this girl at the party who," he rubs his chin before continuing, "well, we used to hang out." His pause after the words "hang out" tells me it was more than just hanging out. "Anyways, she tried to get me to sleep with her last night, and I declined. I told her I was seeing someone, and that's when Brian overheard what I said and wanted to know who I was seeing." He shrugs and waits for my response.

My lips are on his within seconds. I wrap my hands around his neck and kiss him hard, pulling him into me. Nathan follows my lead and matches my movements but then suddenly pulls away.

"Wait, I'm confused. You're happy that some girl I used to sleep with wanted to sleep with me last night?"

I start giggling. "No, that part I'm not so happy about." I bring my hands up to his cheeks, cupping his face in my hands. "I don't care about your past and how many girls you may have slept with. Well, I care a little, but that's not the point. I'm happy that you said no, and I'm happy that you told people you were seeing someone … whatever that may mean."

"What do you want it to mean?" he asks.

"I umm, I don't know. It doesn't matter," I say and look away nervously.

"Yes, it does. Tell me what you want." His voice is almost a whisper, and his hand on my waist pulls me in closer.

"I want …" I'm trying to find the courage to say it out loud. All I can hear is Kyle's voice in my head saying *"fuck buddies"* over and over again. It really bothered me because I started to convince myself that this was all Nathan and I are with each other, and I don't want that to be true. "I want us to be … exclusive. Not to be seeing other people. Well, what I mean is I want us to be in a relationship. But only if that's what you want too."

I get the words out of my mouth and instantly feel like a slight weight has lifted, but at the same time, I'm now worried about Nathan's reaction. Maybe this is not what he had in mind.

"I want that too," he whispers.

My face lights up. "You do?"

"Yeah, I've been thinking about this a lot," he says. "It bothers me to think about you being with someone else when I only want you to be with me." He starts playing with a strand of my hair in a nervous gesture. "Call me selfish, but I don't want to share." He moves his hand to my cheek and rubs his thumb back and forth over it. "I like you, Natalie. I really fucking like you."

I can't help but smile at these words. We're finally getting these feelings we've had for each other for years out in the open. "I really fucking like you too."

I stand on my tiptoes and bring my lips up to his while looping my arms around his neck. His hands begin to slide from my waist and down to my thighs, where his fingers try to lift the fabric of my dress, but I slowly pull away from him, shaking my head and lightly placing my hands on his chest.

"As much as I would love to have a second round with you, I don't want you to be late meeting your mom."

He sighs deeply. "You're right. I should probably get going." When his eyes meet mine, I'm sure he can sense how nervous I am about officially meeting his mom. "She's going to love you, Natalie."

I force a small smile.

I really hope he's right.

"I'll meet you here at 5:30, ok?"

"I'll be here."

He kisses me on the lips one last time and grabs his stuff to leave. After he shuts the door behind him, I walk over to lock it and then lean back against it.

Nathan and I are officially a couple.

It feels a little surreal, but in a good way. A very good way. I don't think it's possible for me to feel any happier than I do at this very moment.

And I'm sure the smile on my face is the biggest smile I've ever worn in my life.

But within seconds, anxiety fills me.

Brian.

I didn't tell him about Brian because I knew it would upset him, and I didn't want to ruin the day with his family.

And if I'm being honest, I'm still scared to tell him.

I might have lied to him, but it was a necessary lie. I had no choice. It wasn't the right time to tell him everything.

Will there ever be a right time?

The answer to this is easy.

No. There will never be a right time to tell him. But the longer I put it off, the harder it will be to tell him this secret that's been eating away at me for almost a year now.

I have to tell him tonight after we have dinner with his mom and brother. I'm sure Nathan will understand why I have been lying to him about this, and everything will be fine between us. I'm sure of it.

Will it be, though?

twenty-six

NATHAN

My fingers anxiously drum along the table's edge as I wait for my mom and brother at the campus coffee shop. Their favorites are already at the table waiting for them.

"Hi, honey." I look up from my phone and see my mom standing in front of me. She's wearing a huge, beautiful grin and her brown eyes are beaming.

"Hi, mom," I say as I stand up, towering over her, and wrap my arms around her slender body.

After we part, she sits on the chair beside me while my brother Nick walks around her. Our height is evidently not something we inherited from our mom.

"Hey, Nate," my brother says with a head nod before taking the last empty seat around the table.

"Hey, man." I nod back.

"So, what is the plan for today? I'm so excited to see everything," my mom says eagerly.

After I got my DUI last spring, the first person I thought about was my mom. And to say I was dreading that phone call would be an understatement.

I didn't want to be the reason for any more heartbreak in her life. I didn't want to see disappointment flash across her eyes because I knew I wouldn't be able to handle it. But my mom was surprisingly far from disappointed in me. Instead, she was *understanding*. She knew why I did what I did, and although she could empathize with me, she did make me promise after some very stern conversations that I would never do anything like what I did again for fear of jeopardizing my future.

I swore on my life I wouldn't because, even at only five foot three, my mom can be scary as hell when she needs to be.

And maybe I let my imagination run wild, but I couldn't help but think that it wasn't so much that she was scared of me ruining my future. More so that I would become like my father.

A *monster*.

Or maybe this was really just my *own* fear.

She picks up one of the coffees in front of her. "And thanks for the coffee, honey."

"Well, I thought we could first take a quick tour of the campus. Maybe show you some of the sights in the area and then," I pause, not sure what my mom's reaction is going to be, "I thought we could meet up with my girlfriend, and then all of us could go out to dinner in the North End if that's ok?" I rush the words out of my mouth, nervously waiting for her response.

No one explains to you that the first time you tell your mom you have a girlfriend is one of the scariest fucking feelings you will ever experience. My heart is thundering in my chest, but I try to play it cool by taking a sip of my coffee, acting as if her reaction will make no difference to me.

But that's not true at all because my mom's approval matters to me … a lot. Call it mommy issues or simply call it what it is: a boy who grew up watching his mom suffer at the hands of her abusive husband, only to then have to spend his childhood quickly turning into the man she needed to take care of her. To make her proud. To make her feel safe. And to make her happy.

Something that asshole would never be able to do.

Her eyes go wide, and her smile gets more prominent. "You have a girlfriend?" She brings her hands to her face with excitement. "I was beginning to think I would never hear those words leave your mouth."

"Ok, we don't need to make this into a big deal or anything," I say, feeling my face getting hot as I rip off a piece of the blueberry muffin in front of me and shove it in my mouth. But the relief I feel from her words has at least caused my heartbeat to slow down to a normal human speed.

"Well, it's about time," she says. "Forget about the tour. I want to meet your girlfriend!"

Laughter escapes from me as I see she's ready to jump off her seat. "Well, I told her we would pick her up around 5:30, so we still have plenty of time for the tour, and also, you might already kind of know her."

"I do?"

"Yeah, umm, it's Natalie Spencer." I wait for her to soak in this information. She knows Natalie. Or at least she knows who she is from seeing her around the Gordons' home over the years.

"Oh my goodness, I remember Natalie. What a beautiful girl! I have never been properly introduced, but you know how much I adore her mother, Nancy. Such a nice family," she adds.

God, it feels like a hundred bricks have been lifted off my shoulders, and for the first time this morning, I feel like I can breathe. Not that I was scared my mom wouldn't approve of Natalie — because I knew she would — but I just needed to hear her say these words out loud to me.

I smile, and my mom smiles back and then takes my hand on the table.

"I'm so happy for you, honey."

"I'm happy too, mom."

"Well, not that all of this lovey-dovey talk isn't fun, but are we going to start this tour soon or what?" Nick asks, which causes both my mom and me to laugh.

* * *

After a couple of hours touring every square inch possible on campus with Nick and my mom, and even having time to show them Faneuil Hall, I park my car in front of Natalie's apartment building.

"You guys wait here. I'll go get Natalie." I jump out, noticing my mom examining herself in the rearview mirror, confirming that she's just as nervous about this introduction as Natalie is.

Making my way through the lobby, I see James, the nightly concierge on duty with whom I have recently become acquainted.

"How are you doing this fine evening, Mr. Thomas?" he asks.

"James, I told you just to call me Nate, please. And I'm good. Just taking out Natalie to meet my family for the first time."

James lets out a deep whistle. "Oh boy. I remember having to do that many moons ago with my in-laws. Best of luck to both of you." A slight chuckle escapes from him.

"Way to make a guy nervous," I joke while looking down at my watch. "Well, I have to get going, but same time tomorrow?"

"Same time tomorrow, my friend." He has a warm, gentle smile and waves as I step onto the elevator.

After arriving on the fifth floor, I knock on Natalie's door, feeling a little nervous myself, but I don't plan on letting her know this. The girl is nervous enough for both of us. She opens the door and stands there looking lovely as ever in that same damn gorgeous dress she was wearing when I left her earlier.

"Are you ready, beautiful?" I feel the anxiety radiating off of her body.

"Ready as I will ever be," she says, putting what I assume to be a fake smile on her face.

"It's going to be fine. My mom is very excited to meet you, and I won't leave your side. I promise." I kiss her on her forehead and take her hand in mine, intertwining our fingers.

When we walk out of the lobby entrance, I see my mom standing outside the car, leaning back against the door. I start to say, "Mom, this is—" but my mom cuts me off.

"Oh, Natalie, it is so nice to finally be properly introduced to you!" She wraps Natalie in a giant bear hug. "I couldn't wait for Nate to finish with the tour. He was taking forever!"

"Jeez, mom," I interject, but she ignores me as she fawns over Natalie.

"Mrs. Thomas, it is so nice to meet you," Natalie replies with a radiant smile.

Seeing the two most important women in my life looking so at ease with each other is really pulling on my heartstrings.

"Oh please, just call me Linda," my mom says. "And what a gorgeous dress!"

"Oh, thank you," Natalie politely responds as her cheeks turn the lightest shade of pink.

"Ok, well, we should probably get going," I say, sliding into the driver's seat.

Natalie sits in the back with Nick, and I hear them say hi to each other while my mom gets into the passenger seat. When we arrive at the restaurant in the North End, I give my keys to the valet service so that we don't have to deal with finding a place to park in the city. The restaurant is pretty busy, but I had made a reservation, so we are seated promptly at a big booth in the corner of the main dining room, giving us plenty of privacy. Natalie takes a seat on one side, and I slide in beside her. My brother and mom sit opposite us.

"This place is really nice," Natalie says, scanning the menu in front of her. Then she looks up at me and smiles, and I can see that all previous doubts have vanished from her mind.

The young waiter comes over to introduce himself, and he pours us each a glass of water then leaves to give us a moment with the menus.

"So, Nate, how are your classes going?" my mom asks.

"They're going pretty well. A lot of my credits were transferred over from my other school, so I'm still on track to graduate on time."

"Well, I'm very glad to hear that, and Mark told me that Tom is very pleased with your work at the club. He says he's never had anyone work as hard as you," she adds, quickly looking down at her menu.

"Yeah, I've enjoyed working at …" but a thought disrupts me. "Wait, when did you see Mark?" I look over at Nick. He brings his menu up high to cover his face.

Why do I feel like I'm missing something here?

Without looking away from her menu, my mom responds, "Oh, you know, here and there, I suppose." She brings her attention over to Natalie. "And Natalie, how are your classes going, dear?"

Natalie looks like she is about to answer her when I cut in. "Sorry, but what does 'here and there' mean?" I look over to Nick for support, but he hasn't moved a single muscle this whole time and continues to hide behind his menu.

"Well, Nate, if you must know, Mark and I have been spending time together. He enjoys my company, and I enjoy his. We have a lot in common, and to be honest, I don't feel like I need to explain myself when I am your mother." My mouth falls open in shock, but my mom doesn't notice since every word she spoke was said to the menu in front of her and not to me.

Mark?

The same Mark who gave me my first job. The guy who did everything he could to find me a job in Boston so that I would be able to continue working while attending school. And the same guy who has, for several years, played the part of the father figure I had been missing and needing in my life.

Looking across the table at the woman in front of me, knowing the turmoil she's gone through in life, I realize how significant this moment is.

"Mom." I reach my hand across the table and gently place it on top of her shaking one. "I'm happy for you, really."

She finally looks up at me. "You are?"

"Of course, I am. I'm just surprised is all. A little heads up would have been nice." I squeeze her hand lightly in assurance as I glare at Nick, who just shrugs. "He's a great guy who has been pretty important in my life. You deserve nothing but the best, and Mark is right up there."

"Thank you, Nate. I can't tell you how relieved I am to hear this." She squeezes my hand and uses her other hand to wipe away the single tear rolling down her cheek.

"Well, I'm glad that's out of the way," Nick says as he finally lowers the menu in his hands, which makes us all laugh.

My mom clears her throat and turns her attention back to Natalie. "Sorry for the family drama. We aren't usually this exciting."

"I don't mind. It's exactly how my family and I are." She smiles.

My mom smiles back, looking favorably between Natalie and me. "Well, where were we? Oh yes. So, Natalie, how are your classes going?"

"They're going really well. I'm just taking care of my general studies first. Then I'll be focusing more on my major."

"And what are you majoring in?"

"Well, right now, I'm entered as an English literature major. I'm hoping to start writing professionally after graduating, but I've been thinking of applying for a double major in business as well." Natalie tucks a loose strand of hair behind her ear before glancing at me, hopeful my mom will be pleased with her response.

I didn't know Natalie was planning on double majoring, and I'm genuinely impressed. And from my mom's expression, I can tell she is also just as impressed.

"Wow, that is quite remarkable," my mom responds. "Nate, you failed to mention how accomplished Natalie is." I can see Natalie's cheeks flush from the compliment.

"Ok, ok. Nick, how's everything going for you?" I ask my brother to take the spotlight away from Natalie. She rests her left hand beside my thigh, and I take her hand in mine, rubbing my thumb back and forth across her soft skin.

I know meeting your boyfriend's mom can be a lot, but damn, *my girl* is killing it right now.

"Can't complain. I made the varsity basketball team at school. We don't start until November, but they wanted to get a head start in tryouts, so I've been practicing a lot." He shrugs.

I can't help but notice that he looks just like I did at that age.

"Man, that's awesome!" I respond. "Congratulations! We'll have to play one-on-one soon."

"That would be great," Nick replies.

The young waiter returns with a breadbasket and takes everyone's orders. When he walks away, my mom turns her attention back to me. "So, Nate, you have a pretty big birthday coming up. Do you have any plans?"

"Umm." I notice Natalie's eyes widen, probably because I never mentioned my birthday to her, but I didn't think it was that big of a deal. "Well, Brian was planning on throwing the usual Halloween party, but he has a football game that night, so it looks like Tim is going to throw it instead. Nothing too crazy." I look over at Natalie, who has now removed her hand from mine.

What did I say?

"Well, maybe it's a good thing Brian won't be there this year. That boy has always been a handful, even for his own parents." My mom has never been a fan of Brian, so I just roll my eyes and let her continue. "I know. I know. He's your friend, so I'll shut up about that, but promise me you and Natalie will stop by your aunt and uncle's house first for a birthday dinner and cake with all of us. I know they would love to see you." My mom takes a piece of bread and begins to butter it as she waits for my answer.

"Sure thing," I respond. As long as I'm with Natalie on my birthday, that's all that matters to me.

As my mom and brother begin discussing what kind of cake to get, I notice Natalie remains quiet. I put my hand on her thigh and rub it slowly back and forth, making sure no one else can see. In return, she places her hand on top of mine, intertwining our fingers, and looks at me with a little smile. For the rest of the dinner, that is where we keep our hands.

After we all eat more than our fair share of delicious Italian food, we get up from our seats and saunter out of the restaurant in a bit of a food coma.

"I'll get the car from the valet," Nick says as he runs off in that direction.

"I'll go with you," Natalie adds before catching up with him, giving my mom and me a chance to talk.

"Well, Nate, I really like her," my mom says as we stand in the cold air, engulfed in the busy nightlife of Boston.

"I knew you would. She was nervous all week with the thought of meeting you." I give a slight laugh.

"Well, she had absolutely nothing to be nervous about. She's polite, friendly, accomplished, absolutely stunning, and you love her." She looks at me as I raise my eyebrows in question. "I know these things, dear. I'm your mother." She puts her arm through mine, and I shake my head laughing at how right she always is. "But there is something else I need to talk to you about, honey." She looks at the ground, unsure how to begin, and then back up at me. "They still can't find him."

I instantly know who she is talking about and run my hand through my hair in frustration. "I don't understand. There are only so many places he could be. How can they not find him?"

"I know. Trust me, I understand your frustration, but it's ok. I don't want you to worry. Your brother and I will continue to stay at your aunt's house. Your father has no idea where we are. We're safe."

"This is all my fault." I look down to the ground in shame. This all could have been avoided if I had just had Nick call the police instead of insisting on taking care of things myself. "I should be with you two while he's still out there." I feel my eyes watering and do everything I can to hold back the tears.

"Nate, the only person to blame is your father," she says very seriously. "And I don't want you to be with us. I want you to be here at school making a life for yourself and having fun with your girlfriend."

A tear manages to escape from my eye, and I wipe it away as quickly as I can, but she's already seen it. Her eyes mist over, and her slender arms quickly wrap around my torso.

"I love you, Nate," she says into my chest, her voice muffled. "Everything will be ok. You'll see."

"I love you too, mom."

She squeezes me before letting go. We both turn when we hear a horn and see Natalie and Nick's faces inside the car. On the ride back to Natalie's apartment, Natalie and I sit quietly in the back seat holding hands, while I try not to let the thought of my father ruin the success of tonight's dinner.

After Nick pulls up in front of Natalie's building, I step out of the car with her.

"I'll be right back. I'm just going to walk Natalie up to her floor, and then I'll take you guys to your hotel," I say.

"Ok. Natalie, once again, it was very lovely meeting you, and I hope we see more of each other soon." My mom steps out of the car and hugs Natalie for the second time tonight.

"I'd like that a lot," Natalie responds as she parts from my mom's embrace.

A few minutes later, Natalie and I step off the elevator. After she opens the door to her apartment, she unexpectedly pulls me inside with her, wrapping her arms around my neck and standing on her tiptoes to reach my lips with a soft brush from her own. Her eyes, filled with desire, connect with mine right before she presses her lips down hard and hungry.

Goddamn.

I tug her body firmly against mine, letting her feel all of *me* as my hands travel down her waist. But just as my hands grip her voluptuous ass, causing me to forget all about the fact that my mom and brother are in the car waiting for me, she breaks the kiss and moves her lips over to my ear where she whispers, "Hurry back."

As she pushes me out into the hallway, she smiles playfully and winks right before closing the door, leaving me standing here trying to catch my breath.

Did I also mention I'm hard as fuck?

Great.

twenty-seven

NATALIE

I lean back against the door and proudly smile as I picture the look on Nathan's face right before shutting the door on him. *He definitely wasn't expecting that.*

Pushing myself off the door, I walk into my bedroom and change into an old baggy T-shirt and a pair of pink fuzzy socks before throwing my hair into a messy bun. I walk into the kitchen, pour myself a heaping glass of wine, and then plop myself down on the couch before bringing a soft throw blanket over my legs.

Nathan's mom was lovelier than I could have imagined, and thinking about how nervous I'd been all week to meet her only feels silly now. She's kind with a warm disposition and clearly loves both of her children a lot. It's hard to envision a woman as lovely as her spending years of abuse at the hands of her estranged husband — someone she once loved. I can only imagine how strong she had to be during those times, not just for herself but also for her sons, which breaks my heart.

I let out a deep breath and lie down on the sofa, moving my head onto one of the pillows until I'm comfortable.

I try closing my eyes, but per usual, something is gnawing at me, causing my chest to tighten.

Brian.

When Nathan's mom asked about his birthday plans, I instinctively panicked, thinking that it would be at Brian's house like it has been every year. I had quickly thought of a million excuses as to why I wouldn't be able to go. Food poisoning. Migraine. Cramps. But hearing that it wasn't going to be at Brian's house and that Brian wouldn't even be there this year considerably relieved me. Maybe Nathan and I would actually be able to enjoy his birthday … together.

Ugh, Natalie, you can't put this off any longer. You said you were going to tell Nathan the truth tonight, and that's exactly what you are going to do. No more secrets.

I put one of my hands behind my head as I stare at the ceiling. I'm going to do it. I will tell him everything, no matter what might happen between us. And I will tell him as soon as he gets back here before I let anything change my mind.

Because I can't continue holding onto this secret for much longer. Sometimes it feels so suffocating. Almost *paralyzing*. And I want to know what it feels like to breathe again without fearing Brian. I want to know that there will be a day when my body won't shut down whenever it hears his name. I want to know I can sleep without worrying he'll haunt me in my dreams.

I want to feel … ok.

I let out a deep breath as I bring the wine glass to my lips, finishing every last drop. As I am about to get up and pour myself a second glass, the front door swings open, and I sit up on the sofa in alarm. Nathan walks in, slamming the door behind him. He leans against it with his eyes closed, trying to catch his breath, looking like he just ran up all five flights of stairs.

Oh my God. Did he?

"You know I was just teasing when I told you to hurry back," I say in between laughter.

Sounding quite winded, he says, "The elevator was taking too long, so I just ran up the five flights of stairs. I couldn't get here fast enough." A big mischievous smile appears on his handsome face.

"Looks like someone needs to add more cardio to their workouts," I tease.

His eyes move from the empty wine glass in my hand back to my face. "Now that you mention it, there is a *cardio* position I've been wanting to try with you."

Damn, he knows just what to say to turn that throbbing pulse on between my legs. "Oh really? Because I've been wanting—" but I stop myself. I need to tell Nathan the truth. Right now.

I can do this. Deep breaths.

My palms begin to sweat, and my pulse quickens as I set the wine glass on the table beside me. I look straight at Nathan, feeling ready, or ready as I will ever be, for what I am about to tell him. "Nathan, there's something I need to talk to you about."

His sweet smile fades, and he confidently strides toward me with darkened eyes that hypnotize my own until he's standing directly in front of me. "Hold that thought," he notes right before scooping me up from the sofa and throwing me over his shoulder.

"Nathan!" I manage to squeal through a fit of laughter, which sends all notions of Brian to the back of my mind, locked away for the moment, as he takes me into the bedroom.

* * *

A little while later, I'm curled up against Nathan's chest, tracing my finger up and down his muscular arm that's wrapped tightly around my waist.

"I'm very glad you hurried back." I shift under his arm, facing him.

"Oh, baby, so am I," Nathan says before kissing my forehead. He falls back, pulling me onto his chest while keeping one arm wrapped around me and his other arm folded behind his head. "My mom likes you." He starts combing his fingers through my hair, which probably looks like sex hair right now. "And before you think otherwise, she told me herself."

"Well, that's a relief. I don't know why I was so worried. I just knew how important this was to you and wanted it to go perfectly.

But I'm so glad I met her. She seems like a really incredible mom."

"She is." He stares at the ceiling, lost in thought.

"She's lucky to have such a great son like you," I add, meaning every word. Nathan doesn't say anything. "Hey," I bring my hand up to his cheek, "what's wrong?"

"I wish there was more I could do for her. For them. I can't tell you how much it bothers me that I'm here in Boston while the two of them are practically forced into hiding. Sometimes it feels like the guilt is just eating away at me." I can feel his body tense beneath me with frustration.

"There's nothing for you to feel guilty about. This is your father's doing, not yours." The wince he makes at the word "father" doesn't go unnoticed. I nuzzle my head into his chest before asking, "Are they any closer to finding him?"

"No. There has been no sign of him. Maybe he left for good this time." He starts running his hand up and down my back, giving me goosebumps. "But I don't know. Something just doesn't feel right."

"What do you mean?"

"Well, it's just they've never not been able to find him before. This time feels different. I mean, the last time I saw him, so much anger raged in his bloodshot eyes. It's like he had no ounce of my father left inside him. I saw only a monster. And it scared me." He goes quiet, waiting for a reaction from me, but I don't want him to know the fear I feel at this moment, so I hold him tighter, unsure of what the right thing is to say.

As if he's reading my thoughts, Nathan says, "It's nice being able to talk to you about this. I know it's a lot to take in, but just having you here listening to me means more than you know."

"That's what girlfriends do." My lips touch his cheek, and I bring the blankets up around me as exhaustion takes over.

He smiles at my words and pushes my hair away from my eyes. "I guess that makes me your boyfriend then, huh?"

I nod then yawn. He tenderly grabs my face in his hands and goes in for a kiss as he flips me over onto my back. Within a split second, he has me pinned under his body, restraining my hands above my head.

Holding himself above me, he looks achingly into my eyes. "There is something else I want to talk to you about before you fall asleep, beautiful."

I can feel my nerves set in motion. "Yes?"

"I'm sorry that I hadn't mentioned my birthday plans. It's not that I didn't want to tell you, I just never really looked at birthdays as a big deal, so I forgot about it until my mom mentioned it. I didn't even find out until last night that Brian and Tim had been planning something." He stares into my eyes, waiting for me to say something, but the mention of Brian creates an instant panic that I try to conceal by closing my eyes and turning my face to the side. "And I don't know. After what happened last year …" he pauses like he doesn't know how to finish his thought.

What does he mean by *after what happened last year?*

My eyes open in a panic.

Can he hear my heart pounding?

"I mean, well, I can tell it upset you earlier, and that wasn't my intention at all. So I'm sorry about that." He kisses the tip of my nose.

My subconscious screams at me to tell him the truth, but my mouth won't open. Why won't my mouth open?

"I almost forgot, was there something you wanted to talk to me about before I pulled a Tarzan and Jane on you?" he jokes.

Tell him, Natalie!

But I can't.

Oh God, I can't.

"It … it was nothing. I don't actually remember anyways." Why is this so hard for me? Why can't I just tell him?

It's anxiety holding me back, bounding me to silence.

Nathan begins to gently nibble at my neck. "Am I getting your pulse racing, baby?" I shake my head up and down, unable to tell him the real reason why my heartbeat is accelerating.

"So, there is one last thing I want to ask you." He looks down at me with a slight blush on his cheeks. "Would you be my date for the party?"

"Really?"

"Only if you want to go. If you don't want to go, I'm totally fine spending my birthday with you, curled up on the couch, watching a movie. Maybe get some pizza. End the night with you just like this because it's impossible for me to keep my hands off you." His eyes graze my entire body before locking with mine, starting an immediate ache between my legs as his tongue slides out over his bottom lip. "As long as I'm with you, I don't care where or how I spend my birthday."

Is it possible for a heart to stop working at eighteen? Because between the anxiety-induced heart rate, the throbbing between my legs, and the sappy heart flutters, I don't know how much more it can handle.

"I would love to go with you." I smile at him. "But now I have a question for you."

"Yes, beautiful?"

"What do you want for your birthday?"

"Hmm ..." He looks like he is mulling something over when suddenly he presses his hips firmly against mine, allowing me to feel his hard length. Then, while still pinning my hands above my head, he moves his lips next to my ear and whispers, "You."

* * *

It's the night before Nathan's birthday.

The night before the night that changed my life.

The night that Nathan still does not know about.

Ugh, I know. Trust me, I know.

Nathan and I pull into the driveway of my family's home, ready to get the weekend started. I called my mom a few nights ago to let her know we would be spending the weekend here, and she couldn't have been more excited. It made sense for us to stay at my house, seeing that Nathan's aunt and uncle live nearby, which is where he will have his birthday dinner. And Tim lives only a few blocks from my parents' house, where Nathan's party will be. Our plan is that Nathan will go to his birthday dinner without me so that I can spend some time with my family, and then the two of us will meet at Tim's house.

And as long as Brian isn't there, I'm sure everything will be fine. *I hope.*

Nathan shuts the car off, and I turn to look out the window, noticing how gorgeously decorated the house is for Halloween. It is my mom's favorite holiday after all, so I'm not the least bit surprised to see cobwebs covering every window, carved pumpkins lining the porch, and inflatable ghosts scattered all over the front yard.

I'm happy to be home to see my family. My mom told me that my dad has been doing well, which is wonderful. Still, I can't help feeling nervous about bringing Nathan to an official family dinner. Probably because this will be the first time I have ever brought a guy over to meet my parents. Cue the avalanche of anxiety trying to make its way to the surface.

"Wow, who does that Audi belong to?" Nathan asks, looking over at the little black convertible in front of the garage.

"Oh, that's mine," I respond with a shrug.

"But I've never seen you drive it. Come to think of it, I've never seen you drive." Nathan looks at me with furrowed brows.

"I know," I say, hoping he will drop the topic.

"May I ask why you won't drive that beautiful piece of metal?"

"I don't know." I look out my side window.

"Natalie?" I can feel his eyes on me.

I take a deep breath, ready to get this out of the way. "Ok, I was in a horrible car accident when I was a kid. My mom and I were on the way to a tennis lesson when a truck ran a red light and drove straight into our car." I look down at my hands folded on my lap. "The driver of the other car became paralyzed from the impact. My mom had a broken wrist, and I … well, I had a broken arm, a cracked rib, and a sprained ankle." I can see from the corner of my eye that Nathan is watching me intently. "So yeah, I'm scared to be behind the wheel of something like a car that can do that much damage to someone. But my parents think if they buy me something cute, I'll just magically start driving. It usually stays in the garage, but I'm guessing my mom was taking out her Halloween decorations and must have forgotten to put it back inside." Nathan doesn't say anything, and I start feeling stupid. "It's silly, I know."

Nathan's hand wraps around one of mine when he says, "Hey, it's not silly." I turn my face toward him. "I understand. That sounds pretty scary. And don't worry, I'll gladly be your personal chauffeur. Just know I accept payment in the form of kisses, and long-distance trips will cost you a little extra." He does his best to wink, and the failed attempt starts an eruption of laughter between us.

I can tell this guy anything, and he'll never judge me. Ever.

Tell him about Brian!

"Is that how you got this scar?" he asks as he runs his thumb over the tiny indent above my left eye.

I shake my head to indicate no. I didn't realize he had ever noticed my scar before. *Now Natalie.* "Nathan," I start to say quietly, but he speaks over me, not hearing my words.

"Looks like your mom is happy to see you." He's looking toward my house, where my mom is standing on the porch waving at us to come in.

"I guess that's our cue." I squeeze Nathan's hand before opening my door. I can tell he is nervous, which makes me nervous since he is never nervous. We both make our way up the front steps of the porch, where my mom eagerly greets us.

"Hi, guys! Did you hit any traffic?" she asks as she pulls me into a hug.

"No, we made great timing," Nathan responds as he follows us inside. My mom takes Nathan in her arms, hugging him like she's known him forever.

"Well, dinner is just about ready. There are a few last-minute things to finish, and then we can eat. I think your dad is in the dining room if you want to join him. Jason and Grace should be here any minute." She heads back into the kitchen.

I turn to Nathan. "So far, ok?"

"So far, ok," he says as he kisses my forehead, takes my hand, and leads us to the dining room.

We find my dad sitting at the head of the table and reading a book titled *How to Live Stress-Free.* When he hears us enter the room, he beams and then quickly glances at our intertwined hands before recovering as he gets up to greet us. Parting hands with Nathan, I give him a hug.

"Natalie, it's so nice to have you home tonight."

"I'm so glad to be home. How are you feeling?" I ask, noticing how good he looks.

"Never better. Your mom has me on a whacky diet, but other than that, I'm great!" I can tell he means it.

"Well, I'm happy to hear that, dad." As we separate, my dad's focus turns to Nathan.

Nathan holds his hand out for my dad to take. "It's nice to finally meet you, Mr. Spencer."

My dad holds out his arms wide and says, "I apologize, but we are huggers in this family." I roll my eyes in embarrassment as my dad wraps his arms around Nathan. "It's a pleasure to meet you, Nate." He lets go of Nathan and pats him on the back. "Hey, aren't you the one who led both the high school baseball and basketball team to the championship a few years ago?"

Nathan cracks a smile, and I can tell he is starting to feel relaxed. "Yes, that was a good year, sir."

"Please call me Robert," my dad insists.

Voices approaching the dining room catch my attention, and I turn to see Jason and his girlfriend, Grace, enter the room.

"Hey, guys," I say, giving a little wave.

"Hey, Nat! I didn't know you were coming home tonight." Jason looks genuinely happy to see me.

"Surprise!" My mom shouts as she walks in holding dishes of food. She places them on the table in front of everyone. "I thought it would be a nice surprise for you, Jason, since I know how much you've missed your sister."

"Not true," he says as his cheeks begin to redden. I'm glad I'm not the only one in the family whose cheeks give their emotions away.

"Oh, Jason," I say, walking over to him and squeezing him as tightly as I can manage.

"Ok, ok, get off of me," he says with a chuckle.

"I've missed you too." I take a seat at the table. Jason and Nathan shake hands, and Jason introduces Nathan to Grace. Nathan then sits beside me, Jason and Grace sit across from us, and my mom and dad sit at both ends of the table.

"Isn't this a lovely sight," my mom states as she looks around at everyone. I swear her eyes are beginning to tear up. "Ok, well, everyone, dig in!"

Nathan dishes some food onto my plate before getting his own and tells my mom throughout the evening how delicious everything is. My dad and Nathan talk about sports and Nathan's job at the Yacht Club in Boston and how he'd someday like to manage or own a marina, which makes my dad very happy to hear. Next, Jason and Grace discuss their plans for an upcoming ski trip that they will be taking during winter break. Then my mom tells everyone about her plans for her and my dad to attend a stress management retreat. The eye roll from my dad tells me how excited he is about this. As I look around at everyone talking and getting along so well, warmth spreads through me.

I take my left hand and find Nathan's hand under the table, already waiting for mine.

When everyone has finished eating, my mom gets up to start clearing the table. "So, I picked up almost every flavor of ice cream imaginable and thought you guys could find something for us to watch in the family room tonight."

"Let me help you with that." Nathan picks up some plates from the table and takes them to the kitchen.

Jason and Grace follow suit, but my dad and I stay behind. I hear laughter from the kitchen as Jason tries to convince Nathan he can beat him in any sport. I love my brother, but I know with certainty that Nathan would crush him in any physical competition.

My dad is staring off at the kitchen when he says, "I like him."

"I like him too," I respond.

"I think you picked a good one. If he hurts you, though, I will have to kill him," my dad says while casually shrugging his shoulders.

"Dad!"

"What? I'm your father. I have to say that," he says, laughing.

I shake my head and grin. "I'm really glad you're doing ok, dad."

"I am too, sweetie," he says softly and puts his hand on my shoulder.

Our sweet moment is over when my mom pokes her head in the dining room and says, "Come on, you guys, your ice cream is melting."

"We better not keep the woman waiting," my dad says as he gets up from his seat. "Speaking of ice cream, don't forget we still have our ice cream date to schedule."

"I haven't forgotten. Can't wait," I remark with a smile, following my dad into the family room where I find Nathan sitting on the loveseat with a space beside him. I sit next to him, and he hands me a bowl of ice cream.

"I know cookies and cream used to be your favorite when we were younger, so I was hoping it still might be?" Nathan asks quietly.

Something so little as remembering my favorite ice cream flavor melts my heart. "You would be right." I nestle closer to him as he pulls a blanket over our bodies.

Jason is about to start the movie, but when I look around, I notice my mom isn't here. "Wait, where's mom?"

"Happy Birthday, Nate!" On cue, my mom walks in with a beautiful birthday cake for Nathan. I had no idea she was planning on doing this. "We won't embarrass you and sing happy birthday, but we are all so glad you are here tonight with us and just want you to have a great birthday." She smiles and holds the cake in front of him, waiting for him to blow out the candles.

"Yeah, man, happy birthday!" Jason exclaims with a fist pump.

"The big two-one! Don't get too shit-faced tomorrow."

"Jason. Really?" My mom shakes her head but the rest of us chuckle. "But actually, Nate, that reminds me. Please keep an eye on this one tomorrow night, won't you?" She looks over at me before continuing, and my heart stops. "I don't want to get a call from the hospital again like last year telling me that you slipped and fell on ice trying to get home before curfew." She shakes her head, trying to rid herself of the memory, then a slight smile appears. "Well, at least we can laugh about it now, right?"

"R-right," I whisper.

"Natalie won't be out of my sight tomorrow night. I promise," Nathan says, looking protectively at me. His hand grips mine tighter, and I'm hoping he doesn't feel my fingers shaking wildly. But then his eyes lock with mine, and the longer I get lost in them, the more I see something in them I've never seen before. *Fear.*

I hear my dad clear his throat, oblivious to the tension felt between Nathan and me, and I instinctively look over at him. "Ah, I barely remember my twenty-first birthday. My buddies and I pretty much drank our body weight in every kind of alcohol you can imagine. In fact," my dad says, but my mom turns to him, giving him a death stare, and he quickly decides not to finish his story. "Well, never mind that. Happy birthday, Nate."

"Happy birthday!" Grace chimes in. I really need to set some time aside to get to know her better, especially seeing how much she means to my brother.

"Time to make a wish!" My mom announces, distracting Nathan from his thoughts.

"Wow, I don't even know what to say." His eyes hop from one person to the next before landing on me. I'm the only one close enough to see his eyes starting to mist over. It occurs to me, looking around, that this is undoubtedly all Nathan has wanted most of his life. A family. Or, more accurately, a happy family. And although he has his amazing mom and brother, I'm sure he always felt like a piece was missing: his dad. I hold back tears wanting to avoid making a scene.

Before blowing out the candles, Nathan clears his throat and says, "Thank you. This means so much."

About an hour into the movie, everyone except for Nathan and me has fallen asleep. There's a heaviness weighing down my eyelids, so I take Nathan's hand in mine and lead him up the stairs to my bedroom. I sit on the edge of my bed, watching as he removes his clothes. He stands in front of me with just his boxer briefs on, making me flush, even though I've seen his god-like body many times before.

"Come here," Nathan says and holds his arms out.

I stand up, but before walking over to him, I slip out of my jeans and throw my top on the floor beside me. Then, slowly, I move into his arms, pressing myself against his defined chest.

Nathan begins to hum a song, which sounds like one of the old jazz songs I've previously heard playing in his car. Our bodies sway in unison to the melody as I stay wrapped in his embrace. His chin rests on the top of my head. The only light in the room is from the full moon that illuminates through the bay window, providing a soft spotlight on us.

"It's midnight," Nathan whispers in my ear, still swaying our bodies back and forth.

"Mhm," I reply, keeping my eyes closed, lost in the comfort of his arms.

"So far, this is turning out to be my best birthday ever." He takes my hand and twirls me away from him before he spins me back into his embrace.

I stand on my tiptoes, bringing my lips to his but pause less than an inch away. "Happy birthday, Nathan," I whisper before finally pressing my lips to his. He wraps his arms tightly around my waist before he picks me up and sets me down in my bed.

NATHAN

I'm finally twenty-one. *Twenty-fucking-one.* The legal drinking age in the good ol' United States. And to say I am ready to start acting my age tonight is an understatement.

After waking up next to Natalie and celebrating my birthday — twice — enjoying a stack of fluffy birthday pancakes with Natalie's family, and beating Jason in some one-on-one at the basketball courts in town, I pull up in front of the local gym to pick up Nick. The two of us will head to our aunt and uncle's house for my birthday dinner before I take off for the final event of the evening, the big Halloween birthday bash.

Nick throws his sports duffel bag in the back seat before hopping in on the passenger's side. "Happy birthday, big bro."

"Thanks. Can't wait to see what you got me this year. There's no way it can beat last year's bottle of floral-scented ladies perfume." I shake my head, remembering the ornate glass perfume bottle shaped like a heart.

"Hey, I'll have you know the hot saleswoman told me it was a bestseller. How was I to know there's a difference between perfume and cologne?"

"Sometimes you scare me." I laugh at the idiot next to me, my brother.

"Sometimes I scare myself," he chuckles. "So, you sure I can't come tonight? I could be the designated driver?" he pleads. I feel for him. I do. But after what happened last year in New Hampshire, there's not a goddamn chance in hell I'm bringing him along. Lord knows I don't need a repeat of that awful night.

"Sorry, Nick. Not happening. Besides, you know mom would kill me if I brought you." Looking over at him, it's not hard to miss the disappointment spreading across his face.

"Fine," he sighs, but he knows my hands are tied, so he doesn't push the issue. "Did you still want to play one-on-one tomorrow?"

"Yeah, of course." I lightly punch him in the shoulder. "I would love nothing more than to whoop your ass in a round of hoops on my birthday weekend."

"Very funny," Nick says, rolling his eyes. "Just because it's your birthday doesn't mean I'll take it easy on you. I've improved a lot since we last played against each other. You'll see."

"I'll be the judge of that, little man," I say with a smug look.

"Little? I'm only an inch shorter than you. Besides, it's not about the size of the player. It's about drive. It's about power ... or at least that's what The Rock claims," he admits with a shrug, making us both laugh.

We pull into the driveway of my aunt and uncle's house and get out of the car.

"Hello?" Nick yells, opening the front door and poking his head inside.

"Come in! Come in!" I hear my mom bellow from inside.

I walk in behind Nick and see my mom and her sister, our Aunt Sheryl, coming toward us.

"Hey, mom," I say as she hugs me.

"Hey, birthday boy! It feels like just yesterday I was dropping you off at kindergarten. Now, look at you, a full-grown man." She removes her arms to wipe away the tears ready to fall from her eyes.

"Mom, please don't cry."

"Let me see him," Sheryl says, pushing my mom out of the way.

"Hey, Aunt Sheryl," I choke out as she squeezes the life out of me. Nick is sitting on the couch enjoying this spectacle.

"Look at how big you are! You need to stop by more often! And where's this beautiful girlfriend your mom was just telling me about?" she asks, looking behind me.

My beautiful girlfriend.

"Oh, Sorry. Natalie is spending some time with her family today before the party tonight. I promise I'll bring her by another time." I reply. "Where's Uncle Harry?"

"Aww, that's too bad. I was so looking forward to meeting her." Sheryl's displeasure is obvious from her facial expression. "And your uncle is off puttering around with his boat, trying to fix something on it. Who knows?" She throws her hands in the air and rolls her eyes. "He should be here shortly, though."

"Well," my mom starts, "I know you're busy today, so let's go into the dining room and start opening presents. And when Harry gets here, we can have dinner and cake."

We all follow her lead into the dining room where I see an abundance of streamers hanging from the ceiling, an enormous fancy-looking cake taking over the center of the table, and a giant birthday banner covering the far wall.

Just as I take a seat at the head of the table, Mark walks in.

"Hey, happy birthday, kid!" he exclaims.

"Hey, Mark. Thanks. It's been a while. How are things?"

"Oh, everything's good. No complaints here. Always something keeping me busy." Mark looks over at my mom, who is beaming with delight that he's here. He sits in the empty seat beside her, wrapping his arm protectively over the back of her chair. "But how are things in Boston? Is Tom a better boss than me?" he inquires with a wink.

"Nah, Tom's great, but I'd say you don't have to worry about your position on the boss-rating meter anytime soon," I say, which gets a good chuckle from Mark. "Thank you again for helping me with that."

"Oh, that was nothing. Tom was short-staffed anyway, so it worked out for everyone."

"Tom told me everything you said about me. If I didn't know better, I might think you like me," I joke.

"What can I say, kid? I guess I have a soft spot for you."

The two of us share an understanding look as I'm reminded that the man sitting in front of me helped me become the man I am today. Even if I had tried, I couldn't have picked a better guy for my mom.

It's silent for a moment until my mom speaks. "Well, these presents aren't going to open themselves."

"Here." Nick throws a horribly wrapped, round object at me, and I immediately know what it is as I catch it mid-air.

"Gee, man, how did you know I needed a new basketball?" I ask sarcastically.

"You haven't even unwrapped it. For all you know, it could be a golf club," Nick protests.

"You're right. Let me just …" I rip the wrapping paper off, revealing an orange basketball. "Wow, what do you know? Definitely a step up from last year's gift, though." We all laugh.

"Sorry, I didn't have time to wrap this." Mark pulls out a solid black piece of luggage from under the table. "I'm told it's the best of its kind. It has an anti-theft lock and a charging outlet for your phone." He looks at my mom before continuing. "It ties in with your mom's gift."

"Here." My mom pushes a white envelope toward me.

I carefully open it and pull out a round-trip plane ticket to Australia. My eyes go wide in disbelief.

How did she know?

"I ran into Brian a few weeks ago. He mentioned going to Australia with some friends over winter break and that he has been trying to get you to go with them. I know money can be tight, but I don't want you to miss out on this opportunity with your friends," she says.

"Mom, this is too much. I can't—" I shake my head, but she cuts me off.

"No, it's not. I wanted to do this. You work so hard in school and at work and always take care of your brother and me. You deserve this, sweetie." Her big brown eyes mist over.

Without a second thought, I get up from my seat and hug her. "Thanks, mom. This is amazing." I look over at Mark. "And thanks, Mark, for everything. Really."

"Anytime, kid," he responds.

"Alright, what did I miss?" Uncle Harry asks as he enters the room.

"Uncle Harry!" Both Nick and I say simultaneously, excited to see our favorite and only uncle.

"Hey, you two! Nate, happy birthday! Get anything good?"

"Well, he got a basketball from me, luggage from Mark, and a plane ticket to Australia from mom," Nick chimes in. "So obviously, mine is the best gift so far."

"Clearly." Harry chuckles and sits next to Sheryl.

"Ok, everyone, there are still more gifts to open, food to be eaten, and cake to be cut into before this one goes off with his friends tonight. Oh, to be twenty-one again," Sheryl says then looks off, lost in thought.

"Earth to Sheryl." Harry waves his hands in front of her face.

"Sorry, I was just trying to remember what it was like to be young," Sheryl remarks.

"Oh, you'll always be young in my eyes, dear." Harry takes her hand and places a kiss on the back of it.

"That's because you're as blind as a bat, but I appreciate it just the same. Do you have Nate's gift with you?" she asks.

"Right, yes." Harry gets something out of his pocket and tosses a key across the table.

"What's this for?" I ask, picking up the gold key.

"It's the key to your boat," Harry responds.

"Funny. No, really, what is it?"

"I'm serious," Harry says matter-of-factly.

My jaw drops to the floor. "W-what? I don't understand."

"Well, Sheryl and I know how much you've always wanted one since you were a little kid. Of course, it's nothing fancy, but for your first boat, we thought it would do. We've been keeping it over at Mark's place."

I turn my head to Mark, who says, "Free of charge."

"You guys … I don't even know what to say." I examine the key in my hand, waiting for it to disappear like this is some kind of crazy dream. "Thank you."

Harry leans over to Nick with a big smile. "I still think your basketball is the clear favorite."

* * *

Pulling up in front of Tim's house a few hours later, I notice cars lining the street and taking up both sides of the road. Damn, this is way more people than I expected. I look down at the Superman costume I changed into at Sheryl and Harry's house and start feeling self-conscious.

Nothing a few shots won't fix.

I get out of my car and walk up to the front door that's wide open. As I enter the house, I see various costume choices and start feeling better about my own. There are people dressed as Marvel characters on one side of the big room. The whole cast of *Stranger Things* is on the other side. A group of girls who consider lingerie to be a Halloween costume are scattered throughout. And, per usual, there are the rebels who are wearing their everyday clothes.

The place is packed with people, half of whom I don't recognize. There's loud techno music blaring from a built-in surround sound system, and strobe lights are streaming in one half of the house. Overall, the place looks like a full-out rave, and I'll be surprised if the police don't show up before the end of the night.

"Hey, everyone, the birthday boy is here!" Tim walks over. He's dressed as a cowboy and carrying two drinks with him.

"Hey, man. This place is insane," I say as he hands me one of the drinks.

"I know, right? And look who was able to make it after all." Tim nudges his head toward the kitchen. "Brian, get over here!"

Brian turns, and the second he sees me, his whole face lights up. "Nate, my man! Raced here as soon as my game ended. Twenty-one to nothing, I'd like to add."

"Holy shit." I grin. Even though things have felt off since the last time I saw him, the man is still my best friend. It wouldn't feel right to celebrate my twenty-first birthday without him. And who knows, maybe tonight will help smooth things over between us. "Really glad you're here. And congratulations on the win."

"Fuck yeah! I wouldn't miss my best friend's twenty-first birthday!" His hand lands on my shoulder as he shouts over the deafening music. "Are you ready to get fucked up tonight?"

"Hell yeah, but first, you need to do something for me." I chug down the dark liquid in my cup, finishing the first of many drinks.

"What's that?" Brian looks confused.

"You need to go change."

"What's wrong with what I'm wearing?" he asks, looking down at his clothes, which consist of a dark pair of denim jeans and a fitted white T-shirt. *Not a Halloween costume.*

"Nothing, except for the fact that you told me this was a costume party, hence the Superman ensemble that I have somehow squeezed my body into." I use my hands to emphasize my outfit, making Brian laugh.

"Tsk. Tsk." Tim nods in agreement, looking Brian up and down.

"You're right. My bad." He gulps down his drink and throws it to the side after finishing. "I'll run home and see what I can find. Don't start getting shit-faced without me." He bulldozes his way through the crowd and out the front door at a record speed.

"I'll be right back," I say to Tim.

I begin to walk around, looking for the one person who will make this night even better. Natalie. And I don't plan on letting her out of my sight once I find her, especially after what happened last year. *Fuck.* I honestly don't know if I'll ever know what actually happened, but the memory alone is enough to make me nervous, and I don't want to take any chances, so I pull my phone out of my tight spandex pocket.

Me: Hey are you here?
Natalie: Sorry running late. Be there in five minutes!
Me: No worries beautiful. What costume are you wearing?
Natalie: It's a surprise.

"Nate!" I do a one-eighty and spot Paul making his way over to me among the mass of people. It's hard to miss him when his head almost touches the ceiling.

"Hey, Paul, glad you could make it." I reach my hand up to pat his shoulder, feeling ridiculously small next to him, which is a descriptor I rarely use for myself.

"Yeah, I hitched a ride with Brian. Wouldn't want to miss your big birthday festivities. Nice costume," he adds. "It suits you."

"Thanks. Your costume is …" I look him up and down, trying to figure out who he's supposed to be. "Well, actually, who are you?"

"Dude, I'm Jon Snow from *Game of Thrones*. Obviously." At almost seven feet tall, he stands with both hands on his hips, proudly displaying his costume. A faux fur cape hangs loosely around his broad shoulders, a fake black beard is taped to his face, and a plastic sword hangs from his basketball shorts.

Laughter fills me and I shake my head. "You don't look anything like Jon Snow."

"Why? Because I'm Black?" he asks, furrowing his eyebrows.

"No, because you're about three feet too tall."

Paul busts out laughing before punching me humorously in the shoulder. "Come on. Let's get you a drink. You need to get thoroughly plastered for your birthday."

"Trust me, I plan on it."

twenty-nine

NATALIE

A few hours ago, I was quickly picking through whatever was left at the Halloween costume store in town. Disappointment took over as costume after costume turned out to be a dud. Too small. Too big. Too weird. I was ready to walk out of the store empty-handed, and really, it was my fault for waiting until the very last minute. But then, thankfully, I found it. A costume that, when I tried it on and looked at myself in the mirror, made me feel something I've never felt before: unstoppable. However, standing on the front porch steps of Tim's house in this super tight, cleavage-revealing Wonder Woman suit, I now have so many anxious thoughts running through my mind.

Ugh. Here goes nothing.

After taking a deep breath and reminding myself that this party will be *nothing* like last year's, I walk through the front door and become engulfed in the blaring music. There are so many people crammed in this house that it will probably be impossible for me to find Nathan, so I pull out my phone.

Me: I'm here. Where are you?
Nathan: Kitchen sexy ;)

From his text, I assume he is probably already drunk or at least pretty buzzed.

I get to the kitchen and see Nathan standing with a few guys I don't recognize. As I approach him from behind, I notice the guys blatantly staring at me.

Do I have something in my teeth?

"Hi, birthday boy," I say as I tap him on the shoulder to steal his attention.

He turns around, laughing at whatever they are talking about, but his mouth hangs open when he sees me. "N-Natalie."

"Oh my God. I can't believe you are Superman, and I'm Wonder Woman." My eyes look over his costume, noticing how it shows off every perfectly sculpted muscle. "What are the odds?"

Nathan continues looking me up and down until finally clearing his throat and raking his hand through his hair. "Wow … you look …"

"Hey, man, aren't you going to introduce us?" The very tall guy wearing an oversized faux fur cape nudges Nathan. I'm pretty sure he is trying to look like a character from *Game of Thrones*, but I'm not sure which one.

"Yeah, umm …" Nathan looks at the group of guys and then back at me. "Natalie, this freakishly tall dork is Paul, and you might recognize these other three from the high school baseball team. This is Tim, Eric, and Danny. Guys, this is my girlfriend, Natalie."

"Hi," I say with a slight wave, and they all smile back sheepishly.

"Damn, Nate, how did you end up so lucky?" one of the baseball guys asks, making me instantly blush.

"Hey, guys, I'm going to make Natalie a drink. We'll meet you outside by the fire pit in a few minutes, ok?" None of them acknowledge his words but continue gawking at me, so Nathan emphasizes them. "Ok?"

"Oh yes, yes. Come on, guys. Let's make fire!" Paul shouts as he holds his drink high up to the sky. The four of them quickly go outside into the cold October air.

"Well, they seem nice," I note.

Nathan's dark brown eyes are studying me possessively, causing my breathing to escalate.

"What?" I ask in a whisper.

"Come with me." He grabs my hand, leading me through the house and down the basement stairs until we reach the laundry room. I stand against the washing machine, cramped in the corner of this small room, as Nathan quickly shuts and then locks the door in one swift motion before turning around to face me.

His eyes are intense, practically undressing me with each sweep over my body. My insides start going crazy, waiting for whatever is about to happen. But, before he steps toward me, he pulls down on a string beside him that's hanging from the ceiling, and the place goes dark. The only light in the room is from the full moon shining through the tiny window.

My heart is thundering in my chest, and I can feel his breath on me after he finally reaches me. His hands find my face, bringing his lips down on mine, devouring me. I wrap my hands around his neck, pulling him in closer, moaning into his mouth, letting him know I need more.

Nathan pulls away to bring his mouth down to my neck, kissing the spot where he can feel my pulse rapidly beating before licking the length up my neck.

"Do you have any idea how fucking sexy you look right now?" he practically growls, igniting an inferno within me.

His large hands circle my waist, lift me into the air and place me on the washing machine. A satisfying groan leaves him as he shimmies my blue spandex shorts down to my ankles and then lets them fall to the floor. He slides each knee-high boot off my feet and then stands up tall, coming back down on my lips as his hands start tugging at the bottom of my top, pushing it up over my stomach.

"Wait," I breathe, pulling away from his delicious lips.

He immediately removes his hands from my body, and I see concern flash over his face. "What's wrong? Is this a bad idea?"

"No. It's not that. I like this idea. Actually, I like this idea a lot." His lips turn into a wicked smile. "It's just that, well, what if someone walks in?" I ask as I look over and see how fragile the tiny chain on the door looks.

"No one will walk in here, baby." He stares tenderly down at me. His eyes dart off into the distance and then back to mine, except this time, they have a wanting in them I have never seen before. "I really need you. Every single part of you. Every beautiful inch of you." His finger traces the plunging neckline of my top, causing my breath to become shallow. "But I am not doing anything until you feel comfortable."

He looks around the room then steps over to the dryer, and after quickly unhooking the machine from the wall, he easily slides it so that it stands directly in front of the door, ensuring there's no possible way for anyone to enter.

My mouth opens in shock. I know Nathan works out and has a physically demanding job, but I've never seen that kind of strength before. He moved that dryer like it weighed nothing. *Absolutely nothing.* And I'm left staring at his solid biceps, realizing they are stretching the fabric thin on his costume.

"What?" he asks, observing my face.

"Nothing." I try to compose myself. "You just made that look really … easy."

He takes a few steps to stand directly in front of me. His index finger gently lifts my chin, so our eyes lock, and he asks, "Do you feel more comfortable now?"

"Y-yes," I say as his hands grip the tops of my thighs, eagerly pushing my legs apart. He bends down, becoming eye level with me, only inches away from my face.

His finger starts delicately tracing a line up the inside of my thigh, creating an instant pulse between my legs. "How about now?" he asks, never breaking eye contact.

"Mhm," is all I can get out as my heart pounds in my chest. *Does he know what he is doing to me?*

"And now?" he asks in a whisper next to my ear at the exact moment his finger plunges inside me.

If he didn't know how much I wanted him before, there was no way of hiding it now.

"Oh God, Nathan," I moan. Instinctively, I wrap my arms around his neck, holding onto him for support. One of his hands is positioned on my lower back, holding me firmly in place, and his other hand continues to apply pressure to all the right spots. Over and over again.

His lips glide greedily down my neck in soft kisses.

"Feel good?" he asks.

Yes. Yes. Yes.

I shake my head up and down adamantly, biting my lower lip so as not to scream out when a second finger enters me, and his thumb finds the exact spot that sends me so close to the edge.

"Please don't stop," I whisper in his ear as I feel the buildup of pressure. "I'm so close."

"But I have to." He removes his hand from me and stands up straight, towering over me.

My body shakes in frustration, begging for him to keep touching me.

NO!

"Why'd you stop?" I pant pleadingly.

"Because I need to taste you."

Oh. My. God.

"Oh, fuck me." My hands cover my mouth in complete shock. *I did not just say that out loud, right?*

"Oh, I plan on doing just that," he says. "But first." He pulls at the end of my top and starts lifting it over my head. "We need to take care of this." With one motion, my shirt is off and tossed to the floor. "And next." His hands find the front clasp on my bra. One flick of his fingers, and it comes undone. I watch his fingers slide up the cup's edge, over each breast, and under the straps until they glide down my arms and off my body.

"Natalie." He stares at me, looking lost in his head. "The word beautiful isn't enough to describe you right now." My cheeks give away my embarrassment, which causes Nathan to smile. "I love it when you blush." His hand caresses my cheek, and he bends down to kiss me softly, but as his hips press against me, I can feel him. *All of him*. His arousal informs me how much he wants me.

I put my hands on his chest, still covered by his costume, and break our kiss. "I don't think it's fair that I'm sitting completely naked on a washing machine while you are fully clothed."

"You're right. Let me take care of that." He reaches behind and removes the red cape before pulling down on a zipper. Within seconds he is standing in front of me, wearing absolutely nothing. "Better?"

"Much better," I retort as I find it almost impossible to take my eyes away from *him*. Seeing how hard he is for me is the biggest turn on, and I can feel every part of me wanting this man.

Every. Single. Part.

He runs his hand through his hair. "God, I don't know how long I'm going to last, Natalie. You have no idea what you're doing to me right now."

His dark eyes gaze down at my body, while his hands cup each of my breasts. I shiver as his thumbs start making little circles over my nipples, exposing how turned on I am. He lowers his head to take my breast in his mouth, and that's when his tongue replaces his thumb and starts making the same circles but even faster this time. I lean back and close my eyes, enjoying every second his tongue dominates me, creating an immediate throbbing between my legs.

But after only a moment, he pulls away, causing my eyes to open. *Will this torture ever end?*

"Ok, now where were we before? Oh, right." A mischievous grin appears on his face as he kneels on the floor and places both hands on my thighs, parting my legs so he can see all of me. His eyes look starved, like a man lost in the desert seeing water for the first time in too long. He licks his bottom lip and then lowers them to my skin, kissing a perfectly straight line to his target area.

"Wait," I say as I place my hand on his head. "It's *your* birthday. I should be—"

"No." He shakes his head. His eyes burn into mine, and his hands move up, gripping my waist. "All I want for my birthday is you." He pauses before emphasizing, "More specifically, I want you coming all over my tongue." And with that, he dips his head between my legs where his tongue starts its sensual assault.

I grab a handful of his soft hair and moan out his name, unable to hold it in. It feels so good. Too good. Almost too much for me to handle.

I start twisting away, but his hands press firmly down on my legs, pinning me to the washing machine, while he consumes me. I try to find something to hold onto, but there's nothing in arm's reach, so I grip his shoulders as his tongue continually strikes against me.

Damn him and his incredible tongue.

That familiar pressure between my legs starts building, and I don't know how much more I can take as I shamelessly ride his face.

"Nathan … I'm so close …"

Suddenly, his lips move to the top of my slit, sucking on my most sensitive spot at the exact instant two fingers shove inside me, and I'm a goner.

Figuratively and mentally gone as everything around me starts fading away.

I'm breathing hard, gasping for air, and holding onto the edge of the washing machine for dear life.

My whole body shudders as I lightly try to push his head away, unable to take any more of his tongue's thrashings.

He pulls his mouth away from me and quickly stands up, licking his lips with an appreciative groan. "Now, that was the best birthday present anyone has ever given me. So fucking delicious, Natalie. But we're not done yet."

Nathan bends down, reaches for his costume on the floor, and pulls out a condom from the pocket. My glossy eyes can't seem to look away as he hastily tears the wrapper and places the condom on himself, stretching it over every hard inch.

"Ready, beautiful?"

I shake my head up and down, and that's all it takes for him to enter me. I call out his name and am about to fall back, but he catches me in his arms.

"I've got you," he breathes.

Our lips meet feverishly. The need we both have for each other at this moment is undeniable.

I dig my nails into his back as the pleasurable pressure returns, and each thrust becomes harder and faster. My legs start shaking, and Nathan can feel my back arching in his hands.

"You feel so fucking good," he rasps between each thrust, driving my ass across the smooth surface and right up against the control panel.

Ding. What was that? But I don't need to wonder for long because the washing machine begins to shudder beneath me.

"I think the washing machine just turned on," I pant.

Nathan looks behind me, and a playful grin forms on his face. "Let's use it to our advantage then." He reaches for the panel, turning a knob as far as it will go.

A moment later, the whole machine steadily shakes beneath me, vibrating every square inch of my body. He turned the spin setting on high.

"Nathan …" I whimper, squirming beneath him.

"Look at you, baby. Taking it like such a good girl." His thrusts get deeper. The vibrations get stronger. And my body is on the edge of shattering.

I can feel the orgasm looming as my body tenses in his arms. Leaning my head back, I close my eyes, waiting for the all-consuming pleasure.

"Together, beautiful," he groans, giving one final thrust, sending me into oblivion. He holds my trembling body securely against his chest, both of us finishing at the same time.

Nathan's heart, thundering in his chest, mirrors my own.

He reaches for the power button on the machine to shut it off, probably after noticing how drained I feel while I cling to his body for support.

A few silent minutes pass as we both hold onto each other. Nathan rests his head on my shoulder, catching his breath, while I bury my head into his chest, cherishing this feeling of pure ecstasy.

"I don't know what I would do without you tonight," he says into my neck.

His words make me smile, and I hold onto him tighter, if that's even possible.

"Unfortunately, we should probably get going before anyone starts looking for us." Nathan lets out a deep sigh, kisses my forehead, and separates from me.

My body instantly craves him.

"I suppose you're right," I respond.

Nathan bends down to pick up his costume and puts it on before helping me with mine. Every piece of my outfit is scattered on the floor around us. He hands me my bra and top first then takes each of my legs and steps them inside my spandex shorts. He finishes by sliding my boots on each foot. Once again, he moves the dryer, putting it in place before turning back and lifting me off the washing machine with ease.

When my feet hit the ground, I realize my legs feel like Jell-O, so I reach out to him for support. "I don't think I'll be able to walk straight."

Nathan gives an arrogant little smirk. The man is proud of himself, and honestly … he should be. "Don't worry. I'm not letting you out of my sight tonight." His lips land softly on my forehead, and his hand intertwines with mine, leading us out of the laundry room.

When we walk out of the basement, I notice that everyone at this party is too wrapped up in their own worlds to notice that we were missing.

"Let's get you a proper drink," Nathan suggests as we enter the kitchen. He starts rummaging in the fridge and comes out with his arms full of different liquors.

"That sounds great to me. I'm pretty thirsty."

I watch as he starts pouring different liquors into a cup and swirls them around. Proud of his concoction, he hands me the drink and waits for my reaction as I take a sip.

"Oh wow, this is really good." Half of my drink is gone within seconds.

"Whoa, slow down, Wonder Woman. I don't want to have to carry you out of here." Nathan laughs.

"Make me another?" I ask as I hand him my empty cup.

"I don't know if I should be turned on or disturbed at how fast you just drank that." He begins to make another drink and hands it over, which produces a big smile from me.

This feeling of … well, I can't put my finger on it, but it feels almost painfully too good to be true.

Nathan is the best thing that has ever happened to me.

"Want to head outside to the fire pit to see where the guys went?" Nathan asks.

"Sure—" My body freezes.

He's not supposed to be here. Nathan said he wouldn't be here.

Quickly, I'm overtaken with a shudder that has my heart beating in a state of panic. My palms become clammy, and my mind races. It's always the same physical reaction to his presence.

Oh, God, no. No. No. No.

"What's wrong, Natalie?" Nathan asks, staring into my eyes. He follows my gaze and sees Brian enter the kitchen.

"Hey, man, I've been looking for you for like twenty minutes," Brian says as he walks in. "This was all I could find to wear. Hope it passes your approval."

Nathan stares at what Brian is wearing.

A football jersey. *Brian's football jersey.* The football jersey I wore when running out of Brian's house last year.

"That football jersey … I've seen it before." Nathan looks like he is trying to remember something.

"Yeah, dude, it's my old football jersey from high school. Can't believe it still fits me," he says, looking down at himself. "Well, it's a little tight, but at least I still look good, right?" An obnoxiously loud chuckle leaves his mouth.

Nathan turns his face to look back at me. There is anger in his eyes like I've never seen before, which heightens my panic.

He knows. But how?

He turns his attention back to Brian and takes two steps closer to him, keeping me behind him as his hands hang by his sides, clenched into giant fists.

"That's your jersey?" he asks Brian, anger radiating in his voice.

"Yes, why? Are you ok, Nate? You look a little pale." Brian furrows his brows in confusion.

"It was you," Nathan says softly like he's lost in a memory.

"What?" Brian asks, now looking around Nathan and right at me. His steely eyes find mine, and I swear my heart has stopped beating.

Nathan stays silent for far too long, and all I can do is wait as the realization hits him like a ton of bricks. "You son of a bitch!" Nathan swings at Brian, pounding his fist hard into the side of Brian's head.

Brian stumbles backward, shaking his head before his eyes go wide, and he pushes Nathan forcefully against the counter. Nathan's body then crashes into mine, sending me to the ground, thus spilling my drink all over myself.

"What the fuck?" Brian roars.

People start crowding around the kitchen to see what's causing the commotion. I get up from the floor as Brian and Nathan continue to go at it like two lions fighting over their place at the head of the pack.

"S-STOP!" I try to yell loud enough over the cheers from the spectators, but it's pointless.

Nathan slams Brian hard against the fridge, shifting it out of place. "She's not your fucking type?! You fucking liar!" Nathan screams, sending another fist to the other side of Brian's head.

"She wanted it!" Brian shouts back. "And don't let her tell you otherwise." He swings his arm right into Nathan's stomach, causing him to lose his breath as he smashes into the counter.

Nathan stands up, and the fury displayed on his face is

terrifying. His eyes are bloodshot, his lips are bleeding, his hands are still clenched into fists, and his body is convulsing. He goes in fast toward Brian and knocks him hard against the wall attempting to bring his hands up to Brian's neck. But before he succeeds, Paul and a few other guys come running in from around the corner, pulling Nathan off of him.

"Whoa, whoa, guys, what's going on?" Paul squeezes between them and puts both arms up.

It takes two guys to hold back Brian as he and Nathan separate. They are both standing there, breathing hard and fast. The adrenaline and testosterone running through their bodies are clearly evident.

"I don't fucking know. Why don't you ask that slut over there!" Brian yells, pointing at me, which causes all eyes in the room to land on me. Nathan is silent. Stone-like even. He leaves his back in my line of vision. Finally, Brian pushes everyone's arms off him and storms out of the kitchen. "I'm out of here! Happy fucking birthday!" The front door slams shut, indicating Brian's left. *Thank God.*

I can feel everyone's judgmental eyes on me. Everyone except for Nathan, who continues to keep his back toward me. An unnerving silence surrounds us, even with the deafening music still playing.

After what feels like an eternity, Nathan finally speaks. But there's a vehemence reverberating in his throat that frightens me. "I asked you if anything happened between the two of you."

I nod, unable to find any words. I lied to him. And it's my fault that everything just went down like this. My eyes are brimming with tears, but I hold them back, not wanting to cry in front of all these people I don't know.

And then, Nathan turns around, facing me. His eyes pierce my skin like daggers.

"You fucking lied to me, Natalie!" Nathan shouts as he slams his fist onto the counter beside him. Paul is still keeping a solid hand pressed up against Nathan's chest.

"I know." I look down at the ground finding it hard to breathe. "I'm so sorry."

"You're sorry?" He scoffs at me. "You hooked up with my best friend and didn't even have the nerve to tell me! How can I trust you if you deliberately lie to me?"

I can no longer hold back the tears as they escape one by one down my cheek. But wait … *what did he say*? I realize from his words that he doesn't actually know what happened between Brian and me. He doesn't grasp at all what happened to me that night or what has caused me to have nightmares for so many sleepless nights. He only *thinks* he knows. But maybe if I could just explain everything to him as I should have so long ago, he would understand. "It's … it's not what you think, Nathan," I manage to say through sobs.

"Then tell me, Natalie! Tell me right fucking now because this is not how I planned on spending my birthday," he roars.

I look around to see even more sneering faces. I have become a source of entertainment for everyone at this party. My body is telling me to run, but my feet feel super-glued to the floor.

"Not here," I whisper, not even sure Nathan can hear me.

"I don't believe this." Nathan turns around, no longer facing me. And I can feel an invisible weight lift from my body, but it immediately returns as he turns back around. "You even told me you were a virgin. And I stupidly believed you." He stares at me coldly, and from the corner of my eye, I see Paul look down at the ground, knowing that his friend has just crossed a line.

And just like that, my heart sinks like the Titanic — fast and violently grim — to the very bottom of a deep abyss. Before I have time to notice the new stares coming my way, I run. And don't look back.

The cold air whips across my exposed skin as I make my way to the end of the road, wishing I hadn't left my coat at home. My pace slows as I walk for another five minutes, thankful that no one drives by me to witness the mess that I am.

Deep breaths, Natalie. You're almost home.

But as I turn onto my street, feeling relief at the sight of my house, I'm pulled forcefully from behind and shoved painfully to the ground.

"Where the fuck do you think you're going?" I hear the snarl and look up to find Brian leering down at me. An unrecognizable *monster*. One of his eyes is practically swollen shut. Patches of black and blue skin surround it. Dry blood trails down his face, and his bottom lip is split down the middle. His only good eye is bloodshot, telling me he's intoxicated or on something. Or both.

"Br-Brian," I stutter, barely able to breathe.

"Aww, are you scared, Natalie?" He reveals an evil smile. "You should be."

I try to crawl away from him. My fingers dig into the dirt beneath me, but he keeps stepping closer.

"Brian, please … please stop. You don't need to do this," I beg with tears streaming down my face.

"Oh, Natalie. We wouldn't have a problem if you had just kept your fucking mouth shut." He shakes his head from side to side as if disappointed in me.

"I di-didn't say anything. I swear."

"Oh really? That's funny because Nathan's fist to my face tonight tells me otherwise." He brings his hand up to his head and wipes away the dry blood.

"I promise. I promise I didn't say anything," I plead, knowing my words mean nothing.

Brian starts laughing, like really laughing. And I'm scared out of my mind. "I don't understand. All you had to do last year was let me fuck you. But instead, you made everything into a bigger deal than it needed to be. You denied me. And no one denies me, Natalie. Especially not you. An entitled bitch with a stick up her ass."

Sobs take over me. There's no reasoning with him. I know this all too well.

"Why?" he asks.

"Wh-why what?" A crunching noise, almost like someone walking on leaves, catches my attention, causing me to look around, hoping to spot anyone for help, but we're alone.

"Why, Nate?" He looks menacingly into my eyes.

And it hits me. Brian is jealous of Nathan. He doesn't understand why I chose Nathan over him. It is all finally making sense. Nathan has what Brian wants and will never be able to have. *Me.*

"Why?" he bellows.

"Because it's always been him," I choke out my confession, staring right back at him, unwavering.

He looks up at the night sky. "It could have been me."

"No," I say sternly. "No, it couldn't have been because you are nothing like him. And no matter how hard you try, you will never be like him."

This revelation pisses Brian off.

He takes another step toward me, sickeningly eyeing my body. "Always dressed like a slut, aren't you, Natalie? Didn't you learn anything after last year?" He takes another step, and I start crawling back until I'm directly against a tree and have nowhere to go. "You know, I remember so clearly what you looked like on my bed. I think about it all the time. Those perfectly round—"

"I'll tell him. I-I will. You take one more step, and I'll t-tell him everything." I try my hardest to sound brave. Not scared in the least, but it's useless. My body is trembling as my words come out shaky through hysterical sobs.

"Go ahead. Who do you think he'll believe? You, the girl he just started fucking? Or me, his best friend? Please, go tell him. It will be so satisfying to watch." He laughs mockingly.

I look down, defeated. *He's right.* Brian is Nathan's best friend. The whole reason why I tried to stay away from Nathan in the first place was because of this. So scared that Brian would find a way to get what he wanted. *Me.* This is my fault.

"God, the only thing I regret is that I didn't fuck you," he growls. "You had to go and kick me right in the balls, Natalie, didn't you? Can't say I saw that coming. Didn't know you had a fight in you." He shakes his head adamantly from side to side. "But don't you see? All that did was piss me off." His beady green eyes narrow. "But I won't make the same mistake of letting you get away this time."

I freeze. Flashbacks come back to me like I'm living déjà vu. "Please … don't."

"You put one hand on her, Brian, and I swear to God, I'll fucking kill you."

thirty

NATHAN

Everyone around me is staring as I stand in the kitchen breathing hard and erratically, trying to wrap my head around what just happened.

Natalie and Brian.

I can't believe it, and I don't want to believe it.

Brian, my best friend of so many years.

And Natalie. Well, my feelings for Natalie aren't something I've ever experienced before. Just the thought of her gets my heart racing like an idiot. Never mind how insanely hard my dick gets.

But the thought of the two of them together makes me nauseous.

Did he touch her the same way I do? Did she moan out his name in pleasure the same way she says mine? Did she fall asleep with his arm wrapped around her slender body? Did she kiss him the way she kisses me? Like each kiss could be our last.

Fuck. I lean over the sink, feeling like I'm about to hurl at any second.

"Ok, everyone, the show is over," Tim yells at the crowd in the kitchen. Once they all disperse to enjoy the party again, he turns to face me. "I'll be right back. Going to look for a bandage for that pretty face of yours." He pushes through a group of people and disappears up the stairs.

"Care to explain to me what just happened?" Paul grabs a frozen bag of vegetables from the freezer and throws it at me. I catch it and bring it up to my busted lip. "One minute I'm enjoying an ice cold beer out by the fire with a beautiful girl sitting on my lap. I mean a *beautiful* girl, and then the next thing I know, I hear people cheering on a fight. Not in a million years did I think I would be coming into this house to break up a fight between you and Brian." He raises his eyebrows for dramatic effect, but it's hard for me to take him seriously in his ridiculous costume.

I look down at the spatters of blood on my costume and shake my head in disgust. "Brian and Natalie." Saying their names out loud together makes my stomach churn all over again.

"What about Brian and Natalie?" Paul asks, confused.

"Something happened between them. A year ago." I run my hand through my hair and close my eyes. I feel overwhelmed by everything.

"How do you know?" he asks.

"I just know." Flashbacks from that night begin to haunt me. Images I had continually tried to forget. But now, I can't stop them from appearing. I see Natalie lying motionless against a tree. Blood is dripping down her face, falling onto the fresh white snow. I yell for her as my legs move faster than they ever have before. I kneel beside her and shake her shoulders, yelling for her to wake up as terror fills me. She mumbles softly when I wrap my jacket around her and lift her in my arms. Within a minute, an ambulance pulls up. I watch in fear as they drive away with the girl I love. And as they turn the corner, a greater fear grips me.

The fear of never telling the girl you love that you love her.

But for the first time, I re-watch this scene in my head and realize she was wearing Brian's football jersey. Why hadn't I recognized it at the time? But more importantly, why was Natalie bleeding? I remember her mumbling to the paramedics that she slipped on ice, but something didn't feel right about her words then, and they don't feel right now. They felt untrue, but why would she have lied?

"Nate, man." Paul leans against the counter next to me. "You know Brian sleeps with anything that has a pulse. That's how he's always been." He puts his hand on my shoulder. "And if we're being honest, it's not like you're some kind of saint yourself."

"Don't remind me." I scowl. I get it. I've hooked up with more girls than I care to admit.

Paul sighs before calmly saying, "The past is the past. You can't be mad at both of them for something they did before she even started seeing you."

"Point taken, but it makes my blood boil just to think about it." I can't get the image of the two of them together out of my mind, and it's killing me. *Someone please end my misery.*

"Well then, don't think about it," Paul says with a slight shrug. "And Nate, I hate to break it to you, but you are never going to find a girl like Natalie again."

"I know." Fuck, do I know this.

"And I don't know, man, but there was something in Natalie's eyes. The way she looked at you tonight before the WWE smackdown in the kitchen, it was like you were the only one in the whole house she had eyes for. And Natalie doesn't seem stupid to me. She isn't about to mess up what you guys have for a real asshole like Brian," Paul says. I look at him, surprised. "Hey, the guy may be our friend, but you know just as well as I do how much of an asshole he can be. But for whatever reason, we're all still friends with him."

"Yeah, I know, but why wouldn't she have told me about her and Brian? I thought she knew she could tell me anything, especially after I told her about my ..." But I stop myself, not wanting to bring my father into the mix. "I don't know. Something doesn't feel right." I look around the place, noticing so many unfamiliar faces enjoying the party. "And why wouldn't Brian have said anything to me? We all know he likes to brag about every girl he's ever been with. So, what makes Natalie different?"

"I don't know." Paul removes his hand from my shoulder and picks up the beer sitting next to him. "Did Brian maybe have feelings for Natalie?"

"Not that I know of. Actually, he talked shit about her the last time I saw him. Really fucking pissed me off."

"Maybe he's just jealous that you're hitting that and not him." Paul shrugs, and I give him a death stare. "Whoa, I'm just stating a fact."

I bring a beer to my lips and take a refreshing sip. The cold liquid on my swollen mouth is soothing. "I don't know. Maybe." I stand there silently, contemplating what I am about to say aloud for the first time about any girl. Ever. "The thing is … I love her."

Paul spits his drink out of his mouth. "Did I just hear you correctly?"

"Yeah, you did. I have for a very long time. Just never had it in me to tell her."

"Well then, I suggest you go after your Wonder Woman and talk to her before it's too late," Paul says.

"You're right. Shit! I can't believe what I said to her and in front of everyone." I throw the bag of vegetables against the wall. "Was it as bad as I remember?"

"I mean," Paul scrubs his hand over his jaw before continuing, "you probably shouldn't have mentioned the whole virginity thing in a house full of people."

I cover my face with my hands in remorse. Those words jumped off my tongue before I could stop them. "If I were her, I would never want to see me, let alone talk to me, again."

"Yeah, but thankfully, she's not you." Paul gives a hopeful smile.

"I need to go find her."

"Give me your keys." I give him a quizzical look. "I've mostly been drinking water the whole night. How do you think I keep this physique in such good shape for the ladies?

"Oh, jeez. Let's go, ladies' man." I give a slight eye roll.

We hop in my car and start driving toward Natalie's home, where I'm guessing she went.

"Do you think she'll forgive me?" I ask Paul, looking out the window and wondering how badly I fucked things up between us.

"I guess you're about to find out," Paul responds, turning down Natalie's street.

"Stop!" I yell, causing Paul to slam on the breaks. I put my face right up against the glass to get a better look at the dark figure lurking in the woods. "Is that … Brian?"

"Oh shit," Paul remarks, seeing the shadowy figure outlined on the edge of the woods. "And is that Natalie on the ground?"

"Fuck!" I reach for the door handle.

Paul presses his arm against my chest, stopping me from getting out of the car. "Wait, man. He doesn't see us from this angle. Go stand behind that tree and see if you can hear them and figure out what's going on. I'll move the car down the street."

I can't wait another second. Natalie is in trouble, and this is all my fucking fault. I jump out of the car and quietly stand behind a tree out of sight. Then, pulling my phone out of my pocket, I hit record and wait.

"Oh, Natalie. We wouldn't have a problem if you had just kept your fucking mouth shut," I hear Brian growl at her.

What the hell is going on?

"I di-didn't say anything. I swear." Natalie's voice comes out sounding so small. Frightened.

"Oh really? That's funny because Nathan's fist to my face tonight tells me otherwise." I see Brian wiping at the blood near his eye. It looks like I messed him up pretty badly. Good.

"I promise. I promise I didn't say anything," Natalie pleads.

Didn't say what?

"I don't understand. All you had to do last year was let me fuck you. But instead, you made everything into a bigger deal than it needed to be. You denied me. And no one denies me, Natalie. Especially not you. An entitled bitch with a stick up her ass."

What the fuck did Brian do to her!?

It takes everything in me to keep my feet planted on the ground when all I want to do is wring Brian's burly neck.

"Why?" he asks.

"Wh-why what?" Her voice quivers, breaking my heart.

Paul quietly walks up behind me. He sees my phone in my hand and immediately knows what I'm doing.

"Why, Nate?" The longer Brian stares down at Natalie, the more rage consumes me.

Natalie remains silent as tears rain down her innocent face.

"Why?" he bellows.

"Because it's always been him," she chokes out through a sob.

Oh, Natalie.

"It could have been me," Brian responds dryly.

This fucker is jealous.

Paul looks at me with an *I told you so* face.

"No," she says harshly. She takes a couple of deep breaths, shaking her head adamantly before continuing. "No, it couldn't have been because you are nothing like him. And no matter how hard you try, you will *never* be like him."

This doesn't make Brian happy. I can see it in how his knuckles tighten by his side, virtually turning pure white.

He steps toward her, eyeing her disgustingly, and every second of this is torturesome to watch.

I won't let anything happen to her.

I won't let him hurt her.

I won't give the motherfucker a chance to lay one finger on her.

"Always dressed like a slut, aren't you, Natalie? Didn't you learn anything after last year?" He takes another step, and the second she crawls back against the tree with nowhere else to go, I move to jump in, but Paul pulls down on my arm, making me wait. "You know, I remember so clearly what you looked like on my bed. I think about it all the time. Those perfectly round—"

"I'll tell him. I-I will. You take one more step, and I'll t-tell him everything." Natalie's words come out trembling. Her whole body is shivering from the cold and fear.

"Go ahead. Who do you think he'll believe? You, the girl he just started fucking? Or me, his best friend? Please, go tell him. It will be so satisfying to watch." He laughs with a vengeance as he sneers down at her.

I don't know this monster.

"What the fuck?" Paul whispers.

My eyes don't move from Natalie. I watch as she wraps her arms around her legs, and her head drops down in complete defeat. There's no way she can believe him, right?

"God, the only thing I regret is that I didn't fuck you," he growls. "You had to go and kick me right in the balls, Natalie, didn't you? Can't say I saw that coming. Didn't know you had a fight in you." He shakes his head adamantly from side to side. "But don't you see? All that did was piss me off." He pauses before continuing. "But I won't make the same mistake of letting you get away this time."

Natalie's face turns as white as a ghost when she looks up at him. "Please … don't."

Enough!

I have more than enough evidence against him, and besides, I can't take one more goddamn second of this.

"You put one hand on her, Brian, and I swear to God, I'll fucking kill you," I roar, stepping into view.

Brian's head whips around, eyes wide like a deer caught in headlights. *Busted.*

"Nate … I … I told you she was a slut. She came running after me, begging for more, and I told her—"

"Enough, Brian! I heard the whole fucking thing! Every fucking word!"

Brian's face shows no emotion until, after a few seconds, he slowly nods in understanding. There's no point in lying anymore. "Ah, well, what can I say? Guess she is my type."

I have to fight the impulse not to beat that smug grin off his face. Not while Natalie is here, at least.

"Natalie, please come here, baby." Natalie scurries off the ground and is over by my side in seconds, pressing her beautiful tear-stained face into my chest. She's shaking uncontrollably, and I kiss her forehead with force before walking her over to Paul. "Can you please put Natalie in the back of my car to get warm? I need to finish this," I say calmly, not wanting to scare Natalie with how I am really feeling at this moment.

Like a man about to kill another man.

"Of course," Paul responds.

I look down into Natalie's iridescent eyes and see nothing but sadness. "I'll be right back for you, I promise." The tears continue to stream down her cheeks, but she nods in understanding.

Paul eyes Brian. "You're dead to me." Then he takes his coat off and wraps it around Natalie before walking her to my car.

Turning to face Brian, fury overtakes me. "Well, do you have anything to say?"

"Like you said, you heard it all." He crosses his arms over his chest. "What more is there for me to say?"

"We grew up with her. You should have been someone she felt safe with. Someone she could trust." I shake my head, disappointed in the man standing before me. The man I now realize I don't know at all.

"What do you want me to say, Nate? That I was jealous of you?" He throws his hands up in the air wildly, anger evidently stirring inside him. "Fine. I was fucking jealous of you."

"Jealous of what?"

"The way that girl looked at you like you were the goddamn greatest thing to ever happen to her. Never once did she look at me like that. And I wanted it."

"Jesus, Brian. So what? You couldn't take no for an answer?" I step closer to him, bending down to get aggressively in his face.

"Guess not." He smiles wickedly.

"God, you're fucked up, Brian." I glance away from his beady eyes, trying to rein in the rage inside me before looking back at him. "And this friendship ... it's over. I'm *done* with you. I don't ever want to see your fucking face again. Do you understand me?"

His eyes go wide in shock at my harsh words. "You're really

going to end our friendship over that whore?"

All I see is red.

My fist finds his face so fast that he doesn't have time to see it coming. Fresh blood pours out of his nose as his body slams onto the cold ground. I keep him pressed firmly down with my body, and my hands wrap forcefully around his neck, crushing his windpipe. "The only thing I have left to say to you is if you ever go near Natalie, talk about her, or even think about her again, I will kill you. Life in prison? I would gladly serve the time. Because I would die for that girl, and I will be damned if I ever let you hurt her again. Oh, and as an extra precaution, I recorded the *whole* conversation you just had with Natalie. So, if she decides to press charges, that's up to her. But I'm warning you: one slip up on your part, and that recording will find its way to the police, fucking ending you. For good."

I release my hands, noticing the bruising already forming on Brian's neck as he gasps for air. He looks like a fish out of water as he brings his hands up to his beefy throat. With fists shaking by my sides, I resist the urge to pound the living shit out of him, straighten back up, and walk to my car.

Because if I don't walk away now, I might actually kill him.

Opening the back door, I find Natalie wrapped in Paul's jacket like it's a giant blanket. Sliding in beside her, I'm overcome by the heat Paul has turned on full blast, probably trying to keep Natalie warm.

"Nathan," she whispers.

"I'm here, baby." I wrap her up in my arms, holding onto her for dear life. She's still shaking, even with how warm it is in here, so I lift her onto my lap. "I'm so sorry for everything. God, I really fucked up, Natalie."

Slowly, she shakes her head. "I-I ne-need to tell you everything."

"Ok, beautiful, but let's get you home first. I think a hot shower would do us both some good. How does that sound?"

She nods in agreement and then nuzzles into my chest, closing her eyes. I keep one arm tightly wrapped around her waist while the other drapes securely around her legs.

Making eye contact with Paul in the rearview mirror, I nod to let him know we're ready to go home.

thirty-One

NATALIE

"I'm going to take care of you, ok?"

Nathan's looking down at me like I'm a piece of glass ready to shatter at any minute as his hands lightly cup both sides of my face. I'm feeling emotionally and physically exhausted from tonight, so without hesitation, I say, "Ok."

We both stand outside the walk-in shower as he fidgets with the knobs to get the water to the perfect temperature. Scalding hot, just the way I like it.

My parents left this evening to spend a few nights at their house in the Cape, and Jason is staying over at Grace's house, leaving just Nathan and me alone. Well, almost alone. Paul is currently passed out and snoring noisily in one of the guest rooms at the end of the hall.

I like Paul. He's a big guy with a soft center, reminding me of a giant teddy bear you just want to hug.

Nathan strips himself from his costume, revealing every newly formed bruise and cut on his body, and tosses it to the side before turning to look at me. He waits for my approval, so I nod. Then his hands pull off the top of my outfit, along with my bra, before he kneels to remove my boots and spandex shorts. When he stands up, his eyes narrow in on my arm, and he grips me there gently. I look down and notice a deep black and blue mark on my skin caused by Brian grabbing me forcefully before throwing me down to the ground. My eyes move up to Nathan, who is barely able to control his fury.

His voice comes out rough. "You won't ever have to fear him again, Natalie. If that asshole even gets within ten feet of you, I will kill him."

His threat is a *promise* to me. A promise I know he will never break.

And it's at this very moment that I try so hard to think of the reason why I never told Nathan the truth in the first place. But I can't. This man loves me. And, no, he has never said those three words to me, but he doesn't have to because I feel it with every bone in my body.

He. Loves. Me.

"Don't cry, beautiful. It breaks my heart." His hands come up to my face, wiping away the tears from my cheeks with his thumbs. Tears I didn't even know were falling until now.

He steps into the shower and holds his hand out for me to take and follow him in. The hot water raining down on my back instantly relieves my achy muscles, and slowly I feel the tension radiating off my shoulders. Nathan reaches down for the bottle of body wash that sits on the shelf. Flicking the cap open, he inhales the heavenly aroma of peaches and apples and smiles.

"Now I know why you always smell so delicious."

He pours the body wash onto his hands, rubbing them together before lathering it all over my skin, even getting on his knees to scrub the dirt off my legs. Taking the bottle from him, without saying a word, I lather his body, washing away the dried blood on his skin until he is spotless.

Next, Nathan washes my hair, massaging the products into my scalp before rinsing them out, leaving me feeling completely clean from head to toe. He looks me up and down, inspecting his work to make sure he didn't miss anything. I get the feeling he had been trying to wash away every trace of tonight, knowing it won't be as easy to fix what can't be seen.

Physically, I look the same. But mentally, I'm not.

Pressing my face into his chest, I say, "Thank you."

His long arms wrap around my waist, pulling me in closer. He strokes my wet hair before saying, "Let's dry you off and get into bed."

"That sounds good to me," I respond, holding him a little tighter, not ready to let go because I know that when I do, it will finally be time to tell him *everything.*

But first, there is something I need to tell him that I should have told him years ago. Three little words that have been patiently waiting for their moment.

I love you.

* * *

I walk out of the bathroom wearing one of Nathan's oversized T-shirts and find him sitting in my bed, positioned with his back against the headboard, and wearing only a pair of black boxer briefs. He lifts the blanket and pats the space between his legs, motioning for me to join him. And I do.

My back melts into the contours of his chest as my head fits comfortably against his broad shoulder. He gathers the blankets around us and then brings his arms under the blankets to conceal me in his warmth.

I could be so content staying exactly like this forever.

Nathan doesn't say anything. He doesn't push me. He just waits. And after a few minutes of silence, I decide it's time.

"Nathan, *before I tell you* … everything, there is something I should have said to you a long time ago." My heart begins to beat rapidly, but there's no turning back now, and even if I could, I don't want to. "I've felt this way for a while, probably longer than I care to admit. And for so long, I was scared at the thought of saying these words out loud, not knowing how you would feel, so I kept them locked up. But I'm not … I'm not scared anymore." I realize I'm rambling, so I turn my body a little so that I can look into his eyes before saying, "I guess what I'm trying to say is that I—"

"I love you, Natalie."

I'm stunned into momentary silence as relief begins sweeping over me. "You do?"

"I do." He brushes my hair back behind my ear. "I'm sorry to cut you off, but there was no way I was letting you say it first." His hand lightly caresses my cheek. "From the moment I wrapped my arms around you wearing that shirt covered in ice cream, I knew you were the girl for me."

"You've liked me since then?" I ask, surprised by his truth since this moment happened years ago.

"No." He shakes his head adamantly before continuing. "I've *loved* you since then."

Just when I thought I had hit my limit on the number of tears I could cry in one night, they slowly but surely begin to stream down my cheeks.

"I love your beautiful smile. I love the shade of pink your cheeks turn when you blush. I love how you look when you're absorbed in one of your smutty books." I open my mouth to protest, but he stops me. "Don't even try to deny it. You may have everyone else fooled with those discreet covers, but I've seen what's inside your books, you dirty girl, and it just makes me love you more." My cheeks flush as I bite my bottom lip because he's absolutely right. "I love how close you are to your family and how you would do anything for them. I love getting lost in your gorgeous grey eyes. I love that I can tell you anything without judgment. I love the way you feel in my arms, just like this. I love when we kiss because every time we do, it makes me feel like everything is right in this messed up world. I love absolutely every damn thing about you, Natalie."

I'm speechless.

If there is only one thing I am sure of right now, it is that this man has always been and will always be the love of my life.

"I love you, Nathan. And even though I was pissed at you for getting your ice cream all over me those many years ago, I secretly loved every second of it." The most heart-stopping smile appears on Nathan's face, only causing the happy tears in my eyes to spill out even quicker.

Our lips meet with a whole new desire in them. Nathan brings his hands up to both sides of my face, bracing me to him as we show each other the meaning of these three words we have professed out loud to each other for the first time.

Nathan slowly pulls away, breathless, pressing his forehead to mine. "The day I moved to this town, my whole world was upside down, and I thought I would never know what it felt like to be happy again. But hearing you say that you love me, well, I don't know how it's possible for me to be any happier than I am right now."

My heart.

I bury my head into his chest, clinging to him, never wanting this moment to end but knowing it needs to.

Nervously, I look up at him, and his face slowly drops in understanding.

"As much as I don't want to ruin this moment, a moment that I am going to think about over and over again, I need to tell you what happened last year. I can't put this off any longer."

Nathan brings his arm around my waist. "Ok, beautiful. I'm here."

You can do this, Natalie.

I take a couple of deep breaths, but it feels like it's not possible for me to get enough oxygen into my lungs as the nerves take over. Nathan lightly squeezes my hand in encouragement, and that's all it takes for the words to start pouring out of my mouth.

"Last year, Vanessa told me about a Halloween party she and Brian were planning on having at their parents' house while they were out of town. And when I found out it was also a birthday party for you … well, I hadn't seen you since that night on the beach, so I showed up at their house wearing a little black dress and devil horns, showing more skin than usual, hoping you'd notice me." I shake my head, feeling embarrassed at this confession. "But about five minutes after I got there, I saw you in the corner with some girl I didn't recognize. You were sitting on a couch surrounded by a group of people, and that girl was sitting on your lap with her arms wrapped around your neck. That's when I realized I was stupid for even thinking there might have been something between us." Shrugging my shoulders, I look down, remembering how badly it killed me to see that girl with Nathan because I wanted to be her.

"Natalie, I—"

"It doesn't matter anymore." I give him a slight smile, but his face looks pained.

"To help with the disappointing sting, I drank — a lot. Vanessa and I both did. Eventually, Vanessa became pretty incoherent, so I took her to her room to pass out, figuring I would check on her later. When I returned downstairs, I started getting the spins, so I kicked off my heels and somehow made my way to the kitchen where I thought making something to eat might help. But while I was peaking in the fridge, I felt someone's bulky arms slide around my waist, pulling me up against them. I couldn't comprehend what was happening because I was in my own little drunk world at this point in the night."

I close my eyes as I remember every dreadful detail from that night. The smell of tequila engulfed me from Brian's hot breath against my neck. The weak feeling in my body was no match for Brian's strength. The way everyone around me was too drunk to notice what was happening.

My pulse speeds up as the anxiety sets in, making me feel like I'm living through that night all over again.

"Hey," Nathan says, stirring me away from these thoughts, "we can finish this tomorrow if it's becoming too much for you."

"N-no," I shakily insist. "I need to finish this now."

"Ok," Nathan says, concern etched in his brows.

Come on, Natalie.

After clearing my throat, I continue.

"Well, as you probably guessed, it was Brian. I thought he was just joking around, so I attempted to push his arm away, but his grip around me only tightened. He told me he had to show me something upstairs then grabbed me by my arm, pulling me forcefully up the stairs. I faintly remember telling him I wanted to stay downstairs, but he continued to drag me with him, and I had no strength to get out of his grip. After we made it to the top, he took me into his bedroom. I never once thought I was in any trouble. I mean, I had grown up with him, and I trusted him. Vanessa and I had been friends for over ten years, and in all that time, I looked at him as a sort of brother figure."

God, how stupid I feel now for thinking that.

"The next thing I knew, I heard the click from Brian's door locking, and that's when I realized what was happening." I see Nathan's eyes go wide and immediately look away from him down to our intertwined hands. "I tried to move past him, but he pushed me onto the bed like I weighed nothing. So, I started to scream, but no one could hear me over the music blaring in the house. I remember he found such amusement in all of it, laughing cruelly at me.

Nathan's body tenses under my own, and when I look up, I find him staring ahead with intensity and a matching clenched jaw.

"He … he was trying to pull my dress off of me, and I begged him to stop, but he wouldn't listen. So, I started to fight back with whatever strength I had. Kicking. Hitting. Clawing. It only made him mad. Really mad. So, he hit me. He struck me across my face, causing me to whack my head on the corner of the nightstand next to his bed." I push my damp hair back so Nathan can see the indent on my forehead. "You asked me recently how I got this, and well, that's how."

His thumb slowly brushes over my skin before he leans down to kiss the scar, causing tears to well up in my eyes.

"I remember starting to lose consciousness after that, so I gave up. I laid there, closing my eyes, waiting for it to be over. Brian tore the dress off me like he was ripping a piece of paper in half and spewed vulgar profanities at me while he did it."

Nathan shakes his head in disgust while raking his fingers through his hair. I swear I can see veins ready to burst from his neck, and when he brings his hand back to his side, I witness it transform into a trembling fist.

"Well, he got on top of me, and that's when I thought, *this is it*. His hands were digging into my thighs, leaving bruises of his handprints on me for days after. But before he was able to ... do anything to me, someone pounded on his door, which was the distraction I needed. When he turned his head toward the door, I kneed him hard between his legs, causing him to roll off the bed in pain. I jumped off the bed and grabbed my dress, but it was just pieces of torn fabric, so I grabbed the first thing I saw on the floor, which just happened to be his football jersey. Then, I opened the door and bolted past some guy standing there."

"I ran down the stairs and around the passed-out people on the floor, who I knew would be too drunk to help me. And I continued running outside for a few blocks until I finally couldn't breathe anymore. I don't remember much after that, though, because I collapsed against a tree, and the next thing I knew, I woke up in a hospital bed. I told everyone I left in a hurry because I had missed curfew and slipped on ice. It was the only thing I could think to say. And after getting out of the hospital, I dropped the football jersey off in the Gordons' mailbox, just wanting to be rid of anything that reminded me of that night."

Something wet falls on my chest, and when Nathan's thumb wipes away the tears spilling out of my eyes, I realize the floodgates have opened.

"I should have told you sooner. I was just so ashamed. For so long, I blamed myself. I told myself that if I hadn't worn a dress like that or hadn't been drinking so much, none of it would have happened." Each word comes out muffled through the sobs, but I know he understands me. "And I didn't want anyone to know because I didn't want this to affect anyone else. My parents are best friends with Mr. and Mrs. Gordon. I'm, or I mean, I *was* best friends with Vanessa, and well, you're best friends with Brian." Turning away from him, I whisper, "I'm so sorry."

"No. Don't say sorry. There's only one person to blame, and it's not you. It doesn't matter what you wore or how much you had to drink. He fucking sexually assaulted you, Natalie. And that asshole will regret the day he laid a hand on you. I swear if I—" But he stops himself, taking a deep breath before speaking again. "I will never let anyone hurt you again, Natalie. Never." He smooths out my hair and brings the blanket over my shoulder when he feels my body shaking.

Wrapped up in his strong arms, I feel the safest I have ever felt. "I was lucky that Brian never … well, he never got a chance to do what he wanted to do to me, but it still left me feeling scarred, as if he had. For the longest time, I would have these horrible nightmares, always about Brian. They were so bad that Jason would hear me screaming in my sleep, and he'd run into my bedroom and wake me up to make them stop. When I left for school, I thought they would somehow disappear or stay here in Greenwich, but they came with me to Boston. They didn't stop until I was with you. Every night you stayed with me, they were gone," I say softly.

His head leans down, and he brushes his lips lightly against mine. I close my eyes, feeling at peace. Then, pulling away from Nathan's lips, I take my biggest breath in a year. And damn, it feels incredible.

Nathan watches me carefully. "I know it wasn't easy for you to tell me any of this, but I hope you now know that you can always come to me about anything." I nod, knowing he's right. I should have told him so long ago. "And also, I'm so sorry for what I said at Tim's house in front of everyone. Fuck, I really can't believe I said that." He shakes his head and looks away, shame plastered all over his face.

"Nathan," I press my palm to his cheek, "you thought Brian and I hooked up and lied to you about it. You were angry and jealous. Yeah, it wasn't so great to have a house full of people hear about my virginity." I shrug my shoulders. "But none of what happened tonight would have even occurred if I had just talked to you in the first place."

"Still, it wasn't ok, and I'm sorry." His eyes lock with mine, pleading for forgiveness.

"I think you saving me from Brian tonight made up for it."

He wraps his arms tighter around me before asking, "How does it feel not to have to hold onto this secret alone anymore?"

"It feels … overwhelming but in a good way. It's like this past year I was alive, but I wasn't living. Not really. So often it felt impossible to breathe, like I was being pushed underwater and *drowning*, unable to come up for air, with no one nearby to save me. But I feel ready to breathe again. I feel ready to live again."

And damn, do I feel ready.

Telling Nathan everything has felt like a boulder has been lifted off my chest. But there is still one more person I need to talk to. "I'd like to talk to Jason about all of this. He should know what caused me to have all those nightmares he had to save me from. I'm just nervous to tell him."

Nathan's fingers brush delicately against my arm before finding my exposed thigh, where he traces tiny circles with his thumb. "I'm sure it won't be an easy conversation, but I see how he looks at you, and I can promise you he's going to feel exactly the same way I do right now. He'll appreciate you telling him, and then he'll probably want to kill Brian with his bare hands for what he tried to do to you because he loves you."

"You're right. He's my brother. I shouldn't be scared to—" But then, something occurs to me. Something that I completely overlooked and should have asked Nathan about the moment we got home. "Nathan, how did you know I was wearing Brian's football jersey?"

NATHAN

"Because I was the one who found you." I lean against the headboard with my eyes closed as I wait for her reaction.

"It was … it was you?" she asks, stunned.

"Yes." I nervously run my fingers through my hair, remembering every detail from that night. "I was downstairs, crashing on the couch in the front room, and just about to pass out when I heard the front door slam shut. Curiosity got the best of me, so I stood up to look out the window, and that's when I saw you. You were running barefoot in the snow. And I don't know. I just had this horrible feeling that something was wrong." Natalie doesn't say anything, so I keep talking, reliving this awful memory.

"Without thinking, I ran after you. You were hard to catch up to. I even lost you at one point. But I kept shouting your name, and eventually, I spotted you. You were lying still against a tree. So unbelievably still. It was the scariest moment of my life. As I got closer to you, I saw blood dripping down your face and …"

The image of Natalie on that night appears in my mind, so I open my eyes to make it stop.

"One of the neighbors must have called for an ambulance

because I heard sirens approaching, so I wrapped my jacket around you and lifted you in my arms to get you out of the snow. You were trembling from head to toe. I swear your feet were blue. And when the EMTs arrived, I heard you come to, struggling to tell them that you had slipped on ice. I knew you were lying because I had just followed you, but I didn't know why you would lie."

I look down at Natalie, unsure how she feels about everything I'm saying. "When I saw Brian in that jersey tonight, my mind instantly flashed back to the image of you wearing it, and all I saw was red. I had no idea it was his until tonight."

"Why didn't you tell me?" Natalie asks.

Good question.

"I don't know. I thought you might have remembered, but when I saw you again for the first time at school at the coffee shop, you never said anything about it, so I thought it best not to bring it up."

She nods just slightly in understanding but then suddenly looks at me. "Wait, so it was you who left the pink roses for me?"

"Yeah. I should have handed them to you in person, but I …" I was a coward. "I wanted to make sure you were ok. You were all I could think about for the longest time. I couldn't get that image of you against the tree out of my head. But you just disappeared this past year. No social media or hanging out with Vanessa. You were gone. So, when I finally saw you at the coffee shop, well, I was just so happy to see you healthy and just as beautiful as ever."

Her cheeks turn the faintest shade of pink as her eyes drop. "I'm sorry you had to see me like that."

Everything that Natalie has told me replays in my head. I never knew that Brian had it in him to do something that cruel. Anger radiates through every part of my body as I think about it. I had been right downstairs when Brian attacked her. That part makes me sick to my stomach. The asshole outweighed her easily by a hundred pounds, and there was no way she would have been able to get away if someone hadn't knocked on Brian's door.

Thank fucking God for that person.

Brushing her hair back, I say, "Stop saying sorry to me, beautiful."

"I'm sor—I mean, ok." She bites down on her lower lip.

"Natalie, if I had any idea what had actually happened to you, I would have gone right back in that house to kick Brian's ass. Probably would have done worse if we're being honest. But I never imagined he could actually be capable of something like that. I would never have expected this, even knowing how much of an asshole he can sometimes be."

"There's no way you would have known. It was my fault for not saying anything to you." She stares down at my chest. "I wanted to tell you, Nathan. So badly I did. But I was … scared."

I think back, realizing how many times she did try to tell me.

There was the day at the apple orchard when I could see her struggling internally over something. Then there was the night I told her about my father, and she stood in front of me, ready to tell me everything right before her mom called. And then the night after we returned from dinner with my mom and brother, when she even told me there was something she needed to talk to me about, but like a fucking caveman, I threw her over my shoulder and took her to the bedroom.

This had to have been weighing heavily down on her for so long.

"Natalie, it's ok. You don't need to be scared anymore." I tilt her chin up toward me so that I'm looking into her sorrowful eyes. "But there's one last thing we need to discuss."

"What?"

"I recorded the whole thing tonight between you and Brian." Jesus, just saying his name creates a rancid taste in my mouth.

Her eyes go wide. "How … how much of that did you see?"

"Plenty. And it killed me watching what was going on. Believe me, Natalie, there was no way in goddamn hell I would have let him lay a finger on you, but I knew as soon as I got close enough to you guys that something wasn't right, so I hit record on my phone and waited. I wanted to make sure there was plenty of evidence if you decide to … press charges."

"Oh," is all she says.

"I know this is a lot, and I'm not telling you what to do. But just know I have it if you decide to go that route. And the asshole knows I have it too. I told him in maybe not so nice of words that if he makes one slip up, the recording will find its way to the police. So besides now fearing me, this recording is being held over his head, reminding him to stay the fuck away from you. That is why I can promise you that you don't have to worry about him anymore."

She slowly nods her head in understanding. "Can I think about this? I mean, I probably should press charges against him, but I don't want to make any big decisions right now."

"Of course. You don't need to decide anything right now."

She ponders, twisting her lips like there's something she wants to say but doesn't know if she should.

"What's going on in that beautiful head?" I ask.

"Can I ask you something?" she spits out.

"Anything."

"Would you have believed me if you didn't see it for yourself?"

Her question is an immediate stab to my chest, but I know why she's asking. I heard what that monster said to her. He tried to get inside her head and convince her that I would believe him over her. But I know without a doubt that I would have believed Natalie in a heartbeat if she had come to talk to me. "I would have believed every word you said to me."

She reaches her lips to mine, and we take our time with this kiss. It's soft, slow, and exactly what both of us need right now.

When she pulls away, she puts her head back against my chest and nuzzles into me. I watch her try to stifle a yawn.

"Let's get some sleep," I suggest.

She nods in agreement, too tired to say any more. I move my body horizontally onto the bed and bring her with me. Her long blonde hair splays over my arm, which she uses as her pillow. I wrap my other arm protectively around her waist.

"Sorry that your birthday was ruined," she whispers.

I laugh and shake my head.

This girl.

No, *my girl.*

"Are you kidding me? I started my day waking up next to you, and I'm about to end my day going to sleep next to you. So, I would say that it was a pretty damn good birthday." Lifting my head, I catch a small smile on her face as I lean down to kiss her forehead before pulling the blankets up over her body.

Brian might have been my best friend for half of my life, but it turns out I never knew him as well as I thought. Or maybe I did and, without realizing it, chose to ignore the side of him that made me question why we were even friends in the first place.

The evil side of him eventually overshadowed the good. And there's no coming back from this. I might have lost a best friend, a guy I saw as a brother at one point in my life, but what I've gained far outweighs my loss.

Natalie.

The best thing that has ever happened to me.

Before Natalie, I had never been in love. It wasn't something I felt was missing from my life, but now, knowing what it feels like, I can never go back.

Hell, growing up, I never thought I deserved love, and maybe that's why I never tried to pursue anything with Natalie. Deep down, I knew she would always be more than just a hookup. She was Natalie. She was *my* Natalie.

And being able to say "I love you" to her tonight after so many years already loving her was the most indescribable moment of my life. Thinking about it now, I really don't know why I waited so long.

No one should ever wait to tell the person they love how they feel.

And I hope she wasn't upset that I cut her off to say it, but she deserved to hear those words first. She deserves everything she wants in life, and with me as the guy who will love and protect her, that will be exactly what she gets. Everyday. For as long as she'll let me.

I don't consider myself a romantic, or maybe I am. I don't know. But what I do know, without any doubt, is that this girl sleeping so soundly in my arms right now is the love of my life.

Holding her tightly against my chest, I whisper in her ear, "Goodnight, beautiful. You're safe now."

thirty-three

—⚬—

NATALIE

The aroma of coffee wakes me sluggishly from my deep sleep, but with the weight of Nathan's body pressed against me, his arm wrapped protectively around my waist, and Paul's snores resonating from down the hall, I find myself wondering who could be making it. Carefully, I slide out from under Nathan's arm, throw on my favorite fluffy white bathrobe, and make my way down the stairs and into the kitchen, where I find the coffee-making culprit.

"Hey, what are you doing home so early?" I ask Jason, glancing at the antique clock hanging on the wall and seeing that it is only 8:30 in the morning.

"Just needed to stop by to grab my football equipment on my way to practice. Figured I had a few minutes to make some coffee." He pulls out two mugs from the cabinet in front of him, filling both with the hot liquid, and then hands one to me.

"Thanks." I sigh, staring at the mug's contents.

Jason furrows his brows. "Everything ok?"

"Yes. No. Well, actually …" I pause before blurting, "Can we talk when you get back from practice?"

"Oh God, I knew this day was coming," Jason groans.

"You did?"

"Yeah, and listen, we really don't need to talk about it," Jason says matter-of-factly.

"Well, I think we should talk about it. I mean, you are my brother, and I think you should know—"

"Listen," he puts his mug of coffee on the counter before continuing, "I'm going to stop you right there. If you feel guilty or whatever, don't. You're forgiven. But if it'll make you feel better, just leave a ten on my bureau, and let's promise never to speak of this again," he pleads.

"I'm forgiven?" I ask incredulously. "What are you talking about?" I place my mug of coffee abruptly on the counter in annoyance.

Jason's eyes widen, staring at me like I have three heads. "You're going to make me say this out loud, aren't you?"

I gape at him, feeling so confused, and wait for a response.

He covers his face with his hands as he mumbles, "You took condoms out of my nightstand."

"Oh my God. Oh my God. OH! MY! GOD!" My cheeks rapidly heat up from his words as I now cover my face in embarrassment.

Jason's hands leave his face, revealing he's just as tomato red as I am. "You're the one who made me say it!" Then, noticing the horrified expression on my face, he asks, "What? Is that not what you wanted to talk about?"

"No! God no!" I practically scream.

"Oh fuck, well, now this is awkward."

"You think? God, can you please never bring that up again? It was one time!" I state, throwing my hands in the air dramatically.

"Hey, you're the one who said you had something to talk about. I just assumed that's what it was about," he counters.

We both stand in silence, unable to make eye contact as we drink our coffees, until Jason clears his throat. "So, what do you want to talk about?"

"Let's just talk when you get home," I suggest. "I need to shower and forget this conversation ever happened."

Jason chuckles. "Works for me."

He begins to gulp down his coffee when Nathan barrels into the kitchen.

"Is everything ok? I heard screaming." Nathan's eyes are panicked as he glances around the room, but he immediately relaxes when he realizes it's just Jason and me.

Jason puts down his cup and throws his sports bag over his shoulder. I notice his cheeks are crimson again, most likely from not wanting to tell my boyfriend that he supplied the condoms for our first time together. Guess I can't blame him when he says, "Well, that's my cue to go."

"Wait," I interject, "would you and Grace want to get pizza and sit out by the fire pit tonight? Nathan and I won't be leaving until tomorrow morning."

"Sure. I'll check with the old ball and chains, but I'm sure she'll be down for that," he says before walking out of the house.

Nathan looks at me. "What was all that about?"

"You don't even want to know," I respond, shaking my head.

But he continues to wait for an answer.

"Fine. The first time we had sex, I forgot to get condoms, so I stole some from Jason's room, and I guess he noticed." Giving a slight shrug, I finish my coffee and sit on the counter stool.

He laughs. "You're right. I didn't want to know that."

He then brushes my forehead with his lips before kissing me tenderly. "Did you sleep ok?"

"It was probably the best night of sleep I've had in a long time." And it honestly was because it was the first night in a year that I slept without having a secret weighing me down.

"I'm so glad, baby." His hands grip my thighs as he leans in for another delicious kiss.

"Good morning, love birds."

We separate to find Paul walking into the kitchen, seeming very well rested.

I don't know what comes over me, but like I said, he reminds me of a giant teddy bear. And because I can't help myself, I jump off the stool, walk up to Paul and wrap my arms around him. "Thank you, Paul. For everything."

Paul clears his throat. "Oh, shit, Natalie, don't make me cry," he jokes. "But you're welcome." We separate, and I turn to get him a fresh cup of coffee.

"Do you need a ride anywhere?" Nathan asks.

"Actually, yeah. I was going to ask if you wouldn't mind taking me to my brother's house. Going to stay there the remainder of the semester. Which, speaking of, I didn't get a chance to tell you guys last night because of," he pauses, scratching his head before speaking, "all the excitement, but I'm officially transferring to Linrey University after winter break."

Nathan's face lights up like a little boy on Christmas morning.

"Are you serious? When did this happen?" Nathan asks.

"About a month ago. I wasn't feeling it in New Hampshire, and I was searching for options, and I don't know, it just worked out perfectly." He shrugs his shoulders, accepting the mug of coffee I'm holding out for him to take.

"Oh, Paul, that's amazing." I beam at him.

"I figured you two wouldn't mind being my tour guides. Maybe we can make plans over winter break?"

"Yeah, of course. It'll be nice to see another familiar face in Boston," Nathan replies. "Well, I'll go get my coat, and then we can head out if you want?"

"That'd be great." Paul looks over at me. "Natalie, if you ever need anything, just let me know, ok?"

"Ok," I say with a slight smile.

"Oh, come here. I know you want one more," Paul teases, holding his arms wide for me.

Nathan starts laughing in the background, while I give Paul one more giant hug. "God, she doesn't even hug me like that."

After I let go of Paul, Nathan comes over and scoops me up in his arms. "You're sure you're ok if I'm gone for a little?"

"Yes. Jason will be home soon from practice, and then I want to talk to him, so it'll be good if we have the house to ourselves for that." My stomach churns from nerves, and Nathan can tell.

"It will be fine. I promise," he coaxes. "Just call me if you need anything." He kisses me affectionately, holding my body tightly against his own before placing me back on the ground. "I have a surprise for you when I get back," he whispers in my ear.

"What is it?" I ask excitedly.

"Aww, you know I can't tell you, or it'll ruin it." The gorgeous, mischievous grin on his face already has my heart racing in anticipation.

"You can't just say you have a surprise for me and then leave." I look up at him with the biggest puppy dog eyes I can muster while pouting my lips, hoping to get any hint from him. Unfortunately, I can tell with one look at Nathan that it's going to take more than this to get anything out of him. If Paul wasn't standing by the door, I'm sure there would be *plenty* of ways for me to get him to tell me what my surprise is. But, alas, Paul is by the door, and I'm not one for an audience, so I guess I'll have to wait. "I've changed my mind. I don't like you anymore," I tease.

"That's right, baby. You don't like me. You love me. And guess what? I love you. I really fucking love you."

* * *

Jason remains eerily quiet as he processes everything I just told him. And I mean *everything*. His eyes stare straight ahead, lost in the fire roaring in the fireplace in front of us, unblinking for a humanly impossible amount of time. Neither of us says anything for what feels like an eternity, and just as the silence begins to overwhelm me, he finally speaks.

"Natalie, I don't even know what to say." His eyes drift over to me, looking conflicted with so many emotions. Sadness. Confusion. Anger. Yes, definitely anger.

"I know." I look down at my hands on my lap, worry eating away at me.

"For starters, I want to kill Brian." His eyes wander back to the fire as his fists clench the arms of his chair. "Secondly," he pauses, taking a deep breath before saying, "I wish you had told me when this happened."

"I'm sorry," I say in a whisper. "I don't know. I was just so ashamed. I blamed myself for a while and worried that this would affect others if they ever found out, like Vanessa, Nathan, and mom and dad. I didn't want that." Tears fall from my eyes.

"Nat," he sits up in his chair, "I'm your brother. I love you and would do anything for you. And I would never tell your secret, but the guy is a real asshole. Someone needs to put him in his place. I know you're worried about what this will do to everyone else because that's the kind of person you are, but you shouldn't be. I can't tell you how glad I am that Nate recorded what happened last night. And I'm not telling you what to do, but just know I support you either way." He takes a deep breath, and I look up to see him holding his head in his hands.

"I've been so worried about you this past year. With the nightmares you were having and the days you would just walk around like a zombie, I knew something had happened. I just never assumed …" He looks back at the fire, and I see his eyes watering. "I know you're older, not by much, but I've always felt like I was your big brother. I don't know, maybe it's because of my size, but I'm supposed to be the one to protect you, and I can't tell you how much it's bothered me not knowing what was wrong with you and that there was nothing I could do to help." He covers his face, trying to hide the tears.

"Oh, Jason." I stand up and gently place a hand on his shoulder. "You, sitting here and listening to me is all I need. It's my fault that I didn't come to you sooner. I'm so sorry. You've always been there for me, and I don't know why I thought this would have been any different."

"Don't apologize."

I nod because he's right.

Jason stretches his neck from side to side, frustrated, and I can feel his shoulders tense under my touch. "If I find out he comes anywhere near you again, I will kill him, Natalie. I'll have to."

"Well, you'll have to beat Nathan to it because he promised the same thing."

"I knew I liked Nate." Jason smiles slightly.

"Yeah, I kind of like him too." No, I *love* him.

"But how are you feeling, Nat? Honestly." His eyes search over me with concern.

"Honestly, it's a lot. But just being able to tell you and Nathan has helped. It feels almost freeing. I don't know how to explain it." I look into the fire that has my brother so mesmerized. "But what I do know is I love you, and I'm so lucky to have you as my brother."

Jason stands up and embraces me. I use his T-shirt to wipe away some of my tears, which makes him smile.

He places his hands on my shoulders comfortingly as we separate and says, "Just know I always have your back, no matter what. Ok?"

"How did I get so lucky to have a brother like you?" I ask.

"One of life's many mysteries." He smiles. "Now, what did you say earlier about pizza?"

* * *

I'm curled up on the couch in the living room, a throw blanket over my legs, with the latest romance novel in one hand and a glass of wine in the other as I kill time waiting for everyone.

Nathan and Jason left about an hour ago to play Nathan's brother and friends in a game of basketball, and on their way home, they're going to pick up some pizzas for dinner.

Just thinking about pizza makes my mouth salivate, since my biggest weakness in life has always been bread and cheese.

Damn carbs. I love them. *Almost as much as I love Nathan.* The thought makes me smile like a schoolgirl.

Just as I get to the juicy part in my book, or the "smutty" part as Nathan would say, the doorbell rings, causing my heart to stammer.

Who could that be?

Throwing my blanket off, I creep on my tippy toes and look through the peephole on the door, but all I see is the top of someone's head full of dark brown hair, which lets me know the person is around my height — no immediate threat.

As I open the door, I see a face that I haven't seen in a very long time.

And my heart immediately wants to cry.

"Hey, Natalie, I was wondering if we could talk?" Vanessa asks. She's standing in front of me with her hands in her red peacoat pockets, looking like she just left a magazine photo shoot. But, of course, she was always put together, even when just running errands. This past year I had desperately missed her fashion advice almost as much as I missed the girl in the impeccable outfits. "I don't want to take up too much of your time."

"Umm." I'm completely taken by surprise since she was the last person I expected to be standing on the other side of the door. I mean, I hoped that eventually Vanessa and I would be able to talk about things, but at this moment, I don't feel mentally prepared. Telling Nathan and Jason was one thing, but telling Brian's *sister* would be a completely different conversation. "Sure, yeah. Hi. Come in." I open the door and wait for her to walk inside while I stand by awkwardly.

"We can go in the family room," I say, leading us in that direction. I take a seat on one of the chairs by the fireplace, and she follows suit, sitting in the chair right across from mine.

"So," I tuck a piece of hair behind my ear, "what did you want to talk about?"

"Is there anyone here?" Her big brown eyes dance around the space.

"No. Jason and … Nathan left about an hour ago to play basketball," I say, pausing before Nathan's name.

"Oh," Vanessa responds.

"Yeah, so—"

"Natalie, I know," she cuts in.

"You know what?" I ask. My heart feels ready to jump out of my chest.

"I know something happened between you and my brother, and I'm so sorry." She looks down at the floor, her dark hair covering her eyes.

"H-how do you know?" I only told Nathan and Jason hours ago, and they wouldn't tell anyone. I'm sure about this.

"I heard about what happened last night at Nate's birthday party. Word travels pretty fast around this boring town." Vanessa laughs nervously. "Well, it wasn't too difficult for me to put the pieces together after that."

"Vanessa, I'm so sorry for—"

"Natalie, you don't owe me an apology." She shakes her head adamantly, looking unwaveringly at me. "I don't want to know the details because he is, unfortunately, still my brother, a brother that I have never been very fond of … But what I'm trying to say is, and I don't even know if what I'm about to suggest is even possible, but I'm hoping somehow we can go back to being friends?" She looks up at me with glossy eyes. "I can't begin to say how sorry I am about whatever happened between you and Brian, but Natalie, I've missed you so much. I had no idea why I stopped hearing from you. You were my best friend. My sister. And it felt like half of me died when you cut me out of your life."

One by one, tears make their way down her cheeks, causing the knife in my heart to twist agonizingly from the guilt consuming me.

"I've missed you too," I say through a quiet sob. "I didn't want to hurt you. I thought I was doing the right thing by putting distance between us. I had no idea how to tell you, and I'm so sorry that I let what happened between Brian and me be the reason for pushing you away."

At the same time, we reach across, hug each other tightly and cry into each other's hair.

I'm so overwhelmed with emotions, but saying I'm happy to be here with my best friend right now is a complete understatement.

After a few minutes, Vanessa pulls away and asks, "Do you think somehow we can put this past year behind us and give it a try at being best friends again?"

I'm not sure how we will make things work or if we'll even be able to return to the way things were, but I want to try more than anything. "Yes. Definitely."

Vanessa wipes away the tears from her tanned skin, seeming pleased with my answer. "So, you and Nate, huh?" The size of her grin shows how happy she is about the two of us being together.

"Yeah, who would have thought."

"Me," she says. "I always hoped you two would find your way to each other. Is it serious?"

"Yeah, I think. No, actually I know it is. I love him." I blush as the words leave my mouth.

"Natalie, that makes me so happy." She grabs my hand and squeezes it, producing a smile on both of our tear-stained faces. And it's at this moment I know we will have no problem returning to being the best friends we used to be.

Somehow, we will make this work.

Suddenly, we hear a car pull into the driveway, followed by doors opening and closing.

"Well, I better get going. I have to get my stuff together before heading back to school tonight. But call me sometime, ok?" Vanessa stands up and flattens her coat for wrinkles.

"Yes, I will. I promise." We hug each other one last time before walking to the front door.

Opening it, we find Nathan and Jason with pizza boxes in their hands and mouths wide open in shock from seeing Vanessa.

"Hi guys, remember me?" Vanessa jokes, trying to ease the tension that could quite literally be cut with a knife.

"How could we forget?" Nathan says. His eyes move between Vanessa and me, and a slight smile appears on his face. "Always nice to see you."

"Hey, Vee, everything good here?" Jason asks casually, most likely noticing the dried tears on my face. I think I've set the world record for the most tears cried in twenty-four hours.

But as I look at Vanessa, Nathan, and Jason, only one word comes to mind. "Everything is *perfect*."

I know healing isn't going to be an overnight process, but with these three by my side, there is nothing that I won't be able to do.

thirty-four

NATHAN

"Your marshmallow is on fire!" Jason warns Grace, who quickly pulls her stick away from the heat and blows on it until the flames disappear, revealing a completely singed marshmallow.

"Oops." Grace laughs, falling back into Jason's chest, and he smiles, holding her tighter against him.

After we all ate our fair share of pizza, we came outside to sit around the fire pit to make s'mores. Jason and Grace made themselves comfortable sharing one chair on one side of the fire, while Natalie and I sat across from them.

Right now, watching Natalie pull her marshmallow away from the fire and place graham crackers and chocolate around it, it's not the flames that have me mesmerized but her smile.

"What?" she asks quietly, seeing me in her peripheral vision.

"Come here," I tell her, sitting back in my chair and making room for that gorgeous body to sit on my lap.

Without hesitation, she gets up and makes a new seat for herself on my thighs, purposely rubbing that perfect ass against me.

"Be careful. Wouldn't want your seat to get too *hard* for you to sit on now, would we?" I tease. My arms come around, gripping her thighs, and my lips nuzzle into her neck from behind.

She turns her head over her shoulder to whisper, "Oops." Then she reveals the cutest little devilish smile, which lets me know she knew exactly what she was doing.

God, I love her.

After taking a bite of her s'more, she turns her body so that she can peer up at me. I wipe a strand of hair away from her face before it gets caught on the chocolate that's now covering her plump lips. Leaning down, I kiss those lips, licking the chocolate off them in the process. "I love chocolate," I say, which makes her giggle. She rests her head against me as I hold her tighter. "So, how are things with you and Vanessa?"

"I think … I think we're going to be ok." She gives a slight shrug. "I don't know how it'll work with her still being Brian's sister, but I want to try. I've missed her so much this past year. I just didn't know how to be her friend while avoiding Brian, and I guess I thought pushing her away was the right thing to do for both of us."

"Well, I'm glad she came over to talk to you. I know she's missed you too." Of course, it's not Vanessa's fault when it comes to who her brother is, but I also know this won't be easy for them to navigate.

Natalie purses her lips and nods, but I know there's more on her mind.

"Talk to me, baby," I encourage.

"I spent this whole year isolating myself because I didn't want this to hurt anyone else. I thought everyone would be better off not knowing what happened, but when we were all standing at the door earlier — you, me, Jason, and Vanessa — it was the first time I understood that instead of isolating myself, I should have reached out to those around me who love me. Because of him, I let a whole year of my life slip away."

Her eyes look sad as she thinks about this, and all I want to do is kill that asshole for making her feel this way. But I don't let the anger inside me show. "Hey, don't get lost in your mind dissecting last year and what you may or may not have missed out on. Use it to learn and grow. Not to punish yourself."

She looks up at me thoughtfully. "When did you get all philosophical?"

"When I realized I was in love with a girl who has anxiety and wanted to do everything I can to help her."

Her eyes drift away, embarrassment washing over her face. "It's that obvious, huh?"

"I've known since we were kids, but that doesn't mean it made me look at you differently. It's a part of who you are, but it's not who you are. Do you understand?"

She slowly nods her head.

"Besides, I think the panic attack in the middle of the corn maze kind of gave it away." I try to make light of it, but Natalie doesn't look up at me.

"I thought that would have scared you away," she says softly.

"Baby?"

"Yeah?"

I pull my phone out of my pocket and hold it out for her to take. "Look in the notes section of my phone."

Her brows furrow, but she takes my phone and taps on the screen, which brings her to my notes. I watch her eyes widen when she realizes what she's reading.

"How to help someone you love with anxiety. The ten best things to say when talking someone down from an anxiety attack. Tips to manage anxiety. Foods to help decrease stress. The top therapists in Boston who specialize in anxiety. The best anti-anxiety notebooks." She keeps scrolling, reading close to a hundred different titled notes of research I've found in my spare time, before looking up at me in awe. "You really do love me, don't you?"

"More than you will ever understand." My thumb rubs along her jawline as my hand rests on her neck, feeling her pulse increase. "I know you are strong and capable of saving yourself, but even the strongest people need help. And on the days you feel like you're drowning, I want to be the one that saves you. Mentally or physically, I will always save you."

Her hands clasp around the back of my neck as she pulls herself to me, pressing her lips firmly into mine. My hand grips her thigh, pulling her body against me until I suddenly remember her brother is just on the other side of the fire, hopefully not witnessing any of this.

Pulling away before we take it too far, I say, "Come on. Let's go get you that surprise."

Her eyes light up with an immense amount of excitement. "I almost forgot!"

We both say goodnight to Grace and Jason, then walk hand in hand into the house and up the stairs to Natalie's bedroom.

When we reach her room, I put one hand on the doorknob and then turn around, watching her excitement bubbling over. "Close your eyes."

"What? Why?" She tries to look around me to see what is hiding behind the door, but I haven't opened it more than an inch.

"Please?"

"Fine," she says. Natalie closes her eyes and stands there impatiently waiting for me. It's a sight that makes me want to laugh, but I refrain from doing so.

Taking her hand, I push the door open and lead her forward until we're standing directly in the center of the room. I drop her hand and walk behind her so she can view everything.

"Ok, open your eyes," I whisper in her ear.

Natalie's eyes bolt open then her mouth drops to the floor. "Nathan, what is this?" she asks in disbelief.

Pink rose petals are all over her white comforter. In the center of the bed, I shaped the petals into a giant heart, and in the center of the heart, I placed a small white envelope with Natalie's name on the outside.

"You should open it," I suggest.

She turns to me, still in shock, and then cautiously picks up the envelope but makes no move to open it.

"Go on," I say softly.

Ever so slowly, she rips open the envelope, and that's when I hear her breath draw back.

"Happy early birthday, baby."

"Nathan, are these what I think they are?" Her eyes begin to water, but unlike the tears I witnessed falling from her eyes last night, I know these are happy ones. Because in her hands, she's holding two plane tickets to Paris.

"Do you like it?" I ask, hearing how nervous I sound.

After waking up this morning, I called my mom to let her know the trip to Australia had been canceled due to schedule conflicts, not wanting to tell her what was really going on. I was hoping she could get her money back, but unfortunately, I found out the ticket was nonrefundable. That's when an idea came to me. Take Natalie to Paris. I knew two tickets to Paris would be a lot more than my one ticket, plus the hotel that would need to be top of the line, but I also knew this was what I wanted to do.

Because making this girl happy has become my mission in life.

"Do I like it?" Her eyes dance between me and the tickets in her hand. "Nathan, these ... these are too much."

I shake my head, knowing she would say this. "Don't worry about that. Please. I wanted to do this. Besides, long story short, I haven't had a chance to tell you, but my mom had purchased a plane ticket for me for my birthday to go on a trip to Australia with some friends." I pause, not wanting to say the asshole's name in case it ruins the moment, then continue. "Well, I called my mom earlier today and told her the trip had been canceled, hoping she could get a refund. But unfortunately, the plane ticket was nonrefundable, so I came up with this idea, which my mom thought would be a much better trip anyway. I'm pretty sure she likes you more than me." I laugh. "Anyways, the airline let me use the credit toward the two tickets, and I made up the difference."

"But Nathan—"

"Remember that night at the common?" I cut in.

"Yes," she responds with a slight smile. "How could I forget?"

"Well, do you remember how I asked you 'where is the one place in this whole world you would want to go?'"

She nods her head.

"The way you looked when you told me how you've always wanted to go to Paris, well, I knew, at that moment, I had to make that dream come true for you." I cup her cheek in the palm of my hand, looking down into a pair of wonder-struck eyes. "So, please, let me take you to Paris."

"I just can't believe you did this for me." Her eyes glaze over the tickets in her hand before landing back on me. "No one has ever done something this romantic for me before."

"I would do anything for you, Natalie." I take the envelope from her hands and place it on the nightstand. Bracing her face, I gently brush my lips against hers.

"Nathan?"

"Yes?"

"Take me to bed," she says softly against my lips.

Our lips meet fervently, devouring each other, finding it impossible to get enough. My hands slide down from her face to the back of her thighs, where I grip her, picking her up with no effort. Her legs wrap tightly around me as her hands tug my hair, demanding more of me. I take a couple of steps to her bed and place her right on top of her rose-petal-covered comforter, breaking the kiss to look down at Natalie, wishing I had a camera to capture the most beautiful sight I have ever seen.

* * *

"I can't believe we are going to Paris," Natalie ponders as she stares out the passenger window. Her mind is clearly far away from here, envisioning us walking through the streets of France hand in hand or maybe having sex on every surface of our hotel room that will overlook the Eiffel Tower.

Of course, I'm a guy, so that's what I had been thinking about.

"Well, we still have some time left until winter break starts, but it gives us something to look forward to." I bring her hand to my mouth and place a tender kiss on the back of it.

We left Natalie's house pretty early since we have to make it back to Boston in time for our classes, plus my nighttime shift at the yacht club. And also because when I stepped outside and felt the first real chill of the year, I knew I needed to stop by my mom's house to pick up some of my winter clothes.

Honestly, I'm surprised it hasn't snowed yet.

Jason seemed pretty bummed to see Natalie leaving, but we promised to be back next weekend for a family birthday dinner for her. I think it put his mind at ease, knowing she would be back in just a few days. But he also has nothing to worry about because I plan on keeping Natalie safe by my side.

Pulling into the driveway at my mom's house, I'm surprised to see the front door cracked open. "That's odd." I look around to see if anyone's car is nearby, but I don't see anything. However, just as I put my hand on the door handle, Natalie stops me.

"Nathan," her eyes narrow as she scans my house, "something doesn't feel right. Maybe you should call the police to check it out before you go inside?"

"It's fine. I'm sure Nick just didn't shut the door hard enough the last time he was here or something." I place my hand under her chin and kiss her soft lips. "I'll be right back." I put my hand back on the door handle but then turn back to her. "I love you," I say, which causes her to smile immediately.

"I love you," she responds before grabbing my face and planting a light kiss on my lips. "Hurry back."

As I walk up to the house, a blast of cold air whips at me, causing me to zip up my coat before pushing the front door fully open and slowly entering.

It's unnervingly quiet in here.

"Hello?" I ask, waiting for a response. But I hear and see nothing out of the ordinary, so I close the door behind me and head to the stairs. My foot lands on the first step when I hear a familiar rough voice.

"I knew you would come back sooner or later."

My body paralyzes in fear, and my pulse begins to beat wildly. I turn my head slightly and see my father sitting in a small chair in the living room, staring at me with a crooked smile that sends chills down my body.

"What? You're not happy to see your old man?" he asks with an evil laugh. "Glad to see you're still scared of me, though." He's wearing dirty, smudged, baggy jeans and a ripped, stained T-shirt and is holding a half-empty bottle of vodka. The scruffy, unkempt beard and hair length tells me he hasn't had a shower in a long time.

"What the hell are you doing here?" I demand, finding the courage somehow to speak. A rage is beginning to build inside me, and I'm thankful for it as I regain composure over myself.

"What am I doing here?" he repeats, leering around the house. "I'm your father, goddammit, and I'll go wherever the fuck I want and do what I damn please."

"You're no father to me," I say through gritted teeth, doing everything in my power not to let him get to me. This is not the friendly and caring man I knew as a little boy. This man sitting in front of me is the *devil*.

"The hell I'm not, boy! My blood runs deep through your veins. You are just like me whether you want to be or not." He takes a big gulp from the vodka bottle before throwing it on the floor beside him. "You're a spoiled, selfish little prick. You never appreciated anything I did for this family," he shouts at me with a fury I have never heard from him before.

"What you did for this family? Do you mean repeatedly abusing my mom until she was black and blue all over? Or do you mean when you would spend every hour of the day belligerently drinking until you became so violent that we would all find places to hide in the house away from you, waiting for you to pass out?" I shout back at him. "You destroyed this family!"

"Oh, I see. So you think you understand the meaning of life or something because you're a college boy now? You think you're better than me, don't you?" He slams his fist on the arm of the chair. "Well, you're not! You're a screwup just like me, and that's all you will ever be in this world. You're nothing!"

"I know I'm better than you!" I stare at him, watching these words hit him like a ton of bricks. His face turns bright red.

"You little shit. You don't know anything!" He shakes his head erratically, looking down at the floor. Then in one swift motion, he pulls a handgun out from behind his back, pointing it right at me.

My body freezes, and all the courage I had previously found disappears. "W-what are you doing?" I slowly move my hand to my coat pocket to reach for my phone, but it's empty. *Shit.* I panic when I realize I left it in my car with Natalie. *Natalie.* There is no way I'm moving to my car with Natalie sitting in it. She is safer out there as long as my father doesn't know she's here.

"I'm tired," he says, laughing to himself. "Tired of not having a home, a full belly, and clean clothes." He glances down at his ratty outfit. "I have no one that respects me, and I'm looked down upon by everyone who passes by me in the streets." He laughs even harder like he just remembered something funny. "I used to be somebody. I used to have a purpose until life kicked me in the ass really hard, and you know what, son. Life is hard. And I want you to know, I'm only doing this because I love you, and I don't want you to have to go through what I went through. I won't let the demons get you too." He suddenly sits up straight, inching closer to me.

"Dad, please don't do this." I feel the tears well up as my father stands, the gun still pointed steadily in my direction. My hands are up defensively, and shaking uncontrollably, in front of me. "Please, dad, don't. You need help. We can get you help. Just p-please put the gun down."

"Nathan, is everything ok?" I hear Natalie's voice as she enters the living room. At the same instant, I see my father turn the gun in her direction. Without a second thought, I jump in front of the gun just as he pulls the trigger.

I fall to my knees as a searing pain spreads throughout my side. A scream of agony falls from my lips before I bite down, unable to control the pain that's invading me.

Glimpsing up at my father, seeing the horror in his eyes from what he has just done, I know exactly what he is about to do next. Abruptly, he brings the gun to his head, pointing it at himself. I quickly turn my eyes to Natalie, who is standing frozen and trembling by the doorway.

"Natalie, look at me," I roar, ignoring the pain consuming me. There's no fucking way I'm letting her see this.

Her frightened eyes connect with mine.

"Don't look away from me, baby," I demand.

And that's when the second shot goes off. A loud thud tells me his body has dropped to the floor just feet away from me, but I focus on Natalie, whose eyes haven't moved from mine.

"Nat-Nathan," she stammers, moving to kneel beside me. She can't help herself as her eyes hesitantly begin to peek over my shoulder, but I stop her, not wanting that man to win even in death by damaging another person on this planet.

"Eyes on me, beautiful."

Our eyes meet, both of us unwavering. And as if we can read each other's thoughts, she slowly nods, understanding who the man lying lifeless on the ground behind me is.

Her wide eyes now find the side of my body where my skin is screaming in anguish. With shaky hands, she unzips my coat to reveal a decent amount of blood soaking through my shirt. I slide the coat off my shoulders and then lift my shirt to see the damage. Thankfully, it looks like the bullet only tore through my flesh, missing any actual vital organs. But seeing how much blood is spilling out causes quite a bit of alarm.

As if sensing this concern, Natalie jumps into action. She whips my shirt off over my head and uses it to apply pressure, which stings like a mother fucker.

"H-hold this firmly. I'm call-calling the police." I notice her eyes begging her to let the tears fall, but she's doing everything she can to keep them at bay.

She pulls out her phone and calls, letting them know what happened. After ending it, she throws her phone to the side then moves my hand from the T-shirt and places hers down instead.

"You're wh-white as a g-ghost," she says, focused on the blood-soaked shirt.

"Right back at you," I tease, trying to get her to relax, but instead, her bottom lip shudders. As I regard her closely, I realize that, between the two of us, she is the one who looks like she is about to go into shock.

"Nathan … you … you took a bullet for me." She shakes her head in disbelief before finally glancing up at me.

"Yeah, and it fucking hurts," I joke with her because I think her bottom lip quivering is hurting me more than the actual gunshot wound, but a flood of tears pours down her flawless cheeks. "I'm ok, Natalie," I lie, but I know she doesn't believe me.

Yeah, this is the worst pain I've ever experienced, but there's no way in hell I'm letting her know that.

"I can't lose you, Nathan!" Her whole body is shivering, tears are spilling out, and her hands holding the shirt against me are shaking faster than a leaf on a windy New England day.

She's *drowning*.

"Hey, look at me." She tilts her head up, hardly making eye contact with me. "I'm not going anywhere. Do you understand me?" But as a chill washes over me, I'm not sure I believe my own words.

She purses her lips, barely nodding in acknowledgment. But I can tell she is elsewhere in her head, already envisioning the worst-case scenario as her chest rises up and down at an alarming rate.

"I need you to breathe, baby. Can you do that for me?" I ask, trying to hide the pain in my voice. Fuck, this is becoming unbearable.

She closes her eyes and inhales through her nose before exhaling a long shaky breath through her mouth.

"One more time." Losing so much blood is causing me to feel lightheaded, but I'm fighting with everything inside me to appear ok.

She does it again without question, and I watch as her chest steadies, slowly rising up and down. My free hand, now beginning to tremble, reaches out for her cheek, which she eagerly leans into.

"I will never let you drown, Natalie."

And I've never meant anything more in my life.

She may have spent the past year struggling to get out of the current's grasp over her, but she would never again have to fear that someone wasn't nearby to save her. Because even though she is quite capable of saving herself, I will *always* save her. Whether from herself or others, *I will save her.*

NATALIE

DECEMBER 22ND

Paris is always a good idea.

"Is it everything you dreamed it would be?" Nathan asks as he comes up behind me, wrapping his solid arms around my waist and holding me securely against his chest.

The two of us are standing on the balcony of our hotel room, which features an unbelievable view of the Eiffel Tower as it gleams and twinkles in the night sky. We spent the first five days in Paris exploring the city and, at night, exploring each other.

During the day, we played the part of the perfect tourists. Taking a bus tour to view the city monuments, spending hours in the Louvre, and riding the elevator to the top of the Eiffel Tower, where we took our first photo together overlooking the city below us. We've also had our fair share of French cuisine. Nathan even tried escargot, which I politely declined.

We ventured off to Versailles, where Nathan drove us around the gardens in a golf cart, which I found pretty enjoyable, even bundled up in multiple layers. And last night, we treated ourselves to dinner and a show at the Moulin Rouge, where poor Nathan spent most of the night with my hand covering his eyes.

My fingers intertwine with Nathan's over my stomach, loving the feeling of being wrapped up in his embrace. "This has truly been a dream come true. And the fact that I got to experience all of this with you and because of you, well, I don't have the words to thank you."

I feel him smile as his chin rests on my shoulder. "I think you've thanked me plenty without even using words." My cheeks heat up, and I look over my shoulder at the hotel room behind us, knowing that we have definitely put all my smutty romance novels to shame. His lips press a soft kiss on the side of my neck. "Let's never leave."

"Don't tempt me." We're leaving in less than two days, arriving home in time for Christmas Eve dinner at my family's house with Nathan's mom and brother joining us. And as much as I'm looking forward to spending the holidays with both of our families, I'm already beginning to feel sad about leaving this beautiful city.

After Nathan was released from the hospital, Paris was the last thing on my mind. In fact, even Brian had left my mind because my only priority was Nathan.

He spent the first week living with his mom and brother back at their house, giving them all time together to heal from the pain and loss. No matter how you look at it, good versus evil, it was still a loss, even if it's a loss that I know Nathan finds more liberation in than grief.

When Nathan felt strong enough to return to Boston, he stayed with me, where I was glued to his side, only leaving when I needed to attend classes.

Thankfully, all of his teachers were very understanding of his situation and allowed him to finish the rest of his semester virtually, which I know was a relief to him.

And once Nathan was back on his feet, I knew what I had to do next. I needed to breathe again, and I could only do this by taking back my life — the life I had stopped living.

I started slowly, not wanting to overwhelm myself. Vanessa and I made plans to see each other, and when we did, it felt like no time had even passed between us. I discovered an indoor tennis club near school and began playing matches as if I had never put down my racquet. I made time to go home and attend Jason's football games, cheering the loudest in the stands for my amazingly talented brother. And when I finally felt ready, I did something I should have done a long time ago.

I booked my first therapy session.

And therapy helped me find healing with something I loved to do: write.

It started with only scribbles here and there until, eventually, I couldn't stop writing.

I took something terrible that happened to me and turned it into something beautiful.

My first book.

And although I am nowhere near finished, it feels good giving my mind a place to escape, a place to breathe.

Because sometimes, when I don't have a place to escape, my mind wanders back to the day when Nathan was shot. Back to the moment the blast from the gunshot paralyzed me as I watched him fall to the ground, fearing I had lost him forever. Nathan's eyes locked with mine as a second shot went off, causing my heart to thunder in my chest. My hands were soaked with Nathan's blood as I tried to keep his shirt pressed firmly to his wound to stop the bleeding. I didn't even hear the paramedics when they rushed in to take charge of the situation.

As if sensing where my mind has traveled, Nathan spins me in his arms, lightly pushing my hair away from my eyes. "Hey, where did you go?"

I shake my head, glancing up at the man I love. "Sorry, I guess I got lost for a second."

Leaning down, he presses his lips to the scar above my eye. "Well, let me remind you where you are." He cups my face in his hands and lightly brushes his lips against mine. "You're here with me in the most romantic city in the world. And our story is only just beginning."

"Our story, huh?"

"Well, yeah. The perfect story for your first book. A love story where two people find their way back to each other, all while dealing with shitty situations that life throws their way and, of course, having lots of incredible sex to get through it all."

"Oh, but of course." I smile at him.

"Oh God, please promise me you won't let your parents read this book." He laughs. "I don't need them hating me for the things we do to each other behind closed doors or … on top of washing machines." He covers his face in his hands, shaking his head. "I'll never be able to show my face again."

"I can't make any promises," I tease, wrapping my hands around his wrists to bring them down, revealing his handsome smile.

"Then promise me this." He looks tenderly down into my eyes, caressing my cheek in the palm of his hand. "That the two main characters in your book find their happy ending by spending the rest of their lives loving each other, harder and fiercer than any other book couple before them."

It's ok if you swoon now because I just did.

"That I can promise."

Staring into Nathan's dark brown eyes right before he leans in to kiss me, I know I'm not drowning anymore, not anywhere close to it, because I'm so damn ready to continue our love story.

The End.

thank you!

Thank you for reading my debut novel.

If you enjoyed this love story, I would be forever grateful if you could leave a review on the platform of your choice.

And stay tuned for …

Jason and Vanessa's love story in …

Before I Saw You

She's the sister of the man he hates most in the world.

What could go wrong?

Acknowledgments

To everyone who took a chance by reading my debut novel, from the bottom of my heart, I thank you.

To my other half, my twin sister, Amanda Wanstrath — Thank you for helping me find the courage to publish my first book and for always believing in me.

To my mom and dad, I love you both and hope you never read this book.

To Cory Welch, because let's be honest, this book would never have happened without you.

To my first official beta reader, Amanda Riviera — Thank you for constantly hyping me up after reading each section I sent you. I couldn't have done this without you!

To Meghan Deneen, Caitlin Deneen, Katie Carew, and Steph Keach — Thank you for being the best group of beta readers who continually showered me with support throughout the whole process.

To Ryan Deneen — Thank you for being the biggest Instagram supporter in the family. You are the real MVP.

To Nafeesa and Dave Feinstein — Thank you for listening to me for a solid two hours, trying to tell you what my book is about, and then being there for me with chocolate cake when I'm overthinking everything.

To my dearest friend of thirteen years, Chelsea Hanson — Thank you for always being there for me.

To Hannah Bird — Thank you for answering EVERY question I threw your way. I feel so fortunate to have met you during this whole overwhelming yet also exciting self-publishing process. I truly don't believe I could have published this book without you.

To Joy Mihanni — Thank you, love bug, for always supporting me even from thousands of miles away.

To Emma Sutherland — Thank you for being the best coworker and for putting up with all of my overthinking for the past three and a half years.

To my editor, Karlee Renkoski, — Thank you for cleaning up my mess and turning it into what it is today. I couldn't have asked to work with a better editor, and no one would have been able to calm me down about my comma fears like you.

To my cover artist, Kate from Y'all. That Graphic — Thank you for making me the most beautiful cover I could have ever imagined.

Thank you.

About the Author

Ashley Elizabeth is an author of steamy contemporary romance. Her books will always tell a love story with just the right amount of spice and, most importantly, end with a happily ever after. When she's not reading a romance novel or overthinking everything, you can find her at Starbucks, keeping them in business, or watching Jurassic Park for the thousandth time with her fur baby, Bailey.

Keep in touch with Ashley Elizabeth

Instagram: @ashleyelizabethauthor
Goodreads: goodreads.com/ashleyelizabeth
TikTok: @ashleyelizabethauthor

9 798987 759202